Twelv
Formation

Terry Todd

For Kelly

May this inspire you to develop your own writing gift to the max, for the glory of the one who gave you the gift.

Terry

This book consists of original, historical fiction stories concerning the childhood and development of Jesus of Nazareth. Scripture quotations are from The New International Version (NIV).

Front cover art: 'Madonna con Bambino'
Matita e biacca su carta, 15 x 20 cm
Copyright by Sofia Novelli, painter at Scuola di Arte Sacra- Firenze

Back cover art: 'Ritrovamento di Gesù nel tempio'
Olio su tela, 130 x 90 cm
Copyright by Sofia Novelli, painter at Scuola di Arte Sacra- Firenze

Used by permission.

FIRST EDITION

Dedicated to the grandchildren who inspire me:

Katelyn Frank
Matthew Frank
Benjamin Frank
Timothy Frank
Zechariah Frank
Mackenzie Todd
Gabriel Logan Oakley
Rayn Oakley
Tobin Oakley

Table of Contents

Foreword

Let me be clear from the outset; these stories are fiction. I made them up. They are the product of my imagination. They are historical fiction in that I tried very hard to make them fit within the historical record of Bible times, primarily provided to us in the scriptures. But they were not dictated to me by any angel.

The project began simply enough during the Advent season of 2005. At that time, I was still sending out paper Christmas cards and that year I wanted to include a small gift. So I imagined a simple dialogue between a two-year-old Jesus and his mother. I called it "Second Birthday." It was well received, so the next year I introduced a few more characters and wrote "Third Birthday." Then the project was launched. I wrote most of the stories one at a time over the next several Advent seasons.

The stories became more complicated and longer as I observed my own grandchildren growing and engaging the world on more complex levels. The stories do not form a historical fiction novel. Each of the stories stands alone and is intended to be a glimpse into incidents that might have happened as Jesus grew from an infant to a pre-teen. But the stories do build on one another and the character of Jesus is formed bit by bit.

One might think that we really know nothing of Jesus as a child. I would argue that, since we know him so intimately as a man, we have a good idea of some experiences he and his family must have had along the way toward his maturity. I pray that the reader will receive these stories in the spirit in which they were written and that the stories of Jesus as a child might endear Jesus the man to the heart of everyone who takes the time to read them.

Terry Todd
December 2016

First Birthday
Sojourn in Egypt

Mary had been to the door several times already. Every time she peered out she saw her husband still engaged in a conversation with their landlord next door. She could hear their voices but they were far enough away that eavesdropping was unproductive. She went back to tending the cooking fire and keeping her toddler from tending it himself.

The little dark-haired lad was fascinated by the fire and had watched his mother expertly pushing sticks into just the right places to make the fire leap up from the coals. He wanted to do what he saw her doing. Now that he was beginning to walk, it took constant vigilance to keep him from grabbing sticks from the woodpile and thrusting them into the fire or into the pot of food bubbling over the fire.

It was quite dark before she heard Joseph's voice coming nearer as he called his parting greetings back to the landlord. When he finally came into the house, he cautiously closed the door behind him and bolted it. Then he leaned back against the door as if to keep out something very large and very persistent.

At the sight of his father, Jesus squealed his delight and squirmed out of Mary's grasp and toddled toward him, arms open wide. Joseph scooped up the child with one hand and held him close. Jesus was cooing and babbling but Mary was frozen to her spot by the fire, watching her husband in silent tension.

Finally she found enough voice to say, "What is it?" By way of answer, Joseph shook his head and put his hand over his mouth to warn her to silence. Mary got up and went to him and allowed him to gather her in his free arm. The three of them stood there for several minutes. Baby Jesus reveled in the closeness with the two of them, cooing and patting first his mother's face and then his father's, then his own.

The tension of his parents was gradually mitigated by his inquisitive innocence when he began to poke them each in the eyes and the nose as he tried to produce the words they were teaching him, "Eye, nose..."

Finally Mary pulled away when Jesus poked a finger up her nostril. Laughing in spite of the obvious danger that hung on Joseph's shoulders when he had come into the house, she said, "I've been keeping your supper hot for so long that it is probably worthless now. But I am hungry. Let's eat."

A small square of cloth was spread on the floor. Mary ladled out lentils and onions into two simple bowls and ceremonially laid the flat loaf of bread between them still wrapped in a clean cloth. Cups of water completed the simple arrangement. Joseph finally left his post at the door and came to sit cross-legged on the floor to sup.

After a few bites, Mary whispered and asked again, "What is it? What's wrong?"

In answer, Joseph again signaled her to silence and got up and crept quietly back to the door. In one swift motion he threw the bolt and swung the door abruptly outward, striding through the doorway with his right arm leading the way. Then he stood silently looking left and right and listening carefully. At this sudden activity, Jesus struggled out of his mother's arms and tried to follow Joseph. Mary was just quick enough to scoop him back or he would have toddled right into whatever the danger was that Joseph was confronting.

Joseph bolted the door again and returned to his supper. Finally he said in a very low voice, "I was afraid someone was listening at the door."

"Who? Our landlord?" asked Mary.

Joseph nodded.

"Why would he do that?"

"Shhh… Maybe he wouldn't. He seems too curious about us, though. He kept asking questions about where we were from and why we came to Egypt."

"Maybe he's just real friendly, Joseph. It's not every day he gets news from the homeland."

"Oh, he's friendly alright. But he gets more news than you would think. This town is a major crossroads and there are more of our people going up and down this road than I would have thought possible. And Jacob is on the prowl for all the news he can get."

"Why do you say that?" asked Mary.

"Well, he's a barber, by trade. They always talk while they work and he plies every customer with question after question."

"So what did he talk to you about for so long? You weren't his customer."

"No, I am his new tenant, so I am a captive audience for more than the twenty minutes he gets with most customers. I agreed to stay here at least six months."

"So you were talking about the rent?"

"No, I have already paid him for six months."

Mary finished her supper and began nursing Jesus. She was watchful and quiet for several minutes while Joseph continued to eat. Then she said, "What are you hiding from me, Joseph?"

"I'm not hiding anything," he protested.

"Yes, you are. He said something to you that has filled you with fear. You are afraid to tell me what he said."

Joseph stopped with his spoon halfway to his mouth and stared at her for several seconds. Then he put the spoon back in the bowl, covered his face with both hands and began to shake with soundless sobs. Mary scooted closer to him so that she could touch his knee with her free hand. Joseph wept and wept and Mary squeezed his knee and continued nursing Jesus. Tears were running down her cheeks as she witnessed the depth of the emotion racking her normally stoic husband.

When the baby had truly nursed himself to sleep, she bundled him off to bed and then knelt on the floor behind Joseph and began to knead the tension out of his shoulders, humming a psalm of David almost under her breath. "Oh Lord, our Lord, how majestic is your name in all the earth! You have set your glory in the heavens. Through the praise of children and infants you have established a stronghold against your enemies, to silence the foe and the avenger."

At that point she was interrupted by new spasms of sobbing from her husband. Startled, she stopped and sat down close beside him, looking into his face for some explanation. He wept until he was spent. Then he wiped his eyes on his sleeve and looked into her eyes. He took both her hands in his and then said, "We got out of Bethlehem none too soon."

"What happened?" asked Mary.

"Herod sent special troops to Bethlehem, his own bodyguard. They must have arrived just hours after we left. He set checkpoints all around the city so no one could escape and they went from house to house looking for the one who had been born to be King of the Jews."

"Thank God we had already been warned!" exclaimed Mary. Then in a second thought she gasped, "Oh don't tell me they killed some other child, thinking they had found our son!"

Joseph wept some more before he could say, "They couldn't tell which one was the one to kill, so they killed them all." He again burst into sobbing and shaking and this time Mary wailed right along with him.

They held each other and wept for several minutes. Then Mary said, "How does Jacob know this?"

"Two young men came through last night, kinsmen of Jacob's from the tribe of Benjamin. Their sister's child was killed in the purge. They avenged themselves by killing three of the soldiers. Now they are on the run."

"Are they staying with Jacob?" she asked in alarm.

"No, they only stayed for a couple of hours and then continued. Jacob told them not to stop until they reached the other side of Cush."

"Maybe we're not safe here either," said Mary. "Maybe we should go to Cush or beyond."

"I probably would except that the angel said to take you to Egypt."

"But maybe we should flee to the farthest corner of Egypt," she said.

"We have already paid rent for this place for the next six months. We should stay here unless the angel says otherwise," said Joseph.

Mary got up to wash the dishes and clear away the remains of supper. As she did, she asked,
"Did they kill all the children of Bethlehem then?"

"Just the boys up to two years old," said Joseph.

"Oh, Joseph, that would mean Rebecca's little Lemuel!"

"And Asher's son, Rueben," answered her husband.

"Is there no limit to the wickedness of that man? Does he think he can kill God's Messiah and become an eternal king himself?"

"And we thought that the Romans were our worst enemies," mused Joseph.

As they were settling down for the night, Mary asked, "Did you ask Jacob about where to sell the frankincense and myrrh?"

"Certainly not," replied her husband. "He was already very curious about where we got the gold with which to pay the rent. If he knew I was trying to sell costly spices, he might put two and two together. He knows about the magi who drew Herod's attention to Bethlehem."

"Then what will you do?"

Joseph sighed and was silent for several minutes. Then he said, "Trust God and wait. He has shown Himself to be very interested in this saga. He has not failed us yet."

Mary snuggled close to him and whispered, "Amen."

September 2014

Second Birthday
Recalling the Shepherds

"Mama, tell me a story."

"Oh not tonight, darling. Your mama is too tired." The young mother looked into the big dark eyes of her son and hesitated.

"P'ease tell me a story," he pleaded again.

"It's too late for stories tonight, my dear. It's time to go to bed."

"But my not s'eepy. My wanna story. P'ease?"

Mary wiped her hands on her apron and brushed back her hair from her forehead. "Okay, but only because it's your birthday. How old are you today?"

Her chubby son grinned up at her but did not respond.

"Come on, show me how old you are. Hold up your fingers."

Recognition spread across her son's face and he held up two fingers.

"That's right! Today you are two years old. And because you are two years old today, Mama will tell you a story."

Her toddler clapped his hands in delight and then did his little "happy dance." It consisted mostly of stamping his feet and wringing his hands while turning in circles. He kept it up until he lost his balance and plumped down on his bottom, all dizzy.

His mother laughed in spite of her weariness and said, "Come sit on my lap and I will tell you the story of the lamb and the wolf cub, okay?"

"No," pleaded the toddler, "tell me 'bout da shepuhds."

"What shepherds? I don't know that story."

"Yes you do," the little fellow objected. "Shepuhds come see me."

"Ah, that story. But that one is true. I was thinking of made up stories."

"Tell me 'bout da shepuhds come see me," he said with such earnestness that Mary had to give in.

Mary gathered little Jesus into her lap and held him close while gathering her thoughts. Then she began.

"Well, it was just two years ago tonight, since this is your birthday. And it happened far from here."

"At home?" her son interrupted.

"No, it wasn't at home and it wasn't here. We are in Egypt now, but your abba and I are from a village in Galilee called Nazareth. Well, we had to travel to Bethlehem , the town our ancestor, King David, was from."

"Why?" asked Jesus.

"Because your abba is a descendant of David and he had to go there to be counted. Caesar ordered it so."

"And you too?" her son interjected.

Mary was startled by the question. Was this a normal question for a two-year-old? She was trying to fathom whether his question was simply a childish, "you too?" or whether he was perceptive beyond his years. His eyes were trained on hers intently and sustained her tension for another moment.

"Yes, I am too."

"You go wif Abba?"

"Yes, I went with Abba."

"My go, too?"

"Well, yes, my dear. You went too, but you traveled in my tummy because you had not been born yet. Now stop interrupting and I will tell you the story.

"It was a long journey and it was not a very comfortable one. I was in no condition to walk with you so big in my tummy. Your abba had borrowed a donkey for me to ride on, but that wasn't very comfortable either. I would ride for a while and then try walking for a while. But I couldn't walk very far either.

"By the time we reached Bethlehem it was late. All the other travelers had reached Bethlehem before us and had taken all the available rooms. Your abba asked at place after place but every last room was full. And my time to bring you into the world was upon me. I had to lie down somewhere.

"When Abba told one innkeeper's wife that I was going to have a baby, she had her husband throw some clean straw on the ground in the barn with the animals. And that's where I brought you into the world, dear one. In a barn with the animals."

"Cow say, 'mooo'."

"Yes, a cow said, 'mooo' right then and there," agreed Mary.

"Lamb say, 'baaaaa'."

"Yes, a lamb said, 'baaaaa' soon after." Mary wondered whether he was remembering the story he had often been told or whether, special child that he was, he was remembering the actual events of his first night on earth.

"Shepuhds come see me?" inquired little Jesus, looking up into his mother's eyes.

"Yes, shepherds came that same night. I hardly had time enough to clean you up and doze off for a few minutes before we heard the sounds of people just outside the barn. Men's voices, excitedly looking for a newborn baby. Abba went outside and stood in front of the door to protect us. He wasn't going to let anyone come in.

"When the shepherds saw your abba come out of the barn, they came right up to him and asked him, 'Excuse us sir, but do you know anything about a baby being born in a barn in this town?'

"Your abba was surprised at this question and he still wanted to protect us so he said, 'Who is asking and what business is it of yours?'

'Oh,' replied one of the shepherds, 'don't take it as anything unkind, sir. We are just poor shepherds, sir. We were just out on the hills and had our sheep all settled down for the night when we got the shock of our lives, sir. Angels appeared in the night sky and startled us half to death, sir. A-a-and that's why we've come looking for the child, you see?'

'No, I don't see at all,' answered your abba and was about to chase them all away when another of the shepherds spoke up.

'What he failed to tell you, sir, is that the angels told us about the baby. The first angel told us that our long-hoped-for messiah was born in this town tonight. And he told us that we could find the child wrapped up in cloths and lying in, of all places, a feed trough. Then suddenly the whole sky was filled with angels singing and praising God. That's why we've come looking for a baby in a barn. Do you know something about this?'

"Of course when Abba heard that, he realized that the shepherds meant us no harm and so he brought them in, two at a time, to see you while the others waited outside."

"Why?" Jesus asked.

"Because he didn't want a big disturbance of many rough shepherds coming in all together. You were just a tiny brand new baby. You needed peace and quiet."

"Cow say 'mooo.' Cow not be quiet."

Mary laughed in spite of herself. "You're right, my darling. That cow would not be quiet. She mooed many times all through that night."

"Shepuhds go home?" inquired the now sleepy toddler.

"Yes," replied his adoring mother. "The shepherds went back to the fields that were their home for that night, back to take care of their own little lambs. And my tiny lamb closed his eyes and dreamed heavenly dreams in a feed trough."

"My a lamb?" asked Jesus.

"Yes, my dear. You are Mama's little lamb."

"Night-night, Mama."

"Night-night, my precious one."

Christmas 2005

Third Birthday
Coming Home to Nazareth

"This is where I was a little boy like you. When I was three, I lived in this village and my abba made things and fixed things in this very shop."

"You not a little boy; you my abba."

"I am your abba now, because I have you. But I was not always this big. I started out as a baby, just like you did. And then I got a little bit bigger and I was a little boy. And this is where I lived. I had a mama and an abba just like you do and they took care of me right here."

"Where your Mama?"

"Your grandma is my Mama and your grandpa was my abba."

"No, Grandma is my grandma."

"Right, but she is only your grandma because she was my mama and then I grew up and got married and you were born as my son. She's your abba's mama and that makes her your grandma. My abba's mama was my grandma. Your abba's mama is your grandma."

"Where your abba?"

"My abba died while we were in Egypt."

"Why he died?"

"Well, he was getting kind of old and then he got sick and died."

"Sarah's kitty got sick and died. Some big boys hurt the kitty and kitty got sick and died."

"That's true. It was very bad of those boys to hurt one of God's creatures."

"We go back to Egypt, you fix the kitty? Make Sarah happy again?"

"No, Jesus, we won't be going back to Egypt. This is home."

"You not fix Sarah's kitty?"

"No, people can't do that. Sarah can get another kitty, but the dead kitty can't be fixed."

"Sarah cried 'bout her kitty died."

"Yes, she did. It was very sad."

"Did you cried 'bout your abba died?"

"I'm still crying over him. I only found out about it last night when we got here. Your grandma told me that he died only ten days ago."

"You can fix your abba that died?"

"No, my son," said Joseph, tears welling up in his eyes, "People can't fix abbas or kitties that have died. Only God can do that."

"Why God not fixed Sarah's kitty that died?"

"I'm sure I don't know. He could do it if he wanted to. He must have a higher purpose. But don't you worry; Sarah can get another kitty."

"And you can get another abba?" Jesus asked, looking up into his father's tear-stained face.

"No, I can't get another abba. In this life you can have many kitties, but you only get one abba."

"Don't cry, Abba. Maybe someday God fix your abba." Joseph gathered his little son into his arms and held him while more tears streamed from his eyes.

"Joseph, where are you?" It was Mary's voice.

"I'm here in the shop."

"Have you seen Jesus? Oh there you both are. Is everything alright?"

"Yes, he's fine. I'm fine," Joseph said, dashing the tears off his face with his sleeve.

12

"He crying 'bout his abba died," offered Jesus.

"I'm so sorry we didn't come a few weeks earlier," said Mary.

"We dared not come until that dream. I hardly dared to come even now."

"I know. But I wish you had been able to see your father again. I would have loved to see him, too."

"You can't be serious. After all his evil suspicions about you?"

"I think it would have been different if he had actually seen his grandson."

"Yeah, if he had considered him to be his grandson. That's not a given."

"I'm sure your father would have been won over if he had laid eyes on this precious lamb of ours. Anyway, come. Your mother is here and wants to celebrate Jesus' birthday. At least *she* accepts him as her grandson."

She took Jesus by the hand and led him out of the woodshop where Joseph had always worked with his father and toward the little house on the hill above it. Joseph dried his eyes again and followed after them.

"Hi, Grandma."

"Hello, you sweet thing," she said, gathering him into her lap. "Oh, Mary, he is even more beautiful in the light of day."

"You only say that because you love me."

"No, I say it because I love him. For years I have wanted to be a grandmother. And when God finally grants me my desire, before he is even born, God sends you far away for three whole years. Hmm... he doesn't much resemble my Joseph, though, does he?"

"Well, no."

"He has your eyes. I've always loved your eyes."

"Good morning, Mother."

"Joseph, you've been crying, haven't you?"

"No, mother. I'm fine. How are you?"

"Abba crying 'bout his abba died."

"Well, of course, my dear one," she replied. "I've done my share of crying, too."

"He is your abba, too?"

"No, sweetheart. He was my husband. Just like this is your mama, I am your abba's mama. And his abba was my husband, just like your abba and mama are husband and wife."

The child looked long into the face of this woman in black mourning clothes who was holding him and then said, "Sarah's kitty got sick and died and Sarah cried a lot."

"Who is Sarah?"

Mary said, "Sarah was the daughter of our neighbor in Egypt. She was the youngest of seven and often played with Jesus, though she was almost six years old."

"People can't fix a kitty that's died," said Jesus. "God can fix it, but maybe he had high purples."

"What?"

"Oh, 'purpose,'" said Joseph. I told him that perhaps God had a higher purpose in allowing the kitty to die."

"Oh, Joseph, I am so glad you have come back to Nazareth. I only wish you could have come sooner."

"We wanted to, Mother. But after what Herod did in Bethlehem, we didn't dare. We wouldn't have come now except that I had a dream."

"What kind of dream?"

"An angel appeared to me and said that it was safe to come home. Even so, we didn't feel great about it."

"Did the angel say anything about your father?"

"No, only that those who sought the child's life were dead."

"Well, the shop is still here and your father's tools haven't been confiscated. Perhaps you can finish what he was making and get started here again."

"I saw a couple of broken cart wheels out there."

"Yes, he was going to fix those for Aaron, the leather merchant."

"My abba can't fix died kitties," said Jesus

"No, but I can fix cart wheels with broken spokes."

"He can't fix his died abba, too."

"Nobody can, my sweet. I wish somebody could. He would have loved to see you."

"God can fix died abbas."

"Well, that's true," sighed his grandmother. "I believe that."

"But maybe God has high purples 'bout Abba's Abba."

"Maybe he did, maybe he did. But your Abba's Abba would have loved seeing you. He would have loved having you call him 'Grandpa.'"

"Maybe someday God fix my grandpa and I go see him."

"So be it, child. So be it. Amen."

Christmas 2006

Fourth Birthday
A Child's Prayer

"Mama, I miss Sarah. When can I go play with Sarah again?"

"Sarah lives far away from here. She and her family are in Egypt, remember?"

"Where is Egypt? I wanna go there and play with Sarah again."

"I'm sorry, honey. Egypt is very far away. Why don't you see if Uri can play?"

"Uri is not home. I saw him leave with his abba. Can Sarah come here?"

"Honey, Sarah is too far away. She can't come here. You will just have to find ways to entertain yourself here without Sarah."

"I'm going to pray and ask God to send Sarah here for my birthday."

"Jesus, honey, when you pray, you should ask for God's will to be done, not your own will."

"Why?"

"Because God is above all and has our best interests at heart. If he gives us every selfish thing we ask for, it will ruin our lives. He knows best what we need."

"Then he knows that I need to see Sarah and hear her laugh again."

"Wanting and needing are different. We don't always know what we need."

"I know what I need and I'm gonna ask God to send Sarah here for my birthday."

"Jesus, I know you miss her very much. But if you ask God to send her here, you be sure to also say, 'Yet not my wishes but yours be done.' Because God may very well wish her to stay in Egypt."

"Dear God," began Jesus, earnestly raising his pudgy hands toward heaven and closing his eyes, "Please send Sarah here for my birthday. I miss her and want to see her and hear her laugh again." There was a pause but he did not open his eyes. Then he continued, "But your wishes be done, not mine."

"Good boy," murmured Mary. She reached out with the corner of her apron and wiped a tear off her son's cheek. "Good boy. Be assured that God has heard you and will do what is best."

When the sound of feet was heard outside the door a few minutes later, Jesus sprang up and ran toward the door. He jerked the door inward and discovered his grandmother in the act of raising her hand to knock. "Well, good morning to you..." she began but Jesus dashed past her and then stopped to look in bewilderment at the empty road behind her.

"Are you alone, Grandma?" he asked, looking all around as if something or someone had just vanished before his eyes.

"What kind of greeting is that? Yes, I am alone. Does that surprise you?"

"I'm sorry, Grandma. Good morning."

"Good morning, my grandson. I wish you a wonderful birthday on behalf of myself and your dear, departed grandfather, God rest his soul. I wish he could be here to see you growing up."

Jesus looked longingly down the road once more but in vain.

"Tell your grandmother 'thank you' for her kind birthday wish, Jesus!"

"Thank you, Grandma," he said, but disappointment was clearly written all over him.

"Good morning, Mother," said Mary, kissing her mother-in-law on both cheeks but keeping her flour-covered hands held away.

"Good morning, dear. What's the matter with him? Is he having a bad day?"

"No Mother. He's just missing a playmate he remembers from Egypt."

"I prayed and asked God to send Sarah here for my birthday. When I heard you coming, I thought He had answered my prayer."

Mary and her mother-in-law exchanged glances that expressed questions rather than answers.

"Well, just because God almighty has not answered your prayer yet doesn't mean that He won't. Your birthday is not over yet."

"Mother, please don't encourage him. You'll just increase his disappointment."

"God is God, my dear. Who can say that a child's prayer will lead to disappointment? We should all pray in such faith as this."

Grandmother set her basket down and said, "Come sit on my lap a minute and we will talk of a great answer that God gave me to a prayer that seemed impossible when I prayed it."

She sat down on a bench against the wall and helped her grandson onto her lap. "Tell me, Grandma."

"Well this story takes place almost three years ago in the town of King David."

"That's Bethlehem."

"That's right, Bethlehem."

"That's where I was born."

"Exactly. And that's where you and your mama and your abba were still living when this story happened."

"What happened?"

"Well, your grandfather, God rest his soul, had made a whole wagon load of fine wheels and he took them all the way to Jerusalem to get the best possible price for them. After he had sold them, he went up to the temple to pray. He said that the whole city of Jerusalem was talking about some rich foreigners from far to the east who had come looking for a child who was born to be king of the Jews."

"They were looking for me?"

"Yes, my dear. They were looking for you."

"What happened?"

"Your grandfather learned that King Herod had asked the scholars at the temple and had then told the foreigners to go look for you in Bethlehem and if they found you, they were to bring him word of where to find you. He said he wanted to come and worship you, too."

"King Herod likes me?"

"No, my dear. He was lying. That treacherous old man had other ideas. It had been almost three weeks since the strangers had left Jerusalem and word was out that Herod was very angry that the strangers had disobeyed him. They did not bring word of your whereabouts. King Herod had sent troops on the road to Bethlehem with orders to arrest those strangers and bring them to him in Jerusalem to report what they had found.

"The whole city was talking about it and said that if those strangers weren't found, it would go very badly for the people of Bethlehem. When your grandfather, God rest his soul, got back here and told me what was going on, we fell on our faces before God and prayed for you and your mama and your abba. We were convinced that King Herod wanted to find you and kill you so that he and his sons could be kings forever. We prayed that God would get you safely away from there, but it seemed impossible."

"Why did it seem impossible?"

"Because no one could get there to warn your parents. The soldiers were already sent out. And even if someone could warn them, where could they run to hide? They had no money and no means to get any. How could they escape Herod's great army? But we prayed and prayed. We reminded God of His promise that you would save these people from their sins and that you couldn't do that if Herod killed you. We prayed that they wouldn't be able to find the rich strangers who had looked for you, just in case they knew where you were."

20

"So what happened, Grandma? Did God answer your prayers?"

"He certainly did, my sweet one. As it turns out, the strangers had found you and had brought you rich gifts and gold and they worshiped you. But then God sent them a dream that warned them to avoid Herod. So they went home another way and didn't tell Herod that they had found you."

"Yea! Good for the strangers!"

"Ah, but the danger was not over yet, my grandson. Herod sent soldiers to Bethlehem with orders to kill every baby boy in that whole vicinity since he did not know which child was to be the king. And since he didn't know exactly when you were born, he ordered them to kill every boy up to two years old."

"And the soldiers did that?"

"To their shame, they did. They were under orders."

"But they didn't kill me 'cause I runned away real fast!"

"My dear you couldn't run fast enough. But God answered our prayers for you. He sent an angel who spoke to your father in a dream and warned him to take you and your mother to Egypt. And because the foreigners had given your family gold, you could afford the journey. So you see, God answered our prayers for something that seemed impossible and protected you from King Herod."

"Mother, pardon me if this is lack of faith, but there is a difference between asking God to spare the Messiah from a jealous king and asking God for a birthday visit from a child who has no business traveling from Egypt."

"But Mary, He is the same God. If he can do great things, can He not also do the small?"

"I do not doubt His ability, Mother. Surely He can do all things. But I'm sure he has more important things to do than to bring Jesus a playmate that he misses from our time in Egypt. Why raise Jesus' hopes only to let them be shattered?"

They both turned to see how Jesus was taking all this. They found him listening intently at the door. Before either of the women heard a thing from outside, the little boy let out a shriek of delight, threw open the door with a bang and left the house on a dead run.

Mary left off kneading the bread dough and didn't even stop to rinse her hands. She and her mother-in-law reached the door at the same time and stuck their heads out side by side to see where Jesus was going. They were just in time to see him throwing his arms around a slender girl in dusty traveling clothes with such momentum that he nearly bowled her over, though she was head and shoulders taller.

"I knew you would come! I prayed to God that you would come and He answered my prayer! Oh thank you, God. Thank you." The girl was laughing and wrapped her arms around Jesus and swung his feet right off the ground.

Behind the girl, came Joseph with his arm across the shoulders of the girl's father. "Mary, you remember Jacob?"

"Yes, of course. Welcome to our home, Jacob," Mary spoke in a breathless voice as if not sure whether she were dreaming.

"Jacob, this is my mother."

"Very pleased to meet you, ma'am."

"Mother, Jacob and his family were our neighbors in Egypt. This is his daughter Sarah."

"Yes, Jesus was just telling us about her and praying that she could come for his birthday."

"Well, well for his birthday, huh? It would seem that his prayers were answered."

"Come in. Sit down. I'll make some tea as soon as I get my hands cleaned up."

Joseph spoke up again, "I was busy getting these few things in the market when a large caravan of camels and donkeys came into town. You can't imagine my surprise when Jacob, here, hailed me from the caravan."

The conversation was punctuated by shouts and laughter as Jesus led Sarah on a merry chase inside, outside and all around the house.

"I was delighted to find you so quickly. I wasn't even sure you would be in Nazareth. When you left Egypt, you weren't real clear on where you would settle."

"That's true, we weren't. But I wanted to see my family here and once we arrived and found out that my father, God rest his soul, had passed away, we decided to stay on with Mother."

Mary said, "Where is Rachel? Did she and the other children stay behind? How is it that you are in Nazareth?"

"Rachel is well and sends you warm greetings."

"She wasn't feeling well when we left there just over a year ago. Did she become quite ill?"

"She suffered for a short time and then presented me with twin sons six months ago."

"Praise be to God! Congratulations! Poor Rachel, I thought she was beyond child-bearing. Why Sarah must be..."

"She was six and a half when the boys were born. We thought our family was complete before you arrived in Egypt. But now we have nine children, praise the Almighty!"

"And none of them came with you but Sarah?" asked Mary, incredulous.

"Simeon and Lamech are helping me take a load of cotton goods up to Damascus to sell. They are taking care of the animals. Sarah was supposed to stay home and help her mother with the babies but when she heard we were going to go through Galilee she begged and cried to go with us. Her mother finally agreed, saying that the other girls were better helpers anyway and it would be one less burden on her if Sarah accompanied us."

"How long can you stay, Jacob? You are welcome guests in this house!"

"You are too kind. The caravan will rest here tonight and tomorrow because of the Sabbath. But on the second morning we will have to be on the road early."

"Papa," said a little voice at the door. Everyone turned to look at Sarah. Jesus had his arms wrapped tight around her waist. "Would it be alright if I stay here until you and Simeon and Lamech come back from Damascus? I would be good and help with chores and…"

"Honey, I can't ask them to take on another burden for a month!"

"Hush that kind of talk," said Joseph's mother. "She is not a burden. She is an answer to prayer. I forbid you to take her to Damascus with you."

Both the children shrieked in delight and flew to her to express their unbounded delight by smothering her with hugs and kisses.

"Well," said Jacob with a surprised look frozen on his face, "I've never been one to snatch away answers to prayer."

Christmas 2007

Fifth Birthday
Cousin John

"Mary, you have a visitor," called Joseph, sticking his dusty head in at the door.

"A visitor?" said Mary with surprise. She hurriedly scooped up the sweepings off the floor and threw them into the fire and set her broom against the wall. "Who is it? Welcome them in."

Joseph withdrew his head and an old woman stepped into the dim light of the kitchen.

"Elizabeth!" squealed Mary and rushed to throw her arms around her kinswoman. "I can't believe you've come. Welcome, welcome to our home," she said, kissing both her cheeks soundly. "Every time we go up to Jerusalem I look for you, but I never find you."

"Thank you for your welcome and thank you for thinking of us. No, we don't go up to Jerusalem for the feasts anymore. My Zechariah is confined to his bed most of the time now. And I am not much for traveling myself. But before I cannot travel at all, I was determined to come and see your child and introduce him to his cousin."

"Your son John is with you? Where is he?"

"My nephew Levi brought us here. He and John stopped at the shop where we met Joseph and your son, Jesus. Mary, he is a very beautiful boy."

"Beautiful? You are very kind. Not many would go so far as to say he is beautiful."

"Nonsense," replied Elizabeth. "Every child is beautiful. How much more so the one who is to save all Israel from sin!"

"Ssshhhh," cautioned Mary. "We haven't told him that yet."

"What? You haven't told him he is our long-awaited Messiah?"

"Not so loud, Elizabeth, please! Who knows what ears may be listening?"

Elizabeth stared in perplexity with her hand over her mouth.

"Please, sit down. Make yourself comfortable. I will make some tea. I'm so glad you've come."

At that moment, Jesus burst in at the door pulling John by the hand. "Mama, look! My cousin, John! They have come four days' journey to see us."

Mary studied the boy with interest. He was half a head taller than Jesus with flashing black eyes and a very serious expression on his face.

"Welcome, John. It is wonderful to see you. I stayed with your mother just before you were born but I never got to see your face until now."

John stood in awkward silence looking at this strange woman in her strange house. Then without a word, he crept behind the chair his mother was sitting in and grasped the loose folds of her traveling cloak and looked down at the floor.

"You look like your mother," observed Mary, looking from one to the other.

"That's not his mother," blurted out Jesus. "That's his grandmother."

"It's my mother, stupid," said John with a look of disdain toward Jesus.

"John, sweetie," said Elizabeth, "that's not a nice word. Mind your manners."

"You look like a grandma," said Jesus.

"I do, don't I? That's because God didn't bless us with a child until my husband and I were very old. It's a miracle. Everyone was surprised when John was born to us."

Jesus looked at his cousin with new interest. "How old are you?" he asked.

"I'm five and a half," said John. "How old are you?"

"I'm four but I will be five tomorrow."

"Day after tomorrow is your birthday, Jesus.'

John smirked at Jesus as if to say, I'm older than you and you don't even know when your birthday is. But he held his tongue.

"I thought we would be near his fifth birthday," said Elizabeth, "but I had no exact information. All I had heard was that he was born in Bethlehem, that you had fled to Egypt and that now you were back here in Nazareth. I can't tell you how excited Zechariah was to hear that he was born in Bethlehem."

"Why was he excited?" asked Jesus with innocence.

Elizabeth looked wide-eyed at Mary and back to Jesus and then back to Mary. Jesus looked at his mother's face in time to see her shake her head very slightly.

Finally, Elizabeth swallowed and answered cautiously, "Because it's a very special place to be born. We call it the city of David because that's where King David was born and grew up."

"My abba is from King David's family," said Jesus. "That's why we had to go there. We had to pay taxes there. And then I was born."

"Well, I'm glad you know that much," said the old woman with a meaningful glance at Mary.

The door opened and Joseph came in, leading a solid-looking man who appeared to be in his late twenties. "Mary, this is Levi, Zechariah's nephew."

"Actually, great nephew," the young man said. "My grandfather was Uncle Zechariah's older brother."

"Well, whatever the relation, you are still family. You are welcome here."

"Thank you very much."

As Mary was pouring him a cup of tea, Joseph asked, "How long can you stay, Levi?"

"Actually, I am hoping to travel tomorrow to visit my brother who is a rabbi in Capernaum. I would stay with him on the Sabbath and come back here on the first day of the week to escort Aunt Elizabeth and John back home. Would that be acceptable?"

"Of course," said Joseph. "We would be happy for you to stay longer, but yes, go and see your brother tomorrow. We will take good care of these two until you return."

Jesus and John looked at each other with mischievous smiles and raced out the door to play.

"I'll race you to the corner of your daddy's shop," said John and took off running without waiting to see if the challenge would be accepted. Jesus ran after him, but it was really no contest. Not only did John take advantage of the surprise start, but he was clearly the more athletic of the two. "I won," cried John as he tagged the corner post.

"I won, too," cried Jesus a couple of strides behind him.

"No you didn't. I won and you lost."

"I'll race you back to the house," said Jesus and took off running. This time the surprise start was in his favor and it was all John could do to manage a tie. "We both won," cried Jesus when they both tagged the house together. We both run really fast!"

"Yeah, but I'm faster than you," said John. "I won the first race and tied the second race."

The testing went on from running to jumping and climbing and finally to throwing. As John established his superiority in every category, he began to relax a little. Jesus, though bested in every category, did not at all lose heart. He became enamored of his powerful cousin and when they tumbled through the door back into the house half an hour later, Jesus was bursting with praise for this boy who could do almost anything.

That night the boys shared a pallet in the loft, Elizabeth and Mary shared a bed and Joseph and Levi slept in the main room on pallets on the floor. Levi left the next morning after breakfast and Joseph went out to the shop to work.

Mary was cleaning the table when she heard John ask his playmate, "Did you know I got my name from an angel?"

"Really?" asked Jesus with real interest.

"Yes. My father is a priest and when he went into the temple to burn incense, an angel was standing there. And the angel told him to name me John."

"Wow!" Jesus was completely entranced by this amazing cousin now.

"And my father was so stunned that he couldn't believe the angel so the angel zapped him and he couldn't talk for a long time. And then when I was born and he named me John, then he could talk again."

"He didn't believe the angel?" asked Jesus, incredulous at the thought.

"Well, the angel told him he was going to have a baby, but he and Mama were so old, he couldn't believe it was possible."

"Mama, did you hear that? Did you know that? Did you know his abba couldn't talk?" asked Jesus.

"Yes, I knew that. He was like that when I visited them. He couldn't say a word."

"Your father isn't a priest is he? He's a carpenter."

"That's right. He makes things and fixes things."

"Why did they name you after Joshua?"

"I don't know. Mama why did you name me after Joshua?"

Mary took a deep breath and said, "Son, I wanted to wait until you were older to tell you this, but you were named by an angel as well."

"I was? Did you hear that?" he said, turning to John. "I was named by an angel, too!" Then turning back to his mother he asked, "And Abba couldn't talk for a long time?"

Mary couldn't suppress a sly smile as she looked straight at Elizabeth and said, "Oh he could speak just fine because he believed what the angel said."

John joined back in, "The angel told my abba that I would have the spirit of Elijah." As he said this, John stood on his tip toes and flexed his muscles.

"That must be why you can run so fast and jump so high," crowed Jesus with unabashed admiration. He turned to his mother and asked, "Did the angel say that about me, too, Mama?"

"No dear. He said you would be more like King David."

"Oh boy! You will be like Elijah the prophet and I will be like King David!" The boys were fairly bouncing off the walls by now and their mothers sent them out to work off some of their enthusiasm with more physical contests and imaginary exploits to save the world.

Throughout the visit, John and Jesus enjoyed a friendly rivalry, but there was some tension between Elizabeth and Mary. Elizabeth and Zechariah had approached the raising of their darling in a very different manner than Joseph and Mary had taken with Jesus. Of course, the fact that Herod had pursued the latter child with deadly force would make them more secretive. But John, on the other hand, was a miracle child of his parents' old age. They had tended to spoil him just on that basis alone. But they also had only a few years to enjoy him and train him before their lives on earth would be at an end, unless God intervened.

When Elizabeth found that Jesus knew so little of his destiny, she couldn't help but chafe with impatience. Joseph and Mary, on the other hand, were struggling with the bluntness, if not downright rudeness, of Elizabeth's eagerness to push the education of Jesus along. And if the boys were to play together, things would surely come to Jesus' ears that they had not planned to divulge so soon.

On the evening of the first day of the week, Levi returned from visiting his brother and Joseph and Mary began to relax, knowing that their guests would be on their way back home early the next morning.

After supper, Joseph offered a cup of wine to Levi, who accepted gratefully. Elizabeth wrinkled up her nose and declined. "I'm surprised you even keep it in the house," she said. "Considering the responsibility…" and she rolled her eyes in the direction of the boys playing in the corner.

Joseph and Mary looked toward the boys and then at each other, but neither showed any sign of recognizing whatever it was she was alluding to. Neither of them noticed Elizabeth's astonished gape when Joseph poured cups of wine for himself and Mary.

Levi began to rock back and forth and tell of a rabbinical argument his brother had been caught up in. It involved the possession of a goose by a man who had contracted a skin disease after the goose had been sold to a neighbor. The neighbor then contracted a skin disease and blamed the man who had sold him the goose, but by the time the man contracted the disease, he had cooked and eaten the goose. The two parties were then taking their case to the rabbi for judgment as to who was liable for what. By the time Levi finished his story, heads were nodding and every adult was thinking about retiring for the night.

Jesus came and curled up in Mary's lap as John stood between her and his own mother. Then deciding he was thirsty, Jesus reached out and picked up his mother's wine cup and peered inside.

Elizabeth gasped and as the child put the cup to his lips, she cried out shrilly, "That's wine!" At the same instant John lashed out and hit the cup, knocking it out of Jesus' hand. Everyone came alive in an instant. The wine sprayed across both Jesus and Mary and the cup crashed to pieces on the floor. Mary screamed and Jesus began to cry. Joseph and Levi jumped to their feet and stared about stupidly as if looking for Roman soldiers who had just invaded the place.

"What? What is it?" cried Joseph. "What is all the screaming?"

Elizabeth pounced in with, "Your Jesus almost drank wine! If my John had not acted so quickly, he would have polluted himself. That was well done, John. Good for you. You saved him."

Mary was totally wrapped up in attending to Jesus. She held him tight and examined his face carefully as he continued crying. "His lip is split wide open," she said. "Joseph get me a clean cloth from over there in that basket."

John cowered into his own mother's arms when he saw that Jesus was bleeding. Levi began to gather the pieces of the cup and to murmur apologies. Joseph got Mary the cloth and examined his son's split lip before turning to mop up the spilled wine.

"I'm sorry he got hurt," went on Elizabeth, "but it is your own fault for not training him better. You have to discipline a boy or he will just run wild on you. Just think what a shame it would have been if you had allowed the Messiah to pollute himself with wine!"

During all her blaming and excusing, Joseph and Mary did not reply at all, but just tended to Jesus and to cleaning up the mess. Mary still didn't trust herself to speak. She would not even make eye contact with Elizabeth but focused entirely on stopping the bleeding of her son's lip and in soothing him. Finally, in carefully moderated syllables Joseph spoke, "I take it you are raising John as a Nazarite. Is that right?"

"Well yes, of course. That was the angel's specific instruction for the boy."

"We were not given the same instruction for our son."

"What?" Elizabeth's question was not one of content but of credulity.

Joseph repeated, "We were not told to raise our son as a Nazarite. Wine won't hurt him."

Elizabeth could not give up her belief so easily. "If the prophet is to abstain from wine, surely the Messiah should abstain even more assiduously," she reasoned.

"That is not what we were told by the angel," said Joseph. "We can trust the words of the angel, can we not? Or would you like to suggest that the angel forgot his duty?"

Finally, Elizabeth had the good sense to blush and apologize. "I'm sorry. We just assumed…"

"It's okay. We forgive you."

Elizabeth glanced at Mary to see if the inclusive "we" was warranted. Mary steadfastly refused to take her eyes off of Jesus and continued to comfort him.

32

"Now, I think it is time for all of us to get some sleep," said Joseph. He looked into his son's eyes. "Do you want to sleep with your mother tonight, son?"

Jesus shook his head. "I want to sleep with John in the loft."

John seemed relieved to hear that answer and headed for the ladder himself.

After everyone was settled down to sleep and the house was almost silent, John whispered to Jesus, "I'm sorry about your lip."

"That's okay," whispered Jesus. "I forgive you."

After a brief silence John whispered again, "What did it taste like?"

"What did what taste like?" asked Jesus.

"The wine. What did it taste like?"

"It tasted like blood," whispered Jesus.

Christmas 2008

Sixth Birthday
Educating a Messiah

"Joseph, we have to make a decision. Jesus will turn six next week and we must do something about beginning his education."

"We have begun. Every Sabbath I read the Scriptures with him and he is very alert, watching my finger proceed over the scroll. He is beginning to recognize words and sometimes speaks them out before I can utter them."

"You know what I mean. That is not enough. He should begin his formal education."

"How do you know it is not enough? That is how I learned from my father."

"That may be enough for a boy who is going to be a carpenter. It isn't enough for this boy. He needs to study under a rabbi."

"Mary, there is plenty of time for God to train him in all that he should learn. For now, let him be a child. Let me teach him here at home."

"Part of the reason you learned at home from your father is that there was no rabbi in Nazareth back then. You didn't have the opportunity. Now there is a rabbi and we should take advantage of the opportunity God has provided."

"I don't know, Mary. Rabbi Zuriel has only been here a few months. We don't know him all that well."

"Well, we need to get to know him. Invite him to dinner next week."

"Mary, you know we can't afford formal education just yet. Let me teach Jesus until we catch up on our debts."

"And I say, we can't afford to ignore our responsibility as parents. Invite him to dinner and we can at least see what his terms will be. God will provide."

At that moment a baby's cry interrupted the conversation and Mary hurried to the bedroom. The twins, James and Joseph were only two months old and put tremendous pressure on the whole household, but especially on

Mary. If she could attend to the one before he woke his brother, it would be so much better than having them both crying at once.

She returned rocking Joseph in her arms and murmuring comforts to him, "There, there little Joseph. It's going to be alright. Mama's got you. Everything is going to be fine."

"With two little ones you have no time to be preparing a dinner for a rabbi."

"The Lord will give me strength. Invite him for Wednesday."

"As you wish, my dear."

On Tuesday, Mary nursed the twins after breakfast and left them in her mother-in-law's care while she went to do the marketing. She looked in at Joseph's shop as she started down the hill. "Jesus," she called, "do you want to help me with the marketing?"

"Yes, Mother. Is it alright with you, Abba?"

"That's fine. I can show you this later," said Joseph.

"If you need him, I can manage alone."

"No, no. That's fine. I was just showing him how to sharpen a chisel. I can show him another time."

"Well, I would appreciate his help carrying things."

"Go, son. Your mother needs you and you could use the change of scenery."

"Thank you, Abba."

On the way to the market Jesus carried the empty basket for his mother. "Abba is showing me how to sharpen a chisel. I will be responsible for keeping his chisels very sharp for him."

"Just be careful, son. A sharp chisel is a dangerous thing."

"Abba says that a dull chisel is more dangerous than a sharp one."

"I'm sure you misunderstood, Jesus."

"No, Mother. It seems like a sharp chisel would be more dangerous. But Abba says a sharp chisel cuts with normal pressure. But if a chisel is dull, the carpenter has to push much harder and when he pushes harder he is more likely to slip. And a slip when you are pushing hard is very dangerous."

"Ah… I see. Well, your father is very much wiser than I when it comes to working with wood," replied his mother as they entered the crowded area where goods were on display and people were milling around looking for the best bargains.

"And you are much wiser than Abba when it comes to making good food."

Then skipping ahead he raised his hands toward the sky and sang out, "Thank you Lord of heaven and earth for giving me both a mother and a father." In so doing, his basket bumped the backside of a man who was bent over inspecting figs.

The man bellowed as if he had been stuck with a dull chisel and spun around looking for his assailant. Jesus was struck dumb by the violent reaction and stood wide-eyed and jaw gaping as the man rounded on him and boxed him on the side of the head.

"What on earth kind of wild boy are you that a man of God is not safe in the market place?" he shouted. "Whose child are you? Don't you know any better than to run screaming through a crowd of your elders and abusing them in your folly?"

The man created such a spectacle that all activity and conversation for fifty cubits in every direction stopped. Jesus was covering his bruised ear with both hands and not saying a word, the basket at his feet. Mary drew her scarf across her face and hurried between the irate man and her child. She scooped up the basket with her free hand and wrapped that arm around Jesus. She would have hurried her child out of the situation but the man grabbed her shoulder roughly and spun her around.

"So this wild boy does have a mother?" he said in tones of amazement. "What kind of mother are you that you let this child molest the rabbi of this town in the public market?"

With her face covered to the eyes and her teeth gritted so that she could hardly form words, she muttered, "We are very sorry, Rabbi. We meant no offense."

"Meant no offense?" he cried. "Whether you meant it or not, I'm offended. What kind of town is this, what kind of market, that a rabbi can't even inspect figs without some brat striking him and distracting his holy thoughts? This kind of behavior is not tolerated in Jerusalem, but out here no one knows the meaning of respect!"

"Please forgive us, sir. Did the boy injure you?"

"He injured my office. He distracted me from praising God. I was about to utter glory to God for creating such wonderful figs and for blessing Israel with good food from the earth. But this brat spoiled all that. That is a serious offense to hinder a rabbi from praising God."

"Forgive me, Rabbi, but did you hear the words the child was uttering when he inadvertently bumped you."

"Of course not, I was focused on God," said the rabbi.

"He was praising the Lord of heaven and earth for giving him both a father and a mother."

"Oh, so this brat has a father? What kind of father does he have, a wolf?"

At that, the nearby crowd snickered and Mary hurried Jesus away. She was so distraught that she turned from the market place and hurried back up the hill to Joseph at his shop. On the way home she had not spoken a word or shed a tear. But as soon as she was safely inside the shop, the dam that was holding everything inside her burst. "Oh Joseph," she cried and her legs collapsed under her and she burst out sobbing as she sank into the wood chips on the floor.

Joseph was so startled that he dropped a chisel which nicked his sandaled foot before clattering on the floor. He retrieved the tool and laid it carefully on the workbench before rushing to his wife on the floor. "Mary, what is it? What happened?"

Mary was crying too hard to speak so Joseph wrapped her in his arms and looked at Jesus for an explanation. Jesus was standing silently just inside the door. His eyes were as big as hen's eggs and his skin as pale as parchment. "What happened, son?"

"I think I did something very bad."

"What did you do?"

"I injured the rabbi's office."

"You did what?"

"The rabbi was about to praise God but I spoiled it."

"Son, why is your mother crying?"

"'Cause I made the rabbi angry, I think."

"Mary, what is all this? Are you hurt?"

"No," she finally said between sobs. "I'm not injured, but you have to tell the rabbi that he's no longer invited to dinner tomorrow."

"Mary, I can't do that. I can't invite the rabbi and then tell him I changed my mind."

"Well, then you will have to cook for him and I will go to your mother's house. I won't be under the same roof with that man."

"Come, come, Mary." He lifted her to her feet. "Let me make us a nice cup of tea and then I want to hear this out. I can see that something unusual happened to you. I want to hear all about it."

"Abba, your foot is bleeding," said Jesus.

"Ah, so it is. Well, that's nothing. We will take care of that at the house."

An hour later, Joseph's foot was bandaged, Mary was sipping her third cup of tea and Joseph and his mother were sorting through the shocking details of the marketing trip gone down in disaster.

"You say the rabbi touched you, dear," asked Joseph's mother.

"Yes, I was just going to hurry Jesus away in the crowd but he grabbed my shoulder and made me face him."

"That was not right for him to do that. He had no right. I don't care how offended he was, he had no right to lay a hand on you," her mother-in-law said.

"And he had no right to strike my child," added Mary.

"Well," said Joseph, "Jesus should have been more careful with the basket."

"It was nothing! People get jostled and bumped in the market all the time and they don't react like that," said Mary. "He didn't deserve to be slapped. He didn't need to be yelled at and humiliated. He was just expressing praise to God!"

"Is that true, son," asked Joseph with his arm around Jesus. "Were you praising God when you bumped the rabbi?"

Jesus nodded, "I was thanking the Lord of heaven and earth for giving me you and Mother. But my basket bumped his bottom and injured his office."

"Well, son, the way I understand it, your offense was small. But his response was big. And in his response he offended your office as a child of God. That is a greater offense than yours."

"And he offended my office as mother, too," added Mary. "He is no longer welcome under this roof."

"Well, speaking of offenses," said Joseph, "I can't think of many that are greater than withdrawing hospitality that has been offered. We will have to go through with this. And perhaps the rabbi will be very different in a private setting. We must have caused him embarrassment in public."

"Not half as much embarrassment as he caused us in return," said Mary. "I won't cook for him. I won't!"

"Joseph is right, Mary," said her mother-in-law. "We still have to deliver the hospitality that was offered. I will help you with the cooking."

"There is nothing to cook. I came straight home without doing the marketing."

"Tell me what you need," said Joseph. "I will take care of it."

At the appointed time the next day, the food was prepared, the house was clean and Mary made sure that the twins both needed nursing just when the guest was to arrive. Joseph was pacing, his mother was spinning yarn and Jesus was in the bedroom entertaining one little brother while his mother nursed the other.

When the knock on the door sounded, Joseph stopped stock still, shook his head and sighed before going to receive the unwelcome guest.

"Good day, Rabbi. Welcome to my home."

"Thank you, Joseph. Good day to you. God bless you and your household."

"Thank you, Rabbi. He already has."

"Oh yes, by my coming, heheh... I see what you mean."

"Please, come in."

"Thank you. A very snug little place you have here."

"My father's father built it."

"Oh, so you've always lived out here in the wilds of Galilee. I, personally, don't know how you do it. I was born and bred in one of the nicer parts of Jerusalem. I never even saw a house this small and humble until six months ago."

"Well, as scripture says, 'A man's riches can ransom his life but a poor man knows no threat.'"

"Ah, well said. I can see why you would not need to ransom your life."

"Please, Rabbi, come to the table. My mother is ready to serve dinner."

"Yes, I could do with some sustenance. Good evening, ma'am."

"Good evening, Rabbi."

"Rabbi, would you be so good as to offer the blessing," said Joseph.

"It is my custom to offer the blessing at the end of the meal," said the rabbi. "That way I know how much of a blessing is required." He laughed at his own joke but didn't proceed to pray. So after an awkward silence, the meal was served to the two men.

"So, Joseph, you tell me that you have a boy whom you would like me to educate."

"I do have a six-year-old son."

"And where is he?"

"Uh… he is helping his mother with the two little ones in the back. We have twins just two months old and they are quite a handful."

"Ah, a double blessing. May God cause them to be the deliverance of Israel."

"Thank you. Right now they are a great deal of work for their mother and for all of us."

"Nevertheless, God has blessed you. But you know it isn't proper for a six-year-old boy to be a nursemaid. He should be out here eating with his father."

"I'm sure he will be along in a moment."

"If I am to instruct him, I need to meet him and see if he is a likely lad."

"Well, actually, we've been thinking that we can't really afford to send him to you."

"You are a carpenter, are you not?"

"Yes, I am."

"Well, perhaps I could take some of my pay in goods and services."

"I appreciate your flexibility, but I'm still not sure we can afford an education."

"Oh, I'm sure we can work something out. Perhaps I could take one meal a week at your house, which would reduce your obligation to me. This food is tasty."

"Thank you. May it be health to your bones."

"But there is no meat in it."

"No, we don't often eat meat. It's too expensive for us."

"Well, on the day that I come to eat with you, I would expect there to be meat in my bowl, if not in every bowl."

"I'm thinking that we will have to put off the boy's education for another year, at least."

"Nonsense! Another year of being a mama's boy will only harm the child. He needs to be under the strict discipline of a man if you want him to amount to anything."

"Actually, he's not a mama's boy. I have begun training him in the disciplines of carpentry."

"Well, if that is all that you want for him, I can't help you. But if you want your son to amount to something, to be somebody, I could train him for a much higher calling. Maybe he could even become a rabbi someday, if he has potential."

At that moment the whimpering and cooing that was occasionally heard from the back bedroom turned into insistent wailing. Joseph's mother jumped up to go help with the babies. She soon returned consoling James in her arms, rocking him even as she walked.

"Oh, let me see him," said the rabbi. "Look at those big tears. What a fine fellow you are. You are the very image of your father, you are."

"You think this one looks like me, you should see his twin."

"This is James; his twin is named for his father because he looks exactly like Joseph did at this age," said the proud grandmother.

"And what is the name of the six-year-old who is to be my student?" asked the rabbi.

"Well, we have not yet decided whether he is to become a scholar just yet, but his name is Jesus."

"Bring him out here. I insist. I can tell you in a moment whether he is likely to prosper under my strict hand. 'Spare the rod and spoil the child' is what the scriptures say. And I go by the book."

Joseph hesitated a moment and then got up and went to the bedroom. He was gone long enough for the tension between the rabbi and the grandmother to mount.

"Please, Rabbi, have some more barley and beans," she urged.

"It is good," said the rabbi. "But you can't imagine how much better it would taste with a nice chunk of beef or lamb in it."

Finally, after several more minutes Joseph came back through the curtain carrying a little dark-haired image of himself while Jesus followed reluctantly and followed so close behind his father that he almost tripped him. He was holding his father's hand but also trying to hide behind him to avoid the gaze of the one who had so harshly attacked him and his mother the day before.

"Oh, my goodness, he does look like a little Joseph," said the rabbi, gazing at the baby. "A remarkable resemblance. May he and James be a double blessing on your household."

"Thank you."

"And who is this hiding behind you? Is this my would-be scholar?'

Joseph tried to pull Jesus into view but Jesus just as firmly fought to stay hidden behind his father.

"Come here, young man. I want to look at you."

Slowly Jesus stopped struggling and after more coaxing stood still as Joseph stepped aside.

"Oh, it's you!" exclaimed the rabbi. "No wonder you have been hiding." Turning his eyes up to Joseph, the rabbi said, "I have met this wild son of yours under some very negative circumstances."

"Yes," said Joseph, "I have heard his version of the event. Now let me hear yours."

"Yesterday in the marketplace I was in the very act of opening my mouth to praise God for his goodness in creating such wonderful figs as were for sale there when this…this… child of yours raced by and whacked me with a basket in front of all the people."

"I believe, Rabbi, that it was nothing more than childish carelessness and no harm or insult was intended. Nevertheless, Jesus has something he would like to say."

"Oh, he does, does he? Well then, let him say it."

Jesus took a deep breath and lifted his gaze up from the floor. Looking the rabbi right in the eyes, he said, "I am very sorry, sir, that I injured your office with my basket." Then his courage seemed to fail him and he fled behind his father once again.

"Well," said the rabbi, "first of all, don't call me 'sir.' You are to address me as Rabbi Zuriel bin Gamaliel bin Amminadab. Do you hear me?"

"Yes, sir," murmured the child.

"No, don't call me 'sir.' Call me Rabbi Zuriel bin Gamaliel bin Amminadab."

"Yes, Rabbi."

"Not just Rabbi. It is disrespectful. You are to give me my full measure of honor every time you address me. Do you understand?"

"Yes, Rabbi Zuriel bin Gamaliel bin Amminadab. Can I please go now?"

"Go where?"

"Go away from you, Rabbi Zuriel bin Gamaliel bin Amminadab.

Joseph intervened. "You may go, Jesus."

After a moment, the rabbi said, "This one will not be easy to train, but with enough rod, I might be able to save him."

"I think that under the circumstances it will be better if we not send him to you for a while."

"It will only be a grief to you if you leave him undisciplined."

"His mother and I will bear full responsibility for how he turns out. I think we can face that before God."

"I certainly hope you can," said the rabbi. "Tell me, why do you think this Jesus does not resemble you at all in his features while the two little ones both do?"

"The hand of God marks each of us according to his will, does it not?"

"That is true, Joseph, but this Jesus does not look like your son," said the rabbi with a suspicious glint in his eye.

"Well, Rabbi, thank you for doing us the honor of breaking bread under our roof. And thank you for your prayers."

"Thank you for your hospitality, Joseph. Let me know if you change your mind about my offer."

When Joseph leaned down to kiss Jesus goodnight a little while later, Jesus took his father's beard in both his little hands and said, "Abba?"

"Yes, my son. What is it?"

"Tomorrow is my birthday and I want to ask you for something special."

"Okay, what would you like?"

"I want you to teach me to read the scriptures."

"I can do that."

"And I want you to promise that you will never, ever send me to study with Rabbi Zuriel bin Gamaliel bin Amminadab."

Joseph kissed his son's forehead and whispered, "You have my word."

March 2010

Seventh Birthday
Hearing the Father's Voice

"Joseph, are you here?"

"Good morning, Jonas. I am here."

"Ah, good morning, Joseph. How are you? How is your family?"

"We are well, praise God. And how are you? How is your household?"

"We are well, thank you. Joseph, I have come to ask if you can make a payment on your loan this week. It has been more than a month since you have come to see me."

"I very much appreciate your patience, Jonas. But I am sorry to say that I won't be able to pay you until I finish this table and chairs and get paid myself."

"Oh dear, I was hoping you could show me good faith by paying at least a small sum," replied the creditor. "Do you have a buyer for the furniture, then?"

"I have an interested party, but he has not declared himself just yet."

"That is most unfortunate. When will you finish this project so that he can make a decision?"

"Hopefully by the end of next week, Jonas. I've been held back a bit by family needs, you know."

"Yes, I understand that you have twins and are expecting another little blessing soon. When is the baby due?"

"Any day now. Today, perhaps. My Mary is so tired; she can't imagine waiting another week."

"Well, and then you will have another mouth to feed. You are going to need help in the shop here, aren't you? Can you get any work out of this boy or does he just sit by the window and read all day?"

"My son is very diligent in his studies, but he also is a great help to me in the shop," said Joseph. "Jesus, this is Jonas bin Lemuel. He was kind enough to loan me the money to buy this wood."

Jesus laid his scroll aside and jumped to his feet. "I am honored to meet you, sir."

"And I am pleased to meet you, Jesus. What scroll is it that you are reading?"

"It is the scroll of Samuel the Prophet, sir."

"And you are able to read this scroll?"

"With Abba's help, yes I am. Every morning I sweep out his shop and then study God's word until time for tea. Then I sharpen his tools and work with him on his projects until lunch time."

"And what other scrolls have you read so far?"

"I have read the first two scrolls of Moses, but at first Abba did most of the reading."

"Joseph, do you own these scrolls?" asked Jonas with surprise.

"No, I borrow them one at a time from a rabbi in Capernaum. I can't afford to buy such precious things."

"He is very generous to loan them to you. Is he, by any chance, the customer who is interested in your table and chairs?"

"Yes, he is."

"Well, I hope his generosity extends to making this purchase very soon, for your sake as well as mine."

"I hope so, too."

"Well then, I will let you get on with it. Come to me as soon as you can make a payment, even a small one."

"Thank you. I assure you I will."

"And may the Lord bless you with another healthy child in his perfect timing."

"Thank you, Jonas. Thank you."

"Abba," Jesus said when the visitor was gone, "do you need me to stop reading and help you more?"

"No, my son. Jonas will have to extend his patience for a little longer. Please go on with your reading. Read aloud so that I can hear God's word with you. It is a blessing to me as well as a lesson for you."

"Okay. 'One night Eli, whose eyes were becoming so weak that he could barely see, was lying down in his usual place. The lamp of God had not yet gone out, and Samuel was lying down in the tabernacle of the LORD, where the ark of God was. Then the LORD called Samuel. Samuel answered, "Here I am." And he ran to Eli and said, "Here I am; you called me."'"

Jesus stopped, puzzled. "Why did he run to Eli when the Lord called him, Abba?"

"That will become clear as you read farther, son. Samuel did not know it was God who called him."

At that moment the door burst open and Joseph's mother appeared in a state of great excitement. "Joseph, her time has come. Send Jesus for the midwife and come and help me with the twins."

"Praise God!" said Joseph. "Jesus, you know what to do. Go get Miriam and tell her to come immediately."

Jesus carefully closed up the scroll and tied the cord around it as he had been taught. Then he plunged out the door in the wake of his father and grandmother. As they went up the hill to the house, he set off running down to the center of the village to find the midwife.

As he ran, he thought about God calling to Samuel. Why did Samuel not know it was God who called him? Wouldn't it be obvious? Would God's voice sound like the voice of Eli, the old, blind priest? It must have sounded like it came from a different room, since Samuel ran to where Eli was sleeping. "I think I would recognize God's voice, if he called me," he said to himself.

"Jesus," shouted a male voice, "hey there, Jesus! Where are you going in such a hurry?"

Jesus skidded to a stop, looking up into the clouds, half expecting God himself to appear.

"Are you headed to my house?" asked the same voice, nearer now.

Jesus spun around and saw Shimei, the father of Miriam approaching him from the market square.

"Oh, it's you," said Jesus. "Yes, I was sent to fetch your daughter. My mother needs her now."

"Well, Miriam told me to watch for you, but I had to run over to the market for some eggs and cheese. It's bad timing on your mother's part, son. Miriam is helping another woman and has been with her all night and all morning. Is there anyone with your mother right now?"

"My grandmother and my father are with her, but they have James and Joseph to care for so they really need Miriam, right away."

"Well, they will have to do the best they can on their own for a little while. Tell them to get some water hot and gather all the clean rags they can. I will send Miriam as soon as she can come."

"Thank you, sir," said Jesus and turned to run back up the hill. As he ran, he wondered if God's voice would sound like Shimei's. "Will I know you, if you call me, Lord God. Will I recognize your voice?"

When he arrived back home, he could hear his mother moaning and crying out before he even opened the door. It frightened him and made him feel like he had failed by not bringing the midwife with him. As he pushed open the door, his mother's cries assaulted his ears like accusations. His father turned to him expectantly. He poured out his news and waited for his father's reaction.

Joseph didn't even blink. He was busy feeding the twins and calmly replied by praying aloud for God to bless the work of Miriam's hands and to free her to come in good time. Jesus marveled that his father didn't even close his eyes to pray. He just spoke as if God was in the room, listening. His mother's cries subsided for a moment and Grandmother came out of the bedroom to hear the report.

"Where is Miriam?" she asked. "Is she on her way?"

"Not yet, Mother," replied Joseph, spooning gruel into the hungry mouth of one twin and then the other.

"Why not? It was all arranged. What happened?"

"She has been helping another mother all night and all morning. She will come as soon as she can," said Joseph.

"Lord have mercy," sighed the anxious grandmother and returned to the bedroom to attend her daughter-in-law.

"Jesus," said Joseph, "I am going to try to get your brothers down for a nap. You can go back to the shop and do some cleaning and sharpening for now. I will call you when lunch is ready."

"Yes, Abba."

Back in his father's shop, Jesus found little to sweep up, since the work was interrupted not long after he had done the morning sweeping. It took a few more minutes to hone a proper edge on the drawknife that Joseph had been using. He tested the edge by taking a few experimental pulls on a scrap of wood. He wished he could continue working on the chair leg that his father had begun to shape, but he did not want to spoil the piece. He did not yet have the strength and the experience to keep the project moving forward so as to relieve his father's indebtedness.

So he returned the drawknife to its peg above the workbench and turned his attention back to the scroll. He was still engrossed in the story of God calling out to Samuel in the middle of the night when his father came down to the shop an hour later.

"Are you hungry," asked Joseph, pushing the door open with his foot. "I've brought lunch down here where there is some peace and quiet."

"That's great, Abba. Is mother okay?" He didn't want to go back and hear or even imagine the great cries he had heard her making.

"It is her time of labor and it is never easy, but by God's mercy, I think she will be okay."

"Did Miriam come yet?"

"No, not yet. Hopefully she will come soon. Meantime, your grandmother is a big help to her. Here, we can eat at the workbench. Thank you for cleaning everything up. I've brought some good hot soup that your grandmother made and some fresh bread that the neighbor brought over."

Jesus tied up the scroll of Samuel again and pulled a stool up to his father's workbench. Joseph gave thanks to God and asked for strength for Mary and wisdom for his mother. Then he broke the fragrant bread and gave a piece to Jesus. As they dipped the bread in their soup and began to eat, Jesus looked up at his father.

"Abba, did you ever hear God's voice?" he asked.

Joseph thought while he chewed the bread. After swallowing, he said, "No, son. I don't think I have."

"But he told you to go to Egypt and then to come home to Israel."

"True, but every time God has spoken to me, it has been through an angel speaking to me in a dream. I am always asleep."

"So is that what happened to Samuel?"

"I suppose that might be," said Joseph.

"But in the scroll it is written that Samuel was lying down, it does not say that he was asleep."

"Does it say he was awake?"

"No."

"Then maybe he was asleep and the voice woke him up. It could have been an angel who spoke in a dream, just like what happened to me."

"But Abba, would Samuel fall asleep three more times and each time the Angel wakes him up?"

"Hmmm… That doesn't seem very likely, does it? When we finish our lunch, we will look at the scroll together, okay?"

"I think God spoke to him like he spoke to Moses out of the burning bush."

"Well, that is certainly possible."

"So what do you think God's voice sounds like, Abba?"

"God is God, my son. He can make his voice sound like anything he wants it to sound like. He can make it sound like thunder to terrify people as he did with those who followed Moses or he can make it sound like a small, quiet voice like he did with Elijah."

"So when you hear his voice, how do you know it's his voice?"

"I don't know for sure. But if the Lord Almighty wants you to know that he is speaking to you, you will know. He has ways of getting our attention."

"But Abba," said Jesus, "it would be terrible if God spoke to someone and he wasn't listening."

"My son, that happens all the time. Most people are not listening for God."

"Well, I'm going to listen for his voice all the time!"

After lunch was over they finished reading about God speaking to Samuel and how old Eli had accepted the judgment against him from God's hand.

"Since God wanted to pronounce judgment on Eli, why didn't he speak to Eli, Abba? Why did he speak about Eli to a little boy?"

"Maybe Eli wouldn't listen to God directly."

"But Samuel listened."

"It is not that unusual, my son, for a child to listen to God when an older person is so busy with his own ambitions that his ears are stopped up; he can't hear God."

"Well then, I want to stay a child forever. I want to hear when God speaks."

"I'm sure you will, Jesus. Now I need to get back to the house. If your brothers are awake, Grandma won't be able to deal with them and still help your mother."

"Do you need my help, Abba?"

"No, son, I think you would just be upset by your mother's cries. You can stay here or go out and play, if you like."

"Uri took his father's sheep up over the hill above our house this morning. May I go look for him?"

"I suppose that would be alright as long as you don't distract him from his work."

"Oh, I won't. I will help him take care of the flock."

"Alright, but be back before dusk and don't go past the spring of Rachel, okay?"

"I hear you, Abba; I will obey you. Thank you, Abba."

They parted ways near the corner of the house and Jesus scampered on up the track that was marked by sheep droppings and the tracks of many cloven hoofs. He sang to himself as he went, partly to fill his ears with something other than his mother's cries. But when he was well beyond the house he became quiet in the hopes of hearing the voice of God.

As he walked, he scanned the hillside above in the hopes of finding his friend, Uri. Uri was three years older and was entrusted almost daily with the responsibility for caring for the family flock. It was not a large flock, numbering less than twenty ewes and two rams. But it was a significant part of the family fortune and their care was a sometimes heavy responsibility, particularly in lambing season. Uri did not have the luxury of studying scrolls, but he had lots of time to study nature and the nature of sheep. Jesus crested the hill without finding so much as a lamb.

He proceeded down the other side to the saddle of the next hill and then descended a hundred cubits or so to the spring his father had specified as the limit beyond which he was not to go. In the immediate vicinity of the spring there was plenty of fresh evidence of sheep having been there, but none was there now. Nearby was an outcrop of rock and Jesus scaled that to get a vantage point from which to see farther.

Far down the slope of the next hill he spied a couple of forms lying in the shade of a tree. They were probably sheep, but he could see no shepherd. He watched quietly for a few minutes and then whistled as loud as he could. It didn't seem very loud out in the open, but he tried two or three more times and then watched. At last a third form rose out of the grass and looked around. It was Uri.

Uri waved when he saw Jesus standing on the lookout rock. Then he motioned for Jesus to come. Jesus shook his head and motioned for Uri to come. Uri motioned again and then lay back in the grass. Jesus thought about going but hesitated. His father had given him permission to go seek Uri. But he had also placed a limit and he was already up against that limit. He steeled himself against the temptation and sat down on the rock to wait and watch.

Perhaps half an hour passed before Uri sat up again. Again he waved at Jesus and motioned him to come. Jesus stayed where he sat. He wanted to be with Uri and to talk with him, but he could not forget what his father had said. And since he could not forget it, he could not ignore it either.

Finally, perhaps an hour after they had first seen each other, Uri rose to his feet and began coming up the hill. Jesus watched as the two sheep got to their feet and followed after Uri. Behind those two appeared the rest of the flock slowly walking up the hill in the wake of their small shepherd. Jesus studied them as they came. He would not have been surprised if he had seen Uri circle around behind them to drive them up the hill, but that did not happen. He walked ahead and all of them, without fail, followed him. As he drew nearer, Jesus could see that he often looked back and spoke to the sheep and each time he spoke, their efforts to keep up with him seemed to gain energy.

Arriving below the rock where Jesus sat, Uri looked up and said, "Why didn't you come to me? Didn't you know it was me?"

"Yes, I knew it was you."

"Then why didn't you come?"

"My father told me not to go past this spring."

"Why did he say that? It is not more dangerous down there."

"I don't know why he said it, but that is what he said."

Now that Uri was no longer leading them, the sheep went to grazing and a few went to the spring to drink.
"Why do your sheep follow you like that?" asked Jesus.

"Because I am their shepherd," replied Uri.

"Don't you have to get behind them and drive them where you want them to go?"

"No."

"It looked like you just talk to them and they follow you."

"They do. They know my voice."

"You mean they wouldn't do the same for someone else?"

"Of course not. They will follow my father's voice, because they knew his voice before mine. But no one else's."

"Can I try?"

"Sure, but they won't follow you."

"You climb up here and let me try to lead them."

The two boys changed places and Uri even gave Jesus his cloak and staff. Jesus approached the sheep very quietly and slowly but they withdrew from him as if afraid. He spoke to them in calm tones trying to coax them to follow him away from the rock but they did not show any interest at all, other than to keep a safe distance away.

"See?" cried Uri, leaping down from the rock. He spoke to the sheep and led them in the opposite direction. As one animal, they all fell in behind him and moved wherever he went. "My sheep hear my voice and they know me and they follow me," said Uri.

Jesus sat down in the grass and laughed. "That's amazing," he said. Then he asked, "Why did you not come to me? I must have waited a whole hour before you got up and came this way."

"That was the time of rest for the sheep."

"Couldn't you have brought them up here to rest?" asked Jesus.

"I have to do what's best for them. My father taught me that once the flock lies down and starts chewing the cud, you do not disturb them for at least an hour. When you whistled, I had just got the flock bedded down. It's not good to move them then."

"So you obey your father just as I obey mine," said Jesus.

"Well, in my case, it is not so much obeying my father as it is doing what is good for the sheep. I want to be a good shepherd."

"What would a bad shepherd be like?"

"A bad shepherd does whatever he wants, even if it isn't good for the sheep. But a good shepherd takes care of the sheep and doesn't take care of his own interests, not even his own safety. If a lion or a bear attacks the flock, a really good shepherd will put himself in harm's way to protect the sheep and won't give up, no matter what."

"What if the lion or bear kills the shepherd?" asked Jesus.

"That happens," said Uri. "I had an uncle who was killed by a lion. He fought the lion and killed it to protect his sheep, but he died later from his injuries. He was a really good shepherd."

"Wow. When was that?"

"That was before I was born, but people still talk about him. They call him Uriel the Lion Slayer. My grandfather still has the claws of the lion. I've seen them."

After sitting in silence for several minutes, Jesus stirred. "Well, I'd better be heading back. How much longer will you stay out?"

"When the sun is about to touch that hill over there, I will start back. Supper is served right after dark."

All the way back home, Jesus was imagining having a flock of sheep following him. He imagined having to defend them from a lion and how much he would want to run home to his father's arms for his own safety. He wondered if he would have the courage to stand and fight to defend his helpless flock.

Arriving at his father's house, he could still hear his mother's cries and he wanted to run back to the quiet pasture where Uri was watching his sheep. The sun was getting low now and soon Uri would be talking to the sheep and leading them home. He hesitated, not willing to open the door to the terror inside. Suddenly he heard voices and footsteps rounding the corner of the shop. His heart leapt at the sight. It was Miriam escorted by her father, Shimei.

"Well, young man, we are finally coming. Are we too late?"

"I don't think so, by the sound of it. But you are not too early either."

"Well, nothing truer has ever been spoken."

At that point Joseph swung the door open. "I thought I heard voices. Oh, Miriam, praise God you have come. Please, come right in. We are so glad you're here."

"Good evening, Joseph," said Shimei. "My missus and I would be honored if you and Jesus, here, would come sup with us. This is surely no environment for men to be caught up in and there's probably no one here with a moment to think of your hunger. You can even sleep at our place since there likely won't be much sleeping going on here for a while."

"Oh thank you, Shimei. You are too kind. Jesus and I can sleep over at my mother's house, but a bite to eat would be quite welcome. Just let me make sure that mother can handle the twins now that your daughter is here to help Mary."

Joseph had to feed the twins and it was full dark by the time they got away from the house and started toward Shimei's house in the village. The two men walked shoulder to shoulder though the darkness and Jesus followed behind. In some of the really dark stretches he could hardly see the two men ahead of him. But as they talked with each other, he could certainly tell by their distinctive voices which one was his father, even when they switched sides as they stepped over a canal that the road crossed.

After supper he and his father climbed back toward their neighborhood under the incredible display of stars overhead. When they turned aside to go to Grandma's house, Jesus spoke up, "Abba, will the scroll be safe in the shop tonight or should we go get it?"

"I'm sure it will be safe, but just in case, I can take it to the house when I go to check on your mother."

"Abba, did you know that sheep can recognize the voice of their shepherd?"

"I did not know that."

"Yes! Uri's sheep follow him as he talks to them. I put on his cloak and took his staff and tried to get his sheep to follow me but they ran away from me because they don't know my voice."

"I didn't think sheep were that smart."

As they entered grandmother's house, Jesus noticed that the whole house held the smell of his grandmother. And he could almost hear her voice in this house that had been her dwelling place for so long.

"Abba, could I please sleep up on the roof tonight?"

"On the roof? Don't you want to sleep in Grandma's bed?"

"No, I want to see the stars as I fall asleep." He didn't want to tell his father that he intended to stay up all night if necessary. He wanted to listen for God's voice in the stillness of the night and he was afraid that in Grandma's bed, he would only hear her voice in his head.

"Well that does sound nice, if we can get comfortable enough. Is there still a pallet up there?"

"I think so. And we can take blankets up there, can't we?"

"I don't know why not."

Joseph settled down beside Jesus on the roof. The low wall kept the night breeze from blowing directly on them as long as they didn't stand up. And grandmother's house was just around the curve of the hill far enough so that the sound of Mary's cries did not reach their ears. Joseph waited until he thought his son was sound asleep and then rose softly and tiptoed down the stairs to go and check on Mary and the rest of his family.

As soon as his father was out of the house, Jesus opened his eyes and gazed at the stars. He sat up against the wall and pulled the blankets up around his shoulders. For a long time he just sat and listened intently. Somewhere on the hills a jackal cried. A couple of dogs in the village responded by barking. Then it was very quiet.

Jesus was very alert and excited. He was sure that if he listened with all his heart and mind and strength, he would hear the very words of God. He waited in this expectant state until his tailbone began to ache and slumped back prone on the pallet, snuggled deep in the blankets. His nose and ears were cold but the rest of him was cozy. He found himself praying silently in his heart but his lips were moving much as Hannah did in the tabernacle when old Eli thought she was drunk. Maybe the Lord would answer his prayer as He had answered hers.

"Lord God Almighty, maker of all these stars, maker of me in my mother's womb, I want to hear your voice. In days of old you spoke to Abraham and told him to count these stars. You spoke to Moses and told him to go to Pharaoh. You spoke to Samuel when he was just a boy like me and told him of the terrible judgment that was going to fall on old Eli. I really want to hear you speak to me. I'm listening as hard as I can, Lord. If you speak, I will listen. I don't want to hear an angel speak in a dream, like you did with my father. If I hear an angel's voice, I won't learn to follow your voice. Just like a sheep knows his shepherd's voice and just like I can tell my father's voice from Shimei's in the dark. I want to know your voice and hear it every day. Nevertheless, not my will but yours be done."

He could not tell how long he lay awake and prayed in this manner. It seemed like he prayed for a long, long time. He prayed at least until he was tired of hearing his own voice in his head. Then he stopped and tried just listening for the voice of God again.

The next thing he knew there was a delicious warmth at his back. He snuggled into it and slept in a deep sense of security and the profound knowledge that he was not alone. Then the sound of dogs barking and roosters crowing coaxed him up to the world of consciousness and his eyes opened onto a world where the sun was about to come up over the hill. At first he couldn't remember where he was and then he remembered that he was on the roof of his grandmother's house. He turned and found that the source of that warmth and the sense of security was his father cuddled up against him on the very edge of the pallet.
His father was awake, propped up on one elbow and smiling down at him. He looked tired and happy and his eyes were all bloodshot.

"Happy Birthday, Jesus," he whispered, as if to keep it a secret.

"When did you come back, Abba?"

"Just a little while ago."

"But it's morning; were you gone all night?"

"Pretty much."

"How's mother?"

"She's pretty wrung out, but now she is resting and happy. And she brought a baby sister into the world to honor your birthday."

"Oh, that's great! What will her name be?"

"Since she arrived on your birthday, we want to hear your ideas before we choose a name. How was your night up here on the roof."

"It was good."

"Did you sleep well? You seemed to fall asleep as soon as you lay down."

"I wasn't asleep when you left."

"You weren't?"

"No, I wanted to listen for God's voice."

"Ah, I see. And did you hear the voice of the Almighty?"

A slow smile spread across Jesus' face and then he threw his arms around Joseph's neck and hugged him with such an intensity that Joseph cried out in pain.

"Ouch! Easy, you're hurting me!"

Jesus backed off a bit but took the sides of his father's beard in both hands and trembled with joy and excitement.

"I take it you are trying to say, yes?" asked Joseph.

The boy's face was radiant and his eyes were glistening with tears of joy. He could not speak but he nodded his head with enthusiasm.

"Wow, that's great," said Joseph. "So were you awake or asleep?"

"I – I – I don't know," stammered Jesus, finally finding his own voice.

"So am I allowed to ask what the Almighty said?" asked Joseph.

"He said, 'You are my beloved son; this day I have begotten you.'"

"Wow," whispered Joseph.

"And He said that I am to seek his voice all the days of my life and walk in the light of his words. His words will be a lamp to my feet and a light to my path."

"Amen, so be it," said Joseph. Then, with a big hug he whispered, "Happy seventh birthday, Son."

Christmas, 2010

Eighth Birthday
A Shattered Potter

"This is the word that came to Jeremiah from the LORD: 'Go down to the potter's house, and there I will give you my message.' So I went down to the potter's house, and I saw him working at the wheel. But the pot he was shaping from the clay was marred in his hands; so the potter formed it into another pot, shaping it as seemed best to him."

Here, the boy stopped reading and looked up, "Abba, what does it mean about the potter working at the wheel? Is he trying to repair a cart?"

"No, son, repairing a cart is more my line of work. A potter's wheel is something entirely different from a cart wheel. He uses the wheel to shape the clay into round things."

"How does it work? Does he roll a wheel over the clay?"

"Well, the potter's wheel doesn't roll; it lies in a flat plane and spins around and around this way," said Joseph, motioning with his hands."The potter puts his clay on it and as it spins, he can use a tool or his hands to mold the clay into a round shape. Didn't you ever see old Levi doing that down at the market square?"

"Who is Levi?"

"Well, he was the only potter here in Nazareth from before I was born. He passed away a few years ago as a very old man but I thought maybe you had seen him working."

"No, I've never seen a potter here."

"I guess you were too young. Levi had no children and never took an apprentice. Since his death, this town has no potter anymore."

"What makes the wheel spin? Does it have a handle so he can push it?"

"No, not a handle. I suppose the potter could spin the wheel with his hand, but the ones I have seen are all attached by a vertical axle to a second wheel underneath. It's kind of like a small cart tipped on its side. The potter uses one foot to keep spinning the lower wheel, which causes the upper one to spin at the same rate because, unlike a cart, the axle turns with the wheels. That way he can spin the wheel with his foot and use both hands to shape the clay."

"I wish I could watch a potter work at the wheel."

"That you shall, my son," replied Joseph. "I'm not sure when or where, but we will find an opportunity one of these days. How are you doing with your secret project?"

"Okay, I guess. I don't know if I will get it finished in time for Hannah's birthday."

"Can I see it or is it a secret from me, too?"

"You can see it. Just don't tell Hannah what I'm making for her." Jesus rolled up the scroll of the prophet Jeremiah and tied the cord that kept it closed. He carefully laid it out of harm's way and brought out a small parcel wrapped in a scrap of sheepskin. Unwrapping it, he showed his father the project. The wood originated as a cut-off from the end of a board that Joseph had shortened to use in making a bench. Jesus had marked out a face on the wood and removed some waste wood from either side of the face with a small saw. And he had begun rounding the head with a knife.

"It looks like you are making a doll, is that right?" asked his father. Jesus nodded. "Well, it's a beginning," said Joseph. "I see the head. What is the rest of your plan?"

Jesus picked up a piece of charcoal and marked out arms, a skirt and two feet sticking out beneath the skirt. "Something like that," he said.
Joseph looked at the design and bit his tongue for a moment and then made a careful comment. "I'm sure your sister will love it very much, especially because you are making it with your own hands."
Jesus smiled.

"Have you considered which way the grain runs in this piece of wood?" Joseph asked.

"It runs this way," Jesus said, pointing it out with his finger.

"That's true, son. Do you see any problem with how that will work out in your design?"

"No," said Jesus, "is there a problem?"

"Well, yes," replied Joseph. "Which way is this wood the strongest?"

"What do you mean?"

In answer Joseph went to the box of cut-off scraps under his main workbench. He scrounged through the box until he found two scraps of similar size. "Now look at these two pieces," he said. "Show me which way the grain runs in each of them."

Jesus examined the scraps and said, "In this one the grain runs the long way and in that one it runs across the short way."

"Correct," said Joseph. "Now suppose I hold this piece down tight against the workbench with this much sticking out over the end. And you take this mallet and strike down on the end that is sticking out. Do you think you can break it?"

"I don't know."

"Try it."

Jesus picked up his father's mallet and hit the end of the piece a tentative blow.

"Hit it harder," said Joseph.

Jesus hit it again.

"Harder, still. Go on and really give it a good smack."

Jesus swung the mallet down hard and catapulted the piece of wood out of his father's grasp. He was a little embarrassed and hurried to pick up the piece from where it had landed in the corner.

"Good!" shouted Joseph with a chuckle. "Now that is a tough piece of wood. You couldn't break it, could you? That's because the grain runs lengthwise. Now let's try it with the other piece."
Joseph held the other piece sticking out over the end of the bench in the same way. "Now give this piece just a moderate tap," he said.

Jesus did so and the part that extended beyond the bench broke right off.

"There you go," said Joseph. "Now do you see the problem with your design?"

"Not really," said Jesus.

"Well, here it is," said his father. "The thinnest part of your design is the arms. By having them stick out straight from the shoulders, your plan would have the grain running across the thinnest part, making the arms very fragile."

"So if Hanna drops the doll the arms might break…"

"Almost certainly. In fact, they might well break off while you are carving them."

"But I wanted the doll to be holding its arms out like Hannah holds hers out when she wants to be picked up."

"Well, that can be done, but maybe you should start over with a different piece of wood and plan it so that the grain runs along the arms."

"But I don't have time to start over. Her birthday is just over a week away."

"Well, you can try, but I have strong doubts about your success."

Jesus stood silent in his dilemma for a moment and then Joseph suggested, "Perhaps we could design the doll so that her arms are held mostly down but a little bit reaching out. Like this," he said, making new marks with the piece of charcoal. That kind of looks like she is starting to raise her arms, but it allows the grain to run diagonally through the arms. That will make them less fragile."

"I guess that's okay, Abba. At least I won't have to start all over."

"You will still have to be very careful in carving the arms, though," said his father.

At that moment, the door burst open and James came in. Jesus grabbed up his project and held it tightly to his body, turning his back toward his brother.

"Mama says to come up and… whatcha got there, Jesus?" He tried to circle around Jesus and see what he was hiding.

"It's a surprise for Hannah's birthday and you aren't allowed to see it yet."

"Ah come on, show me. I won't tell her."

"I don't want anyone to see it till it's finished," said Jesus.

"But you were showing Abba," protested James.

"That's different; he's teaching me how to make it," said Jesus.

Joseph intervened. "What did Mama want you to tell us, James? Is lunch ready?"

"Yes. You are supposed to wash your hands and come right now. Will you make Jesus show me what he's making, Abba?"

"No, James. He is allowed to keep his secret for now. Let's go eat, boys."

Once Jesus, his brothers and Joseph were served and beginning to eat, Mary sat down to nurse Hannah. She asked, "What scripture did you read this morning, Jesus?"

"Still reading Jeremiah the prophet, Mother."

"But which part of Jeremiah the prophet?"

"The part where the word of the Lord came to him and told him to go to the potter's house."

"Ah yes… He was supposed to watch the potter work, wasn't he?"

"Yes. I want to watch a potter working the clay on a wheel."

"Well, old Levi is gone or you could have watched him."

"Don't you know any other potters?"

"My Aunt Judith used to work as a potter."

"Your Aunt Judith?"

"Yes, my father's younger sister. You have never met her. She lives in Korazin."

"Where is that?"

"It's on a hill overlooking the Sea of Galilee. It is more than a day's journey from here."

"Can we go see her?"

Mary cast an anxious look in Joseph's direction and said," Well I don't think that is a good idea…"

"Why not," asked Jesus.

"We've not even heard from her for years. She may not even be there anymore," said Joseph.

"If she is still living, she would be there," said Mary.

"She may have died, then?" asked Jesus.

"Your family would have told us if she had passed away," said Joseph.

"The last I heard about her was not good news," said Mary. "And I haven't heard anything directly from her since before we were married."

"Shouldn't we go and check on her," asked Jesus. "Maybe she needs help. Is she sick?"

Joseph and Mary looked at each other trying to come up with some explanation of what they had heard. Then looking at the twins, James and Joseph, listening with big ears, Mary shook her head ever so slightly.

"We really don't know how she is doing," said Joseph. "Would you like some more bread?"

His effort to change the subject didn't deter Jesus. It just made him more determined, but he decided to bide his time until he and his father were alone in the shop again.

When they returned to the woodshop later, Jesus said, "There's something about Aunt Judith that you didn't want to say in front of the little ones, isn't there?"

"Well, yes... said his father.

"Can you tell me?"

"Well, it's partly rumor. We don't know many details."

"And...?"

"You won't repeat this to your brothers?"

"I won't."

"They don't need to know. Judith and her husband Shaul had a son, an only child. The boy and his father were never close. They argued about everything. If Shaul said it was a fine day, Abner, his son, would argue that it was a terrible day. If Abner liked something, then his father could not find a good word to say about that thing. It was always terrible to be around the two of them."

"That could never happen with you and me," said Jesus.

"No, by the mercy of the Almighty, I don't believe it could. But that's how it was with them. Well, Shaul made a choice that turned his son even more against him. He was getting old enough that working in their field was too hard for him. And Abner was so unable or unwilling to work with his father, that the field couldn't be kept profitable anymore. So Shaul sold it and used the money to get a position as a tax collector."

"For the Romans?"

"Yes, for the Romans. He didn't see any better way to make a living since his only son would not take a share of the field work. And then the young man was even angrier with his father and he publicly disowned him."

"A son disowned his father?" exclaimed Jesus.

"If he hadn't disowned his father first, his father would have disowned him. There was just always hatred between those two. And then Abner ran away and joined a rebel movement to fight against the Romans."

"What rebel movement?"

"Back when the census was announced and we had to go to Bethlehem to register, there was a hot-headed fellow here in Galilee named Judas who refused to be registered. He gathered a number of wild young men and decided he would throw off Roman rule, once and for all. Abner joined his rebellion, probably as much to spite his father as it was to support the cause."

"That was eight years ago, when I was born. What happened to them?"

"The Romans easily hunted them down and killed Judas and some of his followers. The rest ran away and the rebellion was over. Abner was one of the ones killed."

"I'll bet Uncle Shaul was really sad when that happened," said Jesus.

"I'm sure he was, though he might have been too proud to admit it. They say he and Judith fought so much after that that they split up. Shaul went off to some foreign country and never came back."

"How sad for Aunt Judith! She was left all alone with no husband and no son."

There was no sound but sharp steel shaving long curls of wood for a few minutes as Jesus sat imagining the terrible realities that went with such a story. Joseph was planing a board, but he didn't seem focused on his work.

"Abba, don't you think we should go and visit Aunt Judith and try to comfort her?"

"I don't know, Jesus. I'll talk to your mother about it."

Before dawn on the second morning after that conversation Jesus and Joseph left Nazareth with a borrowed donkey and some hope that they would find Aunt Judith in Korazin. They even had some hope that perhaps Uncle Shaul had repented of abandoning his wife and had come home. And Jesus cherished the hope that Aunt Judith would show him how she worked the clay on her potter's wheel.

They took turns riding the donkey and walking so that neither one had to walk all the way. And they both carved as they traveled. Jesus was working on the doll to give to Hannah on their shared birthday. And his father was carving a secret project of his own. Whether riding or walking, they both contributed to a trail of chips that marked the way they were traveling.

They stayed that night in Capernaum in the house of Rabbi Zephon, from whom they borrowed scrolls of God's word for Jesus' education. The next morning early, they began climbing to the heights from which Korazin overlooked the Sea of Galilee.

"I'll bet there is a great view of the fishing boats from up there," said Joseph.

"How long has it been since you were up there, Abba?"

"Actually, I've never been there before, son."

"But you know all about the trouble between Uncle Shaul and his son, Abner," said Jesus.

"The family came to Nazareth a few times before I was engaged to your mother. After each visit, half the town was talking about the shameful fighting between father and son. But most of the story I have heard from others, so I don't know how true it really is."

As they neared the top of the climb, the path got narrow and rocky. At perhaps the narrowest and roughest part of the route, they were overtaken by a merchant riding a camel and two servants leading heavily laden camels. Jesus was riding at the time and was absorbed in his carving and in the conversation with his father. As Joseph tried to lead the little donkey to the side of the narrow path to allow the merchant train to pass, the donkey stumbled and very nearly went tumbling off the edge. Jesus cried out as he lost his balance and fell off the donkey and rolled over the edge of the precipice, arms and legs flying.

"My son!" cried Joseph. The merchant and his servants stopped and the servants scrambled to the edge of the trail to look over the edge where the boy had disappeared in a cloud of dust. Joseph, too, was leaning out over the drop off to see what had happened to his son.

The boy had tumbled about thirty cubits down the steep hillside but had arrested his fall by grabbing onto a small hyssop plant.

"Are you okay, son?" called Joseph.

"I think so," he replied. Joseph could tell from his tone that he was shaken.

"Don't move," shouted one of the servants. "I am coming."

He quickly tied a stout rope to the saddle of the camel he had been leading and told his fellow servant to hold the camels under control. Then holding tightly onto the secured rope, he backed off the edge of the trail and started slowly finding his way backward down the treacherous slope to where the boy lay.

Joseph turned to the merchant and said, "Thank you so much for stopping and allowing your servant to help us."

The merchant nodded but said nothing. Everyone was intent on the progress of the servant toward the fallen child. If the child lost his grip on the hyssop, or if the hyssop roots lost their grip on the scanty soil, there could be a tragic outcome. The servant's feet knocked loose several rocks that rolled past Jesus and then fell a long way before they could be heard striking boulders far below. Joseph shouted encouragement to his son. The servant with the camels shouted advice to his fellow as he descended. Blood was beginning to trickle down Jesus' face but he dared not release his grasp to wipe it away.

When the servant was only a few cubits above Jesus, he said, "I will reach out for you but you must not let go of the hyssop until I say so. Don't reach out for me. You must keep holding on. Do you understand?"

Jesus nodded but didn't trust his voice to say anything. The servant took a couple more careful steps and crouched down. Making careful adjustments of his footing, he released the rope with one hand. He was quite at the end of the rope. It was a good thing that Jesus had not fallen any farther. Holding the end of the rope in one hand and crouching on his haunches, he swung the other hand carefully down toward the boy and grasped Jesus' upper arm.

"Now, you are safe, my little friend," he whispered. "You may release the bush."

A great cry of celebration and hope went up from the three men watching at the edge of the trail as the servant helped Jesus to his feet and had him climb upon his own back.

"What on earth is that knife in your hand," asked the servant. "Do you mean to slay me for saving you?"

"No, of course not," said Jesus. "It's Abba's carving knife. I was carving instead of holding onto the donkey. That's why I fell when he stumbled."

"Well hold on tight to me but be careful with that knife, son. If you cut me accidentally, we might both go to the bottom."

"I will be careful," assured Jesus.

Only when Jesus was securely on his back did the servant release his strong grip on Jesus' upper arm. Then he muttered, "Here we go." He grasped the rope with both hands and carefully rose to his feet. With encouragement from above he carefully picked his way back up through the cactus and loose rocks, going hand over hand up the rope secured to the camel. When he was nearly to the top, Joseph grabbed onto one of his arms and the other servant grabbed the other and together, they brought the servant and the almost lost boy back onto the rough trail.

"May the name of the Lord be praised!" cried Joseph. Everyone was gasping with relief as the boy was returned to his father's loving arms. "You are hurt, son. You are bleeding."

"I didn't lose your knife, Abba."

"I don't care a fig about the knife, son. I almost lost you! Your head is bleeding. Are you alright?"

"I'm fine, Abba. I think I bumped my head on a rock. I will be fine, really."

The merchant brought over a skin of water and wetting a small cloth, wiped the blood out of Jesus eyes. Then producing a flask of wine he offered it to Jesus, saying, "Here, have a drink. This will help restore you to yourself."

After Jesus had taken a drink, the merchant offered it to Joseph. "That was very nearly a bad ending for you, my good man."

"I can never thank you and your servants enough for your kind assistance, sir," said Joseph.

"You are a stranger here, are you not?"

"We are from Nazareth," said Joseph.

"And where are you going?"

"We are going to Korazin."

"To Korazin," repeated the merchant with surprise. "Well, this is the right road, but we don't get many visitors in Korazin. May I ask what your business in Korazin might be?"

"We are looking for Judith, the potter," said Joseph. "Do you know her?"
"There is no potter in Korazin, and never was a potter named Judith, as far as I can recall."

"Oh," said Joseph, "surely you are mistaken. Judith is my wife's aunt and has been a potter for many years in Korazin."

"Well, perhaps you are mistaken yourself. The only potter in Korazin in my lifetime was a man named Shaul and he has left the country in disgrace."

"That Shaul was Judith's husband," said Joseph. "But I don't believe he was ever a potter."

"I used to buy pottery from him," said the merchant. "He always represented it as his own work."

"Perhaps he helped his wife in the pottery, but she was the real artist. Do you know how she fares since Shaul left?"

"No, I have no idea. I never met the woman."

"Do you know where she lives?"

"No, I'm sorry. I do not."

At that moment they were interrupted by a loud cry from Jesus. Everyone turned quickly to see what had upset him. He bent to pick up something in the dust, right under the little donkey he had fallen off of.

"What is it, my son?" asked Joseph in alarm.

"Look," said Jesus, holding out the doll he had been making for his sister. "I dropped it when I fell and the donkey has stepped on it."

Joseph saw that one of the arms was broken off. "Oh dear, that is too bad," he said. So saying, he put his arm around Jesus and comforted him as tears began to flow.

"Well," said the merchant, "a broken toy is a small price to pay. At least you still have your life, young man."

Joseph continued holding his son and whispering comforting words to him. The merchant gave a signal to his two servants to prepare the camels to move on.

"Well, sir, we must finish this climb and get on with our work. Is there anything else I can offer you?"

"Nothing at all, sir," replied Joseph. "Thank you again for stopping and helping us."

"Don't mention it," said the merchant. "And I wish you luck in finding your kinswoman. If she really is the potter who made the fine ware that Shaul used to bring me, tell her that I have a market for her work."

"Where will we find you, sir?"

"Mine is the biggest shop in the bazaar. You can't miss me. Just ask for Simon."

"Thank you again," called Joseph as the merchant mounted the lead camel and urged her into motion.

When the three had gone out of sight, Jesus wiped his eyes with his sleeve and said, "I'm sorry for crying, Abba."

"Don't be sorry about crying," said his father. "I understand your loss. But you can carve another doll."

"Not before Hannah's birthday. But, maybe you can fix this one. Can you?"

"When we get home, I could try gluing the arm back on, but it will always be weak and will probably break off again."

"I so wanted to surprise Hannah with something nice that I had made for her and now it is spoiled."

"Well," said Joseph, "why don't you keep carving on it for practice. And maybe I will come up with an idea of how to fix it." Jesus nodded and wrapped the two pieces of the doll in the scrap of sheepskin and put it away. With that, they resumed their own journey up the trail toward Korazin.

Just at the edge of town, they stopped at the well to get a drink and water the donkey. A few young ladies hurried away from the well as they saw the strangers approaching, but one older woman was busily scrubbing clothes in a tub nearby. She watched with curiosity as Joseph and Jesus approached and drew water.

"Greetings, good woman," said Joseph. "A fine day for cleaning clothes, is it not?"

The woman nodded but did not reply.

Joseph took another sip of water and then ventured, "We are strangers here."

"You are not telling me anything I don't know," said the woman.

Joseph looked at her in surprise. "Perhaps you could direct us to our goal, if you know your way around Korazin."

"I should think I do know my way around Korazin," said the woman. "I've lived here since I was a girl."

"Then surely you can direct us to the home of Judith the potter."

"That I will not do, sir," replied the woman as she went back to her washing with energy.

"But I thought you knew your way around."

"I know every man, woman and child in Korazin."

"And Judith is gone?" asked Joseph.

"Just why do you seek her?" asked the woman, stopping her work for a moment.

"She is my kinswoman," replied Joseph. "My wife's father's sister."

"You should turn around and go back where you came from," said the woman.

"So Judith has moved away?" asked Joseph.

The woman bit her lip and went back to her washing. Joseph waited for a moment and then tried again.

"We have wasted a two-day journey, then. Can you tell us where she has moved to and when she left?"

By now the woman had washed the last piece of clothing and was hanging it over a bush to dry in the sun. She emptied out her tub and dried her hands on her apron and then looked Joseph in the eye. "I never said she left. But you obviously don't know what has become of your kinswoman. And she will not want to see you."

"How can you say that?" asked Joseph. "This boy is her niece's son whom she has never met."

"You should turn around right now and take the boy back to his mother. It will be no blessing to him to meet his great aunt in the condition in which you would find her. And she won't want to be seen."

Joseph was silent a moment as he took in what the woman was saying. Into the silence Jesus spoke,

"Perhaps Aunt Judith is the one in need of a blessing."

The woman regarded the boy for a moment and held her tongue. Then Joseph added, "We are aware of some of the great sorrow that has come upon Judith. Perhaps it would do her good to have a visit from us."

"You don't understand what has become of her, sir," said the woman. "She is a fallen woman. She doesn't need a visit from a kinsman and a boy. She is a disgrace to the whole town. If it were up to me, she would be taken out to the edge of this hill and flung off the precipice. It would cleanse the town of evil and would serve as an example to the younger women for years to come!"

So saying, she shook out the wrinkles in her skirt, turned with a flourish and stormed toward town with her nose held a fair bit higher in the air than God had originally placed it. Joseph was shaken by this revelation and by the fierce attitude of Judith's fellow townswoman. He stood a moment in silence watching the back of the woman as she stalked away in righteous indignation. "Maybe we had better turn back…" he began to say.

Jesus had already begun to lead the donkey after the woman. He stopped and turned to his father. "Abba, come. Aunt Judith needs us." And he walked after the woman toward town.

When they began to come among houses Jesus approached two boys near his own age who were playing in the street. "Excuse me," he said, "where could we find Judith the potter?" They didn't know. Their mother stuck her head out the door to see what these travelers were seeking. When Jesus told her, she pulled her head back in and closed the door with a bang.

Next, they came upon an older man sitting against the wall only half awake. Joseph shook him gently by the shoulder to rouse him, but when the man looked up, Joseph knew he was more drunk than sleepy so he hastily withdrew.

But Jesus squatted on his haunches and looked the man full in the face. The man seemed surprised. Joseph put his hand on Jesus' shoulder and said, "Come, son. We will ask elsewhere."

But Jesus remained squatting before the drunk and looking into his face. The man sat up a little straighter and said, "Hello, little man. Fine day to you."

"Thank you, and a fine day to you, sir," replied Jesus.

"Who are you, that you are not afraid of me?" asked the man.

"I am the great nephew of a woman of this town. I have come to look for her."

"Young man," said the drunk, "I know every woman in this town and most of those in Capernaum. Just tell me who you seek and I will guide you to her."

"Judith the potter is my mother's father's sister. Please take me to her."

"Judith…" stammered the man and stared at the boy stupidly."

"Do you know her?" coaxed Jesus.

"Yes, of course, I know her but… you are her kin?" he asked in wonder.

"Yes, I am. Where is she?"

The old man began to struggle to his feet and Jesus and Joseph took hold of him to help him up. Once he was on his feet, he leaned against the wall for a moment and then said, "This way. It's not far."

He was a little bit unsteady, and Jesus took hold of his hand and walked beside him. Joseph came behind, leading the donkey. The farther they walked, the steadier the man became and after a few turnings through narrow alleys, he stopped in front of a house that looked all but abandoned. There was a gateway but the gate was broken on the ground. There was a small yard that hadn't been cared for by loving hands for years and flies buzzed around some old sheep bones in front of the door.

"Is this it?" asked Joseph.

"This is it," he said, nodding his head with certainty.

"What is your name, sir?" asked Jesus.

"I am called Jonas."

"Abba, do you have any coins to spare to thank our friend for this service."

Joseph looked skeptical and may have been thinking that the man would certainly put any reward to poor use, but he got out his purse. Jesus looked into the purse and selected two coins. Giving them to Jonas, he said, "We thank you, Mr. Jonas. Go in peace." Jonas took the coins eagerly and said his goodbyes.

As he rounded the corner out of sight, Jesus and Joseph walked through the open gateway and up to the door. Joseph kicked the sheep bones aside and Jesus went right up to the door and tapped on it. "Aunt Judith," he called. "You have visitors."

Silence.

"Aunt Judith," he called again, knocking louder on the door.

Still no response. After the third attempt, Jesus thought he heard someone moving inside. At that moment a couple of girls came down the alley past the house with water jugs on their heads. When they saw a man and a boy at the door of Judith's house, they pulled their shawls across their faces and steadying their jugs with the other hand, they ran, tittering all the way to the corner. They looked back only briefly before rounding the corner out of sight.

"Aunt Judith," called Jesus, louder than ever.

The door creaked and opened only a crack. A woman's voice was heard, "Who are you?"

Joseph spoke, "Aunt Judith, I am Joseph, the husband of your niece, Mary."

"Aaaiiii," cried the voice and the door slammed shut.

"Aunt Judith," said Jesus. "Don't be afraid. We have come to visit you."

"Go away," wailed Aunt Judith. "You cannot see me like this."

Joseph said, "We have heard of your great misfortune. We have come to comfort you."

"You cannot comfort me. No one can comfort me. God Almighty has cursed me and no one can undo the cursing of the Almighty."

"Aunt Judith," said Jesus, "I want to see your face."

The door opened a crack and Aunt Judith asked, "Who is this child?"

Joseph said, "This is your kinswoman's son. This is Mary's son, Jesus."

"Please let us in, Aunt Judith," pleaded Jesus. "We have come all the way from Nazareth to see you."

"You cannot see me like this," wailed Judith. "I am a mess. This house is a disgrace. And I don't even have any water to wash my face."

"We know where the well is," countered Jesus. "We will bring you water. What do you have for us to carry it in."

"Just a minute," she said and shuffled away from the door. When she returned, she pushed a pair of earthen jugs out the door but was careful to stay out of sight while doing so.

"We will be right back," promised Joseph and they turned to go fetch water.

When they reached the main road, Joseph said, "Take the donkey and go get the water. I am going to find the bazaar and buy some food."

"Yes, Abba," said Jesus and hurried on his way.

When they returned to the door of Judith's house, it was clear that she had come out and swept the yard in front of the door step a little bit. The sheep bones were no longer in evidence.
 They called out to her and this time she opened the door to receive the water, but still kept herself out of sight. "Thank you," she said. "This is

very kind of you. Now give me an hour, please, to clean up a bit. I was not expecting guests."

"Of course," said Joseph.

While they waited for Aunt Judith to make herself and her house presentable, they wandered around to the back of the house where they found what appeared to be a small, disused stable with the roof sagging almost to the ground in the middle of one side. "Wow," said Joseph, "this hasn't been used for a while. Let's see if we can make room for the donkey in here." He found an old pitchfork hanging on the wall and began to throw moldy straw out into the sunlight to dry. Under some of the straw he found a rusty sickle and said, "see if you can cut any fresh grass with this old thing."

Jesus took it and searched through the clutter that was on the workbench in the corner but he could find no whet stone. He took the sickle outside and went to the corner of the stable where the cornerstone was exposed. It wasn't ideal, but it was better than nothing and he began to knock some of the rust off the sickle blade by carefully stroking it across the corner of the stone. After several minutes of effort, he still didn't have much of an edge, but he tested it and found that he could cut the overgrown grass growing on the north side of the stable.

By the time Joseph finished cleaning out a snug corner in the stable, Jesus came in bringing armloads of fresh-cut grass enough for bedding and fodder. He unsaddled the donkey and gave him a thorough brushing while the donkey ate. As he brushed the animal, he spoke to it with a soft voice and soothing words of gratitude for faithful service. He urged the donkey not to feel bad about stepping on the doll and breaking it. "I know you didn't intend to ruin anything. These things happen. You are completely forgiven," said Jesus.

Joseph found an old wooden bucket that they would be able to fill with water for their tired little beast of burden. Jesus took the bucket and went back to the well again. When he returned, he found his father examining the roof structure on the side of the stable where it so badly sagged. "Look, son," he said. "This beam had a knot right near the place where it was supported by this post."

"A knot often is a weak spot, Abba. You taught me that."

"Exactly. And the weight of the roof caused the weak spot to give way so that the beam fell and the post punctured the roof. Then the post was exposed to rain until it warped so badly that it is only good for firewood."

"Can you fix it, Abba?"

"I could if I had my tools and some good materials."

"There are some long pieces of wood lying up against the wall of the stable on the north side," said Jesus.

"I'll go see what there is," said his father. "In the meantime, you take that fork and clear away the moldy straw here where the roof is broken. Throw it on that pile outside. After it dries a bit we can burn it up."

Joseph went out to see what materials were against the barn. What he found was half a dozen sturdy fence posts but nothing suitable to replace a roof beam. Nevertheless, he sorted through them and found the two stoutest and straightest ones and shook the grass and dust off of them. He carried them around the stable and back in to where his son was working.

"Abba, look what I have found under the straw!" cried Jesus. "Is this a potter's wheel?" he asked.

He was grabbing handfuls of the old straw and sweeping them aside in great excitement. And what was revealed underneath was, indeed, a dusty and somewhat decrepit example of a potter's wheel.

"Yes, Jesus," replied Joseph. "That's exactly what that is."
He joined his son in digging away the detritus of years to reveal the rest of the remarkable tool and workbench of the potter.

"How does it work?" asked Jesus.

"Well, this wheel up here is where the potter throws the wet clay. And this wheel underneath is the treadle that the potter turns with his foot so that the upper wheel spins round and round."

"It does look a bit like a cart that's turned over," said Jesus.

"Yes," said Joseph. "But a big difference is that the axle turns with the wheels. If you jack up a cart and spin one wheel, the other one doesn't turn. But the axle on a potter's wheel is fixed on both ends so that the one wheel turns the other." Jesus tried spinning the wheels while his father was explaining but the wheel was so dirty and in need of lubrication that it hardly moved at all.

"It doesn't seem to work," said Jesus.

"I'd guess it hasn't been used for several years. Perhaps it needs a little attention. There is no grease left on these bearings," he said, pointing out the points where the axle was supported just under the top wheel and a shackle that held the axle just above the bottom wheel. He gripped the upper wheel in both hands and rocked it left and right. The wheel made some gritty, noises and dirt came out from where grease should have been.

"Can you fix it, Abba?"

"Well, I suppose if I had my tools and some grease, I might get it going again. It doesn't appear to be broken."

At that moment a shadow fell across the wheel and they both turned to look at Aunt Judith.

She was only a few years older than Joseph, but she looked like she had been through a terrible war. She held a scarf carefully over most of her face, but her eyes had dark rings around them. They looked dull and full of pain. She was moderately tall but was stoop-shouldered and kept her eyes cast down except for a hasty glance at her visitors. Jesus took one long look at her and began to weep. He went to her and threw his arms around her and just sobbed and sobbed.

Judith tried to pull away at first but the child's grip was very determined. She relented and wrapped one arm around him and began to weep herself. Finally Joseph approached them and put one hand on Jesus' shoulder and the other on Judith's and he began to weep with them.

The donkey in the corner stopped munching on his fresh-cut grass and pricked his ears toward the threesome for a moment and bent to suck up some cool water from the bucket.

Judith was the first to speak. "I can't believe that my wheel is still here," she said. "Shaul said he had sold it."

86

"It was under that old moldy straw," said Jesus.

"I thought it was gone," she whispered.

"It doesn't work very well," said Jesus, "but Abba can fix it. He can fix almost anything."

Judith glanced up at Joseph. She dashed the tears from her eyes with her shawl and then averted her eyes again.

Joseph spoke, "If I can borrow some tools from someone, I can take it apart and clean it. Then if I grease your wheel I can have it working again, I'm sure, Judith."

"You needn't bother, Joseph," she said. "I cannot get any clay."

"Where did you get clay before?" asked Jesus. "Did you buy it in the bazaar?"

"No, I dug it myself from our clay pit," she said.

"So, can't you dig it there again?" queried the boy.

"No, not since Shaul sold the field."

"I heard that Shaul sold the field, but your clay pit, too?" asked Joseph.

"The clay pit was at the end of the field, where the upward slope gets steep. Now I have no clay and no money to buy any. I don't even have any tea in the house. I can't even offer you a cup of tea."

"Ah, that's no problem," said Joseph. "I have just been to the bazaar and I have brought tea and bread and cheese and olives…"

"Do you have any wood to build a fire, Aunt Judith?" asked Jesus.

"Not really," said Judith, looking ashamed. "I have been having a hard time lately. I don't have much of anything."

"I can gather some dry branches from that tree behind the stable," said Jesus and hurried to do so. Joseph was already digging in the saddle bag to produce the goods he had bought in the market. By the time the sun went down, they were sitting around a cloth on the floor of the little house drinking hot tea and sharing a meal.

"Mary sends her love, Aunt Judith," said Joseph. "She wanted to come with us but we have three smaller ones at home and they keep her quite busy."

"I always loved Mary," said Judith. "I'm glad she can't see what has become of me. Please don't tell her how bad it has gotten."

"Mary knows a fair amount about your great sorrow. She knows about Abner's joining the rebellion and what became of him," said Joseph. "And she knows that Shaul abandoned you and went far away. She sent us to bless you and bring you some encouragement."

"Bless her heart," said Judith. "And bless you for making the journey. But I wish you hadn't come."

"But we are glad we have come," offered Jesus.

"I am not glad," said Judith. "I am ashamed of what has become of me but I am cursed by the Almighty and I cannot escape his judgment."

"The kingdom of God is very near," said Jesus. "It is not too late to repent, Aunt Judith."

"Repent of what?" she shouted. "Repent of being abandoned by my husband? Repent of his driving our son to his death?"

"No," said Jesus calmly. "Not that."

"Of what then?" she cried.

"Repent of hating your husband and blaming him for your sin."

Judith had no answer to the boy's words other than a fresh spate of tears.

As she wept, Jesus picked up her hair brush from a small table and stood behind her. He pulled her shawl off her head and began to brush her hair.

"No," she cried. "You mustn't! Don't you understand? I'm unclean!"

"Don't we brush a donkey or a horse when it is tired from a hard journey? Our heavenly father will have mercy on whom he will have mercy," replied Jesus. "Please allow me to do this for you, Aunt Judith. Nobody has cared for you for a long time. But your heavenly father has not cursed you. He cares for you like a husband should."

For the next half hour, he stood behind her brushing the tangles out of her long, graying hair. She wept freely for most of that time and when he had finished, she kissed his hands in gratitude.

"My Abner had gentle hands like yours," she said. "He had no business joining a rebellion. He was not a violent man. He only did it to spite his father after his father became a tax collector."

"Was he killed in a fight with the Romans," asked Jesus?

"No, he was captured alive. They brought him back here and… and…crucified him beside the main road." Judith broke down and wept for several minutes. Jesus climbed into her lap, laid his head on her shoulder and wept with her.

"They wanted to make an example of him in his home town so that no one else would rebel."

"What did Shaul do then?" asked Joseph.

"That coward cut and ran. He didn't even help me bury my poor Abner."

"We heard that he left you but we assumed it was months later," said Joseph very softly.

"No, he left the same night. I don't know if he ran away out of fear or out of guilt, but he didn't even ask for Abner's body."

"So what did you do, Aunt Judith?" asked Jesus.

"Jonas asked for his body and he and I buried him at the end of the field that used to be ours."

"If I had known, I would have come…" began Joseph, but then realized how foolish he sounded.

"You couldn't have come," said Judith. "You were fleeing to Egypt with this lad of yours. Those were terrible, terrible days for everyone in Galilee."

Judith rocked from side to side and relived the grief of those terrible days as she held her great nephew and wept.

After a long silence, Joseph stood up and stretched. "Well," he said, "we need some rest and I'm sure you do, too."

At that moment, there was a knock at the door and a man's voice called out, "Judith!"

Judith blushed and acted flustered. She hurried to the door but opened it only a crack. "Go away," she said in a voice that was full of tension.

"Judith, it's me, Jonas."

"Go away. I have guests," she said but still didn't open the door.

"I know you have guests," he said. "That's why I've come. I brought you something."

"I don't want any. Don't you ever come back here. You're killing me."

"Judith, open the door," said Jonas. "I didn't bring wine this time."

Judith looked at her guests with anguish in her face. She was on the point of crying and she was blocking the door with her foot. Again she said, "Just go away and leave me alone."

There was a long silence and then the sound of shuffling feet. "I'll leave it here by the door, I guess." There was the sound of something heavy being put down by the door and then after a moment, more shuffling steps that disappeared into the night.

"Jonas helped us find you, Aunt Judith," said Jesus softly.

Judith sat down again and let the tears run down her cheeks unchecked. "Jonas isn't a good man, but he is about the only friend I have left in this town," she said.

"And he brings you wine?" asked Joseph.

"Mostly. Sometimes he brings a leg of lamb, but I'm not sure where he gets it. I'm afraid he probably steals the lambs. He may steal the wine as well, for all I know."

Jesus went to the door and then looked back at Aunt Judith. "May I look?" he asked. Judith nodded, wiping away her tears. Jesus opened the door and peeked out. "Firewood, mostly," he reported. "But there's something else." He stooped down for a minute and then came in carefully carrying something cradled in his hands. He brought it to Aunt Judith.

"Oh, a bird's nest," she said. "with part of an eggshell still in it. He does have a soft heart when it comes to God's creatures."

Jesus went back to the open door and brought two small bundles to his aunt. "He also brought these," he said.

"Tea and sugar!" she exclaimed. "He probably stole these. He doesn't work and never has any money."

"I don't think he stole these," said Jesus. "We gave him a little bit of money for guiding us to your house. He might have bought the tea and sugar for you."

"For me and my guests. I shouldn't have been so hard on him, but he just drags me down," she said.

"Maybe he's ready for a change," suggested Jesus.

"I suppose anything is possible," muttered Judith. "I know I am ready for a change."

Joseph finally finished the thought he had begun to voice and which Jonas had interrupted. "Well, I think we had better go bunk down with the donkey and get some sleep. We can talk more tomorrow."

"You are not going to sleep in the stable, Joseph. I have a perfectly good bed in Abner's room and the two of you are going to use it."

"But Aunt Judith," objected Joseph. "What about your reputation."

"I don't have any reputation left to lose," said Judith. "And you are family. I'll not hear of you sleeping in a stable."

"Well, it wouldn't be the first time, would it, Abba?" said Jesus, winking at his father.

"No, it wouldn't. But I guess there really is no need to spurn a perfectly good bed, either."

When the roosters in the neighborhood began to crow the next morning, Jesus crept out of the house. It was barely light and the sun would not be up for nearly an hour. He had it in mind to go to the well to wash his face and hands and to bring some water back. But by the front door, he found a bucket of water already waiting. He was surprised that Aunt Judith would be up before him and had already made a trip to the well and back. He decided to go and cut some more grass for the donkey.

Upon entering the stable, he found Jonas brushing the donkey and talking to it. And the manger was already full of fresh-cut grass. And there was a second bucket of water provided for the animal.
"Good morning, Jonas," whispered Jesus. "You are up very early this morning."

"Yes, I am," said Jonas.

"Did you bring the water?" Jonas nodded.

"And cut grass for the donkey?" Jonas nodded again.

"Well thank you very much. That was very kind of you."

"Oh, not so much kindness," muttered Jonas. "More like paying my rent." He looked at Jesus sheepishly and nodded to where his own jacket lay on some of the cleaner straw in the corner of the stall.

"You slept here last night?" Jonas nodded.

"You don't have any other place to stay?"

Instead of answering, Jonas offered, "I know where I can get some more firewood, too."

"We still have some from the supply you brought last night," said Jesus. "Aunt Judith was so pleased with the bird's nest you brought her."

Jonas smiled shyly. "The young birds fledged more than a week ago or I wouldn't have moved the nest," he assured Jesus.

"The birds have nests but you don't have a place to lay your head, do you?"

"I made my nest here last night," he said with a smile.

"Well, I am going to go stir up the fire and make some tea. When Abba and Aunt Judith wake up, you shall share breakfast with us. Don't go away."

"I'll go get more wood, but I'll be back soon." So saying, Jonas hung the donkey's brush on a peg and scooped up his jacket. He was humming a tune when he went out through the stable door.

An hour later, the tea was made and Aunt Judith and her guests were about to sit down to a simple breakfast when they heard a heavy load of firewood being dropped by the front door. Jesus had already told them about Jonas and what he had already been doing that morning. He had also told them that he had invited Jonas to breakfast. Aunt Judith had objected at first but Jesus argued that hospitality offered could not be withdrawn. So at the sound of the firewood, Jesus jumped up and opened the door.

"Come in Jonas," he said. "Be our guest for breakfast."

"Thank you kindly," said Jonas and snatched off his cap as he entered the house, making nervous bows in the direction of Joseph and Judith.

"I'm sure you are hungry after all your hard work this morning," said Joseph.

"I am a little hungry," admitted Jonas.

"Thank you so much for bringing firewood and tea and sugar," added Joseph.

"Don't mention it," said Jonas.

"Now Jonas, you tell me the truth," asked Judith sternly. "Did you steal that tea and sugar?"

"No, Miss Judith," said Jonas with a pained look. "I don't steal."

"I'm sure you do steal," she said, as though proving his guilt would diminish her own.

"Why Miss Judith, I gave that up," declared Jonas. "And drinking, too," he added.

Judith gasped at the apparently outrageous lies. "Why Jonas, you old fool," she cried. "I happen to know you were drunk just yesterday and I don't know where you would have gotten the wine if you hadn't stolen it. So how can you say such an outrageous thing as that you have given up stealing and drinking?"

"I gave 'em up after that," he said without looking at Judith. He did steal a glance at Jesus, though.

And Jesus spoke up in his defense, "Repentance is repentance, whether it is years old or brand new. There is joy in heaven over one sinner who repents. Let's celebrate by breaking our fast!" With that, he offered thanks to God Almighty for the new morning, for the provision of shelter and food and for the mercies of God that are new every morning. When he said, "Amen," they all fell to eating.

"Aunt Judith," began Joseph between bites, "who bought your field from Shaul?"

"I don't have any idea," said Judith. "Shaul never told me."

"I know who bought it," offered Jonas.

"Who?" asked Joseph.

"The richest man in town, Simon bin Nathan."

94

"He bought it?" asked Judith.

"None other," said Jonas. "I used to tend and harvest that field for him before he fired me."

"I didn't know that," said Judith.

"Does this Simon also have a shop in the bazaar?" asked Joseph.

"The biggest one," said Jonas.

"I think we met him yesterday," said Joseph. "We were nearing the top of the steep climb up to this town when a merchant with three camels overtook us and we had an accident."

"What kind of accident?" asked Judith.

"Well, I was trying to lead the donkey aside to let the camels pass and the donkey stumbled,"

"And I fell off the donkey and down the cliff," finished Jesus when his father paused.

"You fell down the cliff?" exclaimed Judith. "You could have been killed!"

"By the mercies of the Almighty, I wasn't," pointed out Jesus. "And the servants who were with the merchant tied a rope to one of the camels and one of them rescued me and carried me back up."

"That would have been Lamech who rescued you," guessed Jonas. "And the other one would have been Rueben. Those are the two that always travel with him when he goes to get more merchandise from Capernaum."

"I didn't get their names," said Joseph.

"That would be them," said Jonas positively. "I know them."

"It would be very interesting if it is that Simon who owns your field," said Joseph to Judith.

"Why do you say so?" asked Judith.

"Because the Simon whose servants helped us, used to buy pottery from Shaul. And he thought Shaul was the one making the pottery. When I assured him that it was Shaul's wife who had made the pottery, he told me, 'If you find your kinswoman and she really is the one who used to make the pottery I bought from Shaul, then tell her that I have a market for her work.'"

"He said that?" gasped Judith.

"He did. So perhaps he would allow you access to your clay pit."

Soon it was arranged that Jonas would lead Joseph and Jesus to Simon bin Nathan in the bazaar so that they could see if, indeed, it was the same Simon whom they had met. And Jonas would try to arrange for Joseph to borrow a few tools, as well.

When breakfast was over, the two men and the boy set out for the center of town. Their first stop was at a carpenter's shop near the bazaar. A sturdy middle-aged man was teaching a young apprentice how to make wheel spokes. He stopped when he saw the three in front of his shop. "Aha, Jonas, are you bringing me customers or trouble?" he asked.

"Simeon, this is Joseph. He is a carpenter in Nazareth and is here visiting a kinswoman."

"Pleased to meet a fellow tradesman," said Simeon, "as long as you are not planning to move here and take some of my business away." He was smiling as he said it but it might have been a question rather than a statement.

"You may rest assured that I am not interested in moving here," replied Joseph. "It is clear from one glance around your shop that it would be hard to take business away from you."

"And what does that mean?" asked Simeon.

"It means that I can see you do quality work."

"Aha…" With that he seemed to relax a bit. "It takes a craftsman to recognize good work. Tell me, who is this kinswoman of yours? I might know her."

"Judith the potter is my wife's aunt," said Joseph.

"Oh, Judith…" said Simeon, and he paused with a glance at Jonas.

"Do you know her?"

"I know about her. I can't say that we are acquainted. I knew Shaul. I considered taking his son as an apprentice, but Shaul dissuaded me. He tried to tell me the boy was no good. His own son, mind you!"

"Yes," said Joseph, "there was tragic bitterness between those two."

"Well, is this just a social call or could I help you with something?"

"Actually, I wonder if I could borrow a few tools to do some repairs at Judith's place. She has been through some really hard times since Shaul left her and she wouldn't be able to hire you."

"That's what I understand. I tell you what, how long are you going to be here?"

"Only today and tomorrow," said Joseph. "On Friday my son and I need to start back home."

"Fine. Then you borrow anything from this shop that you need, as long as my apprentice and I are not using it."

"Well, you are a fine fellow," said Joseph. "Thank you very much. We are on our way to the bazaar but on the way back I will stop in and borrow a few things."

"You are welcome. I like to see a fellow tradesman helping his own family."

They went on from there but as they neared the busy market place, Jonas stopped. "I will wait for you here," he said. "Simon's shop is that biggest one right in the center of the center aisle."

"Why don't you come with us?" asked Joseph.

"No, no, Simon won't want to see me. You will get on better with him if I am not with you."

Joseph gave him a long look and Jonas averted his eyes. "I'll watch for you when you come out," said Jonas.

"Okay, have it your way," said Joseph and, taking Jesus by the hand, he waded into the jostling crowd of shoppers and merchants.

Simon bin Nathan saw them coming and came to greet them. "So we meet again, my traveling friends. Welcome to the finest shop in Korazin. Come have a glass of tea."

"Thank you very much, sir," said Joseph. "You were right in telling us that we would be able to find your shop quite easily."

"Yes, of course," replied the wealthy merchant. "I am a big fish in this little pond, as you can clearly see. I am glad to know that you made it on in to Korazin." Nudging Jesus he said, "And I trust you didn't fall off the donkey any more before reaching the top?"

Jesus took no offense at the jest. "No, sir. We had no more trouble."

"Thank you once again for your assistance," said Joseph, not alluding to the likelihood that the man's urgency to pass them on the steep trail played a part in precipitating the accident.

"Not at all," said Simon as he snapped his fingers at an employee and indicated that he wanted tea for his guests. "And were you successful in finding your kinswoman?"

"Yes, we were," said Joseph.

"And did you confirm that it was she and not Shaul, who made the pottery I used to buy?"

"Absolutely. Shaul never made a pot in his life. But he apparently was not beyond taking credit for his wife's work."

"Hmmph," said Simon. "Not a very honorable man to begin with, then. Even before he became a tax collector."

"Perhaps not, sir."

At this point the employee brought tea to the table. Simon sat where he could continue to supervise all the activity in his very busy shop.

"And does your kinswoman... what did you say her name is?" asked Simon.

"Judith the potter, sir."

"Yes, does Judith the potter still make those fine pieces I used to get from Shaul?"

"She would do so, sir, if Shaul had not sold her clay pit for money to buy the tax collector contract."

"He sold her clay pit?"

"Well, he sold the field to a man of this town but the clay pit was at the end of the field where it slopes sharply upward."

"Indeed!" said Simon. "I myself bought a field from Shaul but I know nothing about a clay pit."

"We wondered if it might be you. We had heard that the buyer's name was Simon."

"Did Shaul sell more than one field?" asked Simon.

"I believe he only had one field to sell, sir."

"Then why didn't he exclude the clay pit? I have no use for a clay pit."

"I have no idea. It seems there were many evidences of spite and foolishness in the man's character."

"Well, tell your kinswoman that she is free to dig clay any time she wants, but she must only sell her work to me."

"How would you feel about deeding that part of the field back to her?" asked Joseph.

"To a woman? I don't believe I could do that," said Simon with astonishment. "Even if I tried, I'm sure it wouldn't be valid."

"Perhaps you could deed it to me, then," offered Joseph. "And I would allow her to have full use of it."

The merchant drummed his fingers on the table and looked steadily at Joseph for a moment and then finished his tea with a gulp, "I suppose I could do that," he said. But I must have exclusive rights to the pottery she produces from that pit."

"Would right of first refusal be adequate?" asked Joseph. Suppose she created something that you did not want to sell; would she have the right to sell such work elsewhere?"

The merchant's face showed astonishment for a second. "I thought you said you were a carpenter," he said. "Are you sure you are not a lawyer?"

Joseph grinned at the feigned compliment. "I am only a carpenter, sir. But I am trying to think of what my kinswoman needs."

"I think she is lucky to have you, Joseph. I will do as you say. Come back tomorrow morning and I will have the documents ready to be witnessed. Now good day to you and please consider my fine merchandise on your way out."

"Sir," said Jesus. "I have a question and a request before we go."

"Okay, little man. What is your question?"

"Do we have your permission to dig up a bit of clay even today, before the documents are witnessed?"

"Yes, of course you do. My word is as good as any witnessed document. I am eager to see what Judith can still produce. And your request?"

"My request is that you hire Jonas to take care of your field again and pay him to dig clay and bring it for my Aunt Judith."

"Why you young rascal, you! How do you know about Jonas? I hope he is not one of your kinsmen as well!"

"No sir. But he has helped us a bit since we arrived in Korazin and he really needs a job."

"Well let me tell you something about old Jonas, young man. He had a job and it is nobody's fault but his own that he has none now. He is a drunkard and a thief and a ne'er-do-well. I will not have him in my employ ever again."

"Jonas has given up stealing and drinking, sir. If you give him another chance, I don't think you will be disappointed."

"He may tell you almost anything to win your favor, my boy. But I saw him drunk in the gutter not a week since!"

"Yes, I know. It was after that that he repented."

"Well, you are mistaken if you believe him," said Simon. "I won't be taken in by him ever again."

"So," said Jesus, "you do not want to be like your heavenly father?"

"Excuse me?" said Simon.

"Surely you are aware that God Almighty gives people second chances. Even after King David sinned terribly in the matter of Bathsheba and Uriah, God's word describes him as a man after His own heart."

"Well, aren't you a surprising young sprig of a man! Your father is a lawyer and you are a prophet of the most high God."

"Then you will do it?" asked Jesus.

"You know what? I'm just enough of an old fool to do that for your sake, if not for Jonas' sake. Yes, I will give old Jonas one month to show me that his repentance means something. But if he steals one tiny thing from anyone or if he gets even mildly merry on wine, it's all over for him."

"God bless you, sir," said Jesus. "I will run and get him right now. We will be your witnesses of the contract with Jonas." And without waiting for Simon's response, he was off and running.

That afternoon, Judith and Jonas led Jesus out to the field that had been sold to Simon while Joseph set about, with the help of some borrowed tools, to get the potter's wheel spinning freely again. As the threesome left the edge of town, Judith pointed up ahead.

"Do you see where that flat slab of rock juts up at a sharp angle that points on up the mountain? That's where the clay is."

Jonas was carrying a mattock and Jesus was leading the donkey which bore the light burden of two empty buckets. Judith was so excited that the other two almost had to run to keep up with her. Soon they came to the border of a field that was planted with wheat.

"This is the beginning of the field that used to be ours," said Judith.

"It doesn't look like anyone is caring for it right now, but I will soon set that right," said Jonas. "Just look at all the tares growing up with the wheat."

"Will you hoe out all the tares?" asked Jesus.

"No, if I do that, it will disturb the wheat and hinder it from growing well. But if you are careful to distinguish between the wheat and the tares," he continued, "You can cut the stems of the tares down low and it will set them back and keep them from producing seed. That will also give the wheat more sun. Then after the wheat is harvested I will tear out the tares by the roots and burn them."

They followed a narrow footpath around the corner of the field. There Judith stopped and offered up a silent prayer. Jesus looked at her for a minute and then looked up at Jonas with his question eloquent on his face. Jonas put his finger to his lips to urge silence. When Judith moved on without comment, Jonas whispered in Jesus' ear. "Abner is buried right here." He pointed down at the very corner of the field.

"No marker?" whispered Jesus.

"Simon doesn't know. Nobody knows." Jesus nodded and stroked the donkey's ears with a gentle hand and then followed Judith. From there they began to climb up toward the base of the tilted slab of rock. The slab itself was many cubits across and rose to a crooked point perhaps a hundred cubits higher than the base. No plants grew on the slab and the surface was marked by erosion from both water and wind. Right near the base there was a cluster of scrub oak growing and there was the chatter of birds in the oaks. A small tributary broke off from the main path and cut right through the scrub oak and that is the way Judith went.

When they emerged on the other side, there was a surprising lack of growth, not even oaks for the last ten cubits or so to where the slab rose up. The soil there was reddish, like the rock slab but where runoff from the rock had eroded the soil, it was yellow underneath. Judith dropped on her knees in a broad hollow where the soil was mostly yellow and bent down and kissed the soil before her.

"This is it," she whispered and once again tears came to her eyes. "Blessed be your name, O Lord God most high," she cried, "for creating this beautiful substance and returning it to my use. May everything that I make from this clay glorify your holy name."

Jesus bent down and touched the yellowish dirt and said, "This is it? This is not clay, it is dust!"

In answer, Judith scooped up a handful of the fine powder and spit into it two or three times. Then she began to work the spittle into the dust. She spit again to add more moisture and continued working the moisture and the dust together. Then she held it out to Jesus and said, "Just feel that. Feel how slippery it is. Feel how fine and smooth it is. Look, when I pinch some off, how it tries to stay together. That, my boy, is clay."

She then touched her tongue to it and tasted the mixture and sighed with great contentment. "I thought my wheel was gone. I thought my clay was gone. To be honest, I thought my life was gone. And here I am hoping again."

She directed Jonas to use the mattock to scrape away any pebbles and any reddish soil and then to fill the buckets with the finest of the fine yellowish soil.

"This yellow stuff is not at all like the soil in that wheat field," said Jonas. "Look how nothing grows in it."

"It was not meant for growing things, Jonas," said Judith. "It was meant for the potter's wheel."

Soon they hoisted the heavy buckets and hooked them over the saddle. The little donkey blew out his breath and swayed a little under the load as they turned him around and headed back through the oaks and down the trail to town.

"When we get this back to the stable, we will need more water from the well and I hope I can find my big old mud tub somewhere in the rubble out there. If I can find that, I can teach you how to tread the water and the dust together to make the most wonderful clay you ever saw," said Judith.

"I think I may have seen it in the rafters of the stable, Judith," said Jonas.

"I surely hope so. Otherwise we will have to work out small batches of clay with our hands."

When they arrived back at the stable, Joseph was just giving the potter's wheel a test spin with his foot.

"There you are," he said. "Watch this." He put one foot on the lower wheel and gave a strong shove. Both wheels spun around quietly for four or five revolutions before coming to a stop.

"You did it, Abba!" cried Jesus.

"Oh, that will do nicely," said Judith and gave it a spin with her own foot. She was smiling and there was a light in her eyes that they hadn't seen before.

"Is this that mud tub you were talking about, Judith," asked Jonas pointing overhead.

"That is it," she cried. "O God be praised. You have lifted up your handmaid out of the pit."

"And he has placed you back in ownership of your pit, your clay pit, that is," cried Jonas.

"And he has redeemed your job, Jonas," added Joseph. "This is turning out to be a pretty fine day."

He helped Jonas swing the heavy wooden tub down out of the rafters. Judith had them empty the buckets of precious yellow clay-dust into the tub. Then Jesus took the buckets and the donkey and headed for the well.

"Jonas, perhaps you could help me with my next project," suggested Joseph.

"Just tell me what to do," he said. "I have to go work in the field tomorrow, but I'm at your service today."

"Well, I've been looking at this sagging section of the roof," said Joseph. "I don't have anything with which to replace that broken beam, but here's my idea. I can take one of these stout fence posts and use it as a splint on the broken beam and use the other fence post to support the structure in the middle of the splint."

"I'm with you, sir. But how will you splint it when you can't line it up straight?"

"Well, I can fasten the splint onto only one side of the break. Then one of us will lift the side of the beam with the splint and the other will lift the other. And Jesus should be able to slip the second fence post in place under the splint if I have it cut to just the right length. Then we can rest the splinted beam on the post and finish binding the whole structure together."

"That's elegant, sir," cried Jonas.

"Well, I wouldn't call it elegant, but it is what we can do with the materials at hand. In the meantime, take this money and go buy whatever Judith would like from the market. We are going to be hungry before much longer."

Before Jonas got back with the groceries, Jesus got back with the water. Judith showed him how to be very judicious in adding only a tiny bit of water at a time to form the clay.

"If you add too much water, it makes soup instead of clay. You can't make pottery from soup. And it takes days for the water to go out of clay once you have too much in it."

She had Jesus take off his sandals and get into the tub. "This work is much too heavy for hands," she said. "And besides, it feels good to have the clay between your toes." She sprinkled small amounts of water onto the clay and had Jesus tread the water and the dirt together. "Whenever you feel a pebble or any grit at all, we need to get rid of that. We want only the purest clay to work on the wheel."

Gradually, the clay began to squish instead of sending up dust spouts with every step. Judith kept feeling the clay and finding impurities to remove and once in a while she would sprinkle a bit more water in one end of the tub or the other.

"Are you going to make some pots tonight, Aunt Judith?" asked Jesus.

"O mercy, child. No. The clay has to sit overnight to allow the moisture to become equal throughout."

"How did you learn to be a potter, Aunt Judith?"

"My mother learned it from her father. She taught me from the time I was this high," she said, holding her hand at about waist level on Jesus. "Those jugs you used to bring water from the well yesterday are the only two pieces of her work I still have."

When Jonas got back with the marketing, Judith told Jesus that he could stop treading the clay and wash his feet. "That clay needs to rest overnight, just like we do," she said. When he got out, she scooped the clay into a mound in the middle of the tub and patted it smooth like a mother pats her baby's bottom and said, "When you get washed up, come up to the house and I will give you a wet towel to put over the clay to keep it from drying out."

Jesus had a hard time falling asleep that night and when he did sleep, he kept dreaming that he and Aunt Judith were spinning the wheel and making all sorts of wonderful creations out of clay. He kept feeling bits of grit or pebble in the clay between his toes and he wanted to go wash his feet. When morning finally did come, he could hardly bear the delay to make and eat breakfast. He wanted Aunt Judith to uncover the sleeping clay and wake up her wheel.

Jonas had again slept in the stable where he kept watch over the donkey and the clay. Or perhaps the donkey kept watch over the clay and Jonas. Jonas breakfasted quickly and hurried off to show himself worthy of his job in the field of wheat. Joseph went back to his idea of repairing the sagging roof of the stable. And Jesus helped Aunt Judith clean up the breakfast things so that she would be able to return to the business of the clay that much sooner.

Finally, she wiped her hands on her apron and said, "Now let's go see about that clay."

"Yes!" squealed Jesus and he skipped out the door ahead of her. Judith brought a small bowl with her and filled it with water from the bucket by the tub.

"What's that for, Aunt Judith?" asked Jesus.

"I keep a bowl of water handy to moisten my hand if the clay tends to stick to my fingers too much," she replied.

She pulled back the cloth that had kept the clay from drying out and dug in her fingers and pulled out a handful of clay. She pinched it and punched it and slapped it into a sphere, passing it from one hand to the other. "Not bad," she muttered. "Here, feel it."

She put the ball of clay in Jesus' hands. "Just squeeze it and pat it and feel how moist it is but not soupy enough to splash. See how it will hold a shape? Now roll it between your hands to form a rope. That's it. Now dangle the rope between thumb and finger. See how it doesn't drip off. That's about right.

"Now make something out of that bit of clay," she said to Jesus.

"On the wheel?"

"No, just with your hands. I'm going to get a bigger lump of clay ready for the wheel."

Jesus began squeezing, rolling and molding with his fingers while Judith got a larger handful of clay out of the tub and began to slap it and mold it into a sphere. She stopped a few times to pick out small impurities. In the meantime, Joseph was coming and going, measuring and sawing boards and fence posts as he worked on various projects around the house and stable. The heavy lifting it would take to repair the broken roof beam would have to wait until Jonas was available.

Jesus took his clay project over to the bench across one end of the stable. He began laying out different pieces and pinching them together. Before he was finished, Judith called out, "Okay, come over here."

Jesus left his project and came at once. Judith pulled up a stool beside her potter's wheel and threw down her double handful of wet clay in the middle of the wheel. She sat down and began to spin the wheel with her foot.

"Now, see how the clay seems to move back and forth?" asked Judith.

"Yes."

"That's because it isn't exactly centered on the wheel. But watch this." She wet one hand and brought it gradually against the spinning clay. With only slight pressure and constant spinning, she smoothed the clay into a lump that seemed to stand perfectly steady on the wheel.

"Now it is centered and I can begin to shape it," she said.

While the wheel was still spinning, she plunged her thumb into the center of the clay and pressed just slightly outward. The spinning lump quickly began to form a deep, round depression in the very center. Wetting both hands, she then placed one hand on each side of the lump and began to squeeze it so that the sides grew taller and closer together. Then putting one hand inside the depression and the other on the outside, she moved her hands gradually closer to each other. The clay obediently extended itself upward in a deeper and deeper but thinner and thinner shape like a vase.

"Oops, there a pebble," said Judith and expertly picked out the offending object halfway up the side, while the wheel continued to spin. She wet her hands again and smoothed out the place where the pebble had left a gouge. She began to flute out a very delicate looking edge at the top of the vase but then stopped and let the wheel come to a halt.

"That's not going to work," she said.

"But Aunt Judith, that's beautiful," whispered Jesus. "It's wonderful how just your hands and clay can make something so beautiful."

"But look at this," she said, pointing to the delicate fluted top. "See how it is sagging? The clay is too wet to hold this fine edge. And there is some grit, too. That won't do."

With that comment, she smashed the whole structure she had made back down to a lump of clay.

"No," cried Jesus. "Why did you do that? It was beautiful."

"It may have looked good to you, but it was not good enough. I can do much better. But the clay has to be just right to hold a delicate edge. This clay is workable to a degree, but it has impurities. And each time I have to wet my hands to shape it, it becomes a little bit weaker."

"Couldn't you have fixed it?" asked Jesus.

"I can make another vase better than that one when I start with just the right conditions in the clay. This lump can be made into something, but not a fine vase like I was trying to do. Here," she said. "You try it."

So saying, she got up and let Jesus sit down at the wheel. "Keep pushing the wheel with one foot and try shaping the clay with your hands. First get the lump centered so that it doesn't wobble from side to side or front to back."

Judith kept coaching Jesus for most of the morning. Every time the piece became flawed, she would just smash it down and start over. When the clay became too wet, she would scoop it off and throw it back into the tub and get a new handful to start over.

By the fifth hour of the day, they had traded positions several times and they had finished shaping several pieces to their mutual satisfaction. These were removed from the wheel by sliding a broad flat "knife" as Judith called the tool, under the piece and lifting it off. These were set aside on the bench to dry.

"After these dry, they still won't be strong enough to use," said Aunt Judith. They are what we call green-ware. Then when they are dry we bake them in a really hot oven over night to make them strong."

"And do you use different colors of clay to make different colors on the pots?" asked Jesus.

"No, there are special paints that you apply to the pots after they are baked and then you bake them again to make the paint permanent."

"These are nice," said Jesus. "But you didn't try to make that beautiful vase again."

"I'm a little bit out of practice, Jesus," she said. "But this has been a wonderful morning and I will soon be making fine vases again. But right now I am going to make some lunch. And if you will be so kind, you can run take Jonas his lunch and eat yours with him in the field."

"I'll do it with pleasure," he replied.

When Jonas came home from the field that evening, he and Joseph did the heavy lifting while Jesus put the supporting post underneath the splint. Then Joseph finished fastening the splint to the other side of the beam and bound the whole joint together to form a solid support for the roof.

"In the morning I will re-roof that portion and the stable should stay dry for a while," said Joseph. "And then we need to start for home."

"I wish you could stay longer," said Aunt Judith.

"I wish we could, too," replied Joseph. "But I must get back to my work and Mary will begin to worry if we are not home soon."

"Thank you for teaching me about making pottery, Aunt Judith," said Jesus.

"You are most welcome, young man. I wish you could stay here and be my apprentice."

"Would you believe that this visit to you was inspired by reading God's word?" said Joseph.

110

"How did that come about?" asked Judith.

"I was reading from the scroll of Jeremiah," said Jesus. "The word of the Lord came to Jeremiah and told him to go to the potter's house for a message. The message was that the potter can reject a pot that he had begun to make and change the clay into something else altogether."

"Well," said Judith, "I guess you saw that illustrated today, didn't you?"

"Yes, I certainly did. Over and over again."

"Well, it means that God is sovereign over us like the potter is sovereign over the clay. He can do anything he wants and we have no more right to complain than does the clay," said Joseph.

"And even if we think we are becoming one thing, he can make us into another," said Jesus.

"Well, that goes for carpenters and woodcarvers as well as for potters," said Joseph.

"What do you mean, Abba?" asked Jesus.

In answer, Joseph reached into his pocket and brought out an object rolled up in a bit of sheepskin. He handed it to Jesus without another word. Jesus quickly unwrapped the object and exclaimed, "Oh, Abba…"

"What is it?" asked Jonas as both he and Judith craned their necks to see what Jesus held.

"It's a doll that I was making for my sister's birthday," said Jesus. "I wanted to make her with arms held out wide but one got broken off. I thought it was ruined but you just made her with arms crossed in front of her. Thank you so much, Abba."

"You still need to carve a bit on her skirt and feet. I think you can manage that on the way home, though."

"I thought she was ruined completely, but you have given her a new life," said Jesus.

"Well," said Judith, "that is a pretty good parable for what happened to me this week. I thought my life was ruined, but the Almighty has smiled on me through your visit and has given me a new life."

"Yeah," said Jonas. "Me, too."

Christmas 2011

Ninth Birthday
A Journey to the Sea

"Abba, I've brought you some soup. Will you sit up and eat?" asked Jesus.

Joseph roused himself and tried to scoot up to a sitting position in bed. Jesus put the soup on the little bedside table and tried to help his father get into a more upright position, plumping the pillow at his back.

"How are you feeling, Abba?"

"The Almighty be praised; I am still alive," replied his father. "But I have had better days."

"Mama has made this really good soup. She asked me to bring you some and see if you could eat it."

"I'm sure it is wonderful soup and I will try to eat some, but I have no appetite. I still feel feverish and I have been having crazy dreams."

"Dreams from the angel Gabriel?" asked Jesus.

"No, not this time, my son. Dreams from the fever, I am sure. God save us from the dreams I am having with this disease!"

"Abba, you don't look well."

"I assure you I am not well."

"Can I bring you anything? A cool, wet cloth to refresh your face, perhaps?"

"Oh, yes. That sounds wonderful, if you don't mind," sighed Joseph.

Jesus left his father sitting up in bed and the soup waiting on the bedside table. He soon returned with a clean cloth and a bowl of cool water. He wet the cloth and wrung it out and then wiped his father's brow, his cheeks and tenderly cooled his father's eyes and nose, rinsing the cloth several times in the process and wringing it out so that water would not run down and wet his father's bedclothes. "Here, let me wash your neck as well, Abba... How does that feel?"

"Oh, that helps, my son. That helps a good deal."

"Now are you ready to try the soup, Abba?"

"Yes, let me try."

Jesus held the bowl carefully to his father's lips and tipped it ever so gently so that Joseph could sip. "Not too much at first, Abba. Just try a little bit and see if it helps."

After sipping a few times, Joseph awkwardly tried to tip the bowl a bit higher and ended up coughing violently for a few minutes. Mary appeared at the door and looked in with concern but decided there was little she could do that Jesus wasn't handling. Jesus patted his father's back and held the moist cloth to his face until the spasm passed.

"Sorry," said Joseph. "I guess I got too greedy. The soup is good, but I am so weak it is hard to breathe and eat at the same time."

"Just rest a few minutes and then we can try a bit more soup if you like," said Jesus. He let his father rest a few minutes and then said, "Now, if you are ready, take a few deep breaths and then hold your breath briefly while I offer you some soup."

That worked and it became a regular routine: a few moments rest, then deep breathing. A pause in the breathing would allow him to sip a bit of soup and then return to resting. In this manner, Jesus managed to get about half the bowl of soup into Joseph before his father just wanted to go back to sleep. Jesus helped him slide back into a comfortable position and tucked him in. "Just sleep awhile, Abba. God keep you and give you strength."

He slipped out of the room and went to report to his mother.

"He ate about half of the soup but he is still very weak, Mama."

"Has the fever left him?" asked Mary.

"No, not completely. It is less, I think, but he still has some fever."

"Well, you need to keep up your strength, too. Have some soup yourself. And there is bread, as well."

As Jesus got himself some supper, his mother was cleaning up behind the twin brothers. When he sat down to eat, she sat down and nursed his little sister, Hannah, who was nearly two years old already.

"Mama," said Jesus, "how long do you think Abba will be ill?

"God alone knows," she replied. "Hopefully he is on the mend now and will soon be back on his feet."

"But how long before he is strong enough to travel to Capernaum?"

"Oh, he won't be traveling any time soon, Jesus. I will be glad when he is strong enough to play with you children and start working in the wood shop again. I would not let him travel for at least a month after a serious illness like this."

She saw the worried look pass across her son's face and asked, "Why?"

"Oh, it's nothing."

"It's the scrolls, isn't it?"

"Well... sort of."

"Can't you just keep studying from the one you have for a little longer?"

"It's not that, Mama. It's that Rabbi Zephon made us promise that we would bring back the scroll before the feast. I am happy to study it longer but I really want to keep the promise Abba and I made."

"I understand your desire, Jesus, but your father cannot possibly travel to Capernaum before the feast."

"Could I go by myself then?" her son asked.

"Absolutely not."

"But I know the way; I've been there many times with Abba," protested Jesus.

"That's completely out of the question, son." Her tone was firm and her jaw was set. There was no point pushing that argument any further.

"Then will you go with me? Please?"

"I see that you are very persistent, but no, of course not. Your father is ill and needs me here. Your brothers and your sister need me here to take care of them. I cannot go out of this door for more than an hour. Just put it out of your thoughts. Rabbi Zephon will understand that promises cannot be kept if God keeps you from honoring them."

"But, if Abba starts to get better. He could take care of the boys and we could take Hannah with us..." pleaded Jesus.

"That is a very big 'if,' my son. Don't bother me about it anymore. I have too much to do here. I can't even think about Rabbi Zephon and what he expects. God will give him grace to accept the delay or he can just find some other solution for the meantime. Your father is ill and I am not budging from here. Now eat your supper and leave me in peace."

Jesus looked very somber and ate very slowly but he didn't say anything for a long time. When he finally did speak, he took a different tack. "Can I go about the town tomorrow to try and find someone who can take Rabbi Zephon a message?"

"We will see about that in the morning," replied his mother. "For now, just help me get the kitchen cleaned up and the little ones off to bed."

She hadn't said, 'No.' There was some possibility in her answer of "We will see." That was enough for tonight. Jesus swallowed the last of his soup and began to clear away the dishes.

The next morning Jesus was up before dawn, eager to get his chores out of the way so that he might get permission to scout around town for someone willing to go to Capernaum. Overnight, his urgency to go to Capernaum had not diminished; indeed, his plans had expanded from finding someone to take a message, to finding someone who would take him to Capernaum. He did not even consider sending the scroll with a messenger. Not only was the scroll too precious to entrust to someone else, but the possibility of exchanging it for another so that his studies could continue seemed impossibly remote if the task were to be entrusted to someone else.

First he brought water from the well. Then he gathered a double load of firewood. His mind was busy with the question of who would bring water and wood if he were gone for a few days. He might prevail upon his friend, Uri the shepherd, to bring a bundle of wood as he came home each evening from tending his flock. But who would bring water?

His grandmother lived nearby, but she was so old that she depended on others to bring her water most days. Sometimes he, himself, brought her water but not every day. He thought about those others who brought water to her; was there anyone among them who might also bring water to his mother? Following this train of thought as he fed the chickens and gathered the eggs, he decided that he would visit Grandmother and ask her who brought water to her.

When he re-entered the house, he found his mother busy making breakfast. "Good morning, Mama," he whispered. "How is Abba this morning? Better, I hope."

"He is still asleep," she whispered back, hugging her first-born to her with one arm while stirring a pot with the other. "I think the fever might be broken. Sleep is the best thing for him right now."

"My chores are all done," offered Jesus. "May I bring Grandmother some water?"

"Bless you for thinking of her, Son. I don't think she will be up this early. Why don't you have some breakfast first."

At that moment, Hannah began to cry. Mary handed the stirring over to Jesus and hurried to quiet her youngest lest she should wake Joseph. She soon returned with Hannah on her hip. Jesus took his little sister in his arms and began cooing to her, walking her around the kitchen so that Mary could return to her cooking. The twins would likely sleep for at least another hour, but Hannah, like Jesus, was an early riser.

And as soon as she was awake, Hannah wanted to eat. Jesus scooped up a crust of bread while he walked her around the room and allowed her to begin nibbling on it. But what she really wanted was to nurse. Knowing the routine all too well, Mary took the pot off the fire and set it aside to cool while she nursed her little girl.

"Go ahead and serve yourself some of the porridge, but let it cool before you taste it. Don't burn your mouth."

Jesus complied. He was getting fairly independent around the kitchen. That is often a necessity with the oldest child; mothers have so much that they have to do for the smaller ones and they often rely on the older ones, not only to take care of themselves, but also to help take care of the younger ones. Jesus was no exception. Jesus stirred his porridge vigorously and blew on it to cool it faster. He was eager to be about his mission to Grandmother's house. As soon as possible, he finished his bowl and a piece of his mother's day-old bread.

"May I go and bring water for Grandmother now, please?"

"I don't think she will be up this early, Jesus," protested Mary.

"Well, by the time I bring the water and gather her some firewood, she might be."

"Oh, okay. Go along with you then. But don't wake her before her time."

"Thank you, Mama!" Jesus rushed out the door on his errand.

He went first to the town well to fill his buckets. On the way, he kept both eyes busy searching for any person who might be persuaded to take him to Capernaum. He was also watching for anyone who might carry water to his mother while he was away for a few days. But on the way to the well, he didn't encounter anyone who might serve either of these purposes. He saw Rabbi Zuriel, but quickly dodged out of sight of that pompous man. Ever since the man had insulted him and his mother for a "jostling incident" in the market place, Jesus stayed clear of him, whatever his needs might be.

He saw a couple of men who had brought carpentry work to his father, but they didn't seem like the kind of men who might have business in Capernaum, nor the kind of men who had nothing better to do than help him keep a promise.

Then he spied an older woman walking slowly toward the well with a single clay water jar. She couldn't be of any help to him. Then, with a start, he realized that he was looking at the back of his own grandmother. Running up behind her he called, "Grandmother, what are you doing going to the well? I am on my way there to fetch you some water this very minute."

The old woman stopped and turned toward him. "Well, bless your heart for thinking of me, Jesus. Are you really intending to bring me water? I'm sure your mother needs your help more than I do."

"I have already taken her water and firewood and fed the chickens and collected the eggs. Now I am fetching water for you. Mama said you wouldn't be up this early and that I shouldn't wake you."

"Oh, my; I have been up for quite some time. I have a bit of mutton and some barley and some very nice onions. I had it in mind to make some good strong soup to help your father get back on his feet. But I lacked clean water."

"Let me get the water for you, Grandmother. One of these buckets will hold more than that jug of yours and I will fill two of them for you. If that isn't enough, I will make a second trip and a third. How much water do you want?"

"Two buckets would be a blessing, Jesus. I don't need more than that for today."

"You can sit right here and wait for me or you can start back home. I'm sure I can catch up with you, Grandmother."

"Well, I think I will take a bit of a rest here and then walk back with you, Grandson. It is so good of you to think of me."

"I'll be right back," he called over his shoulder as he trotted away. And soon he came, carrying two full buckets at opposite ends of his carrying pole, expertly swaying so that the water stayed within the moving buckets, swinging in time to his regular steps.

She rose to her feet as he neared and the two of them started back up the hill together. "Who normally fetches water for you, Grandmother? You don't often have to go to the well yourself, do you?"

"I don't mind going to the well myself, Jesus, but the water seems to get heavier every year. I keep switching to smaller jugs to lighten the load but now the jug that I can handle is so small that it is hardly worth the trip. Sometimes my brother, Ezra, sees me at the well and carries the jug for me. Sometimes you fetch me water and sometimes other boys help me."

"Your brother, Ezra? You mean the one the boys make fun of? He's your brother?"

"Why do the boys make fun of Ezra?" It seemed she didn't know. But there was only one Ezra in town… it had to be the same one.

"Well, the boys say he is crazy. Some of them run up behind him and tug on his coat and then run like the devil is after them."

"Ezra is not crazy, Jesus. He is deaf, stone deaf, and has been since he was born. The boys shouldn't make fun of him and torment him. He has never heard so much as a bird singing all these years. He never heard our dear mother's voice telling him what a fine boy he was."

"But he doesn't talk," said Jesus. "He just makes threatening roars at the boys who tease him."

"And how would he learn to talk if he never heard the way we talk? He sees our lips move and he knows that we somehow communicate with each other by doing that. But he can't hear the words so he never learned to form them. He doesn't even know what he sounds like when he roars. He only knows to do that because it makes his tormentors run away."

"Why would our Heavenly Father make a baby boy with ears that can't hear?" asked Jesus.

"I'm sure I don't know," sighed Grandmother. "I have pestered the Heavenly Father all my life about that and He has given me no answer. But I am sure He has a good answer. And if I really needed to know, He would surely tell me."

"I didn't know Ezra was your brother, Grandmother." He hesitated, awkwardly and then added, "I want you to know that I have never teased him but I have seen other boys do it."

"You should warn those boys and tell them about the boys who taunted the Prophet Elisha and said to him, 'Go on up, you baldhead.'"

"What happened to them, Grandmother?"

"Two bears came out of the woods and mauled them."

"Really? Is that in Scripture?"

"Yes, it really is."

"I have never heard that story." Then after pondering this news quietly for some steps, he asked, "Is Uncle Ezra a prophet?"

"No, my dear, he is not a prophet. But the Lord God might take pity and defend him just because he is unable to defend himself. So warn the other boys."

"I will, Grandmother."

They soon reached his grandmother's house. Jesus emptied the buckets into a clay cistern on the hill above the house and ran back to the well to get more while his grandmother began preparing the soup. After three trips to the well, the cistern was brim-full and Jesus sat down to watch his grandmother work.

"Grandmother?" he asked.

"Yes, Jesus?"

"Do you think Uncle Ezra could be persuaded to bring water to my mother, if I had to be away for a few days?"

"And what business does a boy your age have that might keep him away from home for a few days?" asked his grandmother.

"Well, you know that Abba and I borrow scrolls of the Law, the Psalms and the Prophets and study them together."

"Yes, I know that."

"Well, we have a scroll of the Psalms right now that we promised to return to Rabbi Zephon before the Feast of Tabernacles."

"That feast is coming very soon."

"So it is. And I want to keep the promise we made."

"But your father is too ill to travel. How do you think you can keep that promise?"

"Well, I have two problems. The first problem is -- who would take me to Capernaum? The second is -- who could bring water and wood to my mother if I go to Capernaum? The second problem is easier to solve, so I am starting with it. I think Uri, the shepherd, will bring wood for Mother if I ask him. Sometimes I help him. So, do you think Uncle Ezra might be able and willing to bring water for her?"

"Let me think about that. Are you then going to ask me who can take you to Capernaum?"

"Do you have an idea?" asked Jesus.

"I do."

"Who?"

She stopped making the soup and looked right in his eyes. "Uncle Ezra," she said.

Her answer took Jesus' breath away and made his head spin. "Uh... uh... Uncle Ezra?" he stammered.

"Why not?"

"But how would I talk to him? What if he roared at me and chased me?"

"Why should he roar at you and chase you?"

"Well, I wouldn't tease him but he might think I am teasing him if he can't hear what I'm saying." It was one thing to try to dissuade the other boys from teasing Uncle Ezra; it was quite another to think of traveling with this strange and fearsome man all the way to the sea and back.

"Believe me, my brother can distinguish between teasing and trusting."

"Surely teasing and trusting are very different, but I'm not quite sure I am ready to trust him. How would I tell him where we need to go?"

"Have you been there before?"

"Yes, many times. "

"Then I can assure him that you know where you are going and he need only accompany you and protect you. It wouldn't be the first time he was sent on such a mission. It was my brother Ezra, who took your mother to visit Elizabeth and Zechariah before the son of their old age was born. And he went back there three months later to fetch her home."

"He's the one?"

"Yes, he's the one. That was almost ten years ago, but Ezra is still strong and he still travels well."

"Well, I will have to think about it. But if Uncle Ezra takes me to Capernaum, who will bring water to Mother... and to you?"

"As you already said, that problem is the easier one to solve. We will come up with a plan. Now, this soup is ready. I'm going to save out just a bit for my lunch and you shall take the rest home. Unless I miss my guess, your father will love it and it will do him no end of good. This is what I always made for him when he was sick as a boy. It has never failed to do its good work."

When he arrived home with the pot of steaming soup, his mother met him at the door. "Where on earth have you been? I never dreamed you would be gone so long."

"I was with Grandmother. I carried water for her three times and she made this soup for Abba."

"Oh, bless her heart. Let me see." Uncovering the soup, she breathed in its aroma. "Wonderful, this is your father's favorite. Go see him while I serve some of this up for him. He has been asking for you."

Jesus pushed aside the curtain and automatically looked for his father in the bed. The bed was empty.

"Abba?" said Jesus.

"Here I am, Son," said the familiar voice from the dark corner. Though the voice was familiar, it was very soft and low.

"What are you doing out of bed, Abba?"

"A man cannot stay abed forever."

"Are you well, Abba?"

"I am better, but I would not say that I am well. The fever has passed. Your mother wants to freshen up the bed. I am resting here for a bit and then I will get back in bed."

"Oh, Abba, we have been so worried about you."

"You needn't worry about me but you may certainly bring my case before the Heavenly Father. He does all things well. I'm sure I won't be leaving this life until you have no more need of me."

"Abba, we will never outlive our need of you."

"Well, if that is, indeed, true, I should live forever."

"I hope you do. Who would teach me to be a man if you don't?"

By the time Mary brought in the bowl of soup, Jesus and Joseph were wrapped in each other's arms and Joseph had pulled the boy almost into his lap.

When Joseph smelled the soup, he brightened up. "Mary, did you make this?"

"What do you think?" she asked, with a sly smile.

"It smells just like what my mother always made for me. It's wonderful!"

"That's because it is what your mother still makes for you. Do you imagine that I will ever be able to replace her in the kitchen?"

For answer, Joseph began to sip at the edge of the bowl. After just a couple of swallows, he sat back in the chair and sighed so deeply that the whole room seemed to vibrate. "Oh, how much I have missed this wonderful soup. It is exactly what my whole body craved, though I couldn't even put words to the desire."

Jesus laughed for the first time in days and his mother fell to freshening up the bed, removing the bed-clothing that had been soaked by the perspiration driven by the fever of the past days. Jesus refrained from asking questions while his mother worked and his father ate. Soon the patient was resting comfortably back in the fresh bed, leaning back on the pillows and closing his eyes with a sense of peace that hadn't graced that room for at least a week.

When he and his mother retreated to the kitchen, Jesus began to ply her with questions. "Who went with you when you traveled to visit Elizabeth and Zechariah?"

"You ask that as if you already know the answer."

"Was it Abba?"

"No."

"Was it Grandmother's brother?"

"Is that what she told you?"

"Uncle Ezra?"

"Yes."

Jesus was quiet for a moment, so his mother continued. "Your father and I were not yet married. It wouldn't have been understood."

"But Uncle Ezra going with you was?"

"Yes. He is a very respectable man, even if some young fools don't realize that."

"How did you communicate with him?"

"Uncle Ezra is a very sensitive and sensible man. He understands your needs before you even try to communicate them. He anticipates."

"Did you write notes to him?"

"No, Uncle Ezra can't read or write."

"What if you had gotten lost?

"We didn't. Your grandmother and grandfather somehow made it clear to him where I was to go. And I had been to visit Elizabeth a couple of times before."

"Why all these questions, son?"

"Well," said Jesus, swallowing a couple of times to get up the courage to confess his plan, "I was asking Grandmother who could bring you water if I were to be gone for a few days. I was thinking that maybe whoever brings her water when I don't bring it, might bring you some while I am away."

"So you are going away? I hadn't heard," said his mother.

"Well, just in case… You know… in case I find someone who can take me to Capernaum. But then Grandmother suggested that Uncle Ezra might be able to take me. I was just trying to solve the water thing…"

His mother was smiling. He didn't know why she was smiling. Was it because he looked so pathetic? Was it because she had trapped him into telling his plan? Was it because the crisis of Abba's health seemed to have passed? He didn't know what to say so he said nothing and just watched his mother. Perhaps she would say something that would give him a clue as to why she was smiling.

Finally, she spoke. "I should have been afraid on that trip but I wasn't. Traveling with Uncle Ezra was such an unexpected outcome to my dilemma. He treated me like a fragile princess until I showed him that I was pretty good at riding. Then he laughed and kicked up his horse and we all but had a race. And with him as my protector kinsman, nobody gave me anything at all to worry about. When we reached Elizabeth's home, I was almost sorry that the journey was over."

"You rode horses? Not donkeys?"

"Yes, Uncle Ezra is quite the horseman. And can you imagine a man his size on a donkey? No donkey on earth could handle his weight, and his feet would drag on the ground."

126

"He is huge," commented Jesus. "And then three months later he came for you and you got to continue the adventure back to here?" asked Jesus.

"Well yes, but by then I was having sickness every morning and couldn't ride as freely for fear of making you uncomfortable."

Jesus had been too small to notice her morning sickness when his mother was carrying the twins. But he was certainly aware of the effects during his mother's pregnancy with Hannah.

Suddenly his mother swept Hannah up in her arms and said, "Keep your brothers out of trouble, will you? I need to go talk to Grandmother."

She was out of the house before he could do more than gasp, "Okay…" He wondered what she had to talk to Grandmother about and why it had come up so suddenly.

When she came back nearly an hour later, she was humming to herself and looked happier and more interested in life than Jesus could remember ever seeing her. She came in almost dancing and swirled Hannah into his arms as if rehearsing a great show. "Here, Hannah, my sweet. Go tickle your brother and make him laugh, too."

Hannah had caught the merry spirit from her mother but seemed as surprised by it as Jesus was. Mary swept on into the darkened bedroom to check on Joseph. Jesus came close to the curtain that separated the two rooms but could not hear voices on the other side. Then he heard his father snoring and drew away, lest his mother should catch him eavesdropping. He took Hannah outside to see what James and Joseph were doing but he could only wonder what his mother was secretly planning. She obviously had a secret. Maybe it was about the birthday that he and Hannah would share next week. Mama was always coming up with secrets and surprises, especially for birthdays.

That evening Joseph was feeling so much better that he abandoned his bed and came to the kitchen for supper. Mama was glowing with an inner excitement and pleasure that held Jesus' attention more than the food. The smaller children could sense the excitement but probably didn't know that it was coming from their mother. Jesus thought, 'She sure is happy that Abba is getting better.' But he was about to discover that there was more to it than joy over his recovery.

"Joseph, dear, I can't tell you how grateful to the Almighty I am that you are on the mend."

"And so am I, dear Mary. So am I."

Jesus looked from one of his parents to the other. He suspected that Abba, himself, was not aware of whatever surprise Mama was planning. She was so pleased with herself, she could hardly sit still, let alone eat. She was toying with her food and shifting in her chair. She was looking out the window more than she was tending to the little ones.

"Joseph, do you realize…" she began and then broke off, unwilling to finish the thought.

"Do I realize what?"

"No, never mind."

"Never mind what? You seem very distracted. What is going on?"

"I'm just very happy about your recovery."

"We all are, my dear. But you are acting very peculiar. What did you start to ask me?"

"Do you realize that your mother is an excellent cook?"

"Yes, I think I am better informed on that subject than almost anyone else. But why do you bring it up now? Are you feeling alright?"

"Of course! I'm fine. You are the one who has been sick."

"Yes, but you are the one who is not making sense. What is going on?"

Jesus spoke up, "Is it something about Hannah's birthday and mine, Mama? You seem to have a secret."

"Well, yes," said Mama. "That is part of it, I guess."

"You guess?" said Joseph. "You don't know?"

"Joseph, do you realize your mother has been quite lonely of late?"

"Well, no, I didn't know that. I will go visit her as soon as I am able," said Joseph.

"Or, how would it be if she came here for a while, just so she wouldn't be too lonely?"

"That would be fine…"

"And she could cook some of your favorite dishes…"

"That would be excellent…"

"While I go to Capernaum…"

"YES," shouted Jesus leaping up so suddenly that he almost overturned the table.

Hannah was so startled that she began to cry. James and Joseph both screamed and nearly fell of the bench. Joseph was so stunned, he just sat there staring with his spoon halfway to his mouth.

Mary rocked Hannah in her arms as she burst out with her secret, "Jesus has been telling me about the promise you made to Rabbi Zephon and he is so anxious to keep that promise by returning the scroll before the feast. And your mother has agreed to come and stay with you and cook for you and look after the twins. Uncle Ezra is going to escort Jesus and Hannah and me to Capernaum. And I so need to get away from this village for a breath of fresh sea air. You realize I haven't set foot out of this village in six years, Joseph? Six years! Please say we can do it, please?"

Joseph, stalling to recover himself, said, "And what has this to do with birthdays?"

"Well Hannah and Jesus do have a shared birthday coming up; the journey can be a birthday surprise for them."

"Well, it certainly is a surprise for me. I didn't know you needed to get away from here."

"My father used to take us to the Sea of Galilee every year when I was a girl. It was always a special treat. And you know I like to travel. I have journeyed to visit Elizabeth. Then you and I travelled together to Bethlehem and all the way to Egypt and back. After all of that, it is hard to stay just in Nazareth for six years. You truly do seem to be on the mend and your mother is eager to do this for us. You will be okay, won't you?"

During all of this exchange, Jesus was watching his father's expression and holding the tension inside. It was a wonderful plan and yet his father might not approve. Jesus still was not entirely reconciled to the idea of traveling with Uncle Ezra, but if his mother were to come along…that would make all the difference.

Finally Joseph leaned back in his chair and spoke, "I think it is a fine plan and yes, I will be okay. I, too, feel the weight of the promise we made to Rabbi Zephon and this will relieve that concern. You may go with my blessing."

Jesus leaped as high as he could and ran to hug his mother for coming up with the plan and his father for approving the plan and each of his siblings just because he couldn't stop celebrating this good turn of events.

"May I run and tell Grandmother that the plan is approved? When do we start?"

"Slow down, Jesus. I think your grandmother knew that the plan would be approved. And we can't start off tonight. We need tomorrow to make preparations and Ezra needs tomorrow as well. On the second morning we will go, not sooner."

The very next morning was filled with preparations. Mama was preparing by making space in her house for her mother-in-law. She was also setting aside clothing for the journey, both for herself and for Jesus and Hannah. She sent Jesus to the market twice to lay in supplies so that Grandmother would have everything she needed.

Jesus also filled the cistern from the town well and laid in a supply of firewood that would last at least four or five days. And he made Uri, the shepherd, promise that he would bring a bundle of firewood each evening. Joseph would have helped with preparations, too, if Mary had let him. But she was not willing for him to overdo and have a relapse of the illness. That would spoil everything. So Abba was shooed away from anything resembling work and told to enjoy his life of ease while he may.

In the late afternoon, Grandmother made her appearance. The bundle on her back was so large, it looked like Grandmother was moving in permanently. And besides what she herself carried, she sent Jesus back to bring a few bundles that she hadn't been able to carry. Jesus wondered whether she was confused about her mission. When Jesus remarked that she was bringing enough to last for months, she scoffed. "Nonsense. I'm just being prepared. It's better to be prepared than to wish you were."

Once supper was over and everything cleaned up, Grandmother settled near the fire while Mary went over her packing one more time. Jesus sat at her feet and stroked the cat, making her purr for all she was worth.

"Grandmother, tell me more about Uncle Ezra. What does he do?"

"Do? Well, Ezra is old enough now, he pretty much does whatever he wants to do."

"Without hearing, he could not have gone to school, could he? What does he do for a job? How does he earn a living?"

"Well, Jesus, it is true that Ezra didn't spend much time in school. The teachers always gave up on him and the other children were pretty mean. So Ezra gave up on school before he was ten years old. But he is smart! He knows more about animals than just about any person alive. And animals trust him. He has often healed horses when others had given them up for dead.

"Tell him about Samson," offered Joseph.

"You mean Samson and Delilah?" asked Jesus. "I know that story."

"No, son, the story of Ezra and his horse, Samson."

"Well," began Grandmother. "I will have to go back a long way to set that story up right."

"Please do, Grandmother," pleaded Jesus. "I love true stories."

"This one is true, as far as I can tell. When my brother was a young man, he was pretty unhappy. He wasn't good at telling true friends from false ones and that got him into a lot of trouble. Some of his so-called friends used to give him wine and beer and strong drink just to entertain themselves with his drunken exploits. They would get him so drunk he would forget himself and then they would set up fights between him and someone else, usually someone from a different village. They would bet money on Ezra and find some young hothead who wanted to become the giant slayer. If Ezra won the fight, as he usually did, they would buy him more drinks with their winnings. If he lost the fight, they would punch him and abuse him because they had lost their bets. There were many times that he stayed out all night and didn't come home until he had slept off his alcohol the next afternoon. Mother would cry over him and clean him up and Abba, our abba, would just shake his head, not knowing what to do.

"One time a Roman legion camped just outside Nazareth for a couple of weeks. Some of their soldiers got caught in the trap of fighting 'Ezra the Bear,' as his friends called him. After he had thrashed their best fighting men for several nights running, their Legate sent a Centurion to our house. He wanted to talk to our father. 'Sir,' he said, 'your son has a rare talent for fighting and he is stronger than two men. Will you let me train him to be a legionnaire in my company?'

"Abba did not like the idea at first and raised many objections but the Centurion assured Abba that he would personally watch over Ezra's training and make him into the greatest fighter in his whole Legion, even if he couldn't speak Greek. Abba reasoned that Ezra could speak as much Greek as he could Aramaic, so language should be no problem. And he had been racking his brain to find a way to rescue Ezra from the young men who were using him. Perhaps this was God's provision for Ezra. And when Ezra realized that he would get a Roman uniform, regular food and even some money, it was impossible to hold him back. So when the Legion moved on, Ezra marched with them and served in Cesar's army for the next five years.

"We weren't able to find out where his Legion moved on to, and wouldn't have had a clue as to what happened over the course of those years if it weren't for Jeter."

"Who is Jeter?" asked Jesus.

"Well, when Ezra came back to us, Jeter followed him a bit later. Jeter was a wiry little man, a professional soldier from Crete who claims he was in the Legion already when Ezra was recruited. To hear him tell it, he took Ezra under his wing, though it is hard to imagine such a large man as my brother being under such a small wing! But I must confess that when I met him, Jeter did seem to have an uncanny ability to understand Ezra and even to speak for him. He had obviously spent a lot of time with Ezra and, as the story goes, the two of them had saved each other's lives on various occasions.

"But even more surprising than Jeter was Samson. Ezra came home riding the most magnificent black Arabian stallion that anyone in Galilee had ever laid eyes on. Jeter called the horse Samson. That horse arches his neck so high and holds his tail straight up like no horse you have ever seen. He even lifts his hooves so high when he prances that you would think he didn't want to soil them on the common earth. And spirit? Oh my, you would think that he belonged to the Lord God Almighty and was given out only for the Angel Gabriel to ride when he had serious business to conduct.

"The whole town came running to see Ezra riding that stallion and, later, to badger poor Jeter with a thousand questions as to where this horse came from and how it came into Ezra's possession. The horse Jeter was riding was as common and drab as a donkey by comparison to Samson. And everyone knew that something wonderful had happened that Ezra should come home so elegantly mounted.

I will try to make Jeter's long story shorter because you need your rest before your journey. According to Jeter, Ezra took to the life of a legionnaire quite well. The rigorous discipline seemed to do him good and the Centurion would not allow the others to bully him as his friends here in Nazareth had done. He was a quick student of war tactics and even taught the Centurion a few tricks of hand-to-hand combat. And with his size and strength, he soon became a favorite with the whole Legion.

"According to Jeter, Ezra distinguished himself not only in fighting, but also in his devotion to the horses of the Legion. There was only one unit of about 100 cavalry soldiers, but horses were also used to pull wagons with supplies. So there were always horses around the camp. And whenever Ezra had no specific duties to take care of, he could be found among those caring for the horses. If a stall needed cleaning, Ezra would volunteer to do it, just because it brought him in contact with the horses. As he became more trusted, he was allowed to curry the horses and even saddle them. And eventually, if a horse needed doctoring, Ezra was the man everyone turned to. It seemed that his limitations in communicating with people played into a supernatural ability to understand animals, especially horses. And that is what led to his discharge from the Legion and was almost the death of him.

"It seems that one day a new cavalry officer who was called Julius, after the late Caesar, was added to the Legion and he was a very hot-headed and violent man who brooked no insolence from anyone. And you didn't have to be insolent to him to be perceived as insolent by him. Julius arrived riding one very fine horse and leading Samson behind him, (though I think Samson was a name given the horse later by Jeter.) According to the story, Julius had captured the stallion on the battlefield after slaying the Arab prince who had ridden him. Two things were immediately clear to everyone who saw the officer with this horse. First, it was clear that the horse was an unusually fine specimen. Secondly, it was clear that the horse and the man were definitely not allies.

"The horse was plunging and kicking, neighing and trying to bite the horse Julius was riding and trying to bite any part of Julius that presented itself. The officer, meanwhile was jerking the lead rope violently and lashing at the stallion's head with the butt end of a whip, all the while cursing the horse with a loud voice. According to Jeter, it took six men to restrain Ezra from rushing at the man when he witnessed this entrance. This set the stage for Ezra's last battle as a Legionnaire."

"What happened?" asked Jesus.

"After that scene," continued Grandmother, "it seems that Ezra was determined to counteract the cruelty done to that great horse. Even while he was cleaning stables or brushing another horse, his eyes and his heart constantly went toward Samson. He is a very attractive horse, of course, which compels every eye to look at him. But for such a wonderful horse to be in the possession of a cruel man who did not know how to enjoy such a horse, that was unendurable. At least it was for Ezra.

"Every chance he got, he watched the horse. When he could come near it, he came near and just stood or sat quietly in the horse's presence. And whatever it is about Ezra that horses sense, Samson sensed it, too. The horse started coming near Ezra whenever he was around, even before Ezra started offering him treats, such as bits of carrot. That horse would not allow anyone else to touch him, but if Ezra stood at the fence, Samson would come to him. If Ezra did not reach out to touch him, Samson would nuzzle his shoulder as if to say, 'Touch me.' And only after Samson initiated contact would Ezra actually reach out and scratch around the base of an ear or run his gentle hand over Samson's muzzle.

134

"One day when Ezra and Samson were interacting like that, Julius came upon them unexpectedly."

"Oh no!" whispered Jesus.
"Julius shouted, 'Hey there, what are you doing to my horse?' Of course Ezra didn't hear him at all but Samson did. Samson jerked up his head and ran away neighing. Ezra looked around to see what had startled Samson and found Julius about to strike him with his whip. As the lash came down, Ezra caught it in his hand and held onto it so that Julius couldn't strike him and couldn't retrieve the whip, either. Ezra wasn't doing anything aggressive, just defending himself. But Julius was so enraged that he drew out his dagger. Perhaps because his better hand was already tightly held, he was not very quick nor adept with the dagger and Ezra grabbed the officer's wrist and pinned him tightly against the fence."

Jesus was squirming restlessly as he envisioned this violent struggle. His grandmother went on.

"By this time, Julius was very angry and was probably afraid for his life as well. His threats and the scuffle drew a number of people running to the scene, among them Jeter, who had witnessed the whole thing. Two cavalry officers who were riding by stopped to see what the trouble was. Of course, they listened to Julius' version of events first, as he was a fellow officer. 'I came upon this idiot peasant messing with my horse, which he has no authority to do. When I accosted him, he attacked me and would certainly have killed me if you hadn't intervened.'

"The senior of the two officers then looked at Ezra and said, 'Is this true? You may speak in your own defense, soldier. What happened?'

"Jeter, bless his heart, spoke up at that moment and said, 'Sir, if you will allow me to speak, Ezra is stone deaf, so he has no idea what he has been accused of.' Others murmured their agreement with this.

'Deaf, you say?' asked the officer. Again, everyone nearby murmured assent. The officer looked at Julius and asked, 'Did you know he is deaf?'

'How should I know he is deaf? I have never laid eyes on him before. And I have never heard of a deaf man being enlisted in the Legion.'

"'So,' continued the senior officer, looking at Jeter, 'did you witness this whole incident? What did you see?'

"'Well, sir,' said Jeter, 'Ezra here has been alongside of me for nearly five years now and I must say, deaf as he is, I've never seen the match of his gift with horses. Though he can't speak to you and me, he seems to speak the language of the horses. They all know him and trust him. And he has saved several of them from horrible diseases and wounds. He has a healing touch with animals. So he was standing right here at the fence just quiet as a mouse and this officer's horse came up and nuzzled him on the shoulder.'

"'That's an outrageous lie,' shouted Julius. 'That horse is as wild as an antelope. He won't even let me touch him.'

"'I am not saying anything that these others around the stables will not confirm,' said Jeter. 'Though this horse will not trust his owner, he comes right up to Ezra and all but begs him to scratch around his ears.' The senior officer looked around and saw every man but Julius nodding his affirmation of Jeter's testimony. Then Jeter went on, 'When this officer came around the corner and saw Ezra petting his horse, he shouted at him, which frightened the horse away. Ezra wouldn't have heard the shouting but turned to see why the horse was startled and he found the officer bearing down on him with a whip. He threw up one hand and caught the blow of the whip and held on tight. The officer then went for his dagger but Ezra caught his wrist and held it tight. He spun and pinned him against the fence, but did not act in aggression at all. All he did was defend himself against unreasonable attack.'

"Julius burst out in his own defense by saying, 'Everyone was told not to try to handle this horse. No one was to touch him!'

The senior officer responded calmly that a deaf man would not have heard this or any other order and might be excused for responding to something that the horse initiated.

"'If he cannot hear orders, then he is unfit to serve in the Roman Legion, said Julius with some spite.

"'I do not know the man nor how he came to be a Legionnaire, but I am glad that his quickness and his strength have prevented you from causing harm.' Turning to Jeter, he asked, "Are you able to communicate to this Ezra that he is in no wise to touch this particular horse again?' After receiving Jeter's assurance that he could, the officer dismissed the crowd but the fatal conflict was now well set in motion.

"A few weeks passed and, though Ezra did not forego all contact with Samson, he was much more discreet about when and where that contact happened. And though Julius suspected that his horse still trusted 'that idiot peasant' he was not able to catch Ezra violating his restriction. Julius was trying his best to win mastery over the wild horse because there was to be a full-dress review of the Legion in front of Herod in just a few weeks. For the sake of his own vanity, Julius wanted to ride in that parade review on Samson. So he came daily and worked at controlling the animal, but his methods reflected his belief that he had to break the horse. This was very much in contrast to the gentle persuasion that Ezra had been using, but by the time the parade arrived, Julius had succeeded in staying in the saddle a few times and had convinced himself that he would be a glorious inspiration riding such a horse in front of King Herod and his retinue.

"He might even have pulled it off, if Ezra had not been stationed near Herod's review stand, in the front row. That put him on the same side as Julius would come riding along trying to look masterful on the most magnificent horse in the whole Legion. Samson was fidgety but Julius managed to look like a great horseman in keeping some degree of control over the horse. That lasted only until they were almost to Herod's position and Samson saw and smelled Ezra at the side of the parade route. He immediately broke rank and tried to reach the huge man whom he trusted. Julius at first didn't recognize Ezra and just tried to fight the horse back into parade formation. When Samson skittered sidewise right up to Ezra, Julius saw him and became furious that this unfinished conflict should spoil his parade. He lashed out with his whip and began beating Samson, but also aiming every third blow at Ezra, who tried to stand at attention in spite of the uproar. The commotion drew every eye in the King's review box to the scene of the agitated horse, the wildly flailing officer who was trying to keep his seat in the saddle, and the huge infantryman who seemed to be caught up in something quite unexpected. By this time, the horse was frantic and the cavalryman was swearing profusely and beating about with his whip in total abandon.

"When Julius began to use his whip on Samson's head, the horse let out a terrific cry and reared so high he almost went over backward. Julius didn't come off the back of the horse but only because he had grabbed a double fistful of Samson's ample mane. In all of this, he did not lose his grip on the whip because he had a leather thong that looped about his wrist and

137

when he regained his balance, he lashed out again with the whip. But Ezra had seen more abuse than he could stomach and when the whip came down, it came into the outstretched hand of Ezra. Ezra took hold of that whip and gave a violent pull which finished what the rearing horse had begun. Julius left the saddle, pulled along by the leather thong around his wrist and crashed unceremoniously to the ground in the exact spot where he had hoped to be noticed for his horse and his horsemanship.

"The whole parade was thrown into disarray as other horses now shied and reared, keeping their riders fully occupied in staying mounted. King Herod's own bodyguard leapt to the ground and assisted the fallen cavalry officer to his feet. In all the excitement, no one had been able to grab the reins as Samson ran, kicking and bucking through the parade and past the spectators and for a mile or two beyond. Julius was beside himself with shame and fury, but he wasn't badly hurt. The Legate of the whole Legion had been in the seat of honor at Herod's right side and had witnessed the whole incident. Julius demanded Ezra's head and wanted him to be publicly executed on the spot for assaulting an officer. Jeter and others shouted objections and tried to defend Ezra for defending a worthy animal from abuse.

"In the end, Ezra was put in the dungeon with his hands and feet locked in stocks until a decision could be reached as to how to resolve the incident that upstaged the review before Herod. The Legate did his own investigation into the origins of the conflict, which also involved learning about the backgrounds of both men and how they came to be in the Legion. When he presented the results of his investigation to Herod, the king apparently suggested that this was something that should be settled in the arena at Caesarea. It might make for good entertainment.

"Jeter was allowed to visit Ezra in the dungeon and to negotiate the terms of the fight on his behalf. Julius had demanded a fight to the death, saying nothing less than Ezra's extinction could satisfy his honor. Ezra was allowed to choose what weapons would be used. Ezra communicated to Jeter that Julius could use any and all weapons he wanted but that he, himself, would only take a shield. Jeter argued with him that such a decision would be tantamount to suicide, but Ezra would not budge. When Jeter reported that to the Legate, it was scoffed at. Of course that was unacceptable. This was a fight to the death and who had ever been killed by a shield? Jeter went back to argue with Ezra and eventually persuaded him to take an offensive weapon. Ezra chose a club. Again Jeter argued but it was no use.

"The Legate was disappointed at what seemed to portend a very short and one-sided battle, but at last he gave in. It wouldn't provide much entertainment, but at least it would settle the conflict and perhaps restore peace in the ranks.

"Jeter negotiated one other point regarding this battle. He insisted that, if Ezra should win, he should be honorably discharged from the Legion and he should take possession of the horse, Samson. Perhaps the Legate would not have granted this condition if he had had the slightest notion that Ezra could win. He probably believed that the outcome was as certain as if Ezra had been summarily executed the day of the parade, as Julius had demanded. But he agreed to these conditions in the hypothetical circumstances of Ezra winning the battle.

"Julius arrived at the Arena riding in pomp and arrayed with more weapons than a man could handily use. He was not riding Samson, though, which was one small sign that he was beginning to gain some sense. He chose a horse that he could better manage, and hopefully, a horse that wasn't already more loyal to his enemy than to himself. He wore his best armor, a helmet with an ostrich plume died red, and carried a shield. For offensive weapons, he carried a spear for throwing, a sword at his side, a dagger in his belt and tied upon his saddle, his now infamous whip. After he paraded around the arena two laps on his horse he stopped before King Herod and the Legate in their royal box and made his salute. The arena was filled with the whole Legion and a good mix of common people who had come to see the show. The crowd gave Julius polite applause, but there were some catcalls, as well.

"Then Ezra was let in carrying his shield and crude club. He wasn't even wearing a helmet. The crowd let out cries of disappointment and then dismay as they saw what an unequal battle was to be their entertainment. Ezra was deaf to all of the crowd noise and walked, untroubled, to take his place before the royal box. He made his salute but did not even look in the direction of Julius.

"The conditions were proclaimed, loud and clear to the audience and to the combatants, but of course Ezra couldn't hear a word of it. Then they were sent to opposite ends of the arena to await the King's signal. Julius sat and tried to look jaunty and confident. Ezra stood silent with his shield at one side and the club resting on one shoulder. The signal to begin was given and Julius spurred his horse forward. Ezra didn't react at all and something about his strange stillness made Julius wary. Instead of riding straight at his enemy, he rode a wide circle around the perimeter of the arena, trying to size Ezra up. Ezra did not move except to turn slowly to keep the horseman in front of him where his every move would be obvious. After making a circuit of the Arena, Julius arrived back at his beginning point and came to a halt.

"The Legionnaires began to boo; they expected more from a man so well mounted and so well armed. So Julius apparently decided to get this over with. He hoisted his spear to his shoulder and spurred his horse straight toward the spot where Ezra stood rooted to the ground. Ezra didn't even raise his shield. The horse was in full gallop and bearing down on Ezra, who stood defenseless with his shield at his side. If you were watching closely you might have seen that Ezra crouched a bit lower as everyone anticipated the launch of the spear at his massive chest.

"As Julius rose up in his stirrups and reached back to throw the spear, Ezra moved sideways like a cat, landing directly in the path of the charging horse. His sudden movement caught everyone by surprise, especially Julius, who was nearly thrown to the ground by the way his horse shied to the left to avoid running into Ezra.

"As the spear fell harmlessly to the ground and Julius fought to regain his seat, a great roar of excitement and approval went up from the crowd. Ezra skipped back to the left as the horse shot by and he picked up the spear and left his club on the ground.

"Julius rounded the end of the arena and went back to his starting point as some of the Legionnaires began to taunt him. He readied his shield and drew his sword. Without his spear, he would have to draw quite close to Ezra, well within range of being harmed by the spear, if the giant of a man even knew how to use a spear. In his next foray, he concentrated on using the shield to defend himself from the spear, but the enemy didn't even raise the weapon. He just held his shield up as the cavalryman galloped by holding his own shield. The crowd booed again.

"On the next foray, he tried swinging his sword at Ezra, but Ezra fended off his blows with his shield and again didn't even raise the spear. Perhaps concluding that Ezra didn't know how to use the spear, Julius moved in to finish him off. Instead of galloping by, he rode in close and began to rain sword blows like thunderclaps upon the larger man's shield but could do no damage. But while he was trying his best to lop off Ezra's head, he

140

failed to notice what Ezra was doing with his left hand, which held the spear. All Ezra did with the spear was to reach it between the horse's legs and begin to slap it left and right, hitting the horse's legs on the insides. The horse shied left and right violently trying to keep from tripping but not knowing which way to turn for escape. In its mad frenzy to escape the trap, the horse threw the rider to the ground but one foot stuck in the stirrup. Not only did he fall, but Julius fell awkwardly with his sword under him, snapping off the blade half a cubit above the hilt. The horse dragged him by one foot, the length of the arena before he managed to get free.

"By now the crowd was on its feet roaring encouragement to the simple warrior who could not even hear them. Ezra did not pursue his enemy but stood, as before, waiting to defend himself from the next attack. Julius took several minutes to gather himself, dust off and catch his badly frightened horse. Soon the crowd was chanting in unison and taunting the mounted warrior to do his worst. Julius was now without a spear, held a blunted sword and had no ally left in the entire legion or in the arena. Everyone was chanting Ezra's name.

"Julius was being forced to consider hand to hand combat but he had felt enough of Ezra's strength on two previous occasions, that he was afraid should the fight come to that. He uncoiled his whip and rode slowly toward Ezra. Having learned one lesson well, he did not put his wrist through the leather loop. Perhaps it was his intent to distract Ezra with the whip because while he was laying about Ezra from a safe distance with the whip, he threw the remnant of his sword with deadly force at Ezra. Ezra was quick enough to get the shield up and deflect the broken sword harmlessly to the side. Then Julius came in closer, hoping to lay some stripes on Ezra with the whip and hopefully get close enough to use his dagger.

"Ezra held up the spear, not the shield and the whip coiled several wraps around the haft of the spear and at that instant Ezra turned and heaved the spear with such a mighty effort that the whole crowd gasped. He did not hurl the spear at Julius but toward the opposite end of the arena. The whip was jerked out of Julius' hand and flew like the tail of a bird behind the flying spear. Had Julius been wearing the leather loop around his wrist, it is hard to know whether his arm would not have flown with the spear and the whip to the far end of the arena.

"Again the crowd roared. Herod turned to the Legate and said, 'Now, we shall see why he wanted a club.'

"'On the contrary,' replied the Legate, 'you will remember that he didn't want a club. He only wanted a shield. We may be allowed to witness the first man ever to be killed by a shield.'

"'That would be a sight to see,' answered King Herod. 'At any rate, this has turned out to be much better entertainment than either of us imagined.'

"Now Julius was reduced to his dagger. And, just as the Legate had intimated, Ezra left the club where he had first thrown it aside. The best use of a dagger is not from horseback. A man has to be quick on his feet and able to jump backward or sideways on an instant, as well as able to lunge forward to plant the deadly blade in his enemy. So Julius reluctantly dismounted and approached Julius warily on foot.

"Ezra stood, as before, with the shield at his side, watching Julius approach. When he was still a few cubits away, Julius began making threatening motions with the dagger, feinting thrusts from one side and then the other. He circled Ezra in his most threatening display of knife fighting moves, but stayed safely out of reach. Again the crowd began to taunt him and call him a coward. Pushed by the crowd, he began to make an occasional lunge toward Ezra, but Ezra just backed out of reach each time. The taunting grew louder, bringing the whole fight to its climax. The crowd wanted blood and Julius was determined to give them Ezra's.

"He ran at Ezra and struck with all his might at Ezra's face with the point of his dagger. Ezra deftly raised the shield. As the dagger blade pierced the heavy shield, Ezra jerked it sharply down, wrenching the dagger out of Julius' grasp. The crowd roared as Julius floundered in the dust trying to regain possession of his last weapon. Just as his hand closed over the grip, Ezra's big foot came down on his wrist. Julius scrabbled with his other hand to try to retrieve the dagger from the trapped hand but Ezra bent down and wrenched the weapon away from him and then sat heavily upon his chest

"The crowd went wild and assumed that Ezra would now stab the cavalryman to death or cut off his head. Ezra saluted in the direction of the King and the Legate and the crowd roared, 'Death, death, death,' as if to compel the death sentence. The King and the Legate both stood up and side by side, gave the thumbs down signal, approving Ezra's execution of Julius. But at that point, as at so many points in the afternoon, Ezra did something that caught everyone by surprise. He shook one finger in Julius' cringing face and then made the cut-throat symbol as a final threat. And then he stood up and threw the dagger aside and started walking away.

"The entire arena gasped and went silent as they tried to comprehend what they were witnessing. Why would he walk away? Why would he not execute as the King and the Legate had bid him do? Some of them began to exclaim to one another, 'Look at this man! He has not made one offensive move in the whole battle. Every one of his tactics was defensive!'

"The King and the Legate were as astonished as anyone else. But all the astonishment turned to apprehension as they watched Julius roll to his knees and stagger upright. He quickly spotted his discarded dagger and dashed for it. The crowd cried out to alarm the victor of his imminent danger, but Ezra was as deaf to their warning as he had been to their cheering. He continued walking away with not even a backward glance at his enemy. Julius saw his opportunity for vengeance and ran toward the defenseless giant who had humiliated him in front of the whole Legion. The whole crowd was screaming and trying to get Ezra to turn around but he was simply walking away unaware of any danger.

"Julius was no more than three paces from striking Ezra when he himself was struck through by an arrow. His momentum carried him stumbling into the back of Ezra's legs, causing Ezra to fall forward. Before either man could attempt to rise, two more arrows pierced Julius where he lay and the crowd did, in fact, get the blood they had hoped for.

"A formal inquiry was launched to learn where the arrows had come from. It appeared that they had come from three very different angles. And while it was true that the archers of the Legion were arrayed around the top rows of the arena for strategic purposes, none among them could be found who would admit to releasing an arrow nor seeing anyone else loose one. In the end, the matter was dropped, partly for lack of evidence against anyone specific and partly because Julius was already a dead man, condemned by King Herod and by his own Legate, before the first arrow found its mark."

"So Ezra got an honorable discharge and got to keep Samson?" asked Jesus.

"That's what happened," said Grandmother.

"Grandmother," said Mary, "you tell that story so well, one would think you were an eye witness to the whole thing."

Grandmother blushed but defended herself by saying, "Of course I was not there. I only tell the story as Jeter told it to us."

"Jeter came here with Uncle Ezra?" asked Jesus.

"Not with him, no. Ezra just showed up one day on that magnificent horse and the whole town started buzzing. It was a couple of months before Jeter showed up and set all the rumors to rest. By the time we heard Jeter's version of the story, we had made up several dozen stories just out of speculation. But the true story turned out to be better than the ones we had made up."

"So where is Jeter now?" asked Jesus.

"He only stayed here about six months. He was totally devoted to Ezra, but when he realized that all Ezra wanted to do was settle down and take care of animals, he lost interest. He had a restless foot and eventually moved on. He may have gone back to Crete or back to the Roman Legion for all we know."

"Wow, I used to be afraid of Ezra like all the other boys but now I can't wait to meet him. Do you think he will bring Samson tomorrow?"

"I don't think Ezra would go a league from Nazareth without riding Samson," said Grandmother.

It was Jesus' intention to be up before dawn to wait for Uncle Ezra to arrive on Samson, but he lay awake so much during the night thinking about the story of Ezra and his horse and imagining his own journey with him and his mother and Hannah, that he overslept. When he got up, the sun was just coming over the edge of the hill and Ezra was sitting at the kitchen table drinking tea. Jesus was surprised at how much of the kitchen Ezra took up. He had looked huge whenever Jesus saw him in the market but now that the man was in his own living space, Jesus saw him with new eyes. He approached him shyly and didn't know how to act. It seemed pointless to say anything because Ezra couldn't hear him, but it seemed ridiculous to approach someone and not speak. So he didn't approach at all. He hung back just watching the big man sip tea and eat his sister's fresh baked bread. Jesus wondered how early Grandmother had been up to have fresh bread at sunrise.

She saw him hanging back and beckoned to him to come. Ezra followed her gaze and looked over his shoulder at Jesus. Jesus could plainly see evidence on Ezra's face of his brawling past. His ears were thick and misshapen. His nose had been broken multiple times. He had a long scar that ran across his forehead and through his left eyebrow. He was missing his front teeth, both upper and lower. But amidst all the damage, the startling feature of his face was his eyes. Jesus thought that this fighting man's eyes were the most peaceful eyes he had ever seen.

While he was taking in all this, his grandmother took him by the hand and drew him forward, saying, "Jesus, this is my brother Ezra." And turning to Ezra she said, "Ezra, this is my grandson, Jesus."

Ezra smiled and nodded at Jesus, so Jesus nodded at him. Ezra put a big finger in the middle of Jesus' chest and then used two fingers straddling his other hand and made both hands move together in a galloping motion with a questioning expression on his face. Jesus knew instinctively that he was asking, "Do you ride?"

"Yes, I do," replied Jesus and he pointed at himself and then made a similar motion with his own fingers straddling his own other hand. He nodded and smiled as he did so and Ezra seemed satisfied. Mary emerged at that moment carrying a couple of bags and Joseph was right on her heels carrying Hannah, properly bundled up for her first horseback journey. As usual, James and Joseph, the twins, were sleeping in and would miss the excitement.

Mary asked Jesus, "Have you eaten?"

"No, I overslept. I just got up."

Grandmother ushered him to the table where she had already set out a bowl of porridge and she poured him a cup of tea. Ezra reached out both hands toward Hannah but Hannah threw her arms around her Abba's neck and held tight. Ezra chuckled softly and patted her back but did not try to take her from her father.

"Abba," asked Jesus, "are you sad that you aren't coming with us?"

"A little bit," he said, "but I am thankful just to be out of that fever. By the time you get back, I think you and I will have some work to do in the shop."

"How does Uncle Ezra know where we are going?" asked Jesus.

"Like this," answered Mary. She got Ezra's attention and then pointed to him, herself, Hannah and Jesus. Then she made the now familiar gesture for 'riding,' and pointed in the direction of the Sea of Galilee. At that point, Ezra took over and made motions which clearly represented a boat bouncing over waves and fishermen casting nets and drawing them in.

"Okay then," said Jesus, satisfied for the moment that communication was possible. It would be different, but perhaps this plan could work. He finished his breakfast and rose from the table ready to begin this new adventure.

Joseph and his mother followed them out the door to where the horses were tied. One glimpse of Samson and Jesus had a new concept of what a horse could be. He was tall and powerful and magnificent, but he also exceeded anything Jesus had ever seen in the form of horse flesh in terms of spirit and intelligence. The light in his eyes and the vigor of his sensibilities made other horses seem like grass was the only thing that mattered to them. This one, though, was responsive to life. And he was especially responsive to Ezra. He whickered softly as soon as Ezra emerged from the house and moved toward him. He was curious about all of the people, but it was clear that Ezra was the one he trusted. Jesus thought it marvelous the way the horse's ears and nostrils and even his lips expressed curiosity and reacted reflexively to every movement or sound that people made. Even while Jesus was taking in this new experience of Samson, it seemed clear that Samson was taking him in as well.

Along with Samson, Ezra had brought a medium sized bay gelding with a white blaze between its eyes and a small brown mare. The gelding was saddled especially for a lady, for ladies did not straddle horses in those days. They rode with both legs on one side of the horse. Recognizing the saddle, Jesus knew that he would be riding the little brown mare. All of the horses had saddle bags for carrying whatever the travelers might need along the way. Jesus was carrying the scroll of Psalms carefully rolled up in its own waterproof cover. Ezra helped him tie it securely between the saddle bags on the mare and adjusted the stirrups and checked the cinch strap before helping Jesus mount.

In the meantime, Mary was busy stowing her bags on the gelding. When she was ready, Uncle Ezra lifted her as easily as one might lift a doll and placed her gently on the side-saddle. Joseph let her get settled and then handed her the sturdy cloth that she tied around herself and over one shoulder, inside of which little Hannah would settle as if in a hammock. Then Joseph kissed his little girl goodbye and handed her to her mother. Jesus noticed how Abba clasped Mary's hand for a moment before coming to embrace him. The mare was not so tall that Jesus had to bend down very much to embrace him and then, with a wave, Ezra swung to his saddle and they were off.

Jesus marveled at how perfectly proportioned the large man looked once he was on Samson's back. On a donkey, Ezra would have looked ludicrous, his feet almost dragging the ground. But on Samson, he just looked like a big man on a big horse. He and the Arabian stallion just suited each other perfectly, a fact that Jesus would never have guessed from seeing Ezra on foot in the market.

They left the town of Nazareth at a brisk walk. At least it was a brisk walk for the little mare that was carrying Jesus. When he looked ahead to the gelding that carried his mother, and especially to Samson, the pace seemed more leisurely. Those longer legs didn't have to move quite as fast or as often to cover the same amount of ground. Jesus wondered whether the mare could gallop fast enough to make Samson do more than trot. He hoped the mare would be able to keep up with the other two horses.

Ezra looked back often to see how Mary and Jesus were settling in and whether the pace was okay. He didn't seem to worry about the gelding or the mare wandering off on a different path than Samson. They seemed quite comfortable with going wherever Samson led. Rather, Ezra seemed concerned only with the comfort of the riders on their backs.

After they got out of town and had the road pretty much to themselves, Ezra motioned to Mary to take the lead and he dropped back to ride beside Jesus. They rode side by side for a while and Ezra observed quietly and then made some corrections to Jesus' riding style. He showed him to hold the reins in one hand and to give the mare some slack so that she could just pay attention to the road ahead without wondering if Jesus was trying to turn her. He showed him that he should relax his shoulders and flow with the horses movement. Soon Jesus began to relax and imitate every movement that he observed in Uncle Ezra and he began to think of himself as a horseman.

Then after maybe a quarter of an hour, Ezra urged Samson forward with his heels and rode beside Mary for a short ways. He seemed to inquire, through gestures, about Hannah and Mary indicated that she was asleep. Ezra nodded with a big smile and resumed the lead.

After a couple of hours on the road, Jesus began to get a bit sleepy himself. The warm sun and the rocking motion of the horse were lulling him into, if not drowsiness, at least some state of less alertness than that with which he had begun the journey. When they reached a steeper uphill section, he was startled by feeling the mare stumbling under him. He fell forward onto the mare's neck, which made her stumbling worse and the two of them nearly went down together before the mare recovered and he could slip back into his proper position.

This episode had not escaped Ezra's attention and he waited at the side of the trail and let Mary go on ahead. Jesus was embarrassed as if he had caused the horse to stumble. But Ezra didn't seem to be blaming him. Instead, he showed him that if the horse stumbles, the rider should lift up the reins sharply so that the horse would pick up her head. Then he patted Jesus on the shoulder and gave him a thumbs-up signal. Then he dropped in behind Jesus and the mare. After that, both the mare and Jesus were more alert.

When the trail dropped down beside a stream Ezra rode ahead. He dismounted under a shade tree and signaled to Mary and Jesus to stop as well. He took Hannah from her mother's arms and with one hand helped Mary slip softly to the ground. Jesus dismounted by himself. When Ezra led the other two horses to the water, Jesus brought the mare along also. Ezra let them drink for a while and kept murmuring to them and running his hands along their necks as they drank. After just a few minutes, he led them away from the water and tethered them where they could graze in the shade. He dug into one of the saddle bags and brought out fresh apples and dried apricots. Samson seemed very alert to what Ezra was fetching from the saddle bag, but Ezra seemed to give him a gentle rebuke as he walked away.

Mary spread out the cloth that had been Hannah's hammock and she sat on it in the shade of the tree. She put Hannah down to toddle around but gave Jesus orders to keep her out of the water. Ezra brought the apples and apricots to her and they rested together as they all refreshed themselves. On horseback and with an early start, they had every prospect of reaching Capernaum by nightfall. So it was okay to have an interlude here in such a pleasant spot. Ezra fetched a drinking gourd from his pack and dipped fresh water from the stream for each of them.

After several minutes of nibbling on the run, Hannah settled down on Ezra's lap, apparently deciding that he was not so scary. He pretended to go for her apple with his mouth wide open. She squealed in laughter and pulled it away. He tickled her which made her forget to hold the apple safe, at which point he again pretended to try to bite it. She squealed again and then held the apple in her teeth. Ezra growled and pretended to go for the apple but instead kissed her on the forehead.

When Jesus finished eating his apple, he was about to throw the core across the stream but Ezra stopped him. He pointed to the horses. Jesus looked and saw that Samson was not exactly straining against his tether, but there was no slack in the rope either. And he was looking very eagerly toward the humans and their apples with ears forward and nostrils flaring. Jesus intimated that he would give the apple core to Samson, and Ezra confirmed it but grabbed his arm. He showed Jesus not to hold the core in his fingers but to hold his hand flat, palm up, with all fingers straight and together. The core was to sit freely on the palm. Ezra showed with his own teeth what might happen to a finger that was wrapped around an apple core. That was a lesson that Jesus was glad to learn from Ezra and not from personal experience with Samson.

When he approached Samson, the horse whickered eagerly and took some antsy steps against the tether to show his interest. Jesus started holding the core on the flat of his palm long before he was in range. He felt the sweat begin to trickle down his sides as he drew closer and closer to the mighty Samson. He swallowed hard and took two more cautious steps. Samson was so eager and the treat so tantalizingly out of reach, that he strained against the rope and the tether pulled out of the ground. Jesus almost turned and ran but before he could make that decision, the horse had lapped the core out of his hand with his soft, whiskery lips.

Samson tossed his head as he munched the apple and seemed to be saying thank you, so Jesus gasped, "You're welcome." He wanted to touch Samson again and Samson wanted to see if the boy had another apple core, so the two of them made contact again. A thrill went through Jesus. He wasn't sure if it was a thrill of excitement or of fear, but he began to back away. Samson, sensing his freedom, began to follow. But when Ezra got up to firmly re-stake the tether, Samson whirled toward him. When the tether was re-established, Ezra took one last bite out of his own apple and handed the core to Jesus. He pointed to the little mare that Jesus had been riding and although Samson started to follow to beg for a second core, Ezra held him firmly and let the little mare have a share.

When Mary finished her apple, Jesus gave that core to the gelding and all was equal. But of course, one apple remained and Hannah had lost interest in it after only a few baby-sized bites. When Mary was quite sure that Hannah was done with it, she tossed it to Jesus and indicated the horses. Jesus first thought that, of course, he would give it to Samson, but he was checked in his thoughts halfway there. He stood quite still for a couple of moments, deep in thought. Then he walked directly to the little mare who was busily munching grass, not expecting any further treat. He gave the apple to her and rubbed her ears while she ate it. Then he whispered something in her ear and walked back to his mother.

"I thought sure you were going to give that to Samson," said Mary.

"I was going to but then something checked me in my thoughts."

"What was that?" asked Mary.

"I realized that the reason I wanted to give it to Samson was because I want him to like me. He is so beautiful and attractive. And then I thought that perhaps everyone treats him that way because he is so attractive and that probably no one ever notices the little mare. She has worked just as hard as Samson, maybe even harder because she can hardly keep up. If no one ever notices her or gives her treats, how sad is that?"

"I like your thinking," said his mother.

"Besides," added Jesus, "Samson seems a little bit greedy." Mary marveled at her son, not for the first and not for the last time, and nodded approval.

Ezra had gone back to playing with Hannah. She was barefoot and he was playing with her tiny toes. He seemed to be counting off her toes, but of course he couldn't say numbers. Instead, he would touch one toe after another and utter a kind of "uh" sound as he touched each one. "Uh, uh, uh, uh, UH." He would say, each time emphasizing the sound as he reached the final toe. Then he would take up the opposite foot and do the same thing over again. Hannah would laugh at every repetition.

Then he took hold of her hand and did the same thing with her fingers, "Uh, uh, uh, uh, UH." And Hannah laughed. He did the same on her other hand and she laughed again. Then he held his own great hand up before her and she counted the fingers off in the same way, saying, "Uh, uh, uh, uh, UH." That time he laughed and held up his other hand. She began to count off going, "Uh, uh, uh, uh," but before she could count off the last one, he pretended to bite it off and folded it out of her sight from the second knuckle. She laughed and started over, "Uh, uh, uh, UH." The shortened version of the game tickled her no end and she laughed so hard it made Mary and Jesus laugh with her.

Then Ezra held up his hands so that he hid his left hand behind his right and inserted an extra index finger between his right index finger and his thumb. Hannah counted, "Uh, uh, uh, uh, uh, UH!" and doubled over with the hilarity of this funny man's antics with fingers. She laughed so hard that tears ran down her cheeks and her face was rosy red. Mary took her in her arms and rocked her back and forth. She turned her back toward Ezra and tucked Hannah inside her clothing to nurse her a bit before getting back in the saddle.

Ezra turned to Jesus and got serious. He was trying to convey something to him about a man with six fingers on each hand and six toes on each foot. Then he stood on tiptoe and reached as high as he could reach, indicating the incredible height of the six-fingered, six-toed man. He then acted out the part of a very large man wielding sword and spear, a giant warrior.

Jesus nodded with recognition. He had read about a relative of Goliath's who was huge and had six digits on each limb. Almost every parent in Israel had tried to instill good behavior by warning children of Goliath and his kin and what they might do to disobedient children.

Then Ezra jumped up and strode to Samson. He retrieved something from one of the saddle bags and brought it back and gave it to Jesus. It was a sling for casting stones. And it was very cunningly worked. The leather of the pouch was smooth and soft, inviting a caressing touch. The cord was black and beautifully braided, of a kind that Jesus had never seen.

"Look at this sling, Mama," said Jesus. "What kind of cord is this? What is it made of?"

"Ooh, nice," said Mary. "I think it might be horsehair." She pointed at Samson and pinched a bit of her own hair. Ezra nodded. She pointed at him and pretended a braiding motion. Again Ezra nodded. Though he couldn't hear her words, it was clear that he recognized and accepted her praise of his work. He almost blushed. Then he got up and waded into the stream and chose five smooth stones and brought them dripping to Jesus. He dried them off on his clothing and fitted one of them into the pouch. He indicated that Jesus should try hurling the stone at the tree trunk.

Jesus stood up to try but Mary said, "Wait! Not near your sister and me!" She gathered up Hannah and went what she considered to be a safe distance in the opposite direction. Ezra waited to see what Jesus could do with a sling. He swung the stone around his head several times and then let one of the horsehair cords slip out of his fingers in order to propel the stone toward the target. It fell somewhat short and was not directed quite straight toward the tree, either. Ezra came over and showed Jesus how to wrap one of the cords firmly so that it wouldn't slip while holding the other cord loosely between two fingers but clamped firmly by the thumb. Then just lifting the thumb would allow the one cord to slip away. Jesus tried a few more times and was getting the hang of it. On the fifth stone, he hit the tree trunk a resounding thwack and Ezra applauded the effort.

Then Ezra and Jesus found more smooth stones and Ezra reduced them to five, counting them off like fingers, "Uh, uh, uh, uh, UH." Then he indicated that Jesus should stay on this side of the stream while he, himself, went to the other. Once on the other side, Ezra found himself a long straight stick and brandished it like a spear in the one hand while in the other, he held a shorter stick like a sword. Then he went into his raging giant act, roaring and acting very threatening.

When Jesus didn't know how to respond, Ezra motioned for him to use his sling and throw a stone at him. Jesus was reluctant, but Ezra repeatedly urged him to cross the stream and fling a stone in his direction. By this time, Mary and Hannah were watching with rapt attention.

Finally, Jesus crossed the stream and Ezra popped out from behind a bush roaring and threatening with both his weapons. Jesus put a stone in his sling and swung it round and round his head. Finally he let fly and Ezra let out an enormous groan, dropped his weapons and clasped both hands to his forehead. Then he fell full length, face down with a terrible crash. Mary screamed and Hannah began to cry in terror.

"Why did you do that, Jesus?" his mother shouted as she ran to see if Ezra was beyond help.

Jesus shouted back, "I didn't hit him, Mama! He's play acting." Mary either didn't hear him or couldn't comprehend as she pulled up her skirts and splashed through the stream. She handed Hannah off to Jesus as she rushed past, but when she reached Ezra and touched him, He rolled over and looked up into her face. Then he laughed a huge belly laugh to see the real concern in her face. He had only been play acting and Jesus had carefully thrown the stone to one side of him. Mary punched him and he rolled away from her laughing till tears rolled down his cheeks.

Mary marched in annoyance back to Jesus and took Hannah in her arms and crossed the creek. She was done with this silliness and ready to get back on the trail to Capernaum. Jesus was kind of caught in between. He thought the play acting was wonderful fun, but he couldn't ignore his mother's angry response. He stood where he was and when Ezra finally got to his feet, he smiled at him and shrugged his shoulders, looking over one of them at his retreating mother. Jesus and Ezra crossed the stream together and started to make preparations for moving on. Jesus tried to give the sling back to Ezra but Ezra wouldn't accept it. He indicated that it was a gift and Jesus must keep it and practice more with it.

When they had ridden down the trail a little way, Jesus rode up beside his mother and asked, "Mama, are you really mad?"

"No, I'm not mad now."

"You seemed pretty angry back there. Uncle Ezra and I were just having fun."

"I understand that now. And I admit that it was kind of funny. I was embarrassed that I was drawn into it and didn't realize it was play acting. I thought you had really wounded or killed him."

Jesus smiled and rode for a few minutes in silence. Then he asked, "Who taught Uncle Ezra about David and Goliath? And how?"

"I can't imagine," said his mother.

"But he clearly knows the story of David and Goliath. He wanted me to play the shepherd boy. He even knows how many stones David took from the stream. And he played Goliath right after telling me about a giant with six fingers on each hand and six toes on each foot."

"Your grandmother has told me that their father used to tell stories from the Scriptures to her and Ezra and to the other children in the neighborhood. Sometimes they even acted the stories out. Maybe Ezra got it from those childhood experiences."

"Well, seeing him today playing with Hannah and play acting with me, it makes me wonder why anyone is afraid of him."

"You were afraid of him not three days ago, son."

"That's true, Mama. But now I wonder if he is play acting when boys tug on his clothes in the market and he roars and chases them."

"It's possible, I suppose. But I don't think the boys know he is play acting."

"Not the ones I know. They are really terrified."

They rode on in silence for another half hour and then Jesus said, "Sometimes Abba and I play a game while we travel to make the road less boring."

"I'll bet I know what that game is," replied his mother.

"Do you know it?"

"One person recites a line of scripture and the other person has to tell an application of the scripture and then add the next line, right? Then the first person has to give an application."

"Yes, that's it. How do you know that game?" asked Jesus.

"I dare say I have traveled with your father just as much as you have, though not recently."

"Do you want to play?" asked Jesus.

"Of course," said his mother. "You start."

"Okay. 'The Lord is my shepherd, I shall not be in want.'"

"That means I am not on my own to figure life out. It means I have someone who watches over me and seeks my good. I am not abandoned; I can turn to my shepherd and know that my needs will be addressed."

"Good," said Jesus. "And the next line?"

"'He makes me lie down in green pastures.'"

"That means that my shepherd not only takes me to pastures that are abundant, but he stops me from eating too much. He makes me lie down even when there is more that could be eaten, because he knows that I won't digest my food well if I do not lie down and chew my cud. A sheep without a shepherd will keep eating more and more until it is sick, but my shepherd treats me the way the Lord treated the Israelites when he gave them manna. He gave them plenty but would not allow them to gather extra because it would spoil. And he forbade them to gather on the seventh day because he knew they needed to rest."

"Wow," exclaimed his mother, "You have thought about that one a great deal!"

"The next line is, 'He leads me beside quiet waters.'"

"Okay," said Mary, "my shepherd knows that food is not enough, I also need water, just as the Israelites needed water and the Lord caused water to flow for them from the dry rock. He also knows that sheep are timid and reluctant to drink if the water is noisily splashing over rocks, so he leads me to places where water runs quietly and I can drink without fear."

Jesus nodded. And Mary added, "'He restores my soul; he leads me in paths of righteousness for his name's sake.'"

"That means," said Jesus, "that my shepherd takes care of my heart needs and does not lead me carelessly down any path that suits him at the moment. It means that his reputation is at stake. If he leads me in paths that are not good for me and unnecessarily dangerous, people will call him a foolish shepherd. It also means that he goes before me on the path, not sending me into any place that he has not gone first."

"Have you and Abba already done this Psalm before?" asked Mary.

"Several times," admitted Jesus a little bit sheepishly.

"It shows,' said Mary. "I can hear your father in some of your answers."

"The next line," said Jesus, "is, 'Even though I walk through the valley of the shadow of death, I will not fear the evil one, for you are with me.'"

"That means," said his mother, "that my shepherd is Sovereign God, who alone has authority over life and death. The evil one may threaten me and try to do me harm, but my shepherd has the final word. If he is with me, then I will live and not die. But it means that our sovereign shepherd is familiar with danger and allows us to become familiar with it as well. And if he should allow me to die, he it is who holds the power to raise me up again. Therefore I am to fear God, and not fear death.

"The next line is, 'Your rod and your staff are a comfort to me.'"
Jesus said, "The shepherd's rod is a weapon, a club, with which he attacks wolves, bears and other enemies of the sheep. Therefore, I am comforted because my shepherd is prepared to defend me from those who would destroy me. His staff is the stick by which he guides me into a path or into the fold where I can safely rest at night. It is the stick by which he retrieves a lamb that has fallen into a ravine and the instrument by which he counts his sheep to know if any are missing. A shepherd without a staff would not be able to do his job. Therefore, I am comforted to know that my shepherd is equipped with the tools he needs to take care of me.

"'You prepare a feast before me in the presence of my enemies.'"

"This means," said Mary, "that although my eyes may be focused on some terrible possibility that confronts me, my shepherd may be at work preparing something very special for me. I should keep my eyes on the shepherd, and not panic at the sight of enemies. Like what happened in the days when Ben Hadad and the Aramean army had besieged Samaria for many days. There was no food left in the city and the whole city was ready to perish but Elisha the prophet told the King that the next day, the siege would be lifted and food would be cheap. The servant on whom the King depended scoffed at this prophecy and Elisha told him that he would see it but not taste of it. By the next day, the whole army of Ben Hadad had fled in terror, leaving their tents full of good food for the city of Samaria. But the man who had scoffed was crushed to death by those rushing to get the food. Therefore, I should look to my shepherd and depend on Him, no matter how the enemy surrounds me."

"That's a good one, Mama!"

"'You anoint my head with oil,'" said Mary, quoting the next line.

"That means that my shepherd has selected me for some special role and has set me apart from the other sheep. This is what we do to signify the lamb that we will sacrifice for Passover; it signifies special honor just as Samuel set David apart to be the next king over Israel by anointing his head with oil. It was years after the anointing that David actually received his crown, and in the years in between, David never tried to take the power of the kingship for himself because he respected the special honor Saul had received when he was the first king to be anointed over Israel. He was confident that if God had Samuel anoint him King, then he would be king, though Saul tried on numerous occasions to kill him. He knew that since God had chosen him, he could not fail to become king.

"Mama?"

"Yes, Jesus?"

"Have I been anointed with oil?"

"No..."

"Will I be?"

"I don't know..."

"But if a king gets anointed with oil, wouldn't you think that the Messiah would be? Isn't that what Messiah means? 'The anointed one?'"

"Yes, that's what it means. But I don't know if you will literally be anointed with oil. There is no one like Samuel living these days."

"But if the Messiah is not anointed with oil, how is he set apart?"

"I believe," said Mary, "that God can set apart a person for a special role without any human being applying ceremonial oil on them."

"Can you give me an example?"

"I can."

"Who?"

"Me."

"Huh?"

"Every daughter of Israel for the last several hundred years has dreamed that she might be chosen to be 'the virgin who would conceive and bear the son, upon whose shoulder the government would rest and whose kingdom would never end.' The angel Gabriel came to me and said, 'You have found favor with God. You will become pregnant and bear a son and you are to call his name Jesus, for he shall save his people from their sins.' Nobody anointed my head with oil, but that is just an outward symbol. God set me apart for this role, even though no anointing oil was involved."

"That… that… I've never thought about it that way," said Jesus, awestruck as he gazed at his mother. "Wouldn't you have been more confident that you were really God's anointed if someone had anointed you with oil?"

"I never even thought about oil," said Mary. "The angel's words were enough for me."

"What did you say?"

"I said, 'May it be to me as you have said.' And just knowing that the angel had spoken for God, gave me courage to go on, even on the long road to Bethlehem, even when Herod sought to kill you. God had said that I would bear the Messiah; why should I question his power to bring it to pass?"

"Why indeed?" said Jesus. He grew very quiet after that and forgot all about the game.

In early afternoon they emerged from the hills and came to the town of Tiberias on the shores of the lake. They could smell fish on the sea air before they could actually see the water. Ezra rode alongside Jesus and

158

made a show of sniffing in the sea air and showing evident pleasure in the experience. He made a wiggling motion with his flat hand held thumb uppermost in front of him. It was clear to Jesus that he was indicating fish swimming. Then Ezra pretended to eat a fish and rubbed his belly with pleasure. Jesus was surprised once again at how much he and Ezra could understand each other, despite the inability to use language.

The travelers rode through the town right along the waterfront and stopped for a lunch of freshly grilled fish right by the beach just north of town. The horses were tethered across the road where they could browse a bit. Jesus took charge of his little sister and allowed her to wet her bare feet at the edge of the sea. Then they played along the water's edge and threw stones at the waves.

They didn't linger very long after refreshing themselves as they had some miles to go yet. From Tiberias the road followed the shore of the sea northward through Migdal, in which there was an ancient tower, or at least the remains of one. The road beyond Migdal was so broad and smooth and the travelers so eager, that they trotted for a ways and then broke into a gallop along the beach. Ezra gave Samson his head and let the wind whistle through his ears for nearly a league, by which time they had left Mary and Jesus far behind. Just when Jesus was beginning to worry that he would lose sight of their guide and protector, he saw Samson wheel and come racing back towards them. By that time, the little mare was getting quite winded and even the gelding was happy to slow to a walk as they saw Samson approaching. Ezra raced past them and then turned Samson toward the water and he and Samson cavorted in the shallow water until they got back to the other horses.

Samson was barely breathing hard and looked like he was ready to go again, but Ezra calmed him down and let him have a drink at the edge of the sea. The other horses followed his example and then they rode on to Capernaum, which is at the north end of the Sea of Galilee, also called the Sea of Tiberias.

Upon entering the town of Capernaum, Ezra deferred to Jesus, who knew his way to Rabbi Zephon's house. The rabbi occupied a small house near the center of town but not next to the sea shore. The rabbi was not at home but his wife, Elsaba, sent a neighbor boy running to the synagogue to tell her husband that they had guests. Elsaba invited them to come in and have some tea, but Jesus and Ezra stayed outside with the horses while Mary accepted the hospitality for herself and Hannah.

Soon the boy came trotting back with the Rabbi hurrying behind him. "Good evening, Rabbi Zephon," said Jesus.

"Good evening to you, my little scholar. I am so pleased to see you. Your father didn't make the trip with you?"

"No, my father has been ill, but thanks be to the Almighty, he is recovering. This," he said, indicating his large traveling companion, "is Ezra, my father's uncle."

"I am honored to meet you, sir," he said, nodding up at Ezra. Ezra nodded back.

"Uncle Ezra cannot hear or speak, but he is a wonderful horseman and traveling companion," offered Jesus.

"The Almighty be praised," said the rabbi. "I can see that the Lord has provided him with a wonderful animal to ride."

"Yes, he has," said Jesus. "His name is Samson. Uncle Ezra won him in the arena at Caesarea when he served with the Roman Legion."

"He served with the Roman Legion, you say? I don't think you should publish that information around here, son. There is a lot of resentment of the Romans in this town."

"I hear you and we need not speak of it at all. But it is a wonderful story how he came to own Samson."

"That part I will gladly hear, behind closed doors, mind you."

"I only heard the story from my grandmother, Ezra's sister, last night. But I will be happy to tell you what I heard."

"I can see," said the rabbi, "that this third horse is carrying a lady. Who else is traveling with you?"

"My mother and my little sister, Hannah. Your kind wife has already invited them in for tea."

"And you all shall be my guests. Come in, come in."

As they began to move toward the door of the house, Ezra resisted and made motions indicating that he wanted to take the horses and find a stable for them. So Jesus and the rabbi took the borrowed scroll and Mary's provisions off the horses. The rabbi pointed out the way for Ezra to find a stable and he ushered Jesus into the house.

"Thank you for returning this scroll before the feast. I was beginning to wonder if you would bring it."

"Abba and I can never thank you enough for allowing us to borrow these precious scrolls. And a promise is a promise. We knew that you needed this one for the feast."

"How did you get on with the Psalms, Jesus?" asked the rabbi.

"Quite well, thank you."

"Did any in particular catch your eye?"

"Many did. Of course David's psalm of the shepherd is very comforting."

"Yes it is. I find it so, myself."

"But the one just before it disturbs me deeply."

"Why is that?"

"Well David writes,
'Dogs have surrounded me;
a band of evil men has encircled me,
they have pierced my hands and my feet.
I can count all my bones;
people stare and gloat over me.
They divide my garments among them
and cast lots for my clothing.'"

"Yes," said the rabbi, "I remember that part."

"When and where did that ever happen to David?" asked Jesus.

The rabbi thought for a minute or two and then said, "I'm not sure that happened to David."

"Then who did it happen to and why did David describe it as if it happened to him?"

"I don't have that answer, Jesus."

"It's something to think about, isn't it?" said Jesus.

"Indeed, it is," agreed the rabbi.

"Rabbi, can you tell me this? When the Messiah comes will someone anoint his head with oil?"

"Hmmm… I'm not sure that scripture tells us that. Perhaps Elijah will anoint him. The prophet Malachi writes that the Lord will send Elijah back to us before the great and terrible day of judgment. But it doesn't specifically say that Elijah will anoint Messiah. You are asking really good questions, my son!"

When Ezra returned, the rabbi and his wife fed their guests a simple dinner of soup and fish and fresh bread. Over tea, Jesus and Mary took turns in telling the story of Ezra and how he won Samson in a "fight to the death" in which he won but did not kill his opponent.

"So how does Ezra make a living now that he is no longer a fighting man?" asked the rabbi.

"He takes care of horses and other animals," said Mary. "He is not a wealthy man but he could probably live off of what he makes in stud fees for Samson. He has single handedly improved the stock of horses around Nazareth over the past several years. And people bring their mares to him from all the surrounding towns, as well."

When the rabbi's wife began to make arrangements for her guests to sleep, Ezra excused himself, making it clear that he would sleep in the stable with his horses. Jesus wanted to join him there but Mary wouldn't allow it. "You would insult the rabbi's hospitality if you refuse to sleep under his roof," she whispered in his ear.

162

Jesus wondered whether Ezra was insulting the rabbi but it didn't seem that the rabbi was offended. Perhaps it was different if a man was taking care of his horses. Or perhaps it was different because Ezra was a stranger to the rabbi until today. And, of course, Ezra was not borrowing scrolls from the rabbi. But Jesus still wished that he could sleep in the straw with Uncle Ezra and the horses.

The next morning Ezra did not show up for breakfast. Rabbi Zephon sent Jesus to the stable to fetch him. Jesus found the stable and the three horses were there but Ezra was not. Jesus asked the owner of the stable and learned that Uncle Ezra had, indeed, slept with the horses but that he had left as soon as there was light in the east. Jesus asked where he had gone and was told, "He went toward the sea."

Jesus went down to the shore but could not see Uncle Ezra anywhere. He asked several fishermen whether they had seen a very large stranger who couldn't hear or speak. He learned that Uncle Ezra had gone out fishing with Zebedee and his brother.

Jesus returned to the rabbi's house and reported this news. They were not particularly surprised and were glad that they didn't have to wait any longer to break their fast. While eating, the subject of their return journey came up.

"It is plain that if Ezra went fishing this morning, he will probably be gone most of the day," said Mary. "And since we won't be traveling today, and Sabbath begins this evening, we seem to be compelled to impose on your hospitality through tomorrow as well, unless there is an inn in this town."

"There are inns in this town," said the rabbi. "but I would be greatly offended if you left our home to go stay in one. A guest is a gift from God. Why would you want to deprive us of a gift from God?" His wife, Elsaba, confirmed the same attitude and insisted that they not even think about an inn.

"Well then you must allow me to help you with preparations for Sabbath," said Mary.

"Nonsense," replied Elsaba. "I have to do a bit of marketing. Why don't you take your children down to the shore and collect shells. Children love playing along the beach and the sunshine and fresh air will do them good."

"Let us help you with the marketing. We will still have plenty of time to go to the sea," said Mary. "And Jesus is very helpful for carrying things."

"Well, okay." said Elsaba. Then maybe I will come to the sea with you for a little while."

"Perfect!" exclaimed Mary.

Rabbi Zephon had only been married three years. He and his wife were still young and there was plenty of time for the Lord to bless them with children. But three years was long enough for them to begin to be a little nervous about their lack of such blessing. Elsaba relished the opportunity to spend some time with Mary and to talk about her concerns, especially since Mary was not connected to all the local gossips.

When the marketing was done and they went to the beach, Hannah was delighted and ran to and fro in her bare feet, sometimes wading into the water a few steps and then running back to her mother. Jesus tried to interest her in building a sand castle, but she was too full of energy to sit still. She wanted to run and splash and chase shore birds that strutted near the waterline.

After watching his sister for half an hour or more, Jesus sought permission to go down the beach to talk to some fishermen.

"Don't go out of my sight, though," cautioned his mother. "And don't get in their way. They have work to do."

"Thank you, Mama," said Jesus and went skipping down the beach.

He drew near to where two men were working on their nets and stood quietly to watch. The men were spreading the nets out and looking for broken or weak spots. They had a large spool of cord from which they unwound lengths for their repair work. Jesus watched to see how they knotted the cord but their fingers moved so fast that he couldn't follow all the movements.

Then he went farther along to where a boy a few years older than himself was stitching the edge of a sail. He watched quietly from a distance but after a few minutes the boy spoke. "Hi."

"Hi," replied Jesus.

"Are you new around here," asked the boy.

"Just visiting," Jesus said. "What are you doing?"

"I'm repairing the edge of this sail where it is frayed. If your sails aren't in good shape, your boat is no good. And if your boat is no good, the fish will have no respect for you. They don't want to be caught by just anybody."

Jesus smiled.

"My name is Simon," offered the boy.

"I'm Jesus. Is this your boat?"

"It is my father's boat, but I get to sail it."

"By yourself?"

"Well, sort of. My father comes with me, but I get to sail it while he handles the nets."

"How old are you?" asked Jesus.

"Almost thirteen," replied Simon. "How about you?"

"Almost nine."

"Have you ever been out in a boat?" asked Simon.

"No, I'm from Nazareth. We are kind of far from the sea."

"Have you ever caught a fish?"

"No, but I would like to."

"Do you want to go fishing with us?"

"You mean with you and your father?"

"And my uncle."

"I'd like that very much. I would have to ask my mother. What time are you going?"

"Tonight about an hour after dark."

"You are making that up!"

"No, I'm not. We always go at night. That's when the fishing is best."

"Okay, let me go ask my mother." Thus saying, Jesus sprinted back to his mother. He breathlessly gasped out his request, "That boy over there is repairing the sail on his father's boat and he invited me to go fishing with him and his father and his uncle."

"Well," said Mary, clearly uncomfortable with the request. "We don't even know them and ..."

"That's Jonah's boy. They are alright," offered Elsaba. "We know them."

"How soon would you be back?" asked Mary.

"Oh, they aren't planning on going out until tonight, about an hour after dark."

"What? Absolutely not," said Mary. "I am not letting you go out on the sea in the dark. Besides, the Sabbath begins at sundown."

"But the fishing is best at night," said Jesus. "Please can I go with them?"

"Not a chance," replied his mother.

Jesus stood silent in his disappointment for a few moments. When Mary and Elsaba returned to their conversation, Jesus quietly walked back and reported to Simon that he wasn't allowed to go at night, let alone on the Sabbath.

"That's too bad," said Simon. "It's really quite safe and sometimes we catch an amazing net full of fish. We hang a lantern over the side of the boat and the fish come to it out of curiosity. One time we caught over seventy large fish in one cast of the net."

Jesus was very disappointed but didn't see any way around his mother's prohibition. And he knew better than to pester her for his own way. Mary was not the kind of mother who could be ignored or disrespected. He continued watching until Simon finished his work and headed home. Jesus watched him out of sight and saw him enter a small hut just across the road from the shore.

Late in the afternoon when the rabbi's household was preparing for Sabbath, Ezra returned. Through animated hand gestures he was able to tell them that he went out fishing but did not catch anything all day. He didn't even see a fish.

Jesus told the Rabbi that a boy had invited him to go out fishing at night but, of course, he wasn't allowed to go.

"Why aren't you allowed to go?" asked the rabbi.

"Because Mama doesn't think it would be safe," said Jesus. "And, of course, it is the Sabbath."

The rabbi was quiet for a minute, studying Mary. Then he said, "I wouldn't worry about the safety if I knew he was with someone reliable, Mary. Who invited him?"

Elsaba spoke up, "It was Jonah's son, Simon."

"Oh, then I shouldn't worry at all. That family is rock solid. They have been fishermen here for generations. Jonah and his brother, Nahum, are very reliable."

"But it is the Sabbath," said Mary, as if that settled the question.

The rabbi twiddled his thumbs in silence for a moment and then cautiously said, "And if Jesus went with me to Synagogue first? Would that mitigate your concern?" He hesitated and then added, "I myself am not a Pharisee about such things, but I don't mean to go against you if you are bringing him up to be more observant…" He was watching her closely, as though trying to read in her face whether he had gone too far.

Jesus pleaded with his eyes but said not a word. Mary looked at Elsaba, and then at Ezra, who was sipping tea noisily, apparently unaware of the conversation. Finally, Mary caught Ezra's eye. She asked him if he wanted to go fishing tonight. He misunderstood and again indicated he didn't even see a fish.

She used gestures to indicate she and Elsaba and the rabbi would sleep but Ezra and Jesus would go fishing. He brightened up considerably and nodded enthusiastically.

Mary turned to Jesus and said, "Can you find your way to Simon's house and ask him if the two of you can join them on their boat tonight?"

"Of course I can," said Jesus and started to jump up.

"No need for that," said Rabbi Zephon. "Jonah and Nahum will be at Synagogue in half an hour and you can ask them there."

"Are you sure," asked Jesus. "What if they don't come?"

"They will come to synagogue on the Sabbath before they go fishing. They always do. And I am sure they will welcome you to go with them."

"Thank you, Mama," said Jesus, throwing his arms around her neck. "I will never forget this."

"Well, I believe in keeping the Sabbath, but there are special occasions when an exception will not kill you. And you may never get another chance to go out on a fishing boat at night."

Soon, Jesus and Rabbi Zephon were on the way to synagogue. Ezra walked in the opposite direction to go check on the horses. The synagogue was in the center of town, a few streets away from the sea. It was a simple building on the outside but comfortably appointed inside. The rabbi introduced Jesus to a very ancient man named Elkanah who was already waiting for the service when they got there. Jesus found a seat and Elkanah waited at the door to greet his friends and neighbors as they arrived. Rabbi Zephon slipped aside to his private prayer room to prepare his own heart for service.

Every time the door opened, Jesus looked up to see if his new friend, Simon, would come in with his father and uncle. Men of all ages were coming in, but apparently boys were not in the habit of attending service. Jesus saw men from various walks of life, but he could not say whether any of them were fishermen. Probably some of them were, but they weren't wearing anything that would distinguish them from men of other professions. And they entered the synagogue conversing only in hushed voices, if at all, so it was not possible to tell from what they were saying to one another.

Then the service began and Jesus stopped watching the door. Elkanah served as the messenger of the congregation. He made his way to various men and assigned them various roles in reading from the law and from the prophets. Then he began by reading out the traditional first blessing, followed by congregational response. After that there was the second blessing, also followed by congregational response. Then Elkanah led the congregation in reciting the shema, "Hear O Israel, The 'LORD' is our god, the 'LORD' alone." Elkanah then read out the third blessing and the congregation once more gave the appropriate response.

That was followed by seven different men of the congregation reading aloud from various portions of the Law, as appointed by Elkanah at the beginning of the service. Then an eighth appointee stood up and read from the prophets.

When it was time for the sermon, Elkanah nodded to the rabbi but the rabbi announced that he would like for his young guest to read from the Psalms. He called Jesus to the front and handed him the scroll and pointed out where he would like him to begin.

Jesus read as follows:
"Ascribe to I AM, O mighty ones, ascribe to I AM glory and strength.
Ascribe to I AM the glory due his name; worship I AM in the splendor of his holiness.
The voice of I AM is over the waters; the God of glory thunders, I AM thunders over the mighty waters.
The voice of I AM is powerful; the voice of I AM is majestic.
The voice of I AM breaks the cedars; I AM breaks in pieces the cedars of Lebanon.
He makes Lebanon skip like a calf, Sirion like a young wild ox.
The voice of I AM strikes with flashes of lightning.
The voice of I AM shakes the desert; I AM shakes the Desert of Kadesh.
The voice of I AM twists the oaks and strips the forests bare.
And in his temple all cry, "Glory!"

I AM sits enthroned over the flood; I AM is enthroned as King forever.
I AM gives strength to his people; I AM blesses his people with peace."

When he was finished reading, he heard tittering among the men of the congregation until the rabbi stood up and cleared his voice, calling them to attention. "Our guest reads rather well for one so young," the rabbi said, "but he is not accustomed to all of our traditions. Please forgive this unintended offense."

Jesus blushed. He knew what the rabbi was talking about. Although the text of the Psalm had the name "I AM" or "Yahweh" in it, it was traditional to substitute "Adonai" meaning "Lord," and not to utter the sacred name aloud, out of respect. Abba had taught him that distinction, but when Jesus had objected that God had told Moses "This is my name forever, the name by which I am to be remembered from generation to generation," Joseph relented. So when Jesus and Joseph were reading to each other, they read "I AM" just as it was written, not substituting "Adonai."

Throughout the rabbi's sermon, Jesus was distracted, thinking about how the tradition of not reading "I AM" was in conflict with what God had told Moses. By not reading the sacred name aloud, they thought they were honoring their heavenly father. But how would future generations remember the name "I AM" if they never heard it? Back in Nazareth he and his father rarely attended synagogue, so they didn't face the contradiction very often.

He heard the door open and wondered whether someone was leaving early or someone was coming late to service. He kept his eyes closed but felt someone slip into the seat beside him. He peeked and found that Ezra was sitting beside him. He wondered what Ezra called God in his own mind. He would never have heard either "I AM" nor "Adonai." He didn't even know that everyone called his stallion, "Samson." But surely he was aware of his creator. It was impossible to imagine the thought processes of a man whose intelligence was not connected to language. But it was clear that Ezra was intelligent.

Ezra put an arm around Jesus' shoulders and gave him a squeeze. It felt good to have even one person there who wouldn't think poorly of him for reading "I AM" out loud.

When the last blessing was read and the congregation had responded, Elkanah closed with a prayer, especially asking for God's blessing and mercy on the fishermen who needed to go out on the sea in the dark. When Jesus looked up, he was a little timid about meeting the eyes of those who might have been scandalized by his reading, but he wanted to find Simon, the boy who had invited him to go night fishing. He did not see him.

The rabbi took him by the hand and led him to a pair of men who had come in after Jesus had stopped watching the door. "Jonah, Nahum," said the rabbi. "Blessed Sabbath to you both."

The men returned the greeting but looked a little sheepish. Jesus figured that might be because they were about to set out on a long night's work and the rabbi might not approve.

"This is Jesus, son of Joseph, from Nazareth, a guest in my house. I think Simon, your son," here nodding at Jonah, "invited him to go fishing with you tonight."

"I heard that his mother wouldn't let him," said Jonah.

"Well, his mother has relented on the condition that you take Ezra here, with you." Jonah turned to Ezra and looked up at him. Ezra nodded a greeting, which Jonah and Nahum returned.

Then Nahum asked, "So, Ezra, do you have some experience of fishing around here?"

Ezra was aware that Nahum was speaking but he looked to Jesus to answer for him. Jesus explained, "Uncle Ezra is deaf and mute, but he likes to fish. He went out all day today with someone but they didn't even see a fish."

"Oh, he's the one Zebedee took out this morning, " said Jonah. "He told me it was a deaf man but he failed to mention how huge he is."

"What else did Zebedee say about him?" asked Nahum. "Was he a helpless burden?"

"Not at all. He said it was obvious that the man had fished before. But they didn't have any luck."

"Well," replied his brother, "I hope he is not bad luck."

"With the rabbi's blessing, perhaps we will have a great night," said Jonah. "And we could use an extra hand if he is not a helpless baby in a boat."

With that it was agreed and they headed out the door. Jesus and Ezra hurried to the rabbi's house while the rabbi himself placated some of the men who were still upset by having heard the sacred name read aloud in their service. Jesus and Ezra grabbed a quick bite to eat and some to carry with them on the boat and hurried down to the shore.

There were several boats preparing to go out and Jesus might not have found the right boat except that Simon was already on board. Jesus called his name and then made for the boat where he heard the boy answer. The boat was pulled in shallow enough that the keel rested on the sand. A rope was stretched taut to a stake up on the beach so that the boat would not drift away before they were all aboard.

When Jonah and Nahum arrived, they were carrying various supplies as well. They stowed them aboard and released the rope. The boat was sitting more heavily upon the sand than the two of them could easily dislodge. Ezra motioned for them to get in and go to the front of the boat. That shifted the weight toward the part of the boat that was floating. Then Ezra gave a mighty shove and the boat moved a couple of cubits. He replanted his feet and really threw his shoulder into it and suddenly the boat was floating freely. Ezra hopped over the gunwale and snatched up the oars. Jonah nodded at Jesus and smiled. It was clear that Ezra was not going to be a burden.

Simon and his father hoisted the sail. Nahum grabbed the tiller and they were away from the shore in another minute. Jonah signaled to Ezra who quickly shipped the oars and sat quietly as the wind in the sail powered the boat in a big sweeping turn. Jesus watched the lanterns on shore shrink smaller and closer together as they went farther and farther into the darkness of the sea. They were not the first boat to leave shore. They could see a couple of lanterns already far out from shore which marked other fishing boats that had started before them. Gradually, other boats set out in their wake until Jesus counted nine lanterns moving out onto the lake.

Simon called Jesus to the bow of the boat. The wind in their faces was exhilarating and the sense of motion was exaggerated. In the bow he could feel every little wave of the sea as the bow rose and fell under their feet. He could hear the water hissing as the bow of the boat sliced forward. When they met small waves, the water would splash up and forward. Simon hung the lantern above the bow and the two of them watched lest they should run into a floating log or an unlighted boat. Jesus wondered how they knew they wouldn't run into dry land but the men seemed to have great confidence that they knew where the lake lay and where it did not.

Overhead, the stars had never seemed brighter. There was no moon, and that always means the stars have a greater intensity. Jesus noticed that he could even see reflections of the stars in the water, doubling the number of visible stars. He reasoned that if you got too close to land, you wouldn't see any reflected stars and you would know that it was unsafe to proceed any further.

While Nahum steered and Simon and Jesus watched, Jonah handled the lines that controlled the sail. Occasionally they would tack around to cross the wind at a different angle. The other boats were doing the same, so that the lanterns seemed to be doing a zigzag dance across the water. The lights on the shore at Capernaum had completely disappeared and Jesus wondered how they would ever find their way back to his mother and sister at the rabbi's house.

After what seemed like hours, but was probably not nearly that long, Simon nudged Jesus and pointed to a faint dot of light that was not moving zigzag across the water. "Migdal," he said. Jesus nodded, remembering having ridden through that town the day before.

"Is that where we are going?" asked Jesus.

"No. We are going fairly near the shore halfway between Migdal and Tiberias," he said. "That's where the fishing is best."

Jesus kept looking at the dot of light and noticed how it gradually expanded and became several lights grouped together. As that happened, it became more believable that he was looking at a town and not another boat that was standing still.

When he gazed around and counted the lanterns of the fishing boats, he could only find six. "Where are the other fishing boats," he asked Simon.

"There are two ahead of us and the rest are back there," he answered, motioning beyond the stern.

"But I see only six. There were more."

"Not everybody comes out this far," said Simon. "There are other good fishing spots but Abba and Uncle Nahum like this one that we are heading to."

"I don't see any stars reflected in the water toward the shore," said Jesus. "Is that because we are so near land?"

"Look overhead," replied Simon. "You don't see any stars in this half of the sky now. Clouds are blowing in. And the air is getting cooler. We could be in for a squall."

Gradually, the lights of Migdal passed on the starboard side but they dwindled to just a few as the residents of that town retired for the night. Another quarter of an hour and Jonah hauled down the sail. Simon left his lookout post and helped his father prepare a net. Nahum stayed at the tiller, keeping the boat pointed into the offshore breeze.

At a nod from Jonah, Nahum let the breeze take the bow of the boat and begin to swing it downwind. As the boat came broadside to the wind, Jonah heaved one end of the net over the side while Simon held the other end. Jonah continued to play out the rest of the net as the boat swung on around and began to drift downwind. Simon worked his end of the net along the side of the boat and across the stern, while Uncle Nahum ducked under the rope by which Simon held it. When the net was stretched across the back of the boat, Simon tied off on the port side and the net was fully deployed behind the drifting boat.

Jonah kept hold of the other end of the net and kept gently tugging on it, trying to sense whether they were making a catch or not. They drifted for several minutes and then Jonah began to gather in the net, pulling both the upper and lower ropes, hand over hand together. Nahum was watching his brother closely and when most of the net was back in the boat, Jonah looked at him and shook his head. Once the net was in, they could all see that they had caught nothing.

Nahum brought the boat broadside again and Simon and his father deployed the net again, as before. That time they left the net down longer and when they retrieved it there were a few small fish in it. Ezra picked one out of the net and showed it to Jesus. Jonah shrugged and signaled

Ezra to throw it back over the side. They hadn't caught anything worth keeping. Jesus and Ezra took each of the half-dozen small fish and threw them back.

On their third attempt, they brought in several more fish that were too small to keep but also one that was greater than the span of Ezra's large hand. On the next cast of the net, they retrieved four of the larger ones and only three of the little ones to throw back. They tried again and caught nothing.

Then Jonah hoisted sail and he and Nahum sailed the boat back toward the shore between Migdal and Tiberias. They wanted to try another pass. By the time they dropped the sail this time, the wind had picked up considerably and no stars were visible anywhere in the sky. The temperature had dropped again and the bow of the boat was rising and falling a good deal more than it had been.

On their first cast of the net, they caught only small fish. On the second, they saw Jonah nodding to his brother and Nahum gave him the thumbs up sign. He waited another minute or two and then started hauling in the net. It became more of a struggle for him so Ezra stood up to give him a hand. The two of them labored to bring the net back aboard and as they came closer and closer to finishing the job, their excitement rose because it was clear that they had made quite a catch. In the end, Simon and Jesus were also pulling on the ropes to get the haul over the side of the boat. When the net came clear of the sideboard, a wiggling, flopping mass of silvery chaos came with it and spread over the bottom of the boat.

Jesus gave a shriek of delight and the men were grinning at each other. Simon was madly plucking fish after fish out of the net and stashing them in the large baskets where the first fish were thrown. Jesus joined him and they shouted out the numbers as they plucked the keepers up and stowed them. They didn't even bother with the small fish until they had counted forty-seven fish worth keeping. Then while they were throwing back the little ones, they discovered a couple keepers among them, so they had taken forty-nine good fish in a single cast.

In the excitement of the great catch, Jesus had not noticed how much the wind had increased. The next cast brought up nothing, so they set about trying to go back to drift across the same spot again. It was with great difficulty that Jonah and Ezra together were able to deploy the sail because of the strength of the wind. Nahum struggled to bring the bow about and the boat took water over the side a couple of times before they were able to tack across the wind to try to get in position to make another pass across the place where the big catch had been made. Suddenly a stinging rain began to blow horizontally across the boat. Jesus could no longer see any lights along shore and only occasionally glimpsed one other lantern, bobbing above the waves for a few seconds and then plunging out of sight. So much water was hitting him in the face it was impossible to tell how much of it was rain and how much was sea spray blown off the tops of waves.

He wondered what had happened to the other boats. He wondered how Jonah and Nahum could tell where they were and which way to go to get back to the good fishing spot. He tried to move back to the bow of the boat to watch but lost his balance on the plunging deck and went down on his knees. Before he could get up, he felt a pair of big hands lifting him up. He looked over his shoulder and there was Ezra lifting him up like Hannah would lift a doll. Ezra set him on his feet but kept hold with one hand to steady him. Then he saw that Ezra was beckoning him to watch what he, himself, was doing.

Ezra had his feet spread apart, one somewhat ahead and the other behind him. With the one hand, he continued to steady Jesus but the other he held out in front of him as though he was gripping reins. He was bending his knees as if on a trotting horse. He was flowing with the motion of the boat, but Jesus knew he was suggesting he ride the boat like he would ride a horse, moving with the motion of the ship, absorbing shocks with his bent knees.

Jesus imitated Ezra and found that he gained a good deal of stability on the bucking, swaying deck. Ezra let him go and he gradually made his way to the bow of the boat without clinging to the gunwale and dragging himself along as he would otherwise have tried to do. By now the wind was whistling through the rigging and the boat was heeling over at alarming angles while trying to pound over the whitecaps coming toward them from windward. Every man and boy of them was soaked to the skin and feeling the chill of the storm.

Jesus' intent in going forward was to keep watch as before, in case any hazards presented themselves in front of the boat. But then they hit a wave particularly hard and the spray nearly knocked him off his feet and put out the lantern. Instantly the boat was plunged into darkness that made it impossible to see even the others in the boat, let alone watch for hazards.

176

Jonah fought his way forward and retrieved the lantern, hoping to relight it, but Nahum started shouting from the stern, "Stow the sail! This is too much strain on the mast!"

Jonah left the lantern and went to try to haul down the sail to relieve the stresses on the mast. There was so much wind in the sail that he and Ezra together could not haul it down. "Go off the wind, off the wind," shouted Jonah. "The mast is cracking!"

"I can't go broadside to these waves or we are done for!" shouted his brother through the roar of the wind. Then with a horrible crashing sound, the mast gave way and the whole boat trembled at the concussion. A deep groan followed and the boat swung wildly out of control.

Nahum left the now all but useless rudder and struggled forward to find his brother pinned between the broken mast and the gunwale, and Ezra struggling to lift the butt end of the mast but hampered by the rigging lines. He snatched his knife and began slashing ropes indiscriminately until with a mighty heave, Ezra roared and raised the mast enough that Nahum was able to drag his brother out of the vice grip that had trapped him. He pulled Jonah to the stern and laid him on a cushion in the bottom of the boat. Whether Jonah was dead or unconscious, nobody knew but they had to try to keep the boat from going down before they could attend to him.

"Simon, throw out the bow anchor! Throw out the bow anchor!" shouted Nahum. Jesus felt, rather than saw, Simon come alongside him and fumble with something heavy at his feet.

"Help me," cried Simon as the boat bucked and swayed. Together they lifted the heavy anchor. "Stay out of the rope!" he shouted. Jesus cleared his feet of the coils and they heaved the anchor overboard. The coils of rope went singing over the edge of the boat and Jesus imagined how terrible it would have been if the anchor rope had caught his foot. The rope kept going out until it was all gone and then jerked taut but the boat didn't seem to change attitude at all.

"The anchor is out but it didn't reach bottom," shouted Simon.

"Well that means we are in deep water. The stern anchor has a longer rope. Take that one forward and tie it to the bow and throw it out as well. But tie it double before you throw it!"

"Yes, Uncle," cried Simon and disappeared into the darkness. The boat continued to plunge and slosh in chaotic movements at the mercy of the wind and the waves. Ezra and Nahum were struggling with the broken mast and the sail, which was fully in the water and threatened to haul the side of the boat under the waves. Nahum was clinging to his knife and trying to sever the ropes that kept the sail attached to the boom and the mast. Ezra kept hold of the corner of the sail and pulled it in as fast as Nahum could cut it loose. Finally, they got the sail all into the boat and together they were able to jettison the mast.

That dealt with the most immediate threat to the boat and allowed it to float more upright. Then they had opportunity to stagger to the stern of the boat where Nahum began checking out his brother. Ezra helped Simon by carrying the stern anchor forward. By then Simon had tied the stern anchor rope securely to the bow and Ezra threw the anchor over the bow. Again, the anchor rope went hissing out over the bow of the boat and became taut without gripping the bottom.

"We're still too deep," shouted Simon. "This one doesn't reach either."

Ezra disappeared into the darkness and Simon went to see what was going on with his father. Jesus stayed in the bow, crouching low and hanging on for dear life. Soon Ezra was back with a large portion of what had been the sail and a piece of fishing net of a similar size. He bound the sail and the net together, corner to corner and tied a piece of the broken boom across one edge of the net and sail combination. He secured the corner ropes to the bow of the boat and deployed his creation into the water. The boom caused the one edge to float on the surface while the weights on the opposite edge of the net caused that edge to sink. The sail filled with water instead of with wind and began to billow out about thirty cubits off the bow of the boat.

Then Ezra took Jesus by the hand and led him back across the dark and slippery length of the boat to the stern. Here he found that Jonah was alive and awake but in a great deal of pain. Nahum and Simon were busy ministering to him. Ezra made sure Jesus was securely settled with those three and he disappeared again.

When he returned, he was carrying the oars and another piece of the sail. Jesus wondered what good a man could do with those oars in such a fierce gale as this. Not even a man as strong as Ezra could hope to row the boat in these conditions. But Ezra was not going to try rowing the boat. He took another length of rope and cut off a section with which he bound one edge of the piece of sail around the handle of one of the oars and then bound the other edge to the handle of the second oar. Then he jammed the blades of the oars down between the stern seat and the actual stern of the boat.

The makeshift sail between the two oars filled with the wind and the bow of the boat swung directly into the wind and stayed pointing into the wind. "Do you feel that?" cried Nahum to his brother. "One of the anchors must have caught the bottom."

Jesus asked, "Why did he throw a net with a part of the sail over the bow?"

Nahum asked, "What did he do?"

"When I was up at the front, Ezra brought a piece of a net up there and a part of the sail and bound them to a piece of wood along one edge. Then he tied the corners to the boat and threw the whole thing overboard. The sail filled with water instead of wind."

"Bless my soul," replied Nahum. "This guy is a seaman! He made a sea anchor! Between that and this little bit of rigging here, we will stay pointed into the wind!" That is exactly what we needed. Eventually, we will reach shallower water where those anchors will find the bottom and keep us from being dashed on the rocks. In the meantime, his rigging will allow the boat to ride this out."

He clapped Ezra on the shoulder and gave him a big bear hug. It was still awfully dark, but Jesus could see Uncle Ezra's teeth and the whites of his eyes. He was smiling!

Jonah had a broken arm and probably some broken ribs, but he was alive. Nahum brought out a flask of wine and gave the injured man a swig. Jonah handed the flask to Ezra and insisted that he, too have a drink. Nahum took a swig himself and then all five of them settled into the stern of the boat to wait.

Jesus drifted off to sleep and when he roused himself, he found that he was nestled against Ezra. It was not yet morning, but there was enough light to see from one end of the boat to the other. Simon and his father and uncle were all huddled together and apparently asleep. The boat was still pointing into the wind and the bow was pounding up and down on huge waves. But the stern of the boat was relatively steady by comparison. The fish in their baskets were flopping in the water at the bottom of the boat. And Uncle Ezra was still smiling.

Jesus snuggled in closer and went back to sleep. The next thing he knew was Simon's voice calling, "Uncle, I see land astern."

Nahum stood up and looked toward the east. "That looks like the country of the Gadarenes," he said. "I don't think we can expect any help from that quarter." He made his way forward and tested the anchor ropes. "The anchors have reached bottom now. If they hold, we can stay here until the wind goes down."

"I think the wind is already a good deal less than it was at the height of the storm," said Simon. "But the waves are still tremendous."

"The waves continue to be dangerous for a couple of hours after the wind calms down," said his uncle.

Jesus noticed that Jonah's arm was now splinted and held in a sling. "How is your father doing?" he asked Simon.

"He is doing okay now but I'm sure he is still in a lot of pain. He can't take a deep breath because his ribs hurt so much."

"Did your uncle splint his arm?" asked Jesus.

"No, your Uncle Ezra did. He set the bone just like a doctor would and then made the splints out of the stays from the sail. He is a man of many talents."

"Actually, he's my father's uncle. He doctors horses and other animals all the time. I didn't know he could doctor people."

"I'm sure glad he was here last night. Abba might have died under that broken mast, otherwise. In fact, the whole boat might have gone down without him," said Simon.

"How did he set the bone?" asked Jesus.

"He had Uncle Nahum hold Abba tight by the shoulders, not by the ribs, of course."

"Of course," agreed Jesus.

"Then he felt all around his arm like he was studying where the bone was broken. Then he pulled hard on Abba's broken arm to get the two ends to line up and guided the bones with his other hand."

"I would think that would hurt a lot," said Jesus.

"I expect it did; Abba cried out and then became unconscious. By the time he came to, Ezra had him all splinted and hung in a sling."

The stranded party dug into their food supplies and settled down to wait. The water from the sea was not the best drinking water, but it was not salty. Nahum told them to just stay calm and wait. He was sure that help would come.

By noon, the wind had let up considerably. The waves were still quite large, but Simon assured Jesus that the storm was past and the waves would grow less and less. His prediction was right on the mark. Two more hours and the waves were not lifting the bow of the boat and jerking on the anchor lines the way they had been all morning. The boat was still rising and falling with the waves but it no longer seemed violent and threatening.

Soon enough, they saw a sail appear to the northwest. Uncle Ezra took down his improvised sail that had kept the stern downwind and the bow into the wind all night. He released one of the oars from the piece of sail but used the other one as a flagstaff to wave the sail back and forth as high as he could reach, hoping to attract the attention of the boat on the horizon.

When the boat got a little closer, Nahum said, "Looks like Zebedee's boat. I'll bet he's coming to look for storm survivors."

Indeed, it was Zebedee and he had three men with him. When they came within hailing distance, Ezra stopped waving his makeshift flag. It was clear they were making for the stricken boat.

"Where is your mast, Jonah?" cried out Zebedee.

Nahum hollered back, "We misplaced it last night. Have you seen it?"

"No, but I have a toothpick you can put in its place," yelled Zebedee.

"Keep your toothpick, it's already been in your mouth," answered Nahum.

"Is everyone okay in that washtub of yours?"

"We are alive, praise the Almighty, but Jonah is hurt some. The mast came down on him. He has a broken arm and probably some ribs."

The boats were close together now and the men hardly had to raise their voices. The wind had settled down to a moderate breeze and the waves were dying down with every passing hour. Zebedee brought his boat alongside and lashed the two hulls together. He hopped aboard and came to examine Jonah.

"How are you doing, old friend?" he asked.

Jonah gripped his friend's hand for answer and didn't say a word. He was struggling to hold back tears of gratitude.

"There, there," said Zebedee. "We'll get you home to your bed and you will be on your feet in no time." Turning to Nahum, he said, "Looks like you did a right proper job of splinting that arm. We can get the doctor to set the bone when we get ashore."

"I didn't splint him, Zebedee," said Nahum. "Ezra here did that. And he set the bone first, too."

"Ezra is the name, huh? He went out with me yesterday morning but we didn't have any luck. Can he talk at all? He never said a word to me."

"He's deaf and mute," said Jesus. "He's my father's uncle. I am traveling under his protection."

"And you are in good hands, young man," said Nahum, "mighty good hands."

"We are all under the protection of the Almighty One," said Jesus. "Why should we fear?"

"Indeed!" said Zebedee. "Well said! And what's your name?"

"I'm Jesus of Nazareth, son of Joseph the carpenter."

"I am Zebedee. And I am going to tow this boat back to Capernaum."

"Let's get on with it, then," said Nahum.

When they got back to Capernaum it was already dark but there were two dozen people waiting on the shore to hear the news and tell their own. Some of the fishermen waded out into the water to help draw both boats up on the sand. It turned out that all the fishing boats had got back safely except for Jonah and Nahum and their crew. Several boats had had a time of it getting back home in the high winds but all had managed it. And none of them had caught more than a handful of fish. They were quite impressed with the haul Jonah and Nahum had brought in.

"It was those very fish that got us into trouble," said Nahum. "If we hadn't had such a good catch on that one pass, we might have given it up and headed for home. But the catch was so rich that it tempted us to go for one more pass."

"One pass too many, it would seem," said Jonah.

The rabbi and Mary were among the crowd waiting for the boats to come ashore. When she saw Jesus and Ezra, Mary covered her face with her shawl so that they wouldn't see her tears of relief. Ezra helped pull the stricken boat up on the sand and Jesus leaped over the side. He ran to his mother and threw his arms around her.

"Don't cry, Mama," he murmured. "I'm alright. And Jonah will get better. And they can put another mast and sail on the boat."

"I am not concerned about an old fishing boat," said Mary. "I'm concerned about you! I could have lost you!"

Jesus held onto his mother in silence for a few minutes, pondering her words. Then he went back to thank Simon and his father and uncle for taking him night fishing. "It was a marvelous adventure, really," he said. Then he added, "Except for you getting injured and your boat getting damaged. May God Almighty heal your wounds and help you to fix your boat."

"Thank you, Jesus. Next time you come to Capernaum the old boat will be as good as new and Jonah here will be strong and fit to haul in an even bigger catch," said Nahum.

"God grant that it be so," said Jesus and took his leave.

The next day, as the party was riding along the shore toward Migdal, Jesus rode beside his mother for a while and then asked, "Mama, do you really believe that I am to be the Messiah, the anointed one?"

"Yes, of course I believe it," said his mother. "The angel declared it. I believed it. That settles it."

"And do you think," asked Jesus, "that the Almighty I AM, would anoint a Messiah and then lose him in a storm?"

Mary bit her lip for a moment and then said, "I am still your mother. It's a mother's job to worry."

Christmas 2012

Tenth Birthday
A Girl with Two Spirits

It was a warm afternoon in the workshop when a voice was heard outside the open door, "Hello?"

"Hello," replied Joseph, stepping toward the door, plane still in hand.

"It is plain to see that you are a carpenter, and it is a carpenter I seek. Are you Joseph?"

"I am. And I believe you are Azor, are you not?"

"Yes, do you know me then?"

"I think everyone in the region knows that you are the owner of the best and largest vineyards in Galilee."

"Ah, you are very kind. I'm not sure my reputation is deserved but that will save us from long introductions. I hear that you are quite accomplished in your own field and there is a point of business where your field and mine intersect. Do you have a few minutes?"

"Yes, of course," replied Joseph. "Please come inside."

Jesus was already dusting off a couple of stools next to a low table just inside the door. This is where his father and customers would sit and chat about possible contracts. He was wiping the table quickly with a shop rag as Azor stepped from the bright sunlight into the shop.

"Ah, I see you have an apprentice," said Azor.

"Yes, I do. He is a very promising apprentice and my eldest son, Jesus."

"Two excellent roles in one person. God keep you, young man."

"Thank you, sir," said Jesus.

"Jesus could you bring us some tea?" asked Joseph. Jesus nodded and quickly slipped out the door and ran to the house.

When he returned a few minutes later with a pot of tea and two tea glasses, his father and Azor were already well into a discussion of his plan.

"Where will this inn be?" asked Joseph.

"I have bought Elihud's large house right on the main road across from the market. My own workers have already begun with the modifications to make it into a very comfortable inn. But I need someone with more expertise to make furniture, especially tables, benches and stools for the great room in which guests will eat and drink."

"I would be very happy to accommodate you. I think you would have to travel to another region to find anyone more experienced than I in making such things," said Joseph. "Just tell me the size and the design of the furniture pieces you would like and the quantity of each. I'm sure we can agree on a fair price."

Jesus poured the tea for his father and his customer and then returned to his own workbench to work on a carving.

Azor sipped his tea and said, "Besides furniture, I would like to have someone make a large wooden sign for the front of the establishment. I have brought a design idea with me." He pulled a small scroll out of his bag and unrolled it on the table in front of Joseph. "It should be two cubits high by three cubits wide and say, 'Azor's Inn at Nazareth' in bold Latin letters and have this figure prominent in the lower right corner."

Joseph studied it for a moment and then looked closely at Azor. "Are you quite settled on that design?" asked Joseph. "Because if you are, you will have to find someone else for the sign."

"This is too hard for you then?" asked Azor.

"Not too hard at all. But I will not carve that image of a foreign god. It goes against the scriptures."

"Ah, I see," said Azor. "That is the image of Bacchus and is universally symbolic in all the Roman Empire of a place where one can enjoy wine."

"I understand that," replied Joseph, "but it goes very much against my conscience to do such a thing. I would advise you to replace that figure or you may find that many people in this town will shun your establishment for conscience sake."

"Well, my idea is to serve travelers at my inn, not so much to serve the local people, although Nazarenes would be most welcome to visit for a meal or to sample my wines and beers."

"That is entirely up to you," replied Joseph. "But I will not make such a sign if that image is to be on it."

"Well, perhaps I should take my furniture order to someone in Tiberias. I'm sure I can find someone there or in Capernaum who will be happy to execute this design for me and do the furniture as well."

"Perhaps you should," said Joseph.

Azor took another sip of tea and watched Joseph carefully for a moment. "I see you are a man of high principles," he said. "I like that in a man. But I am a bit surprised that your conscience is so strong on this point but isn't strong enough to cause you to come to synagogue."

Joseph said nothing and took another sip of tea.

"Look," said Azor, "I don't want to go all the way to Tiberias and then pay for carting to get the furniture delivered here. Perhaps I can just have the sign done elsewhere."

"As you wish," said Joseph. "Are you not open to considering other designs for the sign?"

"What would you suggest?"

"How about a nice cluster of grapes. Would that not clearly tell prospective customers that they can expect a cup of wine at Azor's Inn?"

Azor tapped a finger on the table for a moment as he considered that suggestion. Joseph poured more tea into his guest's cup and waited. Azor nodded his acknowledgement of the tea and took another sip. "I will think about that some while you put together prices for the furniture order."

"Another question about the sign, if you don't mind," said Joseph.

"Yes?"

"Why will you put out a sign only in Latin? Don't you want Aramaic speaking travelers as customers. Being right on the market square, you would do well to serve all of the local people who come on market day."

"Well, I have considered having Latin, Greek and Aramaic on the sign but I don't want it to look cluttered. It must have appeal for every potential customer, so it shouldn't look cluttered and shouldn't look provincial. It is my goal to attract the very finest people who travel through Nazareth."

"Not many fine people travel through Nazareth, you know," said Joseph.

"That is true, but I hope to see that change," said Azor. "And once my inn here is a success, I would like to build others in other cities. I am starting here because it is close to my vineyards and close to my home. But I have plans to expand my business in time."

"I will bring you prices after the Sabbath. Should I bring them to your home?"

"Bring them to me at the project site. Next week we will be there doing the modifications to the building itself. And that will give you a taste for where the furniture will be used."

"I will do that," promised Joseph.

As Azor stood up to take his leave, he stopped to look at what Jesus was working on. "What have we here, young man?" he asked.

"This panel will be the lid to that box," replied Jesus, pointing to a long wooden box nearby.

"That is a very traditional design, the pomegranates alternating with bells. That must be a box to hold a sacred scroll. Am I right?"

"Yes, sir." said Jesus

"May I ask who commissioned such a box? Was it Rabbi Zuriel?"

"No, sir. It is for our own use."

"For your own use? Do you own a sacred scroll?"

"No, but we borrow scrolls one at a time for my education."

"From Rabbi Zuriel?"

"No."

"I thought not. He's is unlikely to loan you a worn out sandal. So from whom do you borrow sacred scrolls, young man?"

"From a rabbi in Capernaum."

Azor looked at Joseph for confirmation. Joseph nodded his agreement and said nothing.

"So here in Nazareth we have an observant family who travels all the way to Capernaum to borrow scrolls for the purpose of education," observed Azor. "You surprise me in your determination to get your son an education, but it does not surprise me that you don't send your son to Rabbi Zuriel to study. I know the man too well. My sister used to send her son to him but that didn't end well and I don't know of anyone who will entrust his son to him anymore. This town cannot go on like this."

Neither Joseph nor Jesus gave any verbal response to Azor. They just waited in an awkward silence. Then abruptly, Azor shook Joseph by the hand and said, "Thank you for the tea. I will look forward to seeing you next week."

After the Sabbath, on the first day of the week, Joseph asked Jesus, "Would you like to go look at Azor's project with me?"

"Of course!"

"Go first and practice your reading from the scriptures while I make a proposal including prices for Azor. Then we will go see his project together."

"Yes, Abba. I will gladly go see this work of his."

When they set out together about an hour later, the sun was warm and the sky was clear. Their sandals kicked up dust along the path and birds sang in the trees overhead.

"Abba," said Jesus, "why is aged wine preferred over new wine?"

"That is a surprising question from a boy your age," replied his father. "Where did you come up with that question?"

"From the scroll of Isaiah that I am reading. Isaiah refers to wine quite often. And in the portion that I read this morning he says, 'On this mountain the Lord Almighty will prepare a feast of rich food for all peoples, a banquet of aged wine... the best of meats and the finest of wines.' I have heard people boast about aged wines before, but here even scripture affirms that aged wine is best."

"It is common knowledge that most wines get better with time, but I don't know why. It would be a question to ask Azor."

"Will you ask him, then?"

"Why don't you ask him yourself?" said Joseph.

"I might," said Jesus.

As they approached the market, the roads filled up with people bringing produce in from their fields, with merchants hauling carts of goods and with a small mixed flock of goats and sheep that were being brought for sale. There was even an Arab with three young camels he hoped to sell. Boys were running through the streets playing tag or carrying bundles for their mothers. There was an atmosphere of excitement as was usual on market day. Joseph was hailed by various neighbors and some former customers as they came into the center of the activity.

They arrived at Azor's project before Azor, himself. Workmen were already busy about the place and one, who introduced himself as Shaleth, was the man in charge of the workers.

"Azor told me to watch for you," he said. "He is coming soon. Come in and see what we are doing here."

190

"He told us only a little about the project," said Joseph. Is it just this house, then, that will be his inn?"

"Actually, he has bought this small house next door, as well. We plan to join them together and remove most of the common wall separating them. Also, we will be adding a room to the back of the larger house to accommodate storage and a larger kitchen."

"What about the second story of the main house?" asked Joseph.

"We are going to broaden the stairs and cut an opening through the wall to the roof of the smaller house. That will provide an outdoor seating area that overlooks the marketplace."

"That will be interesting in fair weather..."

"And in foul weather, we still have the large dining room on the ground floor," added Shaleth.

"What about sleeping quarters?" asked Joseph. "Azor did not ask me for prices for beds."

"That part of the plan will not be developed yet. We have enough beds for a few rooms already but Azor wants to put all available resources into establishing the dining and drinking portion first. Lodging will be developed as a later phase when the first phase has become profitable."

"I see," said Joseph. "Well we should get out of your way. You have much to do and the workmen are waiting for your guidance. We will wait outside."

"Can I get you any tea while you wait?" asked Shaleth.

"No, thank you. That can wait until Azor arrives. We will just have a look around the market."

"As you wish. But if you would like to sit down, we do have a place here for you to rest. And I will order tea any time you ask."

"Thank you," said Joseph, "You are very kind."

Joseph and his son left the construction project and crossed the busy road into the even busier market. Jesus was accustomed to helping his mother at the market, but it was unusual for his father to leave the familiar workshop and to mix with the hustle and bustle of market day. Where they entered the market, most of the merchants were offering the produce of their own gardens and fields. Some were selling pomegranates and dates, others had fresh vegetables. A man with only one eye was proffering many spices of various colors. Pungent smells emerged from cloth sacks with the tops rolled down to display his goods. Father and son were drawn along by the sights and sounds and smells. Joseph was not really shopping for anything the way that Mary would, so their path was random and their pace relaxed. But steadily, they were moving away from the produce portion of the market and toward the distant corner where baskets and wooden articles were being offered.

Joseph stopped to chat with a young man who was selling canes and shepherd's crooks. The young man was carving on a stick while he waited for customers. Jesus could see that the young man was lame in one foot and that he might have been driven into his vocation more by necessity than by the prospect of financial success. Next to his wares there was an old woman selling wooden platters and bowls.

"How are you this fine day, Auntie?" asked Joseph.

"I am, by God's grace, what I am," she replied. "I am getting too old to be sitting here in the hot sun waiting for customers. And my husband, Seth, is too old to continue making these bowls and platters. His strength is failing and I don't know what we will do."

"I'm sorry to hear that, for sure," said Joseph. Turning to Jesus he said, "Son, this is Auntie Hobal. Her husband Seth used to help your grandfather with some carpentry work when I was just a boy. Auntie, this is my son, Jesus."

"Bless you, Jesus," said the old woman. "Bless you and may you be a blessing to your father in his old age."

"Thank you, Auntie," said Jesus. "Are you my father's aunt, then?"

"It's not quite that simple, son." she replied. "My younger sister married a cousin of your father's but he has always called me 'Auntie' and my Seth, 'Uncle.' Bless his heart."

192

"What news do you have of your daughter, Layla, and her husband," asked Joseph.

"I haven't heard a thing from her in over two years," said Auntie. "She married the son of that wine merchant over in Cana and for a while, we would get word of her through occasional travelers. But we haven't heard anything now in ages."

At that moment, they were interrupted by Azor's hearty greeting, "There you are, Joseph! Shaleth told me you were wandering around in the market."

As Jesus and his father turned toward this interruption, there was a more profound interruption from nearby. A loud trumpet was sounded to garner the attention of everyone in the market. Everyone turned toward the sound and a few who were seated got to their feet and stood at attention. All business transactions came to an abrupt halt and the voice of the young man with the trumpet cried out, "Attention all who would do business in these districts. Rabbi Zuriel bin Gamaliel bin Amminadab has arrived to bless this place with his presence and with his intercession on your behalf. Bow your heads and listen as Rabbi Zuriel bin Gamaliel bin Amminadab lifts his voice to the heavens."

The trumpeter was standing on a dais at the edge of the market, a platform raised for the purpose of allowing the town fathers to address the residents on matters of common interest. The trumpeter bowed deeply to the rabbi and stepped aside so that the full glory of the rabbi might be revealed to the people in the market. The rabbi was arrayed in a long robe of the finest material with bells and tassels sweeping just above the dais. The robe was embroidered with a design that evoked the image of Aaron's ephod, and lent a reflected glory to the rabbi of this rather humble town. Large phylacteries were dangling from both wrists and prominent on his forehead.

The rabbi stepped to the very edge of the dais and raised his voice in the most somber tones over the hushed crowd of merchants, shoppers, children and stray dogs. "O God of the heavens and the earth," he bellowed. "I thank you that you have heard the prayers of these humble peasants of Galilee and have sent them a rabbi of your own choosing, to enlighten them, to bring them before your throne in their great need of forgiveness..."

The rabbi went on and on in his prayers, making it very clear to all who heard that these poor, needy sinners of Nazareth had been blessed far beyond their deserts by a learned and wonderful rabbi who came to extend to them the call of repentance and the opportunity to escape the curse of their uneducated state. Among those who apparently did not hear nor want to hear the rabbi's prayer was Azor. He took Joseph by the arm and very pointedly led him out of the crowded market into a back alley. Jesus scuttled in their wake, looking back over his shoulder at the rabbi who went on with his carefully prepared sermon in the form of a prayer.

Azor led Joseph and Jesus through the side streets and alleys to escape the scene of the market. "I can't abide that arrogant son of a donkey," he muttered as they went. "He seeks his own glory with every word that he utters. He doesn't tell me anything about the heavenly father, but only about himself. And I already know more about him than I want to know."

"What do you know?" asked Joseph.

"You know how eager he is for everyone to think of him as a Levite and that he has a special anointing from God? Last year when I was in Jerusalem I asked around among rabbis that I know. Even they consider him a very ambitious sham."

"Really?"

"Yes," Azor said, "He is of the tribe of Issachar. He had an ancestor named Levi, alright, but it was not the son of Jacob. This Amminadab, his grandfather, to whom he is always referring? Amminadab was the son of a textile merchant named Levi. But he plays it as if he were a direct descendant of Aaron the brother of Moses."

By circling around the center of town, the three were able to enter Azor's project by a back door long before the rabbi gave up his grip on the market place. Once inside, Azor asked Shaleth to send for tea and led Joseph and Jesus to one of the back rooms that was somewhat closed off from the workmen and from the market.

With a visible effort, Azor turned from the subject of the rabbi to the subject at hand, Azor's Inn at Nazareth. "Shaleth, my foreman, has showed you around, yes? What do you think of our little project, Joseph?"

"It is very interesting and not exactly a little project, " said Joseph.

"Do you like it?" asked Azor. "Did Shaleth tell you about the rooftop dining area under the stars?"

"He did," replied Joseph. "I have a question about the furnishings for that portion."

"Oh, I have already anticipated your concerns," said Azor. "The tables and stools will all be small and portable. When the weather is unsuitable, they will all be gathered into a storage area on the second floor of this house. We can't leave them out in the weather."

"That was exactly my concern. The only other solution would be to put a roof over that area," said Joseph.

"Ah, but that would mean diners could not gaze up at the stars," countered Azor.

"You have a good point, but by bringing all the furnishings into this house you reduce your capacity for lodging," said Joseph.

"True, and that is regrettable. Do you have another idea?"

"What if an enclosed storage area were to be built in one corner of the roof, one that was closed on three sides and roofed over, but open on one side so that tables and stools could quickly be protected but easily accessed when the weather turned fair. Then you would not lose a room that could be used for lodging."

Azor smiled hugely and said, "I like that idea. I like it a lot."

"And if you have a couple of larger tables that two men can carry, designed like this," he said, while drawing with his finger on the table top, "and four or six smaller tables for each larger one. The smaller ones can be carried by one person, and they can easily be turned upside down on the larger ones in the storage area with the stools tucked under the large tables. That way, the storage area only has to be big enough to accommodate the two large tables."

"Excellent!" exclaimed Azor. "How many stools would you recommend?"

"I would think two benches per large table to begin with and three stools per smaller one," suggested Joseph.

"Three? Why the odd number?" asked Azor.

"Just for flexibility," said Joseph. Sometimes a small table will be occupied by only two men, sometimes three. Sometimes, for a larger party you can push two small tables together for four or five people, or draw unused stools from the smaller tables to get eight people around one of the larger ones. If you find that you need more stools, we can certainly make them. But no need to order too many to begin with. They would only be in your way.

"Another suggestion would be that we make the furniture for the dining room of oak, which is very durable but also very heavy. And we can make the tables for your rooftop of cedar which weathers well but is much lighter. That will make the tables and stools much easier to move into and out of storage when necessary."

"I see that you are a very practical man. It will be a pleasure doing business with you."

Soon they fell to the serious business of prices and total numbers of each kind of table, both for the inside dining area and for the rooftop. Azor questioned how quickly a one-man shop could produce such a large order. Joseph assured him that he could hire competent helpers if he had such an order and that even Jesus was a worthy workman as his apprentice.

The deal was struck and the three of them were just emerging onto the street when who should appear but Rabbi Zuriel bin Gamaliel bin Amminadab, striding straight toward them.

"Aha," cried the rabbi, "just the man I want to see."

Azor, Joseph and Jesus stood rooted to the ground in front of the inn. It was too late to escape.

"Hello, Rabbi," said Azor in tones that belied his resentment of the man. "What can I do for you?"

"Rumor has it that you have entered upon a great enterprise here in this house. Is that true?"

"Well," said Azor, "God helping me, I have begun a small enterprise here. But by His help, perhaps one day it can become great."

"I am a bit surprised that you hope in God to bless your enterprise when you have not sought the blessing of your rabbi on the project," said the rabbi.

"Ah, well you know how it is. God blesses enterprises wherever He wishes, even in towns that have no rabbi."

"Well and good," countered the rabbi, "but you are in a town that has been blessed with a rabbi."

"And what a rabbi, too!" exclaimed Azor. "But I know that you are far too important to be disturbed over every little project your inferiors might launch. Would it not be more fitting for a rabbi of your eminence, and a Levite at that, to be serving in Jericho or even in Jerusalem? Your talents seem to be wasted on such a backwater town as Nazareth."

"I am sure that day is coming," said the rabbi. "But for now it seems to please the Lord to humble me by allowing me to suffer in this God-forsaken place. At any rate, I understand you are converting this house to an inn. Is that right?"

"With God's help, I am trying to do that."

"And what is this I hear," continued the rabbi, "that you have bought the house next door as well?"

"It is true."

"And for what purpose did you buy the second house?" asked the rabbi.

"The inn shall be comprised of both houses together," answered Azor.

"Both together?" said the surprised rabbi. "Elihud's house is not large enough for your enterprise?"

"Not as I have envisioned it. Does that alarm you?"

"It does not alarm me, Azor. But it does disappoint me."

"Why does it disappoint you, Rabbi?"

"I had hoped to have that house next door for my synagogue."

"For a synagogue?" said Azor. "But Rabbi, we already have a synagogue."

"That dark little shack where we currently hold synagogue is not worthy of God's glory," said the rabbi. "And it is too small to train up young men into biblical scholars."

"Do you, then," continued Azor, "have young men you are training?"

"Well of course," said the rabbi. "Your own sister's son among them. I thought you knew."

"The last I knew, my nephew is no longer a student of yours and when he quit, he was the last one."

"That was then," blustered the rabbi. "You know nothing of all the fine prospects that I could raise up in this town. For instance, look at this young man here," he said turning to Jesus. But when he actually looked at Jesus he stumbled and said, "Oh dear God. This one has already shown himself to be unsuitable to the life of a scholar. But there are many others, I assure you."

"At any rate," said Azor, "I cannot give up that house as it is part of my plan."

"I plead with you," said the rabbi, "for God's sake and for the sake of this town, won't you give me this small house for a synagogue?"

"Before God and all these witnesses, " said Azor, looking around at the crowd that had gathered, "I cannot give you that house."

The rabbi stood in stunned silence for a moment, veins pounding in his forehead, nostrils flaring visibly. "Very well," he said. "But don't expect that God will bless your enterprise when you so stubbornly refuse to yield to His higher purposes."

With that veiled threat, the rabbi strode away grandly with the boy carrying the trumpet scurrying in his wake.

Jesus looked at Azor. The vintner's eyes followed the departing rabbi and even through his ample beard, it was clear that his jaws were working as if he were chewing something distasteful. When the rabbi turned the corner out of sight, Azor turned and spat vigorously on the ground. Joseph stuck out his right hand to Azor and not only shook Azor's hand, but clasped him on the forearm with the left hand and held on for a moment longer than necessary. Then Jesus saw his father wink at Azor before he released him and turned to go.

Joseph did not turn toward home, but rounded the corner of the market and headed toward the far side of Nazareth.

"Where are we going now, Abba?" asked Jesus.

"Well, son, we have just taken on the biggest order I have ever tried to complete. We are going to need help."

"Who will help us, Abba?"

"Let's go see if Uncle Seth wants to help us," said Joseph.

"But I heard Auntie Hobal say that he is losing his strength and she is worried that he can't continue making bowls and platters."

"I heard that, too," replied his father. "But if you knew Auntie Hobal like I do, you would know that she always emphasizes the negative. We will talk to Uncle Seth. If he lived by Auntie Hobal's predictions and worries, he would have been dead a hundred times by now."

As they approached the edge of town, Joseph turned up a narrow passage between an olive grove and a vineyard. There were stone walls on both sides to discourage untended children and donkeys from straying into mischief. The smell of olives was rich as they ascended to the top of the hill. There the path divided into two parts, one of which ended at a comfortable-looking house with flower beds on either side of the door. Joseph took the other path which led around the house to the back.

At the back was a large outdoor work area that was roofed over but had only one wall, against which was stacked a considerable supply of olive wood. Under the roof there was a man working with a contraption, the likes of which Jesus had never seen. The device held a workpiece and had a springy pole extended above and a treadle beneath. To the treadle was attached a heavy woven strap that wrapped around the end of the work piece and continued on to the springy pole overhead. The man would repeatedly step on the treadle, causing the workpiece to spin. When he took his foot off the treadle the spring pole would pull the strap back up, causing the workpiece to spin the other way. During the downward part of the cycle, the man would apply a chisel to the workpiece and chips would shower down. During the upward part of the cycle, the chisel would be withdrawn just enough to give clearance. Then another downward stroke would send another shower of chips.

Clearly, this was Uncle Seth and clearly, he was not at death's door. He was busy making another beautiful round bowl for Auntie Hobal to sell in the market. Joseph and Jesus came under the roof of the work area and just stood silently watching Uncle Seth at his craft. He smiled and nodded to them but kept up his rhythm of stepping on the treadle and cutting chips off his workpiece for a few more minutes.

When he did stop, he wiped the sweat off his brow with his sleeve and then gripped Joseph by the shoulders and kissed him on both cheeks, murmuring, "Shalom, Joseph, shalom. Thank you for coming to visit me."

"Shalom to you, Uncle Seth. Are you well?"

"I am very well, never better. And seeing you means that my wellness is on the increase, thank the Almighty."

"Uncle Seth, this is my son, Jesus. Jesus, Uncle Seth."

"Honored to meet you, sir," said Jesus, bowing slightly.

"No, no, the honor is mine," said Seth, grabbing his shoulders as he had Joseph's and kissing him soundly on both cheeks. "It is an honor to have lived long enough to meet the grandson of the finest man ever to walk the streets of Nazareth."

Though Uncle Seth's hands were strong, Jesus was surprised at how gentle they felt on his shoulders. In his embarrassment and confusion at the words and at the warmth of the greeting, Jesus was aware of garlic on the man's breath, sweat on his cheeks and wood chips clinging to the hair on his arms.

"Thank you," muttered Joseph. "You are very kind."

"Not at all," countered Seth. "Historical fact. Your father was kinder to me than my own family was. He taught me everything I know, not only about woodworking but about life. He is the one who made it possible for me and my mother and my sister to keep this place after my father passed away. He it was who helped me build this spinning device to shape my bowls."

"You were a very apt apprentice, Uncle Seth. My father depended on you very much."

"Those were good days. You were not any older than this boy of yours when your father first took me on. I was not quite twenty. How old are you, Jesus?"

"Almost ten."

"There you go," said Seth. "I think your father was about ten when I became his father's apprentice."

"And an older brother to me," added Joseph.

"If you have lived here a long time, why isn't your workshop finished?" asked Jesus.

"But it is finished," said Seth. "What do you mean?"

"But three walls are lacking," said Jesus. "Don't you plan to finish this building?"

"Ah, would you have me build walls to block off this grand view?" Seth asked, gesturing with a sweeping hand toward the three sides that were open. "You would close me in with four walls so that not a breath of air would pass over my brow as I work? You would erect barriers to the glorious light of day so that I would need an oil lamp to see what I was doing?"

Jesus laughed. "Now that you put it that way, I see that it is a pretty wonderful workshop. But what do you do when the weather turns bad?"

"Well," said Seth, "when the weather gets so bad that I can't work under this roof, that is indeed bad weather. That isn't very often and when it happens, I can sit in this house and do nothing at all, a Sabbath rest, if you will. Come, sit down. I will make tea."

He gestured toward a small table and stools still under the roof of the outdoor work area, in the corner with the best view of the valley on the back side of the hill. Even where Uncle Seth stepped to make tea was under the shelter of the roof. He added some chips to the smoldering coals and the fire soon blazed up to boil the pot.

"If my Hobal were here, she would make us a fine lunch, one that you would remember," said Seth. "But she is at the market so we will have to make do with tea."

"Yes, we saw her," said Jesus.

"You did? And how was she faring?" Jesus glanced at Joseph with wide eyes and didn't answer.

"She was her usual self," said Joseph. "Not as cheerful as you, of course, but doing okay."

"Ah, my poor Hobal. If she were cheerful, I would think she was not well."

"She did complain of sitting in the sun," said Joseph. "Maybe you and I could rig up a bit of shade for her at the market."

"I did that for her and she complained of being chilled so I took it down."

"Well, there you have it," sighed Joseph.

"If I took away all occasion of complaining, she would complain of having nothing to complain about." Joseph and Jesus laughed.

"So," said Seth, as he brought tea and glasses to the table, "is this just a social call or is something on your mind?"

"Uncle Seth," said Joseph, "I have just received the biggest work order of my life and I can't complete it without help. I'm wondering if you have the capacity to do part of the work for me."

"Well, I have five hundred bowls to make by next week market day, but other than that..."

"Five hundred bowls?" said Joseph in disbelief.

"Well, if I only make four hundred fifty, Auntie Hobal will think I am shirking," replied Seth with a wink. "But she will be lucky to sell a tenth of the ones she already has. Tell me about your order."

When Joseph described the order for tables and benches and stools, Seth's eyes sparkled and his grin spread from ear to ear. He clapped Joseph on the back and hugged him tight. Then he danced about under the roof of the workshop like a little boy, sending wood chips flying. "This is wonderful news," said Seth "Of course I can help you. I can make stool legs by the score on this spinning machine of mine. Your biggest problem will be to supply the wood fast enough."

"And Jesus and I can busy ourselves with making the table tops, the trestles and stool tops," added Joseph. "The oak I can get locally from Jonas, but the cedar needs to be ordered from someone with connections to Lebanon."

"Jonas has connections to Lebanon; you can order all of the wood from him," said Seth. "This will be a merry season indeed."

"It might even be merry enough to put a smile on Auntie Hobal's face," said Joseph.

"Well, don't count on that," countered Seth. "But we will make a good show of trying."

For the next two weeks, there was a great deal of excitement and a lot of work around the workshop as Joseph and Jesus finished off work that was already in progress for other customers. As soon as they had quite finished that, they received a large delivery of oak and began setting up the shop for the mass production of stools, benches and tables. Jesus was busy cutting and shaping stool tops. Joseph was busy splicing table tops together.

Then one day Azor came to the workshop. He burst through the open door without so much as a greeting and stood there red in the face, eyebrows drawn down hard and jaws working but no words coming out. His fists were clenched and in one of them he was crushing a small scroll and he was shaking with rage.

"Well, shalom to you, Azor," said Joseph in surprise. "Are you alright? What is it?"

By way of answer, Azor held out the crumpled scroll in a shaking hand and could not bring himself to intelligible speech.

Instead of taking the scroll, Joseph took hold of the vintner's elbow and shoulder, saying, "Here, my friend. You must sit down before you fall down." He eased the fellow onto a stool and sent Jesus to fetch tea. Only when Azor was safely settled on the stool did Joseph take the scroll and spread it out on the table to read.

By the time Jesus got back, Joseph had read the scroll and Azor had found his tongue. "That rabbi will be the death of me or I will be the death of him!" he was exclaiming when Jesus came through the door.

"Hush, now. No one should talk like that," said Joseph

"But he is driving me crazy," said Azor.

"Don't let his sin cause you to sin," said Joseph. "You must trust that the Almighty will defend you against the rabbi's ambition."

"But the rabbi believes that God is on his side," said Azor.

"His believing that does not necessarily make it so," countered Joseph. "But if God were on the rabbi's side, you don't want to end up fighting against God. Be careful here, my friend."

"So what should I do?" asked Azor. "What is your advice?"

"I think you have to take this matter seriously and stop all work on Nahor's house until the judgment is given. Don't assume you will lose but don't assume you will be delivered. You must be patient and pray that God will render judgment through the priests."

"That is a very difficult thing to believe. Will not the priests simply agree with the rabbi?"

"Not necessarily. Solomon's proverb says, 'The lot is cast into the lap but the decision is from the Lord.' Wait for God to deliver you; don't try to control your fate by yourself."

Azor drank his tea and Joseph poured him another cup. Azor sat silently for a few moments and then asked, "Have you already bought the cedar?"

"We have ordered it," said Joseph, "but it might be another month before it can be delivered."

"Can you cancel the order?"

"I can ask Jonas. But wouldn't that be presuming that you will lose the case?"

"And wouldn't allowing the order to stand be presuming that I would win?"

"Yes, I suppose it would," said Joseph. "Do you believe that the rabbi has a good case against you?"

"I bought the house from Nahor and paid him a fair price. The deal was all done according to our normal customs. Where the older brother is and whether he would raise any objection to the sale, nobody knows. He hasn't been seen in Nazareth for four years. Last word Nahor had was that his brother was going to Cesarea. I suppose they are trying to find him there or find out where he has gone from there. Nahor doesn't even know if his brother is still alive."

"Well, I will talk to Jonas and see if he can just put the order for cedar on hold, not cancel it."

"That would be better than nothing. I just hope this doesn't ruin everything. Without Nahor's house, I never would have bought Elihud's. It's the two together that make this project worth all the expense and all the trouble."

"May the Almighty look upon your troubles and raise you up out of all of them," sighed Joseph.

"Amen," said Azor. "Amen. Thank you."

"In the meantime, just focus on the work in Elihud's house and don't do any more on Nahor's."

"But we've already broken through the wall on both levels. If the rabbi has his way, I will have to pay to restore those walls to what they were."

"Don't worry about that until you have to," advised Joseph.

Joseph poured another cup of tea for his guest. Azor looked out the door for a moment as if he could see into the future. Then he said, "Are you going up to the feast next week?"

"We are planning on it, at least Jesus and I. Not sure about his mother and the little ones. Last year we all went but it is a great deal of trouble to travel with so many little ones. How about you?"

"Oh yes," said Azor. "I always go. Well, "he corrected himself, "I missed the trip three years ago but that was the only one I've missed in a very long time."

"Three years ago was when the river was so high, wasn't it? Everybody had to go through Samaria rather than cross the Jordan."

"Yes, that was the year I missed," said Azor.

"Because you didn't want to go through Samaria?" asked Joseph.

"No, not at all," he replied. "I always go through Samaria. I missed that year because my wife was very ill. I went up a month later to sacrifice a thanksgiving offering for her healing."

"Do you go up alone?" asked Joseph.

"No, my wife often goes with me and her brother and his family sometimes. Shaleth and some of my servants usually go as well. We always form a big party. Why don't you travel with us? Maybe my wife and the servants could help with the little ones so that your whole family could come."

"Thank you, that is very kind. But my wife is too close to bringing another little one into the world. My mother will stay with her."

"Well, at least you and your son should come with us. What's his name?"

"Jesus," replied Joseph.

Azor looked up at Jesus. "Did you finish the lid to that box for the sacred scroll, son?"

"No, sir," replied Jesus. "There is more carving needed to complete the decoration of the lid, but we got busy with your project."

Azor got up and examined the carving on the lid of the box. Though it was put aside for the time being, it was still within easy reach. Azor lifted one edge of the lid and peered inside. "What scroll is that?" he asked.

"That is the prophet Isaiah," said Jesus.

"I trust you are continuing to study, young man. You should not lay aside the scriptures to work on my project."

Jesus smiled. "I am still studying," he said. "And while I work, the words that I have studied continue to fill my head."

"Good for you, son. You are a fine boy. I hope you and your father join us for the annual pilgrimage. Perhaps we could talk about what you have been reading as we travel together."

"I would like that, sir," said Jesus. "As a matter of fact, I have been wanting to ask you a question."

"Me?" said Azor with no little surprise. "What question do you want to ask me?"

"Isaiah the prophet says that God will prepare a feast with 'aged wine' and with 'the finest wine.' Why is aged wine better than new wine?"

"Aha," said Azor. "Excellent question and that is a question to which I can speak. You see, wine is like a woman. You might think that there is nothing more beautiful than a young girl who is just approaching the age of marriage. And if you judge on beauty alone, she might be very desirable. But she has not developed real character yet. She doesn't even know who she is and what she will become. She might develop bad character like a foolish woman."

"Like Solomon's proverb," said Jesus. "'Like a gold ring in a pig's snout is a beautiful woman without discretion.'"

"Exactly!" said Azor. "If a beautiful girl grows under the very best conditions and with the right influences, she becomes a truly wonderful woman. But it can go the other way, too. The same is true with wine. You have to start with a good wine in the first place and then protect it from contamination. The wine continues to develop character after it is sealed in a jug. If you keep it cool and don't jostle it around by moving it every month, some wines become most excellent only after three or four years."

"Thank you, sir," said Jesus.

"You are very welcome. Thanks for asking," replied the vintner.

"Azor," said Joseph. "Some of the furniture that we are making of oak was destined for the part of the dining room that is in Nahor's house. Do you want to reduce that part of the order as well?"

"You already have the materials for all of the oak furniture, don't you?"

"Yes, but we don't have to cut it all up. Jonas will probably take it back if I don't cut it," said Joseph.

"What did we designate for that part of the dining room?" asked Azor.

"One large table, four small ones, two benches and twelve stools," said Joseph.

"No, don't hold back on those," said Azor. "If, God forbid, the rabbi succeeds in blocking me from Nahor's house, I will expand out the back enough to use that furniture."

"Are you sure?" asked Joseph. "I don't want to put you in a bad way."

"No, I'm sure. Complete the original order in oak, but don't take delivery on the cedar yet. Something will work out."

"Very well, we won't finish the oak furniture until after the trip to Jerusalem. Perhaps by then you will know how the matter with Nahor's house will turn out."

"Fine," said Azor. "Do plan on traveling with us, then."

"We will look forward to it," said Joseph.

After Azor had left Jesus asked, "What happened, Abba?"

"Well, Rabbi Zuriel has appealed to the high priest in Jerusalem and the priest has ordered Azor to stop construction on the smaller house until they determine whether the sale was legal."

"How was it illegal?" asked Jesus.

"Well, Nahor sold the house believing he had every right to do so. But the rabbi is challenging its legality because Nahor has an older brother who should have ownership of the house."

"Then how could Nahor sell it if it belongs to his brother?" asked Jesus.

"Nahor argues that his brother abandoned all rights to the house and may not even be alive anymore. Nahor hasn't heard from him in over four years."

"How will the high priest solve this?"

"Well," said Joseph, "he has apparently sent someone to Cesarea to search for the brother or for any word of him. If they find the brother, and if he doesn't agree to the sale, Azor will have to restore the house to the condition he found it in and he will not get to have his roof-top dining area."

"And we will lose a very large portion of our contract?" asked Jesus.

"That could happen," said his father.

"And what if the brother is found and he agrees to selling the house but wants a bigger price?" asked Jesus.

"Then Azor will have to decide whether the house is worth more than he already paid."

"But if the brother is not found?" asked Jesus.

"Then I don't know what will happen," said Joseph. "It partly depends on the high priest and partly on the persistence of the rabbi. If the rabbi refuses to accept the loss of the house, he might try to persuade the high priest to search throughout all of Israel for the man."

"Do you think Rabbi Zuriel is that stubborn?" asked Jesus.

"He might be."

Ten days later, Joseph and Jesus tidied up the workshop and set the work aside for their pilgrimage to Jerusalem. Jesus had finished cutting and shaping a dozen stool seats and had stacked them on top of each other to await Uncle Seth's delivery of the legs. He still had to bore the holes for the legs, but otherwise, they were ready for assembly. His father had constructed the trestles and the tops for two long tables but in order to conserve space in the shop, the parts were stacked across the end of the workshop out of the way. Jesus had swept the shop out and put all the tools in their accustomed places. Now it was time to get ready to travel.

At the house, all was bustle and excitement. Hannah was running from her mother to her father and then to her grandmother, exclaiming loudly, "Abba and Jesus are going to Jerusalem! Abba and Jesus are going to Jerusalem! What wonderful things will they bring us from there?"

The twins, James and little Joseph, were begging to go along on the adventure. Their father repeatedly tried to assure them that they would get to go next year but that didn't satisfy them in the least and both of them ended up in tears. Grandmother was trying to get Mary to sit down and let her handle packing the food bags, but Mary was restless and kept interfering. Mary was only two months away from delivering yet another little one. She was full of nervous energy but tired quickly and sat down, only to pop back up to supervise another bit of the packing.

"Do keep an eye out for Elizabeth and John," said Mary. "I don't suppose Zechariah will be able to travel, but I do hope to get news of Elizabeth."

"I will certainly watch for them," said Joseph, "but I don't think they come any more."

"Well, ask for news of them from anyone that comes from the hill country of Ephraim."

"I will," he assured her.

It seemed to take forever to get the family all settled in for the night. And long after everyone seemed to be asleep, Jesus heard his mother get up more than once and move quietly about the house. He feigned sleep so as not to disturb her and eventually, he must have fallen asleep for he was startled awake by his father's hand on his shoulder. He sat up without a word and slipped down the ladder from the loft. It was still dark in the house but he could see a hint of light in the cracks between the window and the shutters on the east side. His mother was already up and had a fire going to boil some water for tea. She hugged him to her side in a silent greeting and he felt the baby brother or sister move inside her. He hugged her back and realized for the first time that his head came clear up to her shoulder now.

Breakfast was tea and some day-old bread with yoghurt. A handful of dates made it a bit more special than the usual routine and then Joseph and Jesus slipped out the door. They each carried a saddle bag as they walked down the hill away from home and workshop in the half light of dawn.

In the market place, there was already a crowd gathering but it didn't take long to locate Azor. True to his word, he had provided a donkey to carry their saddle bags. He and Shaleth both were mounted on mules. "I think this animal can carry you, too, when you get weary, young man," said Azor. "Those saddle bags will not be much of a burden for him. Why, he will think it is the Sabbath unless we give him more to carry."

"I'm a strong walker," said Jesus. "I don't mind walking all day, do I Abba?"

"He is a sturdy walker," said Joseph, "but he knows how to ride as well. We will be fine, Azor. Thank you for the use of your animal."

"Don't mention it," said Azor. "My wife isn't going this year, so if you didn't use him, he would just be wasting my pasture. Might as well put him to good use."

In a few more minutes, there was a general movement of about 30 Nazarenes who all started out together on the road to Jerusalem. Jesus looked around but couldn't find Uri the shepherd among those departing at this hour. Perhaps he would come later. Or perhaps he couldn't get away from his work for this journey. There were other boys that he knew, but he wished that Uri were coming with them.

"I don't see the rabbi," said Joseph. "Is he going up this year?"

"Oh, you don't think he would miss an opportunity to strut in front of the whole population of Israel, do you?" answered Azor. "He left two days ago."

"Are we going to cross the Jordan River," asked Jesus.

"No," said Azor. "This party will go through Samaria."

"Is that safe to go through Samaria?" asked Jesus.

"Of course, it's safe," said Azor. "Samaritans will do you no harm if you are half-way fair with them."

"Aren't they robbers and cheats?" asked Jesus.

"There are robbers and cheats among them," replied Azor. "And there are robbers and cheats among our own people, as well. But traveling in a party of so many people, I don't think we are at any great risk."

After a long day of travel Joseph, Jesus, Azor and a large contingent of travelers arrived in Scythopolis, at the junction of the Valley of Jezreel and the Jordan Valley. It was the chief city of the region of Decapolis and even boasted a Roman amphitheater.

As they neared the city Joseph called to Azor, "We usually turn aside here and camp in the valley near the stream of water that flows down from Mount Gilboa. Will that be suitable for you?"

"No, no, no," said Azor. "Tomorrow night we can camp near Sychar. Tonight you will be my guests at the nicest inn of Schythopolis."

"You are very kind, Azor," replied Joseph. "But we don't want you to go to such expense on our behalf. We are very happy to camp under the stars. And with so many people traveling, there is probably no room at the inn."

"It is for business purposes that I want you to stay with me at the inn. I have sent word ahead to the owner, so he will have reserved a room for us. And I want you to see this inn so that you better understand what I am trying to build in Nazareth. I insist."

Joseph tried protesting the unnecessary expenditure one more time but Azor was adamant. "It is not that expensive anyway," said Azor. "This man is a customer of mine. He buys a lot of wine and it is good for business that we stay at his inn."

They passed the amphitheater on the way into the city and it seemed that some of the travelers were camping around the perimeter.

"Will there be any competitions in there today?" asked Jesus.

"I don't think so, son," said Joseph. "The main business of the day for this city is to house and feed the many travelers. And the travelers are, to a man, bent on reaching Jerusalem. Tired travelers are not likely to pay for entertainment when they are focused on reaching the temple for Yom Kippur."

The inn was a three-story house on a major thoroughfare not far from the amphitheater. Azor gave the animals into the care of Shaleth. He and the other servant would sleep in the stable with the two mules and the donkey.. The three travelers stamped the dust off their feet and brushed the dust from their clothing. There was a fountain of clear water bubbling up in a small pool beside the entrance. They stopped there and washed their hands and their faces. The owner of the inn met them there before they were finished.

"Ah, my good friend, Azor! Welcome, welcome, I've been expecting you. I saved you the best room in the inn. How are you? You must be tired. Come in and have something to eat and something to drink."

"Gideon, peace be upon you and on your whole house. It is good to see you again. These are my traveling companions from Nazareth, Joseph and his son Jesus."

"You are very welcome here, Joseph. Peace be upon you. May your journey be prosperous in every way."

"Thank you, sir," said Joseph. We are grateful for your hospitality."

"Not at all," said Gideon. "Any companion of Azor's is most welcome here. Just say a prayer for my prosperity when you are in the temple and I will be in your debt."

"We will certainly do that for you, Gideon," said Azor.

"Come in, come in. Don't stand out here like buzzards waiting for the hyena to leave the carcass. Feasting awaits you through these doors."

Gideon ushered them to a table and called servants to come to their attendance. One of them brought a basin of water and a towel and proceeded to wash their feet. Before that was accomplished, there was a pitcher of wine and four cups on the table. Another servant brought a stack of warm flat disks of bread, just out of the oven. In addition to that, they were soon provided with olives, yoghurt, cucumbers, onions, raisins, figs and roast lamb. Gideon sat with them for a moment, sipping at his wine and entertaining Azor with stories and occasional questions about his family and his business. But he often jumped up to greet other guests or to direct his servants in the care of the many travelers who were flowing in and out of his establishment. He had no time to eat.

"Look around you, Joseph," said Azor when Gideon was away. "What do you see?"

"I see a very busy place with tables not as nice as those that I am making for you," said Joseph.

"Do you see how prosperous this house is?" asked Azor. "There is a lot of money that passes from hand to hand in such a place."

"I'm sure you are right," replied Joseph. "But surely it is quieter when it is not three days before Yom Kippur."

"Of course there are busy seasons and slower seasons," said Azor. "But there is great profit in the busy seasons. This is similar to what I want in Nazareth."

"Nazareth is not going to have as much traffic as this city, Azor," said Joseph. "Not in my lifetime."

"True," said Azor. "But it is only the beginning. With the profits of the inn at Nazareth, I hope to build one in Tiberias and maybe even in Capernaum."

"God give you success in all your plans," said Joseph.

"Amen," said Azor. "May the Lord answer that prayer. And you can build me the finest furniture in all of Galilee."

"We will certainly do our best. Won't we Jesus?"

Jesus was very tired from the travel and was feeling quite sleepy from the full stomach and the wine. He nodded happily but could not find words to express his agreement. He soon fell asleep leaning against his father as the conversation drifted on and servants and travelers came and went.

He woke up to the sound of a rooster and looked about him. He and his father and Azor were on pallets on the floor of a room he had never seen before. It was still dark enough to see stars through the windows on two sides of the room. He wondered how he had come to the room. He realized that Abba must have carried him there. He was embarrassed that a boy his age had had to be carried like a sleepy toddler. He snuggled closer to his earthly father and prayed to his heavenly father, thanking him for safety on the journey, for a protective, loving parent and for the excitement of the journey.

Over breakfast, Jesus began to get curious about this place. "Abba, why does this city have such a strange name?" he asked. "Has it always been a Roman town?"

"Not at all," replied his father. "This is a famous place in Israel's history. It used to be called 'Beth Shan' and it was originally given to the tribe of Manasseh. Manasseh never totally drove out the Canaanites who had lived here before them, but they made them do forced labor."

"I didn't know that," said Azor.

"And in King Saul's time, this place was under the control of the Philistines. It was on the wall of this city where the Philistines fastened the headless body of Saul and the bodies of his sons when they found them among the slain up there on Mount Gilboa."

"And the men of Jabesh Gilead came here and stole Saul's body off the wall?" asked Jesus.

"Exactly," confirmed his father. "They stole Saul's body and the bodies of his sons from the wall of this town and carried them back to Jabesh with them. There they burned the bodies and buried their bones under a Tamarisk tree. King David, when he heard what they had done, sent a message to them and thanked them for that kindness to Saul and his family."

"I had heard the story as a child," said Azor, "but I had no idea that this was Beth Shan. So it has always been in foreign hands."

"Not always," said Joseph, "but too often."

That day their path parted from the path preferred by most of the pilgrims going up to Jerusalem. Most people from Galilee chose to go along the Jordan River, crossing where necessary, rather than climb the higher road through Samaria. Bur Azor's party, now about 35 strong, departed for Sychar in Samaria. That, they hoped, would be their last night on the road. It was their goal to reach Jerusalem in one more long day from there.

As they travelled through Samaria, people would sometimes ignore them, and sometimes would stop and stare. The travelers seemed to huddle a little closer together in this land of strangers. Nobody straggled more than a horse length behind the ones in front of them. When they stopped to rest or to have lunch, they always did so in places of solitude, rather than near a village or a house. When they met Samaritans on the road there were no greetings, no kind words, no words at all. Just a nod of the head seemed an adequate and safe greeting. It was clear to the travelers that they did not have rights here and should keep moving.

In late afternoon they passed through Sychar, one of the larger towns in this area. After passing through the town, they only continued a few more leagues to an ancient well. Here they planned to camp for their last night before pushing on to Jerusalem.

"Aren't we still in Samaria, Abba," asked Jesus. "Is it safe to camp here?"

"This site is so important to Jews as well as to Samaritans, that there is a kind of truce that is acknowledged by all in this place," said Joseph. "This is Jacob's Well and this place was once called 'Shechem.'"

Jesus gasped and his eyes got big as he looked around.

"Shechem," he whispered. "Is this where the sons of Jacob destroyed a city?"

"Yes," replied Joseph.

"Because the king's son slept with their sister, Dinah, before marrying her?" continued Jesus.

"Yes," replied his father. "And this is part of the land that was allotted to the tribe of Ephraim when Joshua and the army conquered the land. And this is where they finally buried Joseph's bones hundreds of years after he had died."

"How is it," asked Azor, "that you two know so much about these things? I should pay better attention in synagogue."

"It's not from synagogue that we learned these things," answered Jesus. "We study the scriptures."

"Ah, that's true," said Azor. "You told me that. I am impressed with how much you know for one so young."

"It is because of the work my father has given me to do," replied Jesus, but then he noticed his father giving him a subtle signal to stop.

Azor looked puzzled, but did not pursue the obvious question of what studying the scripture had to do with a carpenter's apprentice.

They were distracted by the approach of several Samaritans from the town. They were led by a very determined young man who strode with confidence toward the party of Galilean Jews. He strode directly up and addressed Azor, probably because he was dressed the finest of the travelers and had the best mule.

"Tell me, sir," he asked in a voice that had a distinct edge to it. "Are you Jewish pilgrims heading for Jerusalem?"

"We are," said Azor.

"And do you come in peace?" asked the young man. "Because if you don't, you won't find this a suitable place to camp."

"Of course we come in peace," replied Azor. "We told you we are pilgrims heading for Jerusalem for the feast. Is that not peaceable enough?"

"On the surface it is," answered the man, "but we have had harsh enough experience of Jewish pilgrims that we are ready to fight to protect our own. I want every man of you to stand forward with his face uncovered. We are looking for one among you who has done us wicked harm."

"Such a man cannot be of our party," cried Azor. "We have traveled all day together and have just arrived from Scythopolis, weary and hungry. None of us has had time to slip behind a tree to relieve himself, let alone do you any harm."

"The harm was done three years ago at this time by one of you Jewish pilgrims from Galilee going up to Jerusalem. We will find that man when and where we can. All others may rest easy enough," said the Samaritan.

"What was his crime?" asked Azor.

By now, there were more than two dozen Samaritans, mostly men and some of those obviously armed, lined up behind their spokesman. Among them was one older woman who was holding a smallish teen-aged girl tightly around the shoulders. The girl looked only at the ground in front of her feet. The young man turned around and motioned for her to be brought forward.

"This girl is my sister, Dunya," he said. "She is deaf and cannot speak an intelligent word. Three years ago on the night that the pilgrims were camping on their way toward Jerusalem, she was playing with the other children in the woods. One of the pilgrims caught her and violated her and left her beaten and unconscious in the forest. She was not quite twelve years old."

The pilgrims all gasped in horror. "I will find that man," asserted the older brother. "And when I do, may God have mercy on his soul because I will have none."

Azor struggled to regain his composure and then said, "If the man is among us, we will not withhold him from you. But we will not give up any man to you without proof that he is the guilty one."

"My sister can identify the criminal," asserted the man.

"Ah, but a woman's testimony is not valid in court," objected Azor. "Do you not have other witnesses or other proof?"

The young man took a step toward Azor and stretched out his neck until their noses almost touched. "In MY court, MY sister's testimony is valid! When we find the villain, he will never live to see any other court!"

"I understand your passion, my man," said Azor, taking a step backward, "but beware lest your passion cause haste and your haste start a war that you cannot win."

The older woman who was holding on to Dunya tugged at the young man's sleeve. "Let Dunya have a look at them, son. If she does not identify anyone then there is no need to antagonize these travelers," she said.

"I agree," said Joseph. "But you, sir," he said to the young man, "would do well to calm down. If the girl identifies one of our party, we will have much to talk about and a thorough investigation should be carried out. Give us your word that you will not rashly attack without that talk."

There was a murmur of assent from the travelers and after a moment of tense stalemate, the young man agreed. The men among the pilgrims all lined up and waited. Dunya was led down the line by her brother and her mother. She was trembling visibly as they neared the first man. She barely glanced at him and shook her head 'no.' Her brother took her chin in his hand and tried to force her to look longer at the man, but he could not force her to raise her downcast eyes. Their mother slapped his hand and admonished him to let her choose how long to look at each one. The girl was guided down the row of men hardly pausing to glance at any of them, shaking her head 'no' at each one. Between those quick glances, she kept her eyes on the ground. She never uttered a sound.

When she came to Joseph, she again just gave a quick glance and shook her head 'no.' But then her eyes fell on Jesus. He was standing in the line next to his father and when Dunya looked at him, her mouth fell open and she just stared at him. Everyone on both sides of the line-up gawked to see who had caught her attention. Jesus squirmed a bit and quietly took hold of his father's hand.

Her brother tried to push her along to the next man in line but Dunya stood her ground and looked at Jesus. "What is she looking at?" cried her brother in frustration. "He can't be the one; he is just a child." Her mother pulled her along and her brother pushed, but still she looked back at Jesus and her jaw began to work up and down but no sound came out.

Finally her brother took her chin in his hand again and forced her to turn her attention to the rest of the men in the line-up. She returned to glancing timidly at each face and shaking her head 'no.'

When she had dismissed the last man in the line, a great sigh of relief went up, not only among the Galilean pilgrims, but also among the Samaritans on the other side of the path. There was no solution as to who had violated Dunya, but at least there would not be a fight between these two parties, neither physical nor verbal.

The young man stepped toward Azor and introduced himself. "My name is Daryush," he said. "Please forgive my rudeness. Your party is welcome to camp here."

"Apology accepted," said Azor. "I don't blame you for wanting to avenge your sister; I dare say I would do the same."

Joseph said, "We thank you for the opportunity to camp here."

"Yes, we do," added Azor. "Perhaps after we get settled, you will come and share a cup of wine by my fire. I would like to speak with you at leisure."

"Thank you for your offer," said Daryush. "I might do that."

While these formalities were being tended to, Dunya huddled in her mother's arms but kept craning her neck to get another look at Jesus. Her interest in him was so intense that he slipped behind his father and would not return her gaze.

Finally, the Samaritans retreated to the town of Sychar and the travelers set about making camp. After a little while, a few Samaritan children slipped out of the town and came to see if the children among the travelers would like to join in some games. Jesus got permission from Joseph to join in the merriment and soon ran into the woods for games of tag and hide and seek.

That evening when supper was over and Azor's servants had cleaned everything up, he and Joseph and Jesus were sitting quietly around the small fire when Daryush strode into the camp. The other pilgrims pointed him in the right direction and he walked into the firelight with a simple greeting that was quite a contrast to his earlier confrontational entry.

"Welcome, friend," said Azor. "Please sit down. Thank you for coming." Rather than calling one of his servants, who had already been dismissed to their rest, Azor himself poured a generous cup of wine for their guest.

"You know that I am a Samaritan," said the young man, "and you offer me a cup of wine?"

"I am not much of a Pharisee about such things," said Azor. "I am building an inn at Nazareth and I hope to serve not only Samaritans but even Romans in my inn."

Daryush sniffed the wine, raised an eyebrow and took a sip. "That is no ordinary wine, sir," he said. "This is not what travelers ordinarily carry about."

"I see that you can appreciate the difference. I am a vintner and I see no reason to drink vinegar just because I am on a journey."

"There is no comparison between this and vinegar," said Daryush. His appreciation was apparent in his face as well as in his voice. He relaxed against the log at his back and released a deep sigh.

"Are you originally from these parts, Daryush?" asked Joseph.

"My family is of Persian origin," replied Daryush. "We have been here in Sychar for many generations. Legend has it that the King of Assyria brought my ancestors here after he had removed the Jews of this place to a land far away."

"Tell us more of the circumstances of what happened to your sister," said Azor. "You say it was three years ago?"

"Yes, three years ago at the time when Jews go up to Jerusalem for Yom Kippur. Perhaps you were with that very party, yourselves?"
"Not I," said Azor. "My wife was very ill that year and I did not go."

Daryush looked at Joseph.

"Nor I," said Joseph in answer to the look. "Jesus here was seven years old, the twins were not yet three and Hannah was the baby. We wanted to go, of course, but the demands of the children were too great."

"It was a much larger party than you form this year," said Daryush. "Perhaps four times as many people."

"Ah yes," said Azor. "That year the Jordan was running very high and many pilgrims used this road to avoid the flooding."

"Only about half of the travelers camped here by the well," continued Daryush. Other smaller groups spread out in the nearby forest, making various small camps scattered through the woods. The children look forward to playing games with the children of the travelers and Dunya, like the others, ran through the forest paths playing games until it was almost dark.

"When she didn't come home with the other children, I went out looking for her. I asked all of her playmates where they had last seen her but none of them had any helpful information to offer. I gathered others from the town and we went all through the forest with torches throughout the night. It was the strangest search party you can imagine, sir, because it made no sense to call out for her, her being deaf, you know."

"And where was she found?" asked Joseph.

"We didn't find her until the afternoon of the next day," said her brother. "She was leagues from here wandering in the wrong direction and tears streaming down her face and no voice coming out. She had a black eye and bruises. Her clothes had been torn off of her and bloodied but she carried them wrapped about her."

Azor and Joseph groaned simultaneously and shook their heads. "Such a thing should not happen to any child," said Joseph. "How much less to a child who cannot cry out for help!"

"Perhaps that's why she was targeted in the first place," said Daryush.

"For that reason and for the reason that she would be less able to describe her attacker," added Joseph. The others murmured their assent.

"Did you pursue the travelers that day to try to find the guilty one?" asked Azor.

"No," said Daryush. "By the time we got Dunya back here, it was dark and the travelers were likely all in Jerusalem. How could we even find the man in that great city and without Dunya to identify him? She was in no shape to travel."

"And when the travelers came back through on their way back to Galilee?" asked Azor.

"We questioned everyone, of course. But no one had any idea what we were talking about. And the guilty party would surely not come back to the scene of his crime and risk being found out. Surely he would go by another road."

"As he might do for the rest of his life," added Joseph.

Azor filled the wine cups again and they all sat looking into the fire, each thinking his own thoughts.

"Dunya used to be such a happy, carefree child," said her brother. Tears were streaming down his face. "Being deaf and unable to speak never seemed to bother her at all, though Mother and I felt bad for her. But she would run and play with the other children any time she didn't have chores to do. And she was always eager and cheerful even when doing her chores. I suppose if she had ever been able to hear and then became deaf, she would feel saddened by the loss. But she never knew what she had lost, so she went on with life as though she was exactly as she was intended by the creator to be."

"And perhaps she was," sighed Joseph. "Until some wicked man stole her childhood."

"That creature stole more than her childhood. He stole her happiness and mine and her mother's as well. And that of our youngest brother, Cyrus. None of us have any happiness or peace since that day. And Dunya is not the same. Some of the townspeople believe she has a demon. From time to time she becomes like a raging wild animal and no one but Mother can calm her down."

"Then your father is no more?" asked Joseph softly.

"No, father passed away a month before Cyrus was born. That was nine years ago next month."

"How old are you, Daryush?" asked Joseph.

"I will be twenty in the spring," he replied.

"You have had to carry a heavy burden for one so young. Is there any way that we can help you?" asked Joseph.

Daryush just sat, silently weeping and brushing away the tears.

"Come to Jerusalem with us tomorrow," said Azor suddenly.

Daryush looked up. "What good would that do?" he asked. "Gentiles are not welcome in Jerusalem during Yom Kippur."

"Nonsense," said Azor. "They can't go into the temple but they are welcome anywhere else in the city. And maybe we can help you find the wicked man who harmed your sister."

"How could you help me find him?" asked Daryush. "Only Dunya could identify him and at times I wonder whether even she could do that."

"Bring her," said Azor "We will be your body guards and escorts."

"She could never go to Jerusalem without Mother," objected Daryush.

"Then bring her, too," said Azor. "The more the merrier.

Daryush paused, thinking about this proposal. Finally, he said, "I confess I have wanted to go search for the criminal among the pilgrims every year.

But the difficulties of being a foreigner with a deaf child in such a throng is more than I can face."

"But you would not have to face the difficulties alone if you travel with us," said Azor. "I offer you the use of one of my mules for your mother or your sister to ride. They can take turns."

"I appreciate your offer," said Daryush. "Let me ask Mother and Dunya about this. We would probably have to bring Cyrus as well."

"That would be fine," said Joseph. "He could play with my son. And if you are under the protection of our party, no one will bother you in Jerusalem."

"I am tempted to accept your hospitable offer," said Daryush. "But I must confer with Mother. I will come here at sunrise to give you our answer."

"That's fine," said Azor. "But don't let the darkness of the night make you forget the sincerity of our offer."

"I would be tempted to come with you at any rate, Azor, if just for another cup of your wine."

With that, Daryush left them sitting around the fire and set off for home.

When they settled down for the night, Jesus snuggled close to his father and whispered, "Abba, can I talk to you?"

"Of course."

"Do you think it will be a problem if Daryush and his sister come with us to Jerusalem?"

"I don't know," answered Joseph. "I was surprised when Azor made the offer."

"So was I," whispered Jesus.

"I was wishing we could help them some how but..." his voice trailed off.

"But what?" asked Jesus.

"Well, it might change the focus of our trip. Going to Jerusalem to confess our sins for Yom Kippur and going there to try to catch a criminal are two very different purposes."

"Do you think Dunya has a demon?" asked Jesus.

"I did not see her do anything today that would lead me to accuse her of that," said Joseph. "She has been deeply wounded but not everyone who is wounded is demon possessed."

Jesus was quiet for several minutes but he was not falling asleep. "Abba?" he asked.

"Yes?"

"When I was playing with the other children, I met her little brother Cyrus."

"Oh?" said Joseph.

"Yes, he is the one who invited me into the games."

"What kind of boy is he?" asked Joseph.

"He is one year younger than me but he is a very fast runner."

"Is he now?" said Joseph.

"But not nearly as fast as his sister," added Jesus.

"She was out there too?" asked Joseph.

"Mm-hmm," said Jesus.

"I'm a little surprised, under the circumstances..." said Joseph, lamely. "I mean, she is by now, what? Fifteen years old, I would say, or near to it. And after what happened to her when playing such games in the past..."

"Cyrus says she is very independent and she does what she wants. And her mother can't keep her in the house all the time. Besides, she doesn't seem that much older. She is small for her age, and very playful." explained Jesus.

"She is small," said Joseph. "I didn't see her playful side, but in that atmosphere, nobody would seem playful."

"But with the children, she is," said Jesus. "Cyrus was leading me a merry chase and when I got winded and stopped under a tree to catch my breath, an acorn fell on my head. When I looked up, there was Dunya on a branch above me. She laughed and swung down and ran so fast I couldn't tag her. Soon she was hiding again in the woods and I couldn't find her. Then she came up behind me so softly I didn't know she was coming until she tagged me and took off running again, fleet as a deer."

"Huh!" exclaimed Joseph. "The poor child deserves to have a little fun, surely."

After a significant pause Jesus said, "Abba?"

"Yes, Son?"

"Is it possible for a person to have two spirits?"

"Two spirits? I don't know what you are asking," replied his father.

"Well, I don't know if I am right, but..."

"But what? Tell me what you are thinking," coaxed Joseph.

"Well, you saw how she stared at me when she was looking for the man who had hurt her, right?"

"Yes, nobody could have failed to notice that. It was very peculiar."

"Well, her natural spirit is happy and playful and full of fun surprises. But it was like a different spirit looking out of her eyes when she stared at me. Her natural spirit likes to be with me just because we are both children and love to run and play. But there is a different spirit in her that is very focused on me. That spirit came to the fore a few times while we were playing. She ignored all the other children, even her brother, and played only with me. It feels unnatural."

"Son," said Joseph with a quaver in his voice, "you are giving me chills up and down my spine. She almost certainly has a demon and that demonic presence has sensed that you are no ordinary child."

"So what do we do?" asked Jesus.

"What we will do is trust in God Almighty and ask His sovereign protection over you. And you should avoid any contact with her."

"But if they come with us to Jerusalem tomorrow, how can I avoid all contact with her?" asked Jesus.

"Well, if she speaks to you, just don't answer..."

"Abba, she can't speak to anyone!"

"True, I had forgotten. But if the demon speaks to you, you are not to answer. And you are not to be alone with her, even for a moment," said his father.

"Just pray for me, Abba. God will have to give us wisdom and protect us in our ignorance. May it be done to me, all that He has planned."

So Joseph prayed, "God Almighty, Ruler of the universe, may your name be hallowed and your will be done on earth as it is heaven. Have mercy on us, o God and be not far from us in our hour of need. Protect my son, YOUR son from demonic activity in this place and along the roads wherever your sovereign will should lead us. Lead us in paths of righteousness for your name's sake. Lead us far from temptation, lead us far from the nets that your enemies spread to tangle our feet. May the wicked be trapped in their own snares and let the innocent ones fly with swift wings into your protection. May your will be done in the matter of this Daryush and his sister. I pray that your justice would reveal the wicked man who harmed this poor child and that his wickedness would be brought down upon his own head. Let the girl's life be redeemed and may your anointed one escape the notice of any demons involved in this matter. Grant us restful sleep and dreams that are whispered into our ears by your angels. And we will give you the glory. Amen."
"Amen," whispered Jesus.

When Jesus opened his eyes in the morning, he lay very still listening. His father and Azor were talking in low voices as they built a fire and got breakfast ready. "Tell me why it is so important to you that Daryush and his sister come with us to Jerusalem," said Joseph. "Your offer was very generous, but it took me quite by surprise."

"I think any man would want to help Daryush avenge his sister's attack," answered Azor.

"Perhaps so," agreed Joseph, "but you seem particularly eager to get involved with this vengeance. Is there anything special involved for you?"

"Well," said Azor, "I have a suspicion that is growing by the hour."

"What is your suspicion?" asked Joseph.

"Do you remember when Rabbi Zuriel came back from Yom Kippur three years ago?"

"Nothing in particular," said Joseph. "Why?"

"He came back with his head shaved," said Azor.

"And he shaves his head every year when he goes to Yom Kippur," replied Joseph.

"That is true now," said Azor. "But it began three years ago. And he didn't shave his head before going to Jerusalem, but before coming back. Now he shaves his head before he leaves Nazareth."

"And that should mean something to me?" asked Joseph.

"Think about it," said Azor. "A man who is guilty of a crime wants to change his appearance so that the victim can't identify him."

Joseph gasped. "You can't be thinking that our rabbi is the one who violated the girl here in Sychar!"

"Why can't I be thinking that? It had to be someone traveling from Galilee to Jerusalem with the pilgrims. He was among them that year. And ever since, he changes his appearance to travel to Jerusalem and back."

"But this year he shaved his head weeks before Yom Kippur. He is doing it because of his religious vows, surely," said Joseph.

"And do you forget that he made a trip to Jerusalem three weeks ago to involve the high priest in the argument about the sale of Nahor's house?"

"Oh, Azor," said Joseph, "I fear you are trying to make the rabbi guilty of this because he is giving you such trouble over that house."

"I must admit that it would benefit me in my case if the rabbi were guilty," said Azor. "But that doesn't mean there is no evidence against him."

"Very thin evidence, if you ask me," said Joseph. "I warn you against making such an accusation."

"Who is making an accusation?" protested Azor. "I can't help but have a suspicion. But I am only going to try to lead the girl past our rabbi and see if she makes an accusation."

"Hush! They're coming now," said Joseph.

Jesus rubbed the sleep from his eyes and sat up in time to see Daryush and his whole family arrive, packed and ready to travel on no less than three donkeys. Dunya and Cyrus were riding on one, their mother on a second and the third was being used as a pack animal.

"Good morning, friends," said Daryush. "My mother and my sister have agreed to this journey."

"That is good news," said Azor. "Welcome. I trust your journey will not be in vain."

"I hope not," replied Daryush. "We won't have to borrow an animal from you, though we thank you for the offer. This pack animal belongs to us and the other two we have borrowed from neighbors. We are counting on your promise of protection from your fellow Jews."

"I don't anticipate a moment's trouble," replied Azor. "We Jews are focused on confessing our sins before God and praying for the redemption of Israel from our enemies, the Romans. Nobody will look at you cross-eyed."

"Nevertheless," replied Daryush, "we are relying on your personal assurance of protection."

"You are within your rights on that point," said Azor. "Have you had breakfast? Will you join us in a bite to strengthen ourselves for the road?"

"Thank you, no," said Daryush. We will go on ahead at an easy pace. You will catch up with us soon enough, I should think."

"Good roads to you then," said Azor. "We will be along very soon."

Soon enough the Jewish pilgrims were fed, packed up and mounted. They followed the dusty tracks left by Daryush and his family for nearly two hours before they came upon them resting in the shade of a large rock near the top of a hill. As the pilgrims approached, Daryush helped his mother and his siblings remount and they fell in near the back of the group. They had not gone very far after that when Dunya and Cyrus pushed their donkey into a trot and passed several travelers to come alongside Jesus. Cyrus was holding the reins and smiling from ear to ear. Dunya fastened her flashing black eyes on Jesus and did not blink. Her gaze was so steady that Jesus blushed and looked away. He kept walking, leading the little donkey that carried his and Joseph's possessions closer and closer to Jerusalem.

"Will we stop somewhere for lunch?" asked Cyrus.

"Probably," said Jesus without looking up at him. He couldn't look up at Cyrus without meeting the relentless stare of Dunya.

"Shall we play tag while we rest?" asked Cyrus.

"Uhh, probably not," said Jesus.

"Why not? We want to play," he said. "My sister always wants to play and so do I."

"I need to save my strength for the road," answered Jesus.

"Why don't you ride for a while so that you don't need so much rest?" suggested Cyrus.

"Well, then the donkey would be spent before we reached Jerusalem," replied Jesus. "I'm okay walking."

"Too bad," said Cyrus. "Maybe tomorrow we can play in Jerusalem."

"Yeah, maybe," said Jesus. "But we might be too busy with Yom Kippur."

They plodded on in silence for a while. Once or twice Jesus stole a glance up at the brother and sister. Every time, Dunya's eyes were watching his every move. When Jesus had had enough of that, he switched to the other side of the donkey that he was leading, desiring to block that persistent stare. Finally, Cyrus responded to his brother's call to come back to their family's position in the procession.

When the travelers stopped for rest and a bite to eat in the early afternoon, Daryush brought his family near to Azor's party but they shared no food or drink. Samaritans might be open to the possibility of sharing a meal, but they were well aware that most Jews had a prohibition against such things. So they sat nearby and ate and drank from their own provisions.

Cyrus ate very little and then came up behind Jesus and tapped him on the shoulder. When Jesus looked up at him, he beckoned him to come and play. Jesus could see that Dunya was waiting behind her brother and was just as eager as her brother to get Jesus away from the adults. Jesus shook his head and returned to his food.

"Come on," said Cyrus. "We can play just for a few minutes."

"No," said Jesus. "I don't want to."

Cyrus would have persisted, but Joseph laid a hand on his arm. "You have his answer," said Joseph. At that, Cyrus and his sister went back to their mother and Daryush, obviously disappointed. Joseph put his arm around Jesus' shoulders and said nothing. Jesus looked up at his father's face and saw him wink.

Late that afternoon, as they began to approach Jerusalem, their way began to join other roads and they began to fall in with pilgrims from many different regions of Israel, all heading to the main city for Yom Kippur. Some were carrying yearling lambs or goats for their Yom Kippur sacrifice. Others had brought money with which to buy a lamb. Many were singing as they approached the city.

"I rejoiced with those who said to me, 'Let us go to the house of the Lord.'
Our feet are standing in your gates, Jerusalem.
Jerusalem is built like a city that is closely compacted together.
That is where the tribes go up -- the tribes of the Lord --
to praise the name of the Lord
according to the statute given to Israel.
"There stand the thrones for judgment, the thrones of the house of David.
Pray for the peace of Jerusalem;
May those who love you be secure.
May there be peace within your walls and security within your citadels.
For the sake of my family and friends, I will say, 'Peace be within you.'
For the sake of the house of the Lord our God, I will seek your prosperity."

Jesus was enraptured with the singing. Sometimes those farther ahead on the road were two or three words ahead of those who were farther behind. But the rhythm of the music tended to bring the various steps of the travelers into unison until the effect was to set a whole group of pilgrims into one stride and one spirit as they moved up the hilly paths together. The sun was growing lower in the sky as the pilgrims were rising higher and higher. They were rising higher in spirits as well as rising to a higher altitude with each step. When one psalm ended, someone would shout out the first line of another. Then all would begin singing that next psalm as hope and excitement mounted in the hearts of all the travelers.

"I lift up my eyes to the mountains --
Where does my help come from?
My help comes from the Lord,
the Maker of heaven and earth.
He will not let your foot slip --
he who watches over you will not slumber;
indeed, he who watches over Israel
will neither slumber nor sleep.
The Lord watches over you --
the Lord is your shade at your right hand;
the sun will not harm you by day,
nor the moon by night.
The Lord will keep you from all harm --
he will watch over your life;
the Lord will watch over your coming and going
both now and forevermore."

As the travelers sang this one, Jesus reached for his father's hand and gave it a powerful squeeze.

Soon Azor rode up alongside Joseph and said, "It will be too late to go into the city tonight. I know a great place to camp right at the foot of the Mount of Olives. There is a garden there and a fresh spring of clear water. I know the owner. I camp there every time I come to a feast."

"That sounds good to me," said Joseph. "There certainly is no point in trying to find a room at an inn. Not with all these throngs coming to the city."

For at least an hour after Azor's party, including Joseph, Jesus, Daryush and his family and two of Azor's servants were settled in their garden camp, other travelers could be heard singing the psalms of ascents as they proceeded up the mountain into the fabled city. Jesus wondered where all the travelers would find places to lay their heads. He wondered what roads these other travelers had covered in their approach to the holy city. And he wondered what kind of spirit was staring at him through Dunya's eyes. He repeated the words of the psalm again which promised that "The Lord will keep you from all harm -- he will watch over your life; the Lord will watch over your coming and going both now and forevermore." He whispered the words into the night as he lay down close to his earthly father in the Garden known as Gethsemane.

While the mixed party breakfasted the next morning, Azor laid out his plan for the day. They would ascend together into the city, leaving his two servants to keep the animals in camp. As they entered the city, they would be particularly watchful for Dunya to react to any man along the way. If she reacted to any man, they would follow him and try to learn where he was staying and whether he might be a Galilean. They would not be too quick to make an accusation, in case Dunya might be deceived by the man's build or clothing being similar to those of the criminal. And if she reacted to no man, then the Jewish half of the party would visit the temple and shop in the market near the temple for supplies necessary to the Yom Kippur feast before returning to camp, again being watchful.

The road into the city was quite crowded that morning and the sounds of pilgrims singing echoed off of every hill and every building as they climbed into the City of David. One time Jesus glanced at Dunya and found her, as usual, watching his every step. He wondered how in the world Dunya would ever identify her attacker when she never looked at anyone but him. Apparently Daryush was bothered by the same thought as he tried over and over to remind her to keep looking at every man they passed. She would glance around at her brother's insistence, but she paid nobody any particular mind, no more than she had when marched down the row of pilgrims in Sychar.

When they were well up into the city, they came to a busy corner of two major pilgrim paths as they converged near the temple. There, on the most prominent corner of he busiest intersection sat a group of young men, all with heads shaved and untrimmed beards, all rocking in unison with eyes closed and chanting the first of the songs of the ascent:

"I call on the Lord in my distress, and he answers me.
Save me, Lord, from lying lips and from deceitful tongues.
What will he do to you and what more besides, you deceitful tongue?
He will punish you with a warrior's sharp arrows, with burning coals of the broom bush.
Woe to me that I dwell in Meshek, that I live among the tents of Kedar!
Too long have I lived among those who hate peace.
I am for peace; but when I speak, they are for war."

Azor suddenly grasped Joseph's arm hard and brought him to a stop near the chanting young men. Joseph looked at him in surprise and Azor pointed with his jutting chin toward the group. There in the front row was none other than Rabbi Zuriel bin Gamaliel bin Amminadab, rabbi of Nazareth. All of the men were either in an ecstatic trance, trying to get into an ecstatic trance or feigning an ecstatic trance. All of the men were younger than Rabbi Zuriel but none was more emphatic in his gyrations and apparent zeal for Israel. And his voice rang out above them all. A Roman centurion was standing where he could easily keep an eye on these emotional Jewish patriots, and it was clear that he had other soldiers stationed at various points along the road within a moment's call if a need for intervention should arise.

Azor, Joseph and Jesus paused to watch Dunya pass but she hardly glanced in the direction of the rabbi and his disciples. Then she looked pointedly over her shoulder at Jesus. Her brother tugged at her impatiently and tried to force her to attend to the crowd and so the whole group moved on.

Soon the party had to go separate ways since Samaritans were not allowed to enter the temple. Azor urged Daryush to stay near the busy market place in the hopes that Dunya would identify someone as suspicious. Azor, Joseph and Jesus approached the temple and changed their focus to the real reason they had come up from Galilee in the first place. They joined the throng of Jewish pilgrims who entered the outer court of the temple and prayed for forgiveness of their sins, prayed for their loved ones and prayed for the Messiah to come.

"How glorious it would be if the Messiah were to appear in the temple at Yom Kippur, eh my friend?" said Azor.

"Glorious indeed," agreed Joseph, giving Jesus' hand a little squeeze. "And when Messiah comes," he added, "Jerusalem will never be the same."

"I'm sure you're right," said Azor. "Then all the wicked ones will be driven out. That will be a glorious day. May we live to see it with our own eyes!"

"Amen," agreed Joseph. "I'm sure you were disappointed that the girl did not scream and point at your main suspect as we passed by."

"Ah, the girl didn't even see him," complained Azor.

"Or she saw him and he isn't the guilty one," offered Joseph.

"I still say it might be him," insisted Azor. "The man is so arrogant. You see how he and his self-styled 'sons of the prophets' are making such a show. They only want to be seen as holy. I'm sure they don't know anything at all about holiness."

Joseph replied, "If the man were guilty as you think he is, would he draw so much attention to himself?"

"I don't know," said Azor. "Perhaps he is sneaky and careful when he is near Samaria but can't resist the opportunity to look good in front of all these travelers."

"Being arrogant does not make him guilty of harming the girl," said Joseph.

"No, but it doesn't make him innocent either," replied the other.

Upon leaving the temple, the men purchased a yearling lamb and Joseph carried it on his shoulders as they sought Daryush and family. When they found them, Azor said, "Well?"

"Nothing," said Daryush. "I think she is weary. She doesn't seem to understand what we are doing here."

"Listen, son," said Azor. "On the way up here we passed a group of men chanting loudly, having their heads shaved. Make sure Dunya pays attention to that group as we pass them going back."

"I will do my best, but I think she only wants to run and play with Jesus and her brother."

"We must get her to focus somehow," said Azor, "especially on that group."

"I will try," said Daryush.

When they reached that corner, the "sons of the prophets" were still going strong. Daryush looked at Azor and Azor nodded in affirmation that this was the group he meant. Daryush stopped and got down on one knee, holding his sister's face in both hands. He waited until her eyes were focused on his and then he darted his eyes to the side, toward the chanting men and then turned Dunya's face toward them. She tried to escape but her brother held her fast and for a moment, it seemed that she understood the gravity of the situation. She looked at each member of the group one by one and then looked back into her brother's eyes. She shook her head slightly and then dropped her eyes. Daryush let her go and patted her on the shoulder. No one else attracted her attention all the way back to camp. No one, that is, but Jesus.

Conversation around the campfire that night was subdued. The distraction of trying to find a criminal while celebrating Yom Kippur did not lend itself to singleness of purpose. The seeming futility of identifying the criminal was on every mind. And the weight of the travel weighed on everyone.

Jesus took charge of the lamb, feeding it by hand and giving it fresh water from the spring. He then tethered the lamb with the donkeys and mules where it soon settled down to chewing its cud. Cyrus came to plead with him to come and play in the olive grove with the other children, but Jesus saw Dunya watching him as intently as ever from behind a tree. He elected to stay in camp with his father and Azor. He didn't want to run through the olive grove as though he had no care in the world. And he didn't want to be far from his earthly father while an alien spirit stalked him from within a playmate's body. He curled up next to Joseph, leaned against him and moved Joseph's arm to surround him.

"Are you alright," asked his father.

"I'm alright," Jesus answered. "I just want to be close to you."

Joseph hugged his son to himself and looked across the fire at the girl watching from behind a tree. He stared back at her until she slunk off to play with her brother and the other children. He felt, rather than heard, the deep sigh that escaped Jesus when she left.

"You know," said Azor, "I think it was a fool's errand to bring that girl here. I don't believe she knows what her attacker looks like. I'm not even sure she understands why we brought her here."

"It's hard to say what she understands," said Joseph. "Just because she didn't identify the one you wanted her to, it doesn't mean she won't identify anyone."

"True enough," sighed Azor.

"And Yom Kippur is far from over," added Joseph.

"I know," said Azor. "But we can't even reason with her. We can't make sure that she knows who we are looking for." Jesus held his peace and fell asleep leaning against his father.

The second day in Jerusalem went much as had the first. They took a different route through the city in the hopes that they might stumble across the attacker, but they were no more successful than on the first day.

On the third day, Dunya's mother declared that she was too tired to go up into the city that day. She would stay in camp and keep Cyrus with her. If Dunya wanted to go with Daryush for one more look, she was welcome to go, but only if she wanted to go. When Dunya saw that Jesus was going into the city, she wanted to go as well. Jesus was to lead the lamb, for this was the great day of the feast and the lamb would be sacrificed.

238

Because of the presence of the lamb, and because of the great crowd, their progress was rather slower than before. Daryush and Azor reasoned that their chances of happening upon the attacker were increased because of the greater crush of people. Joseph kept a watchful eye on Jesus and placed himself between him and Dunya as often as possible, as though by his body he could avert the demon gaze. Jesus focused on the lamb and began thinking about what would await this innocent lamb once they reached the court of the temple.

It was late morning by the time they made their way through the throng to the major intersection where the "sons of the prophets" were again making quite a show of their ecstatic devotion. There were eleven of them this time, their number having been swelled on the great day of the feast by new faces. Eleven shaven heads waved in the air like so many cobras following the piping of a twelfth man, whose head was not shaved. As the party of pilgrims came alongside the chanting and swaying prophets, Jesus' eyes fell upon the piper and at the same moment, the piper's eyes flew open and he stared straight back at Jesus. Then the piper's eyes rolled back in his head and Jesus gasped, "Father, save me!" He dropped the rope by which he had been leading the lamb and grabbed his father's cloak, trying to get out of the musician's eyesight.

Daryush had been leading his sister by the hand and watching her for any flicker of recognition, but when Jesus dropped the rope, the lamb started to dash through the crowd in a panic. Daryush let go of Dunya and lunged after the escaping lamb and Azor took a different course through the crowd, trying to head off the plunging lamb.

In that utter chaos of Joseph responding to Jesus and the other two men chasing the escaped lamb through the crowd, no one but Jesus saw the change that came over Dunya. From the shelter of his father's back, he looked aside at Dunya as her eyes, for once, stared at someone other than him. As she stared at the piper, her eyes were as big as eggs and her mouth flew open and she began to tremble from head to foot. She reached into the bosom of her gown and drew out an object and flung it in the astonished piper's lap. Then before anyone could even see what she had thrown, she drew a slender stone knife out of her sleeve and with an unearthly scream threw herself at the piper.

The girl was lithe and strong, if small for her age, and her aim was deadly accurate. If the piper had not thrown up his hands in self-defense, the blow would likely have gone to his heart. But his reaction caused her blow to go somewhat astray and she drove the knife almost to the hilt into his left shoulder. He roared and fell over backwards as she aimed two more blows in rapid succession at his chest, but alas, the blade of the knife had broken off in his shoulder so that the blows were more like punches than stabs. At that point, Dunya spit in the man's face and fled as fast as she could move, dodging under the arms that tried to grab this slender, girlish attacker.

Everyone was running and shouting. Some were trying to flee, lest they be attacked, too. Others were trying to get to the injured musician to offer aid. Others were dashing after the girl who had created the scene. Jesus plunged into the chaos in pursuit of the deaf girl who had plagued him for three days. As he ran, he prayed. He prayed to his heavenly father for protection, not of himself, but of the deaf Samaritan girl who had apparently tried to murder one of the sons of the prophets.

He ran as fast as he could and kept watching ahead for glimpses of the girl's blue cloak in the crowd. Sometimes he knew which way she had gone simply by the way the passers-by were staring in her wake. It became for him much like a deadly-serious game of hide and seek, but instead of trees and rocks and bushes, the hiding places were people and animals, buildings and markets. After running for several minutes, he found himself in a part of Jerusalem that he had never seen before. He realized that he was barefoot and wondered when and how he had lost his sandals. By this time, he and Dunya had outstripped all pursuit and the crowds were getting thinner. It was easier to keep her in sight. He began to worry about finding his way back. He worried about explaining how he lost his sandals. But most of all, he worried that Dunya would be caught and destroyed with no one to defend her, no one to explain her situation.

Then he lost sight of her as she turned a corner. When Jesus reached the next corner, he saw only a very quiet, normal street scene with only a couple of stray dogs and one donkey tied in front of a hovel. The donkey switched its tail at some flies but did not look at all disturbed, as it should have been if a girl had just dashed past. The dogs looked at Jesus, hoping for some handout, but there was not even any dust in the air to indicate a hurried passage.

Jesus stopped and turned the other direction but saw nothing at all of interest. He retraced his steps to discover what he had missed. Just before the corner he discovered a narrow wooden door that was ever so slowly moving on its hinges. There was no breeze; the door shouldn't be moving unless someone had recently passed through it. He pushed it tentatively and it swung open. "Hello?" he called. No one answered. He pushed it wider and peered around inside. It was apparently a back door into a somewhat disused market place. Tables were placed under handmade shelters as if in preparation for a busy market day. But most of the tables were empty. Perhaps this was a market that only operated on some days. It was certainly not in use today.

Jesus stepped through the door and began to search for Dunya. It was pointless to call for a deaf person, so he moved very quietly, trying to detect any sound or motion that might give away her hiding place. It was just possible that she had run through the market and out the other end before he discovered the moving door, but he didn't think she had. He was completely out of breath; surely she was tired, too, and needing a quiet backwater in which to disappear.

Around the perimeter of the market were some more permanent shops, but they all seemed closed and silent. Jesus walked quietly through the abandoned market looking for any cranny in which a girl could hide.

One of the merchants around the perimeter had a supply of clay pots, but none of the ones sitting outside his door were large enough to conceal Dunya. Under one of the tables he discovered a large crate of rags. He probed among the rags but no girl was hiding there. Then he saw what he was looking for and what, doubtless, Dunya would have been looking for. There was a basket merchant who had a permanent shop along the north side of the market. And in front of her shop was an array of baskets for sale. Among them were two that were large enough for Dunya to hide in and only one of the two had a lid. That had to be her hiding place.

He tiptoed up to the basket and quietly sat down next to it with his back against the wall. He could hear her rapid breathing inside the basket but knew that she would not be able to hear his. Jesus was not quite sure what he would do with Dunya now that he had found her, but he sat and thanked his Heavenly Father that he had discovered her and that, so far, no one else had.

He sat quite still for at least an hour. He heard Dunya softly snoring at one point and prayed that she would have her fill of sleep and that she would be delivered from that spirit that stared out at him through her eyes. She had not slept long when he felt the basket tremble against his right arm. He perceived that she was awake and shifting about in the basket. He watched as the lid of the basket began to rise stealthily on the side away from him. He waited as that side went down and then the side toward him began to rise. He gazed steadily at the widening gap and then Dunya's black eyes met his. She gasped audibly and dropped the lid back down. He continued sitting silently beside her hiding place and slowly the lid went up again. When she looked at him again, he laid his index finger across his lips and winked at her. She continued looking at him for a few more seconds but it was not the unwelcome stare to which he had reacted before. These were the eyes of a frightened girl, not those of an evil being. He thought again of the eyes of the man whom she had attacked. He had only seen them briefly, but he knew evil when he saw it.

Dunya continued to rest in her hiding place and Jesus continued to sit alongside. He still had no idea what he could do, other than be the watchman over her wicker fortress. Just before the sun went down, an old woman came into the market and limped toward where the two children were sitting. When she was only a few paces from where Jesus sat, she started and gave a little cry. "Hello, do I know you?" she asked, peering at him in confusion
.

"No, ma'am, I don't think you do," replied Jesus, hoping that Dunya wouldn't choose that moment to peek out.

"Well, who are you and what are you doing here?" asked the old woman.

"I am a pilgrim from Galilee and I need a place to rest," said Jesus. "Is it okay if I sleep here tonight?"

"Sleep here?" cried the woman. "I barely have room for myself. I have no room for travelers."

"I meant right here," said Jesus. "I didn't mean to ask for room in your house."

"This is no place for a traveler to sleep," said the woman. "And where are your father and mother? Surely you did not come from Galilee alone!"

"I came with my father, but I was separated from him in the crowd. I'm sure I will be able to find him in the morning," said Jesus.

The woman looked at him for a moment in silence. Then she said, "Have you eaten any supper?"

242

"No, ma'am," he answered.

"Well, I don't have much myself, but at least you must come in and share what I do have."

"If you please, ma'am, I'd rather wait out here. Perhaps my father will come looking for me but he would never knock at your door." Jesus felt the basket jiggle slightly against his arm but the woman didn't seem to notice. When the woman glanced away, he bumped the basket sharply with his elbow and hoped that this would convey a warning to Dunya.

The woman muttered something to herself and then reached into the shopping basket she carried on her arm. She pulled out a fresh, flat round of bread and tore it in half. Giving Jesus one of the two pieces she said, "Well I can't have you starve to death on my doorstep. Eat this and I will bring you some water. You must be thirsty."

"You are very kind, ma'am. May our Heavenly Father repay you for this kindness," said Jesus.

She lifted the latch and hobbled past him into her humble dwelling. Before closing the door, she struck a flint and lighted a candle. As soon as the door was closed, Jesus lifted the lid and again signaled Dunya that she should sit very still and stay quiet. He handed her the bread and lowered the lid. Soon the door swung inward and the old woman peered out. "Here," she said handing him a cup of cool water.

He took a sip and said, "Thank you so much. Your kindness will not go unrewarded."

"You can refill the cup at the cistern by the entrance to the market," she said, pointing. "But where are your shoes? Surely pilgrims don't come from Galilee barefoot."

"I had sandals until this afternoon," said Jesus. "I seem to have lost them running here and there in the crowds."

"What a careless child you are," exclaimed the woman. "Why didn't you stop when you lost them?" Jesus just shrugged and took a sip of the water.

"And what have you done with the bread?" she asked.

"I was very hungry, ma'am," stammered Jesus. "And bread is for eating, is it not?"

"My goodness, child. It's a miracle you didn't choke!"

She turned back into the house and soon returned with the other half of the bread that she had torn in two. "Here," she said. "You must be ravening like a wolf."

"But I can't leave you with nothing to eat," protested Jesus.
"It's true that I was planning on eating that bread," she admitted, "but I have other provisions here and you seem to be in dire need."

"I am fine now," said Jesus. "You take this half."

"May the Lord do terrible things to me if I accept that bread back, having given it to a hungry child," answered the woman. She continued to stand there watching him until he tore off a small piece and began to chew it. Then she began muttering to herself again and turned back into her house. When she returned to the door the next time, she brought a large cloak of two sheepskins sewed together. "Here," she said. "Cover yourself with this so you don't become ill from the cold."

"God bless you, dear woman," said Jesus. "My own mother couldn't be more generous."

"God keep you, child," said the woman and disappeared into her house.

Jesus waited for several minutes lest the woman should again appear at the door. Then he quietly lifted the lid to the basket and offered the cup to Dunya. She drank eagerly and tried to give the cup back to Jesus but he indicated that she should drink it all. So she tipped her head back and emptied the cup. When he reached out to retrieve the empty cup, she grabbed his hand and kissed it in gratitude. He tore what was left of his bread and gave half to Dunya and lowered the lid. Before it was completely dark, he found the cistern that the woman had told him about. He filled the cup twice and drained it eagerly. He filled it a third time and carried it back to Dunya.

He heard the woman's shuffling footsteps moving about the house once more, so he quickly wrapped the sheepskin cloak about himself and pretended to sleep, huddled on the ground by the basket in which Dunya was hiding.

The door creaked open and a candle shed soft light on the boy in the sheepskin wrap. The old woman muttered softly to herself and closed the door once again.

When Jesus could hear the old woman snoring, he lifted the lid of the basket and tried to give Dunya the sheepskin cloak. She rejected it and climbed quietly out of the basket. She stood and stretched, obviously glad to get out of the confines of the basket at last. When the moon came up, they tip-toed quietly through the abandoned market place trying to get their bearings. But when a dog began to bark, Jesus reached out and took Dunya's hand and led her back to their refuge for the night. Dunya declined to get back into the basket, so the two huddled together under the sheepskin and waited for what the new day would bring.

Jesus couldn't stop reviewing the events of the day. He wondered what had become of the lamb. He wondered what it was that Dunya had thrown in the lap of the piper. He wondered whether Joseph and Azor were still searching for him or whether they were back at their wonderful camp in the garden. He wondered what had happened to the injured piper and a shudder ran through his whole body when he remembered the way the piper had looked at him. He prayed that the piper would not find them before Joseph and Azor and Daryush did. He imagined Dunya's mother and Cyrus waiting alone at the camp in the garden and prayed that they would not be overwhelmed by fear. He knew when Dunya fell asleep by her regular breathing. He imagined how she had spent the night lost and wounded and alone, the night in the woods after the piper had assaulted her. His tears came unbidden as he thanked his Heavenly Father that she didn't have to spend this night alone. It was a long, long time before he dozed off.

Two roosters began a crowing competition as soon as there was a hint of light on the eastern horizon. Jesus turned over lazily and his hand struck the basket. He awoke with a start and looked about in confusion. He had been dreaming that he was at home in Nazareth keeping his little brothers and Hannah out of trouble while their parents were away. When he realized where he really was, he was alarmed and on his feet in an instant. Dunya was gone.

The moon had set and there was not enough light to see from one end of the market to the other. He hurried toward the cistern but Dunya was not there. He went down the road in front of the market looking right and left but did not see a soul. He returned to the cistern and started up the road above the market, praying that he would find Dunya before she came to any harm. When she popped out from behind a farmer's cart, his heart skipped a beat and he nearly screamed. He wanted to be angry but the look of delight on her face made him remember how much she loved playing hide-and-seek and he couldn't stifle a grin.

Then she surprised him again by presenting him with two beautiful eggs, still warm from being laid. He tried to ask where she had got them from but if she understood his intent, she ignored it. They walked back to the market and both drank deeply of water from the cistern. Then they folded up the sheepskin cloak and laid it neatly on top of the basket in which Dunya had hidden. They placed the cup on top of the cloak. On impulse, Jesus placed the two eggs carefully beside the cup and pointed toward the door. Dunya nodded enthusiastically and the two children walked away, hoping to find a way to return to the safety of their families and camp.

Jesus led the way down the road from the market. He had the sense that the temple lay in that direction. And he reasoned that if he could find the temple, he could probably find his way back to the garden outside the city. But he was worried that near the temple he might also find the sons of the prophets and the wounded piper with the demon eyes. So they proceeded cautiously, trying to see far ahead to ascertain whether their way was dangerous or not. Before they found the temple, they arrived at a colonnade beside a pool of water. They stopped to bathe their bruised and dusty feet.

The light was growing stronger with every minute and they could now see up and down the street. But they did not see before they were seen.

"Jesus!" rang out an excited male voice behind the two children. Jesus jumped and his head swiveled around toward the shout. Dunya's eyes followed his and they both leaped to their feet as Joseph swept down upon them and grabbed one of them in each arm and held them tight. Tears were welling in his eyes and soon overflowed down his cheeks. He began laughing and crying at the same time until tears were flowing from the children's eyes as well. And still he held them and would not let them go.

When he began to regain his composure, Joseph gasped and said, "You cannot believe how I have worried about you two. We searched all over the city until it was too dark to see and we have hardly slept a wink, not knowing where you were or whether you were safe."

"But we have a Heavenly Father watching over us..." said Jesus.

"Of course you do," said Joseph. "But to a worried earthly father that is not always comfort enough."

"Peace, Abba," said Jesus. "We are safe in God's care."

"Thank you Heavenly Father," blurted out Joseph. "Thank you for answering our prayers and setting a secure watch over your children. We are helpless before the evil one except by your protection. May your name be praised forever."

"Amen," said Jesus. "But where are the others?"

"Daryush and Azor and the two servants and I have each taken a different portion of the city this morning to search for you two. We are to meet near the temple at the third hour to report to each other. Cyrus and his mother are at the camp in the garden in case you should find your way there before any of us found you. Praise the Almighty, I was the one blessed with success, double success. For we had no way of knowing whether you were alive or dead, whether you were together or lost separately."

"We have been together. I followed Dunya when she ran through the crowd and lost her for a little while but God led me to her hiding place."

"But where did you spend the night?" asked Joseph. "You must have been cold and afraid and hungry."

"I will admit to being a little bit afraid," said Jesus. "But the Lord was watching over us and sent an angel to give us food and water and a nice sheepskin cloak for warmth."

"An angel?" said Joseph with interest.

"Well, she might just be an old woman but she was God's messenger to us, without a doubt," said Jesus. He proceeded to tell Joseph all about their adventure of the night before. As he told the tale, Joseph looked from Jesus to Dunya and back again as the tale went on.

Finally Joseph released the two children and began to relax. "Well you must be ready for some breakfast and it is only now sunrise. We won't be able to meet the others for three hours. I saw an inn just down there," he said, pointing. "Let's head there."

"I'm sorry to say that I lost my sandals in the scramble yesterday," said Jesus, indicating his bare feet. "And Dunya lost hers too."

"But I found yours this morning," said Joseph. "And I may have found hers as well. It gave me real hope that I was on the right track." He reached into his satchel and brought out two pair of sandals. The children brightened up as they recognized their lost belongings and quickly slipped them onto their feet.

As they started on their way, Jesus said, "Abba I have so many questions. I don't know where to begin."

"Begin wherever you like," replied his father. "I don't know if I have the answers, but feel free to ask."

"Well, to begin with," Jesus said, "Who is that piper with the evil eyes and is he also looking for us?"

"Ah, excellent question, son," said Joseph. "May all of the Lord's enemies end up where he has gone. He will not bother you or Dunya ever again."

"Then... she killed him?" asked Jesus.

"Oh no, she did him no mortal damage," said his father. "That wound would have cost him some blood and no doubt a lot of pain. But that did not bring him to his well-deserved end."

"Then he is still alive?" asked Jesus with some alarm.

"No, no, my son. He is no longer alive, but Dunya is not guilty of his life blood."

"So, what happened?" asked Jesus.

"Well, you remember how crowded the street was and how chaotic the scene even before Dunya fell upon the man."

"Yes?"

"Well it became far more chaotic as soon as she fled. The crowd was stampeding in every direction, some to escape, some to see what was going on. Every man was shouting, every woman screaming. The piper jumped up and tried to flee."

"To flee?" asked Jesus, "or to chase after Dunya?"

"That is not clear," said Joseph. "At the sudden tumult, the Centurion gave the alarm for his troops to rush into the scene to restore order. Five mounted Romans tried to gallop through the crowd and their action made the stampeding crowd completely mindless. People were running in every direction and stumbling over each other in their panic. The piper dashed headlong into one of the horses and was knocked aside, striking his head on the stone pavement. That blow might have killed him, but if that weren't enough, he was trampled by scores of people who were trying to get out of harm's way. Even if he hadn't struck his head, the trampling might have killed him. But it seems very clear that Dunya's knife didn't kill him."

"I wish she could hear you tell this story," said Jesus. Dunya had been watching Joseph's animated face and gestures but of course, could not hear a single word. Jesus tried to tell her the gist of the story through miming. It was easy enough to mime a piper and to mimic his horrible staring eyes. And it was not too hard to convey that the man was dead and finished. It was harder to convey to her that her knife had not killed him, but after miming a collision with a horse and a trampling crowd, he noticed tears welling in her eyes. It seemed clear that they were tears of relief and of hope. Jesus put his arm around her slender shoulders as she was racked with sobbing. Joseph gripped one of her hands and they waited as waves of pain passed over her mind and slowly subsided.

As they continued down the road toward the inn, Joseph glanced at Jesus and said, "You don't seem wary of her any more. What has changed?"

"She doesn't look at me out of someone else's eyes anymore," said Jesus. "Is it possible that the evil spirit returned to the one from whom she had received it?"

249

"I have no idea," said Joseph. "Thank God I am as innocent as a child in such matters."

"I don't know either," said Jesus. "But she has only her own spirit now."

"Praise be to the Almighty," whispered Joseph.

"Amen," said Jesus.

"Who was the piper?" asked Jesus.

"I don't know," said Joseph. "It would seem that he was the one guilty of assaulting Dunya. She had no doubt about his identity as the guilty party."

"No she didn't," agreed Jesus.

"And if that is true, he must have been a traveler on pilgrimage from Galilee three years ago."

"True," said Jesus.

"But that's all I know at this point."

"Did you see what Dunya threw into his lap before she stabbed him?" asked Jesus.

"I only caught a glimpse of it," said Joseph, "but it looked like a philactery with silver ornamentation."

"Do you suppose it was his?"

"I think it must have been. It made me think of the story of Tamar, daughter-in-law of our ancestor, Judah. Remember that she used his staff and his seal to identify him as the father of her child and to prove that she was not guilty of adultery?"

"Dunya must have kept it hidden for three years. Not even her family knew she had it or they would have presented it as evidence long ago."

"And I'm sure the piper did not give it to her willingly as a token. She may have ripped it off of him in the struggle," said Joseph.

They found the inn and soon were sipping hot, sweet tea and sharing fresh bread and yoghurt with a few figs and raisins. They lingered over their breakfast and kept adding details of their overnight fears and adventures. Joseph told how frightened Dunya's mother had been and how Cyrus had cried over being left with his mother while the others searched for his missing sister and playmate. Jesus told of his fright at awakening from a homely dream to find that Dunya had disappeared.

The longer they talked, the more Dunya seemed to relax and settle into a new sense of safety. The warm sunlight made her face radiant and Jesus marveled more than once over the change in her eyes. She still looked at him often, but now it was the same look she had for her little brother, Cyrus.

Finally it was nearing the third hour and time for them to make their way to the designated meeting place. They were the first to arrive and as soon as Dunya understood that they were waiting for the rest of their party, she became very playful. She indicated to Jesus that they should hide. Joseph didn't think it was a good idea and didn't relish the idea of letting them out of his sight again, but her playful spirit was irresistible. Soon the two children were secreted out of sight behind a pen full of lambs that were left over from holy day sales. But they kept watch to see who would be the first to join Joseph.

It wasn't long before Dunya spied her brother striding purposefully toward Joseph and Azor hurrying to catch up with him. Jesus saw that she was trembling with excitement as she gripped his wrist and held him down beside her for another moment. They could tell that the three men were beginning to exchange tales of futility but they could not make out the words. Joseph did well not to glance over his shoulder in the direction of the two hide-aways.

Finally, when Daryush and Azor turned their faces toward the traffic on the temple approach, Dunya slipped to her feet and pulled Jesus up with her. They rushed on tip-toe up behind the men and then Dunya shrieked and threw herself on her brother's back.

Daryush cried out in surprise and staggered under her attack. Azor exclaimed something unintelligible in his surprise and Joseph began to laugh. Jesus danced around the group in delight at the surprise. Daryush extricated himself from Dunya's grip and then swung her off her feet in a bear hug, swinging her in circle after circle as she laughed and he cried and then they both laughed and cried together.

"Why you heartless monsters!" cried Azor. "Have you been playing hide-and-seek this whole time? Where on earth have you been?"

"It was Dunya's idea," said Jesus. "She ran first."

Soon the two servants joined the merry party and with everyone laughing and talking at once, they began their descent out of the City of David. As they neared the corner where the riot had occurred the day before, there were armed Roman soldiers standing at attention on the very spot where the sons of the prophets had been chanting all week. No shaved heads were in evidence anywhere and the crowds were slipping past in somber silence, not daring to glance in the direction of the Romans.

Jesus noticed that his own merry party was also silent and subdued as they approached that intersection.. As they passed under the noses of the watchful soldiers, Jesus saw that the cobblestones under his feet were stained with blood. He wondered if it was the blood of the piper but he didn't dare ask. He glanced at Dunya but she was gazing up at her brother's face and didn't seem to notice.

When they were no longer in range of the Romans, Jesus tugged on his father's sleeve and asked, "Abba, what happened to the lamb?"

"That little fellow got away," answered Joseph. "We were all focused on finding you and Dunya and the lamb apparently ran for its life."

"Then what will we do for Yom Kippur?" asked Jesus.

"Yom Kippur was yesterday and I don't have money for another lamb anyway," said Joseph. "But I am thinking that an offering of two pigeons might be an appropriate way of giving thanks for the safety of our two 'little pigeons.'"

"I'm sorry about the lamb," said Jesus. "He was my responsibility and I..."

"Don't be sorry for concerning yourself with your fellow human being rather than with a lamb that was to be sacrificed anyway," said Joseph. "You did exactly the right thing. I am very pleased with you."

252

The tearful outburst from Dunya's mother as they entered the camp was not a surprise to any of the party, but the intensity of it did threaten to bring everyone to his knees with emotion. As she howled on and on, Jesus thought how lucky Dunya was to be protected from the noise by her deafness. Cyrus was wiping tears from his eyes as well, as he witnessed this reunion, but he soon wanted to run and play in the olive grove. Jesus was tempted to join him just to escape the woman's voluble display of the whole range of human emotion. But he couldn't leave as he was the only one who could put words to a critical part of the story, which had to be told and retold most of the afternoon.

In late afternoon, as they were all spent with emotion and refueled with good food, most of the party lay relishing the return of quiet to the garden. Joseph and Jesus did slip away and go back to the temple to sacrifice the pigeons as a thanksgiving offering to the God of their story, the God who had not only protected the children but avenged the assault on a little Samaritan maiden by striking down the wicked perpetrator.

Over supper that night, Daryush was very quiet. Dunya sat next to him and leaned on him as she ate. She clearly had more appetite than he did and kept urging him to eat. He accepted a bite now and then but it seemed that he was doing it to please her, rather than with appetite. Joseph finally addressed him directly, "Daryush, are you feeling alright? You don't seem quite yourself."

Daryush looked away into the darkness of the olive grove on the hill above the garden and started to speak and then checked himself with an obvious effort. Azor refilled the young man's wine cup and motioned for him to drink. Finally Daryush tipped the cup and took a long pull.

Then he spoke. "It is good that the earth is rid of that villain, but I regret that I did not smash his head with these two hands."

"I hear you," said Joseph. "It is natural to want revenge, especially for harm done to an innocent child. But be glad that this man's blood is not on your hands."

They sat in silence a few moments and then Joseph told the following story. "Our scriptures tell of a time when David was not yet king of Israel and he led a small army of discontented and violent men. It was during the time when Saul was king and was trying to do away with David. David took it upon himself to protect the property of a certain wealthy man, whose shepherds were caring for his flocks in the vicinity of David's hideout. When the wealthy man held a feast at the time of shearing, David sent some of his men to him in hopes of receiving a reward for his protection. But the man was ungrateful and harshly rejected any claim David might have on his hospitality. When David learned of this response, he and his men armed themselves and set out to destroy the man and his whole household. But the man's wife, Abigail, was a wise woman and when she learned what her husband had done, she prepared a generous gift of food and sent it to David by the hand of servants. Then she followed the servants and intercepted David on his way to avenge the insults of her husband. She succeeded in stopping the raid and in changing David's plan. And she said, 'When the Lord has fulfilled for you every good thing he promised concerning you and has appointed you ruler over Israel, you will not have on your conscience the staggering burden of needless bloodshed or of having avenged yourself.' Daryush, there may come a day when you will rejoice that it was not by your hand that Dunya was avenged."

Daryush nodded slowly and took another draft of wine. He held it in his mouth a long time before swallowing and then said, "Those are good words. Thank you for saying that."

Later, the subject of the phylactery came up again. "Oh, you mean this?" asked Azor, fishing the ornamented amulet out of his satchel.

"How did that come into your possession?" asked Joseph.

"I ran into Rabbi Zuriel this morning when I was looking for the children," said Azor. "He gave it to me."

"Did it belong to the piper?" asked Joseph.

"Of course it did," said Azor. "Rabbi Zuriel snatched it up during the chaos yesterday. He told me that he recognized it as belonging to Rabbi Kenan."

"Rabbi Kenan?" asked Daryush. "Is that the name of the piper?"

"Yes," said Azor. "He is... or I should say he was rabbi in Tiberias. He has long been part of that group of chanting hypocrites that gathers there every year at Yom Kippur."

"And Rabbi Zuriel had seen him with this philactery?" asked Jesus.

"Yes," said Azor. "There originally had been two, a matching pair. Zuriel had admired them four or five years ago. Then three years ago Kenan showed up as usual but with only one. He claimed to have lost the other one. After Zuriel had commented on what a pity it was to lose one, Kenan stopped wearing the other one."

"Surely he knew when and how he had lost the one, so he tried to remove the evidence of his crime by getting rid of the matching one," said Joseph.

"No doubt," agreed Azor.

Daryush held the amulet between thumb and finger to inspect it in the firelight. Then he turned questioning eyes on his sister and held it in front of her. She blushed and mimed how she had hidden it in the bosom of her gown for three years and had plucked it out and thrown it into the lap of her attacker.

"And that's why she hasn't let me wash her clothes for these three years!" exclaimed her mother. "I thought it was just her desire to be independent. I do declare, though I am her mother, I don't have half an idea how her mind works! Why wouldn't she show us that evidence?"

"Who knows," said Daryush. "I guess she wanted to keep it safe in her own control against that day when she would see him again."

"And all this time we have doubted that she even knew what we were looking for," marveled her mother.

Azor reached for the phylactery and examined it. "Aren't these supposed to contain tiny scrolls of scripture?' he asked.

"For a religious person, yes," said Joseph.

"Would you be curious to know what this one contains?" asked Azor. There was a general murmur of assent. Azor fumbled with it but could not get it open. Daryush took it from him and with the point of his knife pried up the silver ornament on one end and fished out a tiny yellowed scroll. He handed the scroll to Azor.

Azor studied it for a minute and then handed it to Joseph, saying, "I can't make it out in this light; can you?"

Joseph examined it and declared that the script was too small and the firelight too weak for him to read it."

Jesus was peering over his shoulder and reached for the tiny scroll. Lying down on his back with his head toward the fire, Jesus held the scroll up and slowly read these words: "I will ascend to the heavens; I will raise my throne above the stars of God; I will sit enthroned on the mount of the assembly, on the utmost heights of Mount Zaphon. I will ascend above the tops of the clouds; I will make myself like the Most High."

"Blasphemy!" exclaimed Azor.

"That is from scripture," said Joseph. "But those are the words of Lucifer and are indicative of his great sin. No one should use those words in his phylactery, especially not a rabbi."

Jesus turned softly and placed the little scroll in the middle of the fire. When the scroll was consumed, Daryush threw the silver-ornamented container in after it and they all watched as the leather wrinkled and writhed in the fire like a serpent and the silver disappeared into the ashes.

"I shouldn't wonder that a man with such a phylactery should be demon possessed," said Joseph. "I wonder what other wickedness he has wrought in Tiberias and elsewhere."

"We will probably never know the extent of his sin," said Azor. "The town of Tiberias is well rid of him."

"So will the town get a new rabbi?" asked Jesus.

"I happen to know," said Azor, "that the town of Tiberias will very soon have a new rabbi."

Everyone looked at him curiously. "And the town of Nazareth will be without one, praise God Almighty who answers my prayers."

"What?" exclaimed Joseph. "Rabbi Zuriel is moving to Tiberias?"

"That's what he told me this morning," said Azor with a wide grin. "He told me that he is dropping the case against my purchase of Nahor's house because, as he says, 'The Lord has called me to greater things.'"

"Wonderful!" cried Joseph.

"Hallelujah!" cried Jesus.

Azor continued, "That means that you and I have a lot of work to do back in Nazareth, my friend. Are you willing to leave in the morning?"

"We are," said Joseph.

"Yes, we are," said Jesus.

And they did.

December 2013

Eleventh Birthday
Are You My Abba?

"Good morning, Grandmother. I hope I didn't frighten you by coming in without knocking. Are you alright?"

"Good morning, Jesus. You didn't frighten me; I was expecting you."

"I've brought you some tea."

"Bless you, child. I should be offering you a cup of tea."

"Not until you are on your feet and quite well again," said Jesus.

"Sometimes I wonder whether I will ever feel quite well again," said his grandmother with a sigh.

"God heal you, Grandmother. You need not despair."

He sat quietly while his grandmother sipped at the tea. "Mother would have come herself, but she is quite busy with Hannah and Simon."

"I'm sure she is, bless her heart. How are they doing?"

"Hannah is almost herself again but Mother is keeping her inside. Simon is still quite feverish and cries all the time unless Mother is holding him."

"Ah, the poor child," murmured Grandmother. "I wish I could come and help."

"No more than Mother wishes she could come and help you. This sickness seems to attack the very young and the very … uh…" Jesus stopped lest calling his grandmother very old should be offensive.

"Now don't you feel bad about calling me old, Jesus. It is God's own truth. Why I was already old when you came here from Egypt and that was what? Six years ago?"

"No, Grandmother," said Jesus, "that was eight years ago. I was three when we moved here and now I am almost eleven."

"How can that be?" exclaimed Grandmother. "Has my Jacob been gone eight years?"

Jesus nodded. "He passed just before we arrived and we have been here eight years now."

"Then I am, indeed, a very old woman."

"Grandmother, can I bring you something to eat?" asked Jesus.

"No, my dear, I am not the least bit interested in food this morning."

"Is there anything I can bring you or do for you?"

"Would you check on my garden for me? I have not been out to tend it for over a week. I am sure it is as dry as dust and overrun with weeds."

"I would be happy to do that. I can bring water for your cistern, too."

"Bless your heart; you are a treasure!"

"Don't you worry about a thing. I will see to your garden." And with that, he dashed off and spent the next hour and a half pulling weeds, carrying water and tending to his grandmother's garden.

When Jesus came back to his grandmother's house midmorning, he again entered without knocking and crept to the door of her bedroom. When he found her sleeping, he crept out again and went to see if there was anything else he could do in her garden. He found a few more weeds to pull but soon he was back checking on his grandmother.

She roused out of her sleep when he opened her door. Jesus didn't say anything at first, waiting to see if Grandmother was indeed waking up or only momentarily disturbed. Spying him peeking through the door, she spoke, "Come in, sweet Jesus. I'm awake."

"I don't want to bother you, Grandmother."

"You are no bother. Why would I be bothered to see you?"

"How are you feeling? I peeked in a little while ago and you were sleeping."

"Yes, I drifted off but I'm done with sleep now for a while. How did you find my garden? Was there anything left of it?"

"Yes, of course. Your garden is doing well. I pulled a lot of weeds and watered it thoroughly."

"I suppose the cucumber vines were dead, though, weren't they?"

"Do you mean those vines at the far end with the dark green pointy leaves and yellow flowers?" asked Jesus.

"Yes, do they have blossoms, then?" she asked.

"They were wilted pretty much but I watered them well and the leaves look good again already," he said.

"I don't suppose there were any fruits on the vines, were there?"

"I didn't notice any but I can go look again," he offered.

"Would you? The fruits often hide under the leaves. I would love to have some cucumber yoghurt salad."

"I'll go check," said Jesus and slipped out of the house.
He was back in just a few minutes. "No, Grandmother, I can't find any fruit but lots of blossoms. I think several blossoms have opened just since I watered this morning."

"Well, we can't have fruits without having blossoms first," she replied. "Are there any female blossoms or just male ones?"

"Are you trying to make me laugh, Grandmother?" asked Jesus. "None of the blossoms were wearing skirts or long hair."

Grandmother chuckled in spite of her weakness and exclaimed, "Now that would be a sight to see! Female blossoms wearing skirts! I think it is you, trying to make me laugh. Were there any bees working the flowers?"

"Yes, I did see a couple of bees climbing down inside the flowers. Is that important?"

"Why yes, of course!" said Grandmother. "If the bees don't transfer pollen from the male flowers to the female flowers, the vine will not produce fruit."

"Then you were serious about male and female flowers, Grandmother? I thought you were teasing me."

"And are you so unfamiliar with cucumber vines, dear boy?" asked Grandmother. "It was your father who brought seeds back with him from Egypt."

"I guess I have been too busy in the wood shop and with my studies, Grandmother. I never heard of a plant having female and male flowers."

"Well, cucumber vines do. And here's how you can tell them apart. The first blossoms to appear on the vine are always the male flowers. And the stems that lead to the male flowers are slender right up to the back of the flower. As the vine gets larger, it begins to produce both male and female flowers. If you follow the stem of the female flower out toward the blossom, you come to a wider, fleshier part at the end of the stem just before the back of the flower. That fleshy part becomes the fruit, but only if the bees transfer pollen from a male flower of a different cucumber vine."

Jesus looked dumbstruck for a moment and then said, "Well, I'll go look a little closer." And off he went to the garden once again. When he came back in he reported, "The smallest vine has six blossoms but they are all male. The other two vines have mostly male blossoms but there are two female blossoms on one and one on the other."

"Well, praise the Almighty," said Grandmother. "When I was last able to tend my garden the vines were just beginning to produce male flowers. I am so glad they didn't die!"

"And I'm so glad that you sent me out there. They were really looking sad before I watered them."

"Yes, they require a lot of water. I would be so grateful if you would check on them every couple of days until I get stronger. How about the melons? How are they doing?"

"They were wilted, too, but not as bad as the cucumbers. And they are perking up now that I gave them water."

"Do they have any melons developing yet? I would love to have a bite of melon right now."

"There are a few very small melons starting to swell up and one that is large enough to eat but not yet ripe. I will keep an eye on it and harvest it for you as soon as it is ready."

"Oh, that would be lovely," sighed his grandmother.

"Let me run home and get you some bread and yoghurt right now so you do get stronger. And I can run to the market and see if I can buy any cucumbers or melons."

"No, no, don't seek them in the market, Jesus. I doubt there would be any there and if there were, they would be too expensive."

"I'll be right back, Grandmother."

When Jesus came back he had flat bread wrapped in a cloth and a bowl of yoghurt for his grandmother. "Mother is coming in a few minutes with some tea," he said.

"Bless you, Jesus. Thank you for caring for me."

"Abba is busy adding a room to our house so you can move in with us," said Jesus.

"Oh, he shouldn't do that," said his grandmother. "I will only be in your way. And I love this house. I have my garden here and I can't move it."

"You will not be in our way; we are more likely to be in your way, Grandmother."

"But I am not strong enough to help with the little ones or do the cooking and washing."

"But we would love to have you with us where we can watch over you better, at least until you get strong again," countered Jesus.

"Tell your father not to build that room for my sake," she said. "I prefer my peace and quiet here."

"I can tell him, but he won't stop building it. We need the extra space anyway and maybe you can stay with us just for a week or two until you get better."

"But," said his grandmother, "I'm afraid if I leave this house in my condition, I will never make it back here."

"You are not that ill, surely!"

"I am feeling very old, dear boy. I long to go rest with my Jacob, and with my dear parents, God rest their souls."

"Not too soon, Grandmother. We still have need of you here."

"What do you need me for? I can't do anything anymore," she said.

"You can still tell us stories about the olden days. You know stories that I have never heard. You have answers to questions that I haven't thought of yet. Don't be in a hurry to leave us, Grandmother, please."

"I won't go a day before the Almighty calls me," she replied. "But He may call me soon and when He calls, I won't delay a minute."

She began dipping the bread into the yoghurt and eating, but she did it so slowly Jesus worried that she would fall asleep between bites. Then she looked up and asked, "What scroll are you studying right now?"

"The scroll of Samuel the prophet," said Jesus.

"Would your father let you bring the scroll here?" his grandmother asked. "I would love to hear you reading the scriptures."

"I'm sure he would have no objections. I can do my lessons here as well as there, as long as I am careful with the scroll."

"I won't be able to correct you like he does," she said. "But I would dearly love to hear God's word."

"I'll go ask him," offered Jesus and dashed out the door.

When he returned a few minutes later, he was carrying the box that he had made and carved, inside of which they stored one borrowed scroll of God's word at a time, from which Jesus studied. His mother, Mary, was there, having brought the promised tea. On her lap was his youngest brother Simon, squirming every which way and trying to reach everything on the bedside table. His sister Hannah was standing behind mother apparently feeling a bit shy about being in the presence of her ailing grandmother.

"There you are," said his mother. "I must have just missed you on the path."

"Hello Mother. I went to the shop to ask Abba if I could bring the scroll here to read for Grandmother."

"Are you up for that, Mother?" asked Mary. "I don't want him tiring you out."

"Of course I am up for it," said grandmother. "I asked him if he would."

"Well, I was hoping he would watch his sister for a little while," said Mary. "I want to run to the market and it is so much harder with two little ones in tow."

"Leave her here with us," said grandmother. "It should be safer for Jesus to watch her here than at the wood shop with all those sharp tools."

"But I don't want her to bother you," objected Mary.

"I will deal with that if it happens," said grandmother. "It won't hurt her to hear her brother read scriptures, will it?"

"He won't get much reading done with Hannah pestering him," said his mother.

"Well, whether much or little, it will be fine. You just run along and get your marketing done," said grandmother. "We will get on very well here."

"Okay," said Mary. "Hannah, you be good for Jesus and for Grandmother. I will hurry back."

So saying, she hurried off.

"Hannah, dear, you climb up here on the bed with me," said grandmother. "Jesus will read to us from the scroll of Samuel."

Hannah didn't say a word and climbed onto the bed but kept a little distance between her and her grandmother.

"I don't think Hannah has ever seen you with your hair let down, Grandmother," said Jesus.

"Ah, is that it?" asked Grandmother. She made an effort to sit up straighter and pulled her hair back from her face, quickly tying it in a semblance of a bun. "I usually wear my hair more like this. Is that better?"

Hannah visibly relaxed and her usual smile spread across her face. Now she crawled the length of the bed and snuggled against her grandmother, ready for Jesus to read.

Jesus took the lid off the box and reverently drew out the scroll. "I've been reading this with Abba for some weeks now, but I can begin at the beginning if you like, Grandmother."

"That would be fine," she replied. "Wherever you would like to read, I will be pleased to listen."

Jesus began to read, "There was a certain man from Ramathaim, a Zuphite from the hill country of Ephraim, whose name was Elkanah, son of Jeroham, the son of Elihu, the son of Tohu, the son of Zuph, an Ephraimite. He had two wives; one was called Hannah and the other…"

"That's my name," said Hannah.

"Yes, that's your name," said Jesus.

"My name is in the scroll?" she asked.

"Yes, it is. Right here." He held the scroll in front of her and pointed to the letters of her name. "Right here. These letters spell Hannah," said Jesus.

Hannah smiled and settled back against her grandmother to listen as her brother read further. "He had two wives; one was called Hannah and the other Peninnah. Peninnah had children but Hannah had none. "

Jesus read on for some time. When he came to the story of Samuel as a young boy serving the Lord under Eli, he looked up and saw that his sister had fallen asleep against Grandmother's shoulder. Grandmother smiled and stayed quite still so as not to wake the sleeping child. Jesus stopped reading and just looked at the two of them for a moment. Then he whispered, "Grandmother, can I ask you a question."

"Of course," said Grandmother in a soft voice. "I think she is sufficiently asleep. You need not worry about waking her."

"Yesterday I was reading to Abba and I wanted to stop and ask him a question but James came dashing in and I never got to ask it."

"What did you want to ask?"

"Do you know the story of King David and Uriah the Hittite?" asked Jesus.

"Yes,"

"Why did David send for Uriah the Hittite and bring him home from the war on the Ammonites?"

"Ah, my dear, it was to cover up his own sin," said Grandmother.

Jesus looked shocked. "What sin? David was a man after God's own heart!"

"He was that," allowed Grandmother, "but he was also a sinner and he was trying to hide his sin just as all of us do."

"But," said Jesus, "what was his sin?"

"What he did with Bathsheba," answered Grandmother.

"That's the part I don't get," said Jesus. "He asked about her and when he found out who she was, he had her brought to him but then he fell asleep."

"Ah, well, um... " stammered his grandmother. "There was more to it than that. Did you not read about what Nathan the prophet said to David after this matter?"

"Not yet. I haven't gotten that far."

"Well, that should clear it up for you when you read that part."

"But if you know, why don't you explain it to me, Grandmother?" pleaded Jesus.

"No, ... I think it might spoil the story if I explain it before you read what Nathan said."

"Okay. Shall I read it now?" asked Jesus.

"No, not now," she said. "I think your mother is back from the market." And indeed, at that moment Jesus heard the sound of baby Simon's voice crying and his mother's voice trying to comfort him as she hurried.

Jesus carefully rolled up the scroll and placed it back in the carved container. He opened the door and took Simon into his arms as his mother swept into the room.

"How are you, Mother dear? Oh, how sweet!" she said as she saw Hannah sleeping against Grandmother's shoulder. "When I left she was acting so timid!"

"She warmed up to me soon enough," said the old woman.

"I hope she is not bothering you, Mother."

"Nonsense," said Grandmother. "She is very precious to me."

"Jesus," said Mary, "will you take my basket on home for me and see how your father is getting on with the twins? I'll just nurse Simon and then be home to make lunch."

"Shall I leave the scroll here, Grandmother? Perhaps I can come back this afternoon and read to you," said Jesus.

"Of course. That would be fine."

Jesus took the basket of vegetables home and then trotted toward the workshop. He found the door open and his father bent over his workbench showing James and Little Joseph how to sharpen a chisel. "You see," he said, "just a little oil on the stone and then keeping the chisel at just this angle, I slide it forward to grind off the bluntness and restore a keen edge. I pick up the chisel on the backward stroke and then set it down again at the same angle for the next stroke. If you change angles, you round off the edge instead of making it sharper."

"I get it," said James. "Let me try."

"I want to try, too," said Little Joseph.

When the shadow of Jesus fell across the doorway, they all three looked up.

"Ah, there you are," said his father. "I could use your help if you don't mind."

"Of course, Abba. How can I help you?"

"I need to go and make some measurements on the house and prepare for the adding of a room for Grandmother's use."

"If you tell me what you need, I can get the measurements, Abba," said Jesus.

"I need to do that myself, Jesus," he replied. "But you could help me by training your brothers in sharpening technique while I take the measurements."

At that, Little Joseph let out a groan and James rolled his eyes. Joseph either did not notice or did not choose to respond. He gathered his thoughts and his measuring tools and strode out the door.

As soon as Joseph had left, Little Joseph spoke up, "You don't need to show us anything. Abba already showed us how to sharpen tools."

"Yes," chimed in James, "we've got this covered so you can go study your scroll, Jesus."

Sensing their displeasure but not wanting to disappoint his father, Jesus stayed put. "If Abba has already told you how, perhaps I can watch how you carry out your training," he suggested.

"No, no," protested James. "You should go do something more important, like baby-sitting your scroll."

Ignoring the barb, Jesus said, "But since Abba told me what he wants me to do, I think I should obey him even if you don't agree. Let me see your skill at sharpening that chisel."

Little Joseph balked and said, "You just want to give a bad report to Abba about us so you will look superior."

"Yeah," said James, "there were reasons why Joseph son of Jacob got sold into Egypt."

Little Joseph laughed. "That's right," he said. "It was his arrogance that was the problem. You should be careful how you treat us. We might know some traders headed for Egypt."

Jesus stood quite still for a moment, trying to decide what to say or what to do. Finally, he said, "Little Joe, you are holding the chisel. Here is the stone. Show me what you have learned."

In frustration, his brother started sliding the chisel back and forth on the stone energetically but without the careful precision that Jesus had learned under his father's oversight.

"Stop, stop," cried Jesus. In response, Little Joe worked the chisel even faster and with even less precision. Jesus grabbed his brother's forearms in an effort to save the chisel from any further damage and in the ensuing struggle they both tumbled to the floor. As they fell, James threw himself across Jesus' legs and with their combined weight, the twins pinned Jesus to the floor. Jesus still held his brother's wrists but the chisel was still firmly in Little Joe's grip and the point of it was aimed at Jesus' face.

270

There was a loud roar from the doorway and Joseph Senior dashed in upon the boys, grabbing the chisel out of Little Joe's hand with his right hand and hauling him up against the wall by the front of his clothes with his left hand. "What in the name of righteousness is going on here?" he demanded. "Can't I leave you boys alone for one minute without it turning into a malicious brawl?"

"He started it," accused Little Joe. "He was bossing me around and tried to grab the chisel out of my hands."

"It's true," chimed in James. "Jesus started it. He's just trying to make you turn against us. He wouldn't let us sharpen the chisel the way you showed us."

Joseph turned to look at Jesus. Jesus was still picking himself up off the floor and dusting himself off. "Well?" said Joseph. "What's your story?"

"I'm so sorry, Abba," stammered Jesus. "They hate me without cause. They don't respect me and won't allow me to teach them how to handle a chisel. I can't tell them anything. I was just asking Little Joe to show me his skill, he started madly scraping the chisel all over the stone, ruining the edge. When I told him to stop he did it all the more energetically and wildly. I tried to grab his wrists to keep him from ruining your chisel. But then they both jumped me."

"Don't you lie to our father, you son of a perverse woman…" James' words were cut off by a sharp slap across his mouth.

"Who do you think you are to speak of your mother that way," shouted Joseph. "I will not have such talk coming out of your mouth!'

"But it's from the scroll, Abba!" cried James. "I heard Jesus read those very words."

Joseph looked at Jesus with open doubt all over his face.

"Those are the words of Saul to his son Jonathan when Jonathan supported David," said Jesus. "It was not intended as an example for the children of Israel to follow. It was one of those times when an evil spirit from the Lord was upon Saul."

"So is an evil spirit from the Lord upon you, James, that you should curse your own mother and on you, Little Joseph, that you would threaten your brother with a chisel?" Joseph was staring from one boy to another, at a loss for how to settle this unwelcome skirmish.

James was holding his stinging face in both hands and weeping openly. Little Joseph was cowering near the door but again said, "Jesus started it. He is always trying to boss us around."

"He is your elder brother and I gave him authority over you. If you ever become half as good at sharpening as he is, you will be useful to me in this shop. If you won't learn from him, you will remain a fool."

"See," wailed James, "he is always turning our own father against us!"

At that moment Joseph glanced in Jesus' direction and Jesus motioned with his chin toward the door. Joseph turned and found wide-eyed Hannah peeking around the doorpost at this violent scene.

"Oh... hello Sweetie," he said in a voice he hadn't used all morning. "We're just having a ... a... discussion here. Is lunch ready?"

Hannah nodded solemnly and ran for the house.

The pattern for the rest of that week was that Jesus would bring breakfast to his grandmother and read scripture to her from the borrowed scroll while she ate. Then he would do various chores for her and take care of her garden. Each day she would ask about the development of the cucumbers and the melons. After reporting to her about the state of the garden, he would go back home and report on the state of his grandmother. She continued to be mostly bed-ridden with a slight fever and a cough that she just couldn't shake.

On Friday morning when Jesus reported back to his mother, Mary said, "I don't think we can bring her here for the Sabbath meal this evening; we will have our Sabbath meal at her house."

"Good idea," said Jesus. "I can help you carry things."

"You can help me in other ways, too," she replied. "I want you to sweep out her house and clean the table. Make sure there is plenty of fresh water there and no yeast in the house. Then I want you to run out to Uncle Ezra's and invite him to come share Sabbath meal with us."

"Yes!" exclaimed Jesus. He relished the idea of having the Sabbath meal in his grandmother's house and having her huge, mostly silent brother share the experience with them. And he felt honored to be trusted to go alone to Uncle Ezra's place to deliver the invitation.

He hurried to carry out his mother's instructions. His grandmother perked up a bit when he told her that they were going to celebrate the Sabbath meal at her house. She perked up even more when Jesus told her he was going to go invite Uncle Ezra to join them. She asked, "Are there any cucumbers large enough to make some cucumber yoghurt salad? Ezra loves it with lots of salt and garlic in it."

"I'm afraid not, Grandmother," replied Jesus. "The vines are beginning to set fruit but they are still very small. I can check in town, if you like."

"No, that's alright," she said. "Don't go to extra expense. Is the first melon ripe?"

"Not yet," he said. "I think it will be in a couple more days."

When he finished his chores, he set out on his mission to visit Uncle Ezra and invite him to Sabbath meal. He had been to Uncle Ezra's place a few times with his father, but this was his first time to go there alone. On the way there, he practiced the gestures he thought might clearly convey that he was to come to his sister's house to eat at sundown.

Uncle Ezra lived somewhat out of town where he kept a number of horses and mules of his own and where he doctored animals for neighbors and friends at need. He was deaf and mute which contributed to a great deal of social awkwardness. but he had a wonderful sense of understanding with animals.

When Jesus was getting near his goal, he saw that he was not the only one visiting Uncle Ezra that day. And there was a good deal of excitement on hand. There was a Roman centurion there with another soldier and a servant. All four men were standing at the fenced stables and the horses were in a good deal of turmoil. Samson, the great black, Arabian stallion that Uncle Ezra had brought back from his time as a legionnaire was rearing and neighing and pawing the ground in a perfect frenzy. He was tied securely in a small pen that restricted his movements, but his energy and excitement filled the air. In the pen next to Samson was a grey mare that Jesus had not seen before.

The centurion was speaking Greek and the servant was translating into Aramaic for him, but Uncle Ezra was as deaf to the one as to the other and kept his eyes and his hands on Samson. He was stroking Samson in between the rearing and plunging and making soft noises to try to calm him, but it was having little effect. Jesus hung back and watched the action for a few minutes. The mare was restless, as was every animal in the vicinity, disturbed by the frenzy of Samson. The men were excitable, too, with the exception of great Uncle Ezra.

When the servant glanced Jesus in the background, he motioned for him to come near. "Who are you?" he asked.

"I am called Jesus," he replied. "Ezra is my father's uncle."

"Can you communicate with him at all," asked the servant.

"Yes, somewhat," said Jesus. "What is going on?"

"I am Jotham, a hired servant of this centurion. He brought this mare to be serviced by the great stallion but two days have passed and Ezra has not allowed them to come together. He is wondering why Ezra is keeping them separate and when he is going to fulfill his part of the contract. The mare is obviously in heat and the stallion is ready. What is the problem?"

"I know little about such things," said Jesus, "what do you mean by serviced?"

"You know," said Jotham, using a crude gesture, "serviced! He is supposed to get her pregnant. Make a baby."

Jesus blushed and replied, "I don't know much about horses, but Uncle Ezra is the expert around here. I'm sure he must have his reasons. Did your master agree on a price and pay it?"

"They agreed on a price and half of it has been paid. The other half is not due until the mare is clearly pregnant. But my master is getting impatient. He is under orders to travel to Cesarea in four days. He wants this business cleared up."

At that point, Uncle Ezra noticed Jesus. He stepped back from the heavy fence and greeted Jesus, kissing him on both cheeks and engulfing him in his huge embrace.

Using gestures, but avoiding the crude one Jotham had used, Jesus asked his great uncle when the two horses would come together. Uncle Ezra signaled that waiting was better. The right time would come. He didn't want Samson to hurt the mare or the mare to hurt Samson in their excitement. The mare had to become less frightened of Samson.

Jesus told this to Jotham who then translated the message into Greek for the centurion and his companion. They again expressed their urgency, which needed no translation for Uncle Ezra. He could read their impatience without hearing their words. He signaled that they should return in four more days. Jesus told Jotham that but the centurion rejected that answer. He insisted he would come back in three days. If by that time the mare had not been serviced, then the deal was off and he would demand his money back.

Uncle Ezra agreed to those terms and the party left. When they were gone, Ezra brought grain and water for Samson and the mare and then took Jesus aside for some tea. They sat in the shade where they could watch the two horses. Jesus conveyed the invitation to come for the Sabbath meal to Grandmother's house. Ezra showed real pleasure at the invitation and promised to come. Then he got up and led Jesus to a garden patch behind his simple dwelling. He searched among the leaves and brought out two long cucumbers and gave them to Jesus.

He also picked a double handful of beans to contribute to the meal. And a double handful for Uncle Ezra was a rather generous supply, his hands being so large.

When they went back to the animal pens, Uncle Ezra pointed out how much Samson had eaten and how much water he had drunk. The mare had eaten and drunk, as well. They watched a few minutes longer. When the mare came close to the fence that separated the two and touched muzzles with Samson over the fence, Uncle Ezra grunted with satisfaction and nodded.

Then he released the mare from her pen into a corral that adjoined the pens and continued to watch. When Jesus began to take his leave, Ezra motioned for him to stay. The mare circled the corral a couple of times and then approached the fence that separated Samson from the corral. Samson was straining against the rope that held his halter short at the other end of the small pen. Ezra released the rope and let Samson turn around. When his head came close to the mare's, she did not flee. Samson was trembling from nose to tail. His eyes were bulging and he was sweating. He tried to rear up as if to climb over the gate separating them, but Ezra brought him back to earth and with one hand swung the gate open. He released the rope and let Samson fly. Both horses took off with great energy but the mare only trotted around the corral a few times and then settled down.

Samson, on the other hand, seemed determined to impress this mare with his virility. With his tail held high, he raced around the corral at top speed, kicking and bucking and leaping into the air. When he got near the mare, he slid to a stop and tore off in the other direction in the same energetic manner. For several minutes, Samson prolonged the show until he was quite lathered up. When he began to slow down, the mare trotted alongside him for another lap or two. Finally, she stopped and turned. Ezra and Jesus held their breath as Samson mounted her.

Uncle Ezra clapped Jesus on the back and hugged him tight. Then he sent him on his way back home.

That Sabbath was a very memorable occasion for Jesus because of the mixture of the familiar routines with the disruption of having the Sabbath meal at grandmother's house. Instead of having her come to the meal, they were taking the meal to her. Instead of Grandmother helping his mother with the preparations, Jesus helped make the meal for Grandmother. And having Uncle Ezra come was out of the ordinary, as well. As Jesus cut up the cucumbers and stirred them into the yoghurt, he wondered if Uncle Ezra would come on Samson's back. He wondered if Samson would still be trembling and sweating and overly excitable. He imagined Samson tied outside his Grandmother's house, rearing and neighing. Surely Samson would break free and run away to be with the mare. If that happened, Uncle Ezra would have to run after him. Jesus hoped Samson would not spoil the Sabbath meal.

Half an hour before sunset, Jesus approached Grandmother's house carrying the bowl of cucumber-yoghurt salad. He was anticipating the joy his grandmother would express when she saw that dish and even more joy when she tasted it. He prayed as he walked that God would use this meal to strengthen her so that she could join them on their pilgrimage to Jerusalem as she used to do.

He was disappointed not to find Samson tied in front of the house and began to wonder if Uncle Ezra would come. But when he entered the house, he found him already there. He was sitting beside his sister's bed holding her hand and stroking her hair. Tears were rolling down Grandmother's cheeks. She was not even trying to wipe them away.

Jesus put the bowl on the table and asked, "What's wrong, Grandmother?"

She blew her nose on a handkerchief and said, "Nothing is wrong. I'm just overjoyed to celebrate the Sabbath one more time with my family before I go."

"Grandmother, where are you going?"

"I'm going to go up that hill where my Jacob, God rest his soul, is waiting for me. And I am going to lie down next to him and wait for the resurrection."

"Not yet, Grandmother!" cried Jesus. "Surely not yet! Do you not want to get strong again and enjoy your garden?"

"I'm very tired, Jesus," she said. "I am worn out and I don't think I will see that garden produce anything again."

"I've made you some cucumber-yoghurt salad," said Jesus.

"Did my vines produce cucumbers, then?" she asked.

"Actually, they are about to produce fruit, but these cucumbers are from Uncle Ezra's garden."

"Oh, bless his heart," she said, patting her brother's large hand.

Soon Mary and the other children bustled into the house bringing the rest of the meal and a great deal of noise and confusion. James and Little Joseph unburdened themselves and immediately dashed out to chase each other around the house. Hannah clung to her mother's skirts as she carried Simon on one hip and tried to arrange the preparations on the table.

"Good Sabbath, Mother," she said and soon came to check on her mother-in-law. She greeted Uncle Ezra and squeezed his hands. She kissed Grandmother on both cheeks and said, "You've been crying, Mother! Are you in pain?"

"No, no, I'm just being a sentimental old fool," she said. "I'm sorry to create so much extra work for you. I should be bringing food to your house."

"The Lord gives rest to those He loves, Mother. Just relax and enjoy your Sabbath."

Joseph came in a few minutes later, hands and face still damp from washing up. "Good Sabbath, Mother!" he said. "And good Sabbath to you, Ezra," he said, hurrying to kiss both of them. "I'm sorry I have come so late. I'm working on expanding my house to bring you under our roof, Mother."

"I would tell you to stop," said his mother, "if I thought you would listen but you won't. And you can use the extra space for your own growing family. I'm not going to need very much room at all. I'm getting ready to move up the hill next to your father, God rest his soul."

"Mother, don't be so pessimistic. God willing, you will soon be strong again."

"If He gives me strength, I will be strengthened," conceded the old woman. "But I suspect I'm almost through with my allotted days."

"Joseph, please come light the candles," called Mary. "The sun is setting and we are ready to begin. Jesus, go call your brothers."

Joseph lit the candles and Ezra carried his frail sister to a couch prepared for her beside the table. The Sabbath had begun.

Grandmother leaned against her brother and ate very little. Ezra tried to get her to eat, but she had very little appetite. She did eat some of the cucumber-yoghurt salad when Ezra spoon-fed her. And she seemed to appreciate the efforts everyone made to include her. But she seemed very tired.

"Grandmother," said Jesus, "I do hope you will get strong enough to go with us to Jerusalem this month."

"Oh, dear boy," she sighed. "If I ever see Jerusalem again, it will be a miracle."

"God still does miracles," said Jesus.

"He does," she agreed. "But I don't think I am strong enough to receive a miracle right now. I think the next journey I take will be up that hill to lie down beside your grandfather."

"Mother," said Joseph, "please don't talk like that. Don't give up hope."

"What hill?" asked James. "Where is our grandfather?"

"She means the graveyard on the hill beyond Uncle Seth's place," said Joseph. "My father, Jacob, was buried there just days before we returned from Egypt. That was before you were born."

"Can we go up there tomorrow?" asked Little Joe. "You can see ever so far from up there."

"I think that's a good idea," said Joseph. "The Sabbath is a good time to visit the tombs of our fathers. You can each put a stone of remembrance on his tomb. His parents are buried there, too. That is, your great grandmother and great grandfather along with my little sister who died when she was three."

At the mention of his sister, Grandmother began to weep. And the weeping made her begin to cough. Ezra gently picked her up and carried her back to her bed. Mary and Ezra tucked her in and tended to her until she stopped coughing and fell asleep.

The next day, Grandmother was so ill that Joseph and Mary were both too busy tending her to even think about visiting the graves. James and Little Joe, however, were so insistent on the outing that their father consented to let them go if Jesus would guide them and keep them out of mischief. Jesus agreed.

When they left the house, James was carrying a bag over his shoulder. Jesus asked, "What do you have there?"

"A treat," replied his brother. "A little something special to eat when we get up there."

"Did Mother give that to you?" asked Jesus.

"Yes, Mother gave it to me," said James. Little Joseph agreed.

Jesus thought it was strange that his mother would give such a treat into James' care. Usually such responsibility would be entrusted to the oldest brother. And he had not seen her give it to James. Perhaps his mother had been too preoccupied with Grandmother this morning. He let it pass without further comment, but he was puzzled.

They went through the middle of town on their journey. The market place was deserted and quiet on the Sabbath. Even the usual stray dogs had abandoned the center of town in search of scraps in the rubbish heap. The boys continued up the lane between a vineyard and an olive grove toward the home of Uncle Seth and Auntie Hobal. At the top, they turned right and entered an area on the other side of the ridge where many graves were warmed by the morning sunshine.

"This is grandfather's grave," said Jesus, leading his brothers to a small stone marker near the lower corner of the area. "And those two markers are for our great grandparents."

"Where's the one for Abba's little sister?" asked Little Joe.

"I'm not sure," said Jesus. "I was never told. Maybe it doesn't have a marker."

"Have you ever been up there," said Little Joe, pointing to the highest hill in the region. "Isn't that where 'the leaping stone' is?"

"Yes, it is," said Jesus. "I've been up there just once."

"Why do they call it the leaping stone," asked James.

"I've heard it said," said Jesus, "that when someone feels cheated in love, he goes up there and leaps to his death."

280

"And I heard about an infidel that was thrown off of there when he wouldn't give glory to God," said Little Joe. "Let's go up there and see it!"

"No," said Jesus. "We don't have permission to go up there."

"But there's nothing to do here," said Little Joe.

"Yeah, this is boring," agreed James. "What's the fun of visiting graves?"

"Well, normally Abba tells us stories of the people who are buried here."

"So are you going to tell us those stories?" asked James.

"I don't really know those stories, myself," said Jesus.

"So, let's go to the leaping stone. That place is more interesting."

"Maybe we should go back and ask Abba for permission to go up there," suggested Jesus.

"Fine," said James. "You go ask Abba for permission. And in the meantime, Joseph and I will start going that way."

"Yeah," said Joseph. And the two of them started off on the path toward the leaping stone.

"Wait," said Jesus. "We don't have permission yet!" But he couldn't dissuade them.

He stood still, torn between two obligations. He felt he needed Abba's permission to go but he was also under orders to keep his brothers out of mischief. He couldn't just abandon them in order to go seek permission. Reluctantly, he followed his brothers, calling after them to give up this fool's errand and come home. They ran ahead, trying to get out of the reach of his voice.

When they reached the leaping stone, the view was so grand that they were all silenced for a moment by the sense of being so small and so exposed. They went near the edge and looked down. Below them was a field of boulders that had fallen from these heights. "Wow," whispered James, "it must be two hundred cubits straight down!"

"Look," said Little Joe, pointing. "Isn't that a skull beside that large boulder down there?"

"No, I don't think so," said Jesus. "That's just a rock."

"I think it is a skull," said James. "We should climb down there and see."

"Don't be crazy," said Jesus. "Nobody would allow a skull to remain there. They would get it and bury it."

"Well," conceded James, "that might be a stone but I bet we could find human bones down there."

"I forbid you to go down there," said Jesus. "If you start down there, I am going to run get Abba and you will be in big trouble."

"You are such a girl," said Little Joe. "If you were really our brother, you would show us how to get down there and you would help us look for bones."

"Yeah," said James.

Jesus refrained from retaliating, watching to see if they would relent and stop their mad adventure. "Hey," he said, "what about the treat in that bag? Wouldn't this be a good place to eat it? How about back here in the shade of these trees?"

"No," said Little Joe. "Let's sit right here with our feet dangling over the edge and eat it."

"Yeah," agreed James. Let's enjoy the view."

"Come back a little bit," coaxed Jesus. "The view is just as good from here and we will be safer."

"Girls need to sit where it's safer," said Little Joe. "We men aren't afraid of a little danger, are we, James?"

"That's right," said James. "You stay safe and we will sit like men."

282

The drop was intimidating enough that the twins, daring though they were, sat down and then scooted toward the edge until their feet stuck out in the air. Their feet were not exactly dangling. Jesus sat cross-legged a little farther back but near enough to grab an arm if one of his brothers began to slip.

Then Joseph opened the leather bag and brought out a smallish melon.

Jesus looked at it in surprise and asked, "Where did you get that melon?"

"Mother gave it to us," said Joe.

"I don't think so," said Jesus. "Where did you get that?"

"We bought it in the market yesterday," said James.

"I don't believe you," said Jesus. "You asked to borrow money from me yesterday to buy grapes."

"Yeah," said James. "And you wouldn't give us any!"

"So where did you get the melon," Jesus asked, with growing suspicion.

"We borrowed the money from someone who was more generous than you," said Joseph.

"I think you are lying," said Jesus. "That melon isn't ripe enough to be sold in the market."

"Okay, okay," said James. "We picked it out of our garden. What's the big deal? Who made you judge over us?"

"We don't have a garden this year," countered Jesus. "You stole that out of Grandmother's garden, didn't you? She has been waiting and waiting for the first melon to ripen and you stole it!"

"Grandmother's garden is our garden," shouted Little Joe. "And at least she really is our grandmother, not yours! She's too sick to eat it anyway."

"Don't try to cover up your wickedness with foolish talk," said Jesus. "I am going to tell Abba what you have done!"

"He won't believe you if you do," said Joseph. "He's not your Abba, anyway. He's ours."

"Don't speak like a madman, Joseph!" said Jesus. "You are in enough trouble already. Abba will listen to me. I am his firstborn son."

"No, you're not," said Joseph. "James is, and I was born right after him. You were adopted!"

Jesus was stunned into silence by his brother's audacity.

"That's right," agreed James. "Abba adopted you to save Mama. Everybody knows that. Everybody but you."

Jesus gasped. "What do you mean everybody? If that was true, Abba would have told me."

"They probably didn't tell you because they knew you couldn't handle it," said Joseph.

"Abba told you this?" asked Jesus. He was incredulous at the thought.

"No, Malki told us," said James.

Malki was the little brother of Uri the shepherd. Jesus was sure his brothers were as untruthful about this as they had been about the source of the melon. But he was shaken by their bold accusations and outraged at their callous theft of Grandmother's first melon of the season.

"Do you have your knife," James asked Jesus. "Let's open this melon."

Without answering, Jesus reached out and took the melon from him. Then in one swift motion he stood up and raised the melon over his head with both hands.

"What are you doing?" shouted Joseph, scrambling to his feet. But he was not quick enough to stop Jesus from throwing the melon off the cliff.

"No!" cried James as all three of them watched the melon burst into pieces like a human skull thrown upon the boulders.

"Why did you do that?" shouted the twins in unison.

"I will not taste of that stolen melon and neither will you," said Jesus.

James began to weep openly and Joseph muttered, "I will get even with you for this."

Something in the malice of his tone made Jesus retreat from the edge of the leaping stone.

By the time they got home that afternoon, Jesus had many questions he wanted to ask Abba but Abba and Mother were so anxious and busy taking care of Grandmother that there was no opportunity to talk about what had happened at the graveyard and at the leaping stone. Jesus didn't even find time to tell them about his brothers' outrageous behavior. He reasoned that the family had enough trouble right now. His report on this whole outing, horrible as it was, would have to wait.

As soon as the sun set, the Sabbath was over, so Jesus brought water and tended his grandmother's garden in the failing light. He lamented the missing melon and saw that the melon vine had been damaged when the first fruit had been ruthlessly wrenched off, rather than carefully harvested. He marveled at the wickedness of his brothers and their disregard for truth and righteousness.

Early in the morning on the first day of the week, Jesus ran to Grandmother's house. He found his father already there sitting beside the bed.

"Abba, you are here early," he whispered.

"On the contrary," Abba whispered back. "You are here early; I am here late."

"Do you mean you spent the night here?" asked Jesus.

Joseph nodded. "Actually your mother and I took turns. But I have been here since the third watch of the night."

"How is she?" whispered Jesus.

Joseph shook his head. "She is not doing well. Right now she seems to be sleeping okay, but often her breathing is labored and she moans as if in pain."

"I brought this tea for her, but maybe you should drink it."

"No, keep it here for her. She might wake soon and want it. If you will watch her for a bit, I will go home and get more than just tea."

"Of course, Abba. I will call you if I need you."

After his father left, Jesus sat quietly watching his grandmother and praying for her recovery. It might have been half an hour later that she turned softly in the bed and began to cough. At first it seemed like she would just cough a few times and then go on sleeping, so Jesus held his peace. But the coughing grew persistent and more violent until she sat up in bed. Jesus greeted her softly and patted her shoulder. He found her a handkerchief and she held it to her mouth and coughed more. When she stopped coughing, she examined the handkerchief. Jesus saw that she had coughed up blood with her sputum.

"Oh, Grandmother," he said. "That is not good. Shall I go get Abba?"

"No, don't bother him," said Grandmother. He knows. He was here with me most of the night. Let him get some rest."

"But what can I do for you? How can I help?"

"There is nothing anyone can do for me, Jesus," she said. "My days here are finished very soon now. I hardly have the strength to cough."

"Will you drink some tea? It was hot when I brought it but the heat has gone out of it now."

"I will drink a little," she said.

"I can heat it over the fire," he offered.

"No, I will drink it as it is. If I spill it on me, it won't burn me," said Grandmother.

Jesus helped her steady the cup and she sipped a bit and then leaned back with a sigh. "That's fine," she said. I still enjoy my tea."

She sat quietly for a few minutes and then asked, "Did you go up to your grandfather's grave yesterday?"

"Yes." He wasn't sure what else to say. There were scenes with his brothers that he didn't want to describe to her.

"It is so peaceful there," she said. "He and I used to walk up there every Sabbath and visit his parents' graves. We would sit and admire the view. And he would talk to his mother and father. Can you believe that? It seemed strange to me at first, but he would tell them all about his week and what had happened in Nazareth, just like they were sitting there carrying on a conversation. I found it a bit strange at first."

"Did you ever talk to him up there? You know, after he was buried?"

"Only once, last year. I was sitting all alone up there on a Sabbath afternoon and I said, 'Jacob, I know you are not coming back to me. But one day soon, I will come lie down beside you. Then we will be together again.'"

"Did you cry?" asked Jesus.

"A little bit," she admitted. "But then I felt all peaceful inside. I'm not afraid to go, you know?" She said that as she patted Jesus' hand.

"I know you're not," said Jesus. "Have you been back there since that time?"

"No, that was the last time I went. Next time I go up there, I will stay."

She had another coughing spell. Jesus patted her shoulder until the spasm passed.

Then she asked, "Is that first melon ripe enough to harvest yet?"

Jesus swallowed a wave of emotion before telling her, "No, Grandmother, there is not yet a melon on that vine that is fit to eat." He consoled himself with the thought that he hadn't lied. He could not see any good coming from telling her what had happened to that first melon. In his mind's eye, he saw it bursting on the boulders at the bottom of the leaping stone and a shudder passed through him from head to foot.

"Well never mind that melon," said his grandmother. "If you feel up to it, you could read to me from the scroll."

"With pleasure," he exclaimed. He was always eager to read God's word, but especially if it meant changing from the current topic, fraught as it was with perplexities.

Grandmother continued to decline that week. Each day Jesus would take the morning watch and read from the scroll of Samuel. Sometimes he would have to stop reading her and support her while she coughed violently. Other times he would read, not knowing whether she listened with her eyes closed or whether she slept while he read.

On the fourth day of the week, he came to the end of the scroll and looked up. Grandmother's eyes were closed and she was very still. Something about her posture looked unnatural and he touched her shoulder to restrain her from slumping out of bed. She was limp and lifeless. She had climbed that hill for the last time while he was reading.

"Oh Grandmother," he gulped. "I wish I had seen you leaving! He secured her in the bed and then kissed her forehead. "Good bye, Grandmother," he cried softly. "Good bye. Tell Grandfather hello for me."

Then he ran to find Abba and Mother.

The next couple of days were filled with people, tears, stories and food. Grandmother had outlived many of her own generation, but the children of her friends remembered her warmly from their youth. They came by in family groups, large and small to convey their sympathies, to shed some tears, swap some stories and many brought contributions of food to help the family with the social obligations of losing a family member.

The funeral was on Friday and held early enough in the day so that it would not interfere too much with preparations for the Sabbath. Jesus was watching for Uri the shepherd or his brother, Malki. If Malki really had told James and Little Joseph that Jesus was adopted, Uri would probably know about it. Perhaps he would say that Malki is just a trouble-maker and not to worry about it. Or perhaps Uri hadn't even heard it and it was a vicious rumor, though Jesus could not think of any reason why Malki would start such a rumor. At any rate, Abba and Mother were far too occupied to deal with such questions. And if it were a vicious rumor, no need to bother them. He wished he could have brought up the topic with Grandmother, but…

After Grandmother was buried and the last psalm sung, Jesus stood in a kind of reception line with his parents and siblings and Uncle Ezra receiving condolences from neighbors. When the last stragglers were lining up, Jesus saw Uri slipping away. He almost didn't recognize him because he wasn't in his customary shepherd garb. He was all cleaned up and looked so different without a flock of sheep and no shepherd's staff.

It seemed that Uri would just leave without going through the reception line, but when Jesus caught his eye, he turned and followed the last two women past the family.

Uri muttered his condolences so low that Jesus had to assume that he was speaking the customary words. Jesus thanked him in turn and then before he could slip away he asked, "Who is watching the sheep?"

"Malki is with them but I need to get back," said Uri.

"Could I come see you tomorrow? I need to talk to you," said Jesus.

Uri looked a bit surprised but he nodded. "I'll be out on the hill below the spring. The flock will bed down about the fourth hour. If you come then, I will not be too busy."

"Okay," said Jesus. "I'll try to come."

Uri nodded with one eyebrow raised in curiosity and then quietly took his leave.

The Sabbath meal that evening was a somber affair and everyone was a bit teary-eyed over Grandmother's sudden absence from the family group. Jesus slipped off to bed rather earlier than usual, as soon as evening chores were done.

The next morning he crept out of bed as quietly as possible while there was only a hint of light on the eastern horizon. He stealthily found a bit of bread and some raisins and left the house without anyone being the wiser.

He went first to the graveyard and sat down beside the freshly filled mound beside Grandfather's stone. He munched on the bread as the dawn approached and then he spoke aloud. "Good morning, Grandmother. I came to talk to you. I was so sad that you made your final journey up this hill. I hope you are comfortable lying beside Grandfather like you said you would. We all miss you terribly. Sabbath meal last night was mostly silent and tearful. Your place was empty."

He paused. After the first few utterances, it didn't feel strange to be talking to her. It was sad that she didn't speak back, but there was something encouraging about expressing himself in words that he couldn't yet say in front of live people.

"Grandmother, I wish I had asked you more questions. I wish you had told me every story you ever heard or knew. And… there is a painful matter that came up between the twins and me last Sabbath. I wish I could talk to you about it and hear your response. They were very naughty and sassy with me and… and… they had stolen your melon. I'm so sorry you didn't get to eat your melon. I was really looking forward to bringing it to you. We were up on the leaping stone and they said they had a treat. And they brought out your poor melon. When I asked where they had got it from, they just lied. I got so angry I took the melon from them and threw it off the cliff. I'm sorry… it wasn't ripe enough to eat, you know. But it is so sad."

He wiped the tears from his eyes and then continued, "They said that I'm adopted and that you aren't really my grandmother and… and… that Abba is not my father. If you could talk, I'm sure you would say, 'Nonsense!' and dismiss their words as rubbish. I wish I could hear you say that."

He sat silently for another half hour and watched birds go about their lives in the trees and bushes nearby. He heard roosters crowing and donkeys braying as the town of Nazareth woke up to another Sabbath, just as if nothing had changed, as if no one had died. When a stray dog wandered into the graveyard, Jesus shooed it out and threw a stone after it. He didn't want any dog disturbing the freshly turned soil on his grandmother's grave.

From there he turned and walked up the path toward the leaping stone. Halfway there, he hesitated. It occurred to him that he hadn't said goodbye to Grandmother when he left. But then he reasoned that she had not said goodbye before leaving her bed to make her final journey up that hill. Perhaps goodbyes were no longer necessary. He continued.

The sun came over the horizon just as he reached the top. He sat down cross-legged on the edge of the precipice and allowed the sun to warm him in silence for several minutes. Then he began to address his Heavenly Father, "Hear oh Israel, the Lord our God is one. Thank you my Heavenly Father, that you hear me. Thank you that you know me. Before a word is on my tongue, you know it completely. You were watching down on me and my brothers last week as we disturbed this tranquil place with childish conflict. Have mercy on us, oh God. You saw the wickedness of James and Little Joseph in stealing Grandmother's melon and then lying about it. Forgive them for their childish misbehavior and help me to lead them in paths of righteousness for your name's sake. Forgive me for throwing the melon off this cliff."

He peeked over the edge but could not detect any trace of the melon on the rocks below. Perhaps the melon had fed some of God's creatures in the end. And Grandmother had been too ill to wait for the melon to ripen.

"Father, you heard the malicious words of my brothers and their accusations that I am not their brother. Why do they hate me without cause? What have I done that they want to distance themselves from me and eject me from the family? Surely I am innocent of any harmful wish in their direction, let alone any vile behavior! Vindicate me, oh God, and help me to be an elder brother of the very best kind to them, even if they do not thank me for doing so. Guide me in paths of righteousness for your name's sake."

The sunlight had not yet reached the bottom of the cliff. In the half-light below him, Jesus thought he detected stealthy motion. He shielded his eyes from the glare of the sun and sat very still. After a few minutes, a jackal crept from behind a boulder and, sniffing the breeze, sat down and looked over her shoulder. Two young ones came to her and began tumbling over each other and playfully biting her tail. She continued to watch for any sign of danger but did not detect his presence at the top of the cliff. He thought that this might be similar to how the Lord looks down on his people without their being aware that He is watching. He took the remaining scrap of bread out of his bag and threw it in the direction of the jackals. He watched as it turned over in the air and then ricocheted off a boulder and disappeared into the talus. At the sound of the bread hitting the rock, the female jackal gave a sharp 'yip' and she and her young ones disappeared in a flash. Jesus mused that human reactions are probably often similar when God Almighty looks down on them with pity and supplies what they are lacking.

He watched for several more minutes but the jackals did not reappear. He tired of sitting on the stone and got up to go look for Uri. As he walked, he thought about his brothers' accusation and wondered if it just came out of their general misbehavior. He would have thought so except for their mention of Malki. Why would they throw in a random reference to an innocent party? Malki must have said something that his brothers misinterpreted in their eagerness to oppose him and reject his authority over them. That must be it. Uri would probably clear everything up in a moment.

He found Uri resting in the shade of the rock where he said he would be. Most of the flock was gathered near him, lying down and peacefully chewing their cuds. The exception was a pair of rams who were a bit apart and focused on each other, with occasional head-butting going on between them.

"Shalom, Uri," said Jesus as he came within voice range.

"Shalom to you, little friend. How are you doing?" said Uri.

"I'm doing well," Jesus replied.

"It's too bad about your grandmother."

"Yes, it is," said Jesus. "I was really hoping that she would go up with us to Jerusalem next month. Now I don't even want to go."

"That's understandable," replied the shepherd.

"Uri, I need to ask you a question," said Jesus.

"Go ahead, ask," said Uri.

"It's probably all a misunderstanding, but my brothers said that your brother, Malki, said that I was adopted. They misunderstood him, don't you think?"

"What do you think they misunderstood?" asked Uri.

"Well, James and Joseph were being particularly annoying, as little brothers can be, and they said I was adopted, that I'm not their brother. When I told them not to talk foolishness, they protested that they had heard it from Malki."

"And?" said Uri.

"And I came to you as Malki's older brother to clear this up. I'm sure you will tell me that Malki was just being particularly annoying and made up this rubbish to hurt my brothers' feelings as revenge for some mischief they had done to him." Jesus waited a moment with growing concern and confusion as Uri did not respond.

Finally Uri spoke, "If Malki was being mean, I will thrash him. But I can't tell from what you report that he was being mean about it."

"What do you mean?" asked Jesus. "If people say that someone was adopted when they know he wasn't adopted, that seems unkind, if not downright mean."

"But in this case," countered Uri, "why would it be automatically mean for him to say that about you?"

"Excuse me?" said Jesus in total confusion.

"Why would it be mean to say that you were adopted? In your case it's true. I'm sure no insult was intended."

"B-b-but I'm not!" exclaimed Jesus.

"Do you really not know?" asked Uri. "I'm so sorry. I thought … Well, … your mother and Joseph should have told you by now. It shouldn't have come out this way," said Uri.

"You are making a joke, aren't you, Uri?" said Jesus. "Very funny. You had me going for a minute." He tried to laugh but it was forced.

Uri just looked at him. The obvious discomfort in his face made it clear that this was no joke. Or if it was a joke, Uri was a master at keeping a straight face. And if that was true, he was carrying it too far.

"Come on, Uri. Let's laugh about this now and get down to truth."

Uri was quiet another moment and then softly said, "You really didn't know, then?"

"Enough, Uri! It's not funny anymore. You are taking it too far!" Jesus had a smile frozen on his face but there was no humor in his eyes.

Finally Uri said, "Well it's a shame that it has to come to you this late and I'm sorry to be the one to break the news, but everyone in Nazareth knows that you are Mary's son but not Joseph's."

Jesus felt as if he had been slapped in the face. He couldn't find any words with which to reply so he sat gaping as if he had just watched Satan swallow up the moon. Then tears filled his eyes and overflowed down his cheeks. His head was slowly swinging from left to right and back again but still no words would come.

"Hey," said Uri, patting Jesus on the knee, "it's not your fault. You had no say in the matter."

Sitting cross-legged, as he was, Jesus bowed clear over, his face in his hands and his hands on the ground. There he wept, sobbing audibly for several minutes. Uri patted his back and waited for the spasm of sorrow to pass. He kept murmuring, "It's alright. It doesn't make any difference. I'm still your friend."

Finally Jesus sat up and wiped his eyes. He said, "If this were true, Abba would have told me."

"Maybe he was just waiting for the right moment. He didn't want to hurt you," suggested Uri.

"If it is true, it would hurt no matter how long he waited. I can't believe it's true," said Jesus.

"Well," said Uri, "I suppose the whole town could be wrong and you could be right. But you weren't old enough to give eligible testimony on the subject at the time, you know. But the whole town has talked about it ever since before you were born."

"And what did they say?" challenged Jesus.

"Well, there has always been a lot of speculation as to who was your real father. Not that I was aware of the story back then. I was only three years old myself."

"So who do they say was really my father?" asked Jesus.

"Some say one, some say another. Nobody really knows for sure. Or if they do know, they aren't saying."

"No, tell me!" insisted Jesus. "Who do they say is my father?"

"Look at those rams over there," said Uri. By now a third ram had got to his feet and all three of them were challenging each other and occasionally two of them would butt heads with terrific force.

"Don't change the subject," said Jesus.

"I'm not changing the subject. The talk about town is that when Joseph was engaged to marry your mother, he had a couple of rivals."

"What do you mean, rivals?" asked Jesus.

"Just like those rams," said Uri. "They are rivals wanting mating rights with the flock. Each one wants to plant his own seed in the ewes and to prevent his rivals from doing so. Each one wants his own line to be dominant in the flock. That's why they are competing."

"So you are saying that other men were competing with my father for the right to marry my mother," said Jesus. "Who were they?"

"As the story goes, there was a Hittite named Gershom who left Nazareth about that time and who had bargained with Mary's father for her hand. His disappearance was sudden and a bit mysterious. And there was an Arab trader that offered her father four camels for her but he was unsuccessful. Either one of them might be your father."

"You can't be serious," said Jesus. "Do I look like a Hittite or an Arab?"

"Well," said Uri, "you don't look like Joseph!"

Jesus had heard that often enough in his eleven years. He didn't challenge Uri on that point. "Is that the best story they can come up with?" he asked. "And if I am the son of one of his rivals, why would my father marry my mother? Does the whole town think he is a fool?"

"On the contrary," said Uri. "All the speculation has been about what happened to your mother and what her responsibility in the whole matter was. Joseph has been above reproach, for the most part. Most people respect him for having saved your mother from being thrown off the leaping stone. Of course some take that generous act as proof that Joseph really was your father, but that doesn't seem likely. Apparently he was quite disturbed when she came back home clearly pregnant."

"What do you mean?" asked Jesus. "Came back home from where?"

"Your mother was apparently gone from Nazareth for a few months and when she came back, she was pregnant. So some speculated that she got that way while she was away."

"She went to the hill country of Ephraim, to visit Elizabeth, a relative of ours," said Jesus. "I know that part of the story. She was taken there by my father's uncle, Ezra. I'm surprised the village gossips haven't accused Uncle Ezra of being my father."

"To tell the truth," said Uri, "that version of the story has made the rounds, too. But it doesn't attract many followers. You don't look any more like him than you do like Joseph. And you have your hearing. And besides, Ezra has never shown any interest in women. Most people believe you are the son of Gershom the Hittite."

"I will ask Abba," said Jesus. "He will tell me the truth."

"Yes, ask," agreed Uri. "But I am a little surprised that he hasn't said anything before now. And let me know what you learn. All of Nazareth is waiting for the solution to this mystery."

More confused and troubled than he had been when he arrived, Jesus bade Uri goodbye and departed with the intention of going back to the leaping stone. He had bravely said he was going to ask his father, but his heart was so shaken that he could not face anyone at that moment. As he walked, the vision of Uncle Ezra kept popping up. He pondered what it would mean if Uncle Ezra really was his father. Joseph might marry Mary and raise her child on behalf of his uncle. Without realizing where he had changed course, Jesus found himself walking toward Uncle Ezra's place.

When he was still half a league from where Uncle Ezra lived and cared for animals, Jesus slipped off the road and began to pick his way more stealthily through fields and untended brush. He found a vantage point from which he could see Ezra's place without being seen. He sat down to wait and watch.

Several horses and four or five donkeys were grazing in the fields. Samson was not among them. Either Samson was inside his enclosed stall or Uncle Ezra was away from home on Samson's back. From the vantage point Jesus had chosen, it was not possible to tell. He ate the remains of his stash of raisins and laid back on the ground in the shade to wait.

His mind was spinning with questions such as, "If Ezra is my father, then Joseph is my cousin. And since Ezra is Joseph's maternal uncle, he might not be from David's lineage. So I could not be the Messiah, despite what Abba and Mother have been saying. And why do I refer to him as Abba if he is really my cousin? And if I am the son of a Hittite or an Arab, all talk of my being the Messiah is ridiculous beyond words. Did they just make that up to make me feel better?"

He fell asleep with his head spinning and didn't wake up until the afternoon was well spent. When he awoke, it took him a couple of minutes to realize where he was and to remember why he was there. He sat up and looked out again at Uncle Ezra's animals. There was a young man tending to the animals but Uncle Ezra was not visible. Perhaps he had hired this young man to tend his animals while he himself went on a journey.

Jesus quietly slipped away through the brush and thought about going home, but he was not ready to face James and Little Joseph with their smug insolence. And if they were right that he was adopted, then he had no standing on which to reprove them for their audacious behavior. And how do you go to your father, or to the one you have always thought was your father and ask him, "Who are you and who is really my father?" Or can you go to your mother and ask her, "Who planted the seed in you that I grew from?" You can't ask such questions. It's like telling your parents, "Stop lying to me and reveal your sin!"

Half blinded by the fresh onset of tears, Jesus stumbled onto the path that led to the leaping stone. When he got there, he walked quietly to the edge and looked down. He looked for fragments of melon. He looked for the jackal and her little ones. The sun was at his back now and the boulders at the bottom of the cliff were in shadow. It was getting hard to see anything down there.

He heard a voice behind him sayng, "Have you considered how lovely it would be to leap and end it all?"

He spun around and saw no one. "The voice must be inside my head," he said aloud.

"Whether inside or outside, what does it matter?" asked the voice. "If you are hearing truth, you should act on it."

"Who are you and what do you have to do with me?" asked Jesus.

"What if I am your father?" asked the voice. "Should you not listen well to what I say?"

"Who is my father?" asked Jesus. "If you know, then tell me!"

"It would seem that your father did not care about you if he left you in such ignorance. Unloved. Uncared for. Abandoned."

Jesus wiped tears from his eyes and said nothing.

The voice spoke again, "It must be a terribly heavy burden, not knowing who your father is. One quick jump and you would escape this intolerable situation."

Jesus felt the sweat dripping down his sides, though the heat of the day was long past and the cool of the night was coming on. He shifted his weight from one foot to the other and looked over the edge. It was quite dark in the shadow of the cliff. If the jackals came out, he would not know it.

"You wouldn't even need to jump," said the coaxing voice. "Just a simple step forward and it would be resolved. Your body would be a week's worth of food for those poor hungry jackals. It would be a worthy sacrifice, would it not?"

A tremor passed through Jesus' legs. He was afraid his knees would buckle or that the owner of the voice would push him. He took a step back from the edge. With that step, he found the strength to whimper, "Away from me, you devil!"

He collapsed on the spot and lay trembling and sobbing until it became too dark for him to find his way home. He wasn't sure he would ever have the courage to go home again, but at least in this darkness he didn't have even his wits about him. He crawled farther from the edge until his outstretched hand found the rough bark of a small wild tree. He grasped it with both hands and clung to it as if to a lifeline and cried himself to sleep.

He had troubling dreams about riding a camel across the wilderness trying to find his father. Occasionally he would glimpse some wild Arab fleeing into the distance but he couldn't catch up to him. In another dream, he walked into his father's workshop and said, "Good morning, Abba." But when "Abba" turned around, it wasn't Joseph.

In the middle of the night he woke up, aware of a terrific thirst. His tongue stuck to the roof of his mouth. He felt about him but couldn't find the flask of water he had had with him. He wondered whether he had left it beside Uri and his flock. Or perhaps he had left it near Uncle Ezra's place. He couldn't remember when and where he had last had a drink.

"There is a spring at the bottom of the cliff," said the oily voice in the darkness. "You will find it very refreshing down there."

Jesus trembled in the darkness and reached out once again for the trunk of the tree under which he had taken refuge. After clinging to it for a moment, he considered whether there really were a spring at the bottom of the cliff. His head cleared and he knew there was no such spring.

"Get away from me!" he cried out. "You are the father of lies! You are not my father!"

The voice did not speak again that night. Jesus lay awake for the rest of the night alternately praying and weeping. He didn't leave the refuge of the little tree trunk until he heard roosters crowing and saw a hint of light in the east. Then he sat up and began thinking of the concern he must have caused Abba and Mother. Or... Joseph and Mother. He didn't know what to call him anymore. But he had been away for a whole day and a night. They must be very worried. Or perhaps they are just relieved, he thought. I must be a source of great trouble for them. Maybe their lives would be better if I just disappeared. Perhaps I should steal a camel and just disappear into the desert, he mused. But which way would I go?

As the light grew, he was drawn back toward the edge of the leaping stone. Perhaps he had been afraid to jump because of the darkness at the bottom. Perhaps if he could see the stones at the bottom, they would seem like a welcome refuge. He was pretty sure that a fall from that height would kill anyone. There would not be much suffering. And who cares if a fatherless boy suffers, anyway. No one would miss him. James and Little Joe would probably celebrate. No one would ever chide them for stealing melons again. And no one would tell their father what they had done. At least they had a father and knew who he was.

Jesus crept to the very edge and looked down. No sign of the jackals. He noticed his own feet. He was wearing sandals that were almost brand new. His father had bought them for him to wear to Grandmother's funeral. That is, Joseph had bought them... He thought it would be a shame to ruin them in leaping off the cliff. He decided to take them off and leave them at the edge of the leaping stone. That would serve two purposes. It would give Joseph a clue as to what had become of him... assuming he would wonder and come looking. And it would show gratitude for the gift of the sandals. Someday James or Little Joe would grow into them. Maybe they would wear them and feel sorry for how badly they had treated their half-brother.

He placed the sandals side by side about a cubit from the edge and stepped forward to the edge once again. As he did so, he saw one of the jackals flash from an exposed perch back under a boulder. He remembered how a crust of bread had frightened the jackals the day before. He wondered how long it would take them to get over the shock of a boy's body being shattered on the rocks that comprised their home. He felt the grit of a pebble under one of his bare feet. He shuffled to kick the pebble off the edge and watched as it fell and ricocheted among the boulders below.

He watched as a small bird swooped in to examine the spot where the pebble had come to rest. "No, little sparrow," he whispered. "That is not food for you. But do not worry," he added. "Your heavenly father knows that you have need of food. He will not leave you in need."

The latter sentence, he had uttered aloud and it seemed that the echo of those words resounded in his own heart. "Your heavenly father knows that you have needs. He will not leave you in need." His eyes welled with tears at that surprise and he took half a step backward to ponder the meaning.

As he did so, he heard another voice. This voice was a very familiar one, though colored with a sense of urgency he had never heard in it before, "Jesus! Jesus! Don't jump! Wait!"

He turned toward the voice and saw Joseph running toward him with stark panic in his face. Jesus became weak in the knees and began to stagger dizzily. Joseph reached him in another bound and swept him off his feet in his powerful arms and stumbled back from the brink where they both collapsed in tears.

It was several minutes before Joseph could find a voice for anything other than weeping. Then he said, "Son, what are you doing here?"

Jesus said nothing.

Joseph said, "I have been so worried about you. I went looking for you yesterday afternoon but could not find you. I went to your grandmother's grave, God rest her soul. And I found your water flask there but not you." He held up the flask to demonstrate his discovery and Jesus reached out toward the flask with both hands.

Joseph handed it to him and he drank and drank. He didn't stop until he had emptied the flask. When he put the flask down, he asked, "There is no spring of water at the bottom of this cliff, is there?"

Joseph looked at him quizzically and shook his head, "No."

Jesus nodded and held his peace. He could not bring himself to look Joseph in the face.

"Why do you ask?" asked Joseph.

Jesus dismissed the question with a shake of the head and said nothing more about it.

"Look, Jesus," said Joseph, I know you are grieving over Grandmother's death. We all are! But you have caused us great concern by staying away so long. It is time to come home and get ready for the pilgrimage to Jerusalem."

"I don't want to go this year," said Jesus.

Joseph waited in silence a moment before answering. "I'm sure you don't feel like it, but we should go to honor Grandmother.

Jesus said nothing.

"She wanted to go one more time with all of us but the Lord didn't grant her the length of days to make the journey," said Joseph.

Jesus sat quietly watching the sun rise.

"Look, Son," said Joseph, "You have no idea how your mother and I have worried over you. I searched all over town until long after dark without finding another trace of you. I went to talk to Uri and his family in the middle of the night. He told me that you had spoken with him in the middle of the day but he didn't know where you went from there. We have not slept a wink wondering where you were and praying for your protection."

When Jesus could no longer look at the sunrise for the power of the sun, he slowly turned and looked at Joseph. "Who are you?" asked Jesus.

Joseph recoiled at this question and said, "What kind of question is that? Have you lost your mind?"

"Who are you?" asked Jesus again.

Joseph laid a palm on Jesus forehead to see if he were feverish. Then he said, "I am your Abba! Do you not know me? I am Joseph!"

"I know that you are Joseph," said Jesus softly. "But I think you are not my Abba."

"What?" asked Joseph.

"I am adopted. Tell me the truth. I am not your son, am I?"

"Whoa, whoa, whoa!" protested Joseph. "Who have you been talking to? Of course I am your Abba and you are my son. Who told you any different?"

"James and Little Joe, and Uri... and the whole town knows except for me!"

"Wait a minute. Does this have anything to do with that melon of your grandmother's?" asked Joseph.

"That's when they became so nasty and told me I was adopted. But it has nothing to do with the melon. Either I am your son or I am not. Everyone talks about how much Little Joseph and even James look like you and how I don't. And it explains why they don't respect me and just try to exclude me from everything. It explains why they don't want me in the family because I'm not supposed to be a part of the family and..."

"Enough, enough, stop!" said Joseph laying a hand across Jesus' mouth. "So this is what you have been chewing on. Why didn't you ask me sooner?"

"I'm asking you now. Whose son am I? Gershon the Hittite's? Is that Arab camel trader my real father? Or is it Uncle Ezra?"

"Slow down, son."

"Don't call me son if I am not your son," protested Jesus.

"I have called you my son for almost eleven years and I will not stop now. There are some things you need to know that you did not need to know when you were two and three years old. Some knowledge a man has to grow into."

"I would think a boy needs to know who his father is," said Jesus.

"Clearly the time has come for you to know more than you have been told," said Joseph. "Let me remind you that you have both a Heavenly Father and an earthly father. And I am your earthly father."

"Then why does nobody believe that but you?" asked Jesus.

"Son, there is more to being a father than you realize. God told the children of Israel that if a man dies childless, his brother is to marry the widow and produce children for his brother. In such a case, which man is the father?"

"So you are telling me my father died?" asked Jesus.

"No, but I'm using that to illustrate the fact that fatherhood can be more complex than you think. Another example is when Moses was being raised and he thought he was part of Pharaoh's family."

"So I am adopted," said Jesus.

"No, no. That's not what I meant. That's a bad example."

They sat a few moments in silence, Jesus waiting for an explanation and Joseph searching for words. Before he spoke again, he lay back on the stone with his head pillowed on his hands. He took a deep breath and then asked, "How much do you know about the angelic announcement to your mother?"

Jesus rolled onto his side and looked at Joseph. "Gabriel came to her and told her that she was going to have a son and that she should name me Jesus."

"What else?"

"That I would save the people from their sins."

"Anything else?"

"That's about it, I think," said Jesus.

"Well then," said Joseph, there is an important piece that you didn't hear about."

"What's that?" asked Jesus.

"Your mother asked, 'How can this happen? I don't have a husband.' And Gabriel said, 'The Holy Spirit will come upon you. Therefore, the holy one to be born of you will be called the Son of God.'"

"You mean… you mean… like the Greek 'gods' who were tempted by the beauty of human women?" said Jesus.

"No, not at all like that," said Joseph.

"But a baby animal can't be born unless a father plants the seed in the mother," said Jesus.

"Correct. But in that sense, you don't have a human father."

Jesus was quiet for a few moments and then found the courage to say, "So you are not my abba."

"Jesus, I am your abba. I am the only abba you have ever had or ever will have."

"But you did not plant the seed in my mother?"

"No, I did not. We were not married yet when you began to grow in her body. She went off to see Elizabeth and Zechariah right after the angel's visit. And when she came back she was pregnant. I did not plant the seed that you grew from."

"And you're sure that no other man did?" asked Jesus.

"I was very worried about that very question," said Joseph.

"So how did you settle it?" asked Jesus.

"I was very upset. I thought what any other man would think. I didn't know your mother all that well, you know. My parents had arranged our betrothal. I wasn't absolutely confident of her character. But I didn't want to have the whole town come down on her with cruel accusations and hypocrisy. They would probably have thrown her off this very cliff. I actually spent a night and a day right in this very spot trying to think of a solution. I thought that if she went back to her kinswoman, Elizabeth, people would assume she married the father of the baby and things would quiet down."

"You spent a night and a day up here?" asked Jesus.

"Yes. I even considered throwing myself off the leaping stone as a way to escape my dilemma. But then it got dark and I couldn't bring myself to take that coward's way out because it wouldn't solve your mother's problems. So I crept back up this way," he said, pointing behind them away from the cliff, "and I fell asleep. While I was sleeping the Lord sent an angel into my dream and the angel told me not to be afraid to marry your mother. He specifically told me that you were a child planted by the Holy Spirit. So when I woke up, I went back into town and married your mother. But I planted no seed until after you were born."

"So, how did the seed get there?" asked Jesus.

"I don't know," said Joseph. "God is God. He could just speak the word and the seed would be there."

They were both quiet for a long time. Joseph looked to see if Jesus had fallen asleep. But he was still quite alert.

Finally, Jesus said, "If I am not your son, then I am not of the Davidic line. So I can't be the Messiah."

Joseph replied, "Ah, but you are of the Davidic line."

"How so?" asked Jesus.

"I am descended from David's son, Solomon," he replied. "But your mother is descended from David's son Nathan. Solomon's descendants turned away from God and some of them were very wicked kings of Judah. But you are descended from Nathan and are not contaminated by the wicked kings such as Manasseh, son of Hezekiah."

Jesus lay still for a long time before he spoke again. "Abba?" said Jesus.

"Yes, my son?"

"You are the best abba ever, even if you are descended from wicked kings."

Joseph chuckled and hugged Jesus close.

"And now," said Jesus. "We need to go home and prepare for our pilgrimage to Jerusalem."

306

"Let's do it," said Joseph. And they did.

Christmas 2014

Twelfth Birthday
Alone in Jerusalem

"Abba, may I ask you a question?"

"Of course, son. What is it?"

"What are we going to do with Grandmother's house?"

"Ah," said Joseph. "We haven't made a plan just yet. Why do you ask?"

"Well, I was wondering if I could take the sacred scroll over there to study. It's very quiet there compared to your workshop. And I could still come ask you questions if I get stuck. And it's close to Grandmother's garden, so I could tend the young plants for a break. Please?"

"I think it's a great idea," said James. "Then there would be more room in the workshop for Joey and me to help you, Abba."

"Can I have his tools, since he won't need them anymore?" asked Joey.

"Hold on, hold on," cried their father. "Jesus, does this mean you don't want to work in the shop with me anymore?"

"Not that," said Jesus. "I do want to spend more time studying the scroll, and I like working in Grandmother's garden. Sometimes it seems like I can still feel her presence in that house or in her garden. I miss her and…" He paused, not sure of what more he could say. "And if you do need my help with anything, just let me know. But now you have James and Joey in the shop with you… I'm kind of in the way."

"I do not view you as in the way, Jesus," said Joseph. "You are my best helper."

At that, James rolled his eyes and Joey stuck out his tongue at Jesus but they were sneaky enough to avoid being seen by their father.

"I respect your desire to study more and I think you should. But I may need to interrupt you from time to time because you are an excellent workman."

"Can I have his tools," asked Joey again.

"No," replied their father. "The tools I have given Jesus are to remain his. If you become a good helper like him, you will earn your own tools."

"I appreciate how you are taking care of Grandmother's garden, Jesus," added Mary. "I don't want that place to become a weed patch. We can use the extra vegetables."

"Yes," said Joseph. "And it is better for you to use the house than for it to sit empty. It would be nice to rent it out for some income, but until we find the right family, go ahead and make it your study, son."

"And Jesus could sleep over there and we could send him some bread once in a while," offered James.

"That's enough," said Joseph. "You two boys go and gather firewood for your mother. Jesus, come with me."

Joseph put his arm across Jesus shoulders and together they walked to the workshop. "I know your brothers are making it really awkward for you in the workshop. They are very jealous of you and especially jealous of my love for you."

"They will be happier if I am out of the way," said Jesus.

"But I won't be," replied Joseph. "Sometimes I wish I had a small herd of sheep so I could send your brothers out to tend the sheep and it could be just you and me in the workshop again."

"But when my time comes to enter my ministry, you will need them to help with the carpentry work," said Jesus.

"I know. But there are days when I wish you had been born just to help me in the shop."

"Yes, and there are days when I wish that was what I was born for," said Jesus.

Together they wrapped up the several tools that Joseph had given Jesus for his own, once he had learned to be proficient with them. "Why don't you keep these with you at Grandmother's. That way I won't have to constantly watch James and Joey to keep them out of them." Jesus nodded.

"I knew you would leave the workshop someday," said Joseph. "But I didn't think that day would come so soon." Jesus nodded again and bit his lip.

"Here, you carry the scroll case and I will carry the tools," said Joseph.

Jesus nodded but instead of picking up the case he had carved, with the sacred scroll inside, he threw his arms around his father's neck and wept. "I am not leaving you, Abba. "I just need some space between me and my brothers."

"I know that," said Joseph. "You are still my son."

"And you are still my abba."

Everybody seemed happy with the new arrangement. James and Joey were especially happy and began to be more attentive to their father's training in the workshop. Jesus was more productive in his studies and the whole family benefitted from the produce he was able to coax out of the garden plot. And, at least for the time being, Grandmother's house was not standing empty and attracting vagrants.

Jesus continued to live and eat and sleep as part of the family, but spent the majority of his daylight hours reading the borrowed scrolls and tending Grandmother's garden. Often, after supper, Joseph and Jesus would take a pot of tea and an oil lamp and go back over to Grandmother's house. There they would discuss the scriptures and pray together until the lamp ran out of oil. And occasionally, they would adjourn to the flat roof and continue their discussions and prayers under the stars until the roosters began to crow.

One morning when Jesus was tending the garden, who should appear but Great Uncle Ezra, Grandmothers deaf brother. He came striding up from town with a great hoe over his shoulder, the kind of hoe used for tilling a garden plot but also for general earth-moving projects. Ezra grabbed Jesus with evident pleasure and kissed his cheeks soundly before showing his admiration of his late sister's garden. He made signs to ask, "Are you the one tending this garden?"

Jesus nodded.

"And are you sleeping at this house?" he signed, pointing toward his sister's house with his chin.

Jesus shook his head and indicated that he slept in his father's house around the hill but that he studied in this house. Ezra expressed heartfelt approval of the arrangement. He beckoned for Jesus to follow him and started along the path around the brow of the hill toward Joseph's home and workshop. After a short distance, Ezra turned uphill into a shallow gully that was crowned by an overhang of rock. Jesus followed him off the path, curious to see what Uncle Ezra was up to.

Near the top, where it was becoming hard to walk, Ezra swung the great hoe off his shoulder and leaned it against his thigh. He spit on his hands and rubbed them together as a man sometimes does as he is about to begin a great piece of work. Then he took hold of the hoe with both hands and swung it in an arc above his head driving the blade into the ground almost to the handle. With a heave of his back and shoulders, he pulled the hoe toward himself and a great chunk of earth came loose and rolled toward his feet. Up went the hoe again and sliced down next to the first opening and more dirt was pulled out and down.

Uncle Ezra established a rhythm of swinging the hoe high, gouging into the earth, pulling toward himself and then stepping slightly to the right. In a matter of minutes, he had dug out a strip of earth about fifteen cubits long underneath the rock overhang. The spring rains had ended several days before and the earth was very workable. Ezra then went back to the beginning of his excavation and drove his hoe in again and began working the strip deeper and pulling the loose dirt down toward his feet. When he had finished the second pass across the hill, he looked up from his work and smiled his big, silent smile at Jesus.

Jesus pointed to the work and shrugged his shoulders as if to ask, "What are you doing?"

Ezra used his great hands to show the outline of his planned excavation. Then he indicated posts and a barricade of some sort, enclosing the excavation except for the side that was shaded by the cap-rock. Then he made signs that Jesus recognized as sheep.

Somewhat bewildered, Jesus signaled to Uncle Ezra that he would go and bring his father. Ezra nodded and went back to work. He dashed to his father's shop and was relieved to find him alone inside. "Come, Abba," said Jesus, somewhat out of breath. "Uncle Ezra has come and is making something in the draw between here and Grandmother's house."

"What is he making?" asked Joseph.

"I'm not sure, but I think he means it to be something for sheep," said Jesus. "Come and see."

By the time Joseph and Jesus arrived, Ezra had finished a third pass along his excavation and was clearing away the mass of excavated soil so as to make room for a fourth pass. The excavation extended not just downward but also became wider with each pass so that more and more dirt was being loosened and pulled outward from the hilltop.

Joseph greeted his uncle with the traditional kisses and then motioned at the excavation as if to ask, "What is this?"

Ezra made it clear that he was making a sheep pen. Joseph expressed surprise and then indicated, "I have no sheep." Ezra replied in gestures.

Jesus said, "Is he saying he is going to give us sheep?"

"That's what it looks like," said Joseph. "But if so, it's a great surprise. I don't know why he would give us sheep. Perhaps he just needs to keep his sheep here."

"Why would he need to do that?" asked Jesus. "He has a nice, big sheep pen of his own."

"I don't know, maybe he wants to reduce his flock."

"Or maybe he wants to move into Grandmother's house and move all his animals here," suggested Jesus.

"I can't imagine how that would be to his advantage," replied Joseph. "He has that broad meadow for grass and many pens and corrals. He couldn't take care of all his animals on this hillside."

"How can we ask him what his plan is?" asked Jesus.

"I'm not sure. We might have to wait and see what he does. Why don't you bring him some water to drink?"

"Gladly, Abba. And I can bring Grandmother's hoe and offer to help him."

"Okay, then. I will send someone to call you both when lunch is ready."

By the time Jesus got back, Ezra had worked up a good sweat but was not breathing hard. He received the cool water with joy and took a long drink. His smile broadened at the sight of his sister's gardening hoe. He gestured to show Jesus that he, himself, had made that hoe for his sister. He showed him a mark on the iron head of the hoe and then showed him the same mark on the head of his own great, earth-moving hoe. Ezra pointed to the marks and then to his own chest. Jesus gathered that it was something of a signature, though it didn't resemble any letter of the alphabet. If anything, he thought, it resembled a horseshoe with an eye in the middle.

After another long drink, Ezra got up and showed Jesus how to use the small hoe to break up larger clods and to pull loose dirt down the slope a bit to clear the work area for succeeding passes along the growing sheep pen. Then he went back to his own task of moving a great deal of earth with one great chop and scoop after another.

When Hannah came to call them for lunch, she was wide eyed with wonder at how her brother and Great Uncle Ezra had transformed a rather bleak looking hillside into a great excavation project. "Are you making a place to play?" she asked.

"No, I think we are making a sheep pen," Jesus replied.

"But where are the sheep?" asked his sister.

"I don't know where they will come from," said Jesus. "This is Uncle Ezra's idea and he seems to have some sheep in mind but I don't know where they are or whose they are."

"It looks like a nice place to play," said Hannah.

"Well, someday when it is finished and there are sheep inside, perhaps you can come and play with the lambs."

"That would be nice," said his sister. Then her smile turned to a worried look, "There won't be a ram, will there? I'm afraid of rams."

Jesus laughed, "We'll just have to wait and see. But if there is a ram and if he is mean, I will tie him up so you can play with the lambs. Did you come to call us to lunch? 'Cause we're hungry."

"Yes," Hannah said as she turned to skip away. "But Mama says to wash your hands."

That afternoon when Jesus and Ezra again took a break for a drink, Ezra wanted to see Jesus' palms. Jesus showed them and Ezra immediately pointed out painful blisters that were developing. He frowned with concern and shook his great head. He made a sympathetic noise and then showed Jesus his own hands. They were so calloused and rough they looked like water buffalo leather.

Jesus pointed out on his own hands that he had a few callouses. They had been developed by pushing on planes and saws. But pulling on a hoe uses different muscles and puts different pressures on the skin. The little bit of hoeing weeds that he did in the garden did not prepare him for this kind of excavation work.

Ezra indicated that he should stop excavating and go back to his reading. Jesus was disappointed and relieved both at the same time. He didn't want to be a quitter, but his hands were begging for relief. But as he picked up Grandmother's hoe to leave, Ezra gripped his arm and winked at him. He held a threatening index finger in front of Jesus and then put his hand over his own mouth as if to say, "Don't tell anyone." Then he led him back up toward the capstone under which they were excavating. There was a large bush directly under the place where the rock jutted out the farthest. Ezra led him to the bush and again warned him not to tell. When Jesus nodded and put his hand over his own mouth by way of promise, Ezra reached behind the bush with one great arm and pulled the branches away from the rock. He jutted his chin toward the rock and Jesus looked, expecting to see a snake or a rabbit nestled against the rock behind the bush.

Instead he saw blackness and felt cool air flowing out from behind the bush. His mouth dropped open and he fell to his knees to look into the opening. "A cave!" he exclaimed. Then he remembered his promise and looked up into Ezra's grinning face. He again put his hand over his mouth to confirm his promise and to remind himself to keep the promise. But what a surprise!

Jesus pointed to the cave, then to Ezra and then to his own head in an attempt to ask whether Ezra knew about the cave. Ezra nodded and pointed to himself, to his own head and then to the cave. Jesus wondered who else knew about the cave. He wondered if his own father, who had grown up on this hill, knew about the cave. But he couldn't ask. He had promised.

Ezra was motioning again. He pointed to himself and held his hand palm down about waist high and then indicated he had gone into the cave. Then he held his hand higher and then indicated his considerable current girth and indicated that he could no longer fit into the cave.

To confirm the meaning, Jesus asked by gestures whether Ezra had gone into the cave. Ezra nodded and again held his hand about waist high. So it was true! As a boy Ezra had been inside the cave. Jesus asked whether it was big or small inside. Ezra motioned with his hands and paced off about ten strides, giving Jesus the idea that it was as big as a small house inside. But he indicated that the roof of the cave was not as high as a house roof.

Jesus again looked at the opening to the cave. It seemed too small for a boy his size to crawl through. So maybe Ezra was really young when he went in. It was hard to imagine such a gigantic man ever having been a small enough boy to go through that opening. Perhaps there was no bush there when Ezra went into the cave. He really wanted to see what it looked like inside, but it was too dark to make out any features. And he still had the image of a snake in the back of his mind. So he scrambled to his feet and shook Ezra's great hand with his small, blistered one and again confirmed his promise not to tell.

Jesus went back to his studies at Grandmother's house. At least he sat with the scroll in front of him. But all he could think about was the secret cave. He remembered the story of David and his men hiding in a cave when King Saul went in to relieve himself. He imagined his ancestor's trembling heart as he crept near and cut off the corner of the king's cloak. He wondered how David and his men had covered their tracks at the entrance of the cave so that Saul would not suspect that anyone was near, let alone in the cave. Surely that cave must have had a larger opening since David and Saul were not small boys at the time of that story. And it must have gone back a lot farther than Ezra's cave because David had hundreds of men hiding with him. He wondered if Ezra's cave had any narrow tunnels

316

that went back to larger chambers. He wondered if he would have enough courage to explore the inside of the cave. He would want to take an oil lamp and some rope…

Jesus finally gave up trying to study. He went outside to tend Grandmother's garden. He did a bit of watering and weeding, but his mind was still full of questions about the mysterious cave. He decided Uncle Ezra might need another drink of water. He filled a flask and ran back to the excavation. But there was no one there. The great hoe was left there at the side of the excavation, but no sign of the excavator. Briefly, Jesus wondered if Uncle Ezra had gone into the cave but he knew that was ridiculous. There was no way a normal-sized man could get into the cave, let alone his huge relative. He must have gone home for the day. He began to walk toward the bush, thinking he would just peak into the cave one more time when his brothers, James and Joey came into sight.

"Hey, whatcha doing?" they called in unison. "Where's Uncle Ezra?" asked James.

Jesus tried to look nonchalant and said, "I guess he's gone home for the day if you didn't see him at our house."

"This doesn't look like a sheep pen," said Joey.

"Is it finished?" asked James.

"I don't think it's finished," said Jesus. "It will need a fence to keep the sheep in and the wolves out."

"This would be a great place to play," said Joey. James was trying to pick up the great hoe that Ezra had left on the job.

"Hey, leave that alone. You might hurt someone," said Jesus.

"Don't be so bossy," said James. "I'm not hurting anything."

"It's not yours and it's too big for you," said Jesus.

"Bring it over here," said Joey. "Let's chop out this bush. That will make this even a better place to play."

"NO!" shouted Jesus. He grabbed the handle of the hoe and wrestled it out of his brother's grasp. The violence of the struggle for the hoe resulted in two of his blisters tearing open, but he did not let go.

"Give it back," cried James.

"Oh let him have it," said Joey, throwing a dirt clod in Jesus' direction.

"Good idea," said James. "Let him have it." He picked up a handful of loose dirt and threw it directly in Jesus' face. Joey cackled in glee and they both began to pick up handfuls of dirt and pelt Jesus as fast as they could. Jesus didn't retaliate and didn't flee. He squatted low to the ground and tried to protect his face as best he could but did not release his grasp on Ezra's hoe.

The twins were so intent on their torment of Jesus, they did not hear their mother's shriek or have any idea that she was fast approaching. The first they knew of her presence was the stinging lash of a tamarisk branch across their bare legs. She only got in a couple of brisk strokes before they danced out of range howling at the tops of their voices.

Mary was beside herself as she bent to comfort her firstborn. "What in the world? What is wrong with you boys? Are you bewitched? Are you the devil personified? Oh, I don't know what to do with them.
Come, let me look at you," she said, lifting Jesus face with one hand. "What was it this time? Oh, you have dirt in your eyes! You could go blind! Come, let's get you cleaned up." She half lifted him to his feet. He was still clinging to the hoe. "Leave that here," said Mary. "Let go of it."

Tears were leaving muddy tracks down his dusty face as he stumbled along in his mother's grasp. "Yes, go ahead and cry," said his mother. "The tears will help wash out the dirt. I am so sorry, Jesus. So sorry they treat you like they do."

Supper was later than usual that night because it took so long for Mary to help Jesus get the dirt washed out of his eyes and out of his hair. While she was tending to him, Joseph fed the younger children and got them settled in bed.

When the three boys and their parents came to the table, Jesus' eyes were red and irritated from the dirt they had taken. The twins were subdued,

318

waiting for justice to be administered, all the while thinking about ways to excuse their behavior. The tension in the room was visible in Joseph's face.

"Now, tell me what happened," said Joseph in a voice that suggested he was confronting something powerful and dangerous.

"Jesus was bossing us around again," offered James. "He always tries to spoil our fun and ..."

"Stop," said Joseph firmly. James stopped.

"It's true," whined Joey. "We were just playing and he grabbed the hoe away from James and ..."

"Stop," said Joseph even more firmly. Joey stopped. "Jesus, suppose you tell us your perspective. How did this start?"

Jesus sat very quietly thinking about his promise to Uncle Ezra and trying to find a way to talk about what happened without exposing the cave.

"Well," coaxed his mother. "What happened?"

"Nothing," whispered Jesus.

"Nothing happened?" said Joseph. "I beg to differ. Something happened. Tell us the truth."

"Abba, you know I speak the truth to you. Nothing happened that I am willing to talk about."

"Ah, that is different," said Joseph. "Something happened but you are not willing to talk about it."

"That's it."

"Well I don't know how I am to administer justice if you don't talk about it."

"No justice needs to be administered. Just let it go. Let them go."

"That won't help, Jesus," said Mary. "They were behaving like little demons and they need correction."

"We already got correction," whined Joey. "Look at these marks on my legs!"

"Yeah, and mine, too," added James.

Joseph brushed the twins' complaints aside with a wave of his hand and said, "Jesus, …"

"No, Abba. I won't say more. I forgive them. Just let it be. It's over."

When Jesus rounded the curve of the hill the next morning, there was a horse and cart standing in the middle of the path. He recognized the horse as a smallish mare belonging to Uncle Ezra. The cart was loaded with used wooden posts. Uncle Ezra had already installed three posts in the ground and was digging a hole for the fourth. Jesus wondered how early Ezra had got up. It was clear that more dirt had been excavated in addition to the installation of the posts.

Ezra stopped his work to greet Jesus and show him the progress on the sheep pen. He showed him how he was using rocks to wedge the base of the posts into the holes. Then he unloaded the poles out of the cart and asked Jesus to take the horse and cart to go to the stream and collect more rocks. He showed him what size rocks he wanted and sent him off.

Jesus wondered whether he should tell his father what he was doing. Abba would expect him to be at Grandmother's house studying. He had driven a horse cart only a few times, but the little mare was very docile and knew her job well. Jesus decided to take the extra minute or two to keep his father's trust. He pulled the cart to a stop at the door of his father's shop. The door was standing open and Joseph popped his head out to see who had come.

He was as surprised to find Jesus driving the cart as Jesus was to be driving it. "What have we here, young traveler? Are you off to see the world?"

"No, Abba. Uncle Ezra has started setting posts for the sheep pen. He asked me to go get rocks from the stream."

"Well, he is not wasting any time, is he? Thanks for letting me know."

320

As Joseph was speaking, James and Joey stuck their heads out the door as well. "Can we go too, Abba?" pleaded James.

"No, I need you here. Jesus can do this job just fine on his own," said Joseph.

Jesus could hear the twins whining in jealousy as he clucked to the mare, shook the reins and drove off. He was exhilarated at Uncle Ezra's trust and grateful for his father's blessing. Even more, he was grateful that his father had not allowed the twins to come along. He could easily imagine how badly such an adventure could turn out once James and Joey started playing in the water instead of helping to choose and load rocks.

When he came to the stream, he tied the reins to a small tree near the edge. When he had come upon the mare back where Ezra was working, she hadn't been tied to anything. Ezra had her trained to stand still any time he dropped the reins on the ground in front of her. Jesus was not sure that she would obey him the way she obeyed Ezra. And he imagined certain disaster if the mare decided to trot away while he was choosing rocks.

Picking rocks out of the cool water did not work his hands in the same way as the hoe had done the day before. He was aware of the blisters, but was able to avoid putting too much pressure on them as he loaded the cart with stones. And the cool water soothed his injured hands.

When he got back, Ezra had dug holes for several more posts but had run out of rocks so he had not set more posts. Ezra took the reins from Jesus and led the mare up onto the relatively flat area he had been creating. Then he had Jesus drive the cart from one hole to another while he unloaded several stones at each stop.

When the stones were all unloaded, Ezra patted Jesus on the shoulder and gave him the signal for "good." Jesus wanted to go peek into the cave behind the bush again but also felt the tug of responsibility calling him to his studies. And Ezra was so focused on his fence building that Jesus was too shy to bring up the subject of the cave. And the cave was a secret; you never knew when someone might come along and see you peeking behind the bush.

So Jesus bade his great uncle farewell and went to study the scriptures at Grandmother's house. He was studying the scroll of Isaiah, borrowed as usual from the young rabbi in Capernaum who had become almost a member of the family. Jesus anticipated finishing this scroll before too long and then traveling to Capernaum to borrow another. He wondered which scroll Rabbi Zephon would let him borrow next.

He opened the scroll and began to read these words, "See, my servant will act wisely; he will be raised and lifted up and highly exalted." Jesus thought that these words might refer to the Messiah. Who else would be lifted up and highly exalted, if not the anointed one.

But the next words were, "Just as there were many who were appalled at him — his appearance was so disfigured beyond that of any human being and his form marred beyond human likeness — "So maybe this doesn't mean the Messiah, thought Jesus. The Messiah wouldn't be appalling and disfigured.

"So he will sprinkle (or maybe startle) many nations, and kings will shut their mouths because of him. For what they were not told, they will see, and what they have not heard, they will understand."

Jesus paused in confusion and went back to the beginning of the passage. After reading it a second and even a third time, he was unsure whether this "servant" was the Messiah or not. He would have to ask Abba for help with this part, and maybe even Rabbi Zephon. He decided to go on for the time being.

"Who has believed our message and to whom has the arm of the Lord been revealed? He grew up before him like a tender shoot, and like a root out of dry ground. He had no beauty or majesty to attract us to him, nothing in his appearance that we should desire him. He was despised and rejected by mankind, a man of suffering, and familiar with pain. Like one from whom people hide their faces he was despised, and we held him in low esteem."

Well, thought Jesus, that couldn't refer to the Messiah. The Messiah would be honored and trusted, not despised and rejected. So who could this be referring to? Perhaps to Isaiah, the prophet who wrote these words? Isaiah prophesied at a time of wickedness when Israel was threatened with exile. Perhaps the wicked people of that generation despised and rejected Isaiah and his message.

He read on. "Surely he took up our pain and bore our suffering, yet we considered him punished by God, stricken by him, and afflicted. But he was pierced for our transgressions, he was crushed for our iniquities; the punishment that brought us peace was on him and by his wounds, we are healed."

I'm not sure what wounds Isaiah might have suffered, thought Jesus, but any punishment he might have experienced did not bring peace upon Judah and Israel. Both kingdoms were destroyed and the survivors were dragged into exile in foreign lands. This cannot be about Isaiah.

The next words were, "We all, like sheep, have gone astray, each of us has turned to his own way; and the Lord has laid on him the iniquity of us all. He was oppressed and afflicted, yet he did not open his mouth; he was led like a lamb to the slaughter, and as a sheep before his shearers is silent, so he did not open his mouth." Jesus thought about the night before when his brothers had accused him of bullying them and he had not defended himself. It was partly because of the secret of the cave that he had held his peace. He wondered if the person about whom Isaiah had written held his tongue because of a secret. And if so, what was the secret?

He read on. "By oppression and judgment he was taken away. Yet who of his generation protested? For he was cut off from the land of the living;" Well that settles it, thought Jesus, it can't be about the Messiah. The Messiah lives forever. "For the transgression of my people he was punished." Who on earth can this be, thought Jesus. What king or prophet or priest has ever been punished for the sins of the people?

"He was assigned a grave with the wicked, and with the rich in his death, though he had done no violence, nor was any deceit in his mouth. Yet it was the Lord's will to crush him and cause him to suffer, and though the Lord makes his life an offering for sin, he will see his offspring and prolong his days and the will of the Lord will prosper in his hand. After he has suffered, he will see the light of life and be satisfied, by his knowledge my righteous servant will justify many and he will bear their iniquities."

And who, thought Jesus, could possibly be called "my righteous servant" and who will "bear their iniquities" but the Messiah? He remembered that the angel had told his father that Mary's son would be called Jesus for "he will save his people from their sins." A shiver went up Jesus spine as he considered whether this passage in Isaiah was describing a path he, himself, would have to walk. Suffering? Rejection? Death? Nobody had said anything about death. Everybody knows that the Messiah lives forever, he thought. Rejection he was already experiencing at the hands of his little brothers. Suffering, too, he thought as he remembered the gritty dirt in his eyes and the bruises from dirt clods hitting his ribs. But death? Really?

He turned back to the scroll. "Therefore I will give him a portion among the great, and he will divide the spoils with the strong, because he poured out his life unto death, and was numbered with the transgressors. For he bore the sin of many, and made intercession for the transgressors."

So death isn't the end, thought Jesus. After "pouring out his life unto death" the Messiah would be rewarded. After he has suffered, "he will see the light of life and be satisfied."

"O Lord God, Creator and Sustainer of all that is," prayed Jesus, "is this the path you have laid out for me? Why has nobody told me that mine is a path of rejection, suffering and death? Can a son of man bear this kind of path? Will I be given the strength to walk this path? O Lord God, if it is possible, let there be a different path, a path that I can endure..." He sat weeping for several minutes before he remembered to add what his mother had taught him, "Nevertheless, not my will but yours be done."

He was still sitting before the scroll, reading and rereading this passage when Hannah came to call him home for lunch. As he walked with her past the place where Uncle Ezra had been working so hard, he didn't even look up. All thoughts of exploring the secret cave had been banished from his mind by the discovery about the path ahead of him. The secret of the cave was nothing compared to the secret that he had discovered in the scroll of Isaiah.

Over lunch there was happy chatter from James and Joey. Joseph reported progress in the workshop both with his own work and with training the twins. Hannah held her little brother, Simon, on her lap and tried to feed him from her own portion. Uncle Ezra silently teased Hannah and Simon with finger games and facial gestures.

Jesus sat in his own silence and ate slowly. Mary tried to draw him out: "Abba tells me you hauled stones for Uncle Ezra."

"Yes, I did," said Jesus.

"That sounds like an adventure," said Mary "Did you drive the cart?"

"Yes, Mother."

"And it worked out?"

"Pardon me, Mother? What do you mean?"

"Were you successful? Did the horse obey you? Did you get the stones?"

"Yes, Mother, it worked out."

"We wanted to go with him and help him, but Abba wouldn't let us," volunteered James.

Jesus sat in silence and thought about the sheep being silent before the shearers.

"Are you feeling okay, Jesus?" asked Mary. "Let me see your eyes; are you in pain?"

Jesus let her look in his eyes but only said, "I'm fine, Mother."

"They still look red. I'm worried about your eyesight. Were you able to read the scroll okay this morning?"

"Yes, Mother. I was able to read," said Jesus.

"Then what did you read? Tell us about it."

"Please, Mother, just let me be. I read from the scroll of Isaiah but I don't feel like talking about it."

Mary was about to protest but Joseph nudged her and she held her peace.

After lunch Jesus went back to Grandmother's house and sat down by the garden. He was reminiscing about the time when she was still alive. He thought about how much she loved to garden and how happy it made her to see things alive and growing. He looked at the sprouts of cucumber vine that were beginning to spread out in the sun. He smiled at the thought of her smiling over the growth.

He didn't know how long he had been sitting there when his father came along the path. "There you are, son," Joseph said. "I thought I might find you helping Uncle Ezra."

"Oh, does he need my help?" asked Jesus.

"Not that he indicated," said Joseph. "But I know you are curious about the project so I just thought I might find you there."

"Did you come to get me because you need my help?" asked Jesus.

"No, not really." They sat in silence for a moment. Then Joseph said, "I came to see if you are alright. You were awfully withdrawn at lunch."

"I'm alright, Abba."

"You are not very convincing when you say it that way, you know. Is this about what happened with James and Joey yesterday?"

"No, it's not about that," said Jesus.

"Then what is it about?" asked his father.

After a few moments of silence, Jesus said, "The angel told you that I would "save my people from their sins," right?

Joseph nodded. "That's what he said."

"Did the angel tell you how I would do that?" Joseph reflected for a moment and then admitted that the angel had not disclosed how the people would be saved.

"How do you imagine Messiah will save the people from their sins?" asked Jesus.

"I'm not sure," admitted Joseph.

"Do you imagine that I will tell the people to repent and they will all repent and God will forgive them?"

"I haven't given it a lot of thought, but yeah, something like that," said Joseph.

Jesus picked a stem of grass from the edge of the garden and began to chew the tender end of it. Then he looked at his father and asked, "Have you ever heard anyone say that Messiah has to die?"

"No, of course not," said Joseph. "Messiah lives forever. Everyone agrees on that."

"Isaiah does not agree on that," said Jesus.

"I'm sure you are mistaken, son. You must be misinterpreting something."

"No, I don't think so."

"Come, show me what you are reading. We can clear this up. Messiah definitely lives forever."

Together they went into Grandmother's house and Jesus got out the scroll. He opened it on the table to the place he had marked with a feather when he had been called to lunch. "Right here, Abba. Read from right here until it says, "he bore the sin of many and made intercession for the transgressors."

Jesus sat silently and watched his father's face as he read the passage. As his father's eyes went back and forth across the scroll, his eyebrows grew lower and closer together. At one point, he stopped and went back to the beginning of the passage and methodically worked through it again, this time all the way to the end.

He looked over at his son and then went back and read part of the passage again. Then he cleared his throat and said, "I wanted to believe that this passage was about Isaiah or someone else."

"I know. I tried to do that, too."

"But it's not."

Jesus shook his head.

"I don't know why I have never seen this before," said Joseph. "It's not a passage that I have ever heard discussed at synagogue."

Jesus sat silently chewing on the grass stem.

"We should ask Rabbi Zephon how he reads this passage," suggested Joseph. "Perhaps there is an answer we are overlooking."

"No one ever told me that this was a path of suffering and rejection and death," said Jesus. "Why did none of the angels mention that?"

"You remind me of something that was said, though not by an angel," said Joseph.

"What?" asked Jesus.

"Do you remember us telling you about Simeon, the very old man who was waiting at the temple when we brought you in to present you to the Lord and present the sacrifice of doves?"

"Yes," said Jesus. "He said something like, 'Lord now you can dismiss your servant in peace for my eyes have seen your salvation.'"

"Exactly," said Joseph. "He went on to say that you would be a sign that would be spoken against and that you would cause the falling and rising of many in Israel. Something like that. Your mother would remember better than I."

"A sign that would be spoken against? As in 'We considered him smitten of God, despised? '"

"It fits, doesn't it?"

Jesus burst into tears. His father gathered him into his lap and held him, rocking back and forth and letting his own tears flow freely.

After some time, Jesus wiped his eyes on his sleeve and kissed Joseph on both cheeks. "I don't know if I can travel this road," he said.

Joseph held silence for a moment and then said, "You don't have to travel that whole road today, son. Sufficient to the day is the trouble thereof. When more strength is needed, that strength, too, will be given."

"Abba?" said Jesus. "Can this be our secret? You won't tell Mother, will you?"

"Why don't you want your mother to know this, son?"

"Because she will get all motherly and protective. She will cry so much and, … and … when she cries it takes away what little strength I think I have."

"Okay, I get that," said his father. "At least for now, it will be our secret. But I still think we should ask Rabbi Zephon how he reads this passage."

"Thank you, Abba."

Then turning his thoughts in a fresh direction he asked, "You didn't leave James and Joey in the shop alone, did you? They might wreak havoc without you there."

"No need to worry about that," said his father. "I sent them down to the stream to play. They were so jealous of you when you drove off this morning!"

"Yeah, I heard them whining. Thanks, too, for not sending them with me."

"Oh you are welcome. I wouldn't do that to you. It seems that they are God's messengers to prepare you for rejection."

"If that is their purpose," said Jesus, "they do their job well."

They left Grandmother's house hand in hand and went to see how Uncle Ezra was progressing. When they came in sight of the project, Jesus thought Uncle Ezra had already left. But the cart was still there and the mare was grazing nearby. Then he saw the bush shaking and realized that Uncle Ezra was working behind it.

"What is he doing behind that bush?" asked Joseph.

Jesus wanted to protect the secret of the cave but his father strode right up to see what Ezra was doing. Ezra was down on his knees scooping dirt with his hands and trying to dislodge a large stone that obstructed access to the cave. Joseph tapped Ezra on the back and Ezra came up laughing. His whole face was radiant as he disclosed the secret cave to Joseph. He looked over his shoulder at Jesus. Jesus was quick to point to himself and cover his mouth with both hands. He wanted Ezra to know that he had not given away the secret. Ezra laughed and signaled that it is no longer necessary to keep silent.

"Look at this, Jesus," called Joseph, pushing past Ezra as Ezra backed out of the way. "A cave, right here behind this bush. Right on our family property!"

"Did you not know about it?" asked Jesus.

"No, I had no idea. I have a vague memory of my father talking about discovering a cave when he was a boy, but he would never tell me where it was. I think he was afraid I would go into it and not come out."

"Uncle Ezra told me not to tell anyone. It was a secret until now. He said he went into the cave when he was a small boy but now he doesn't fit."

"Well, it looks like he is determined to make that opening big enough to go in again. Let's help him!"

When they looked around, Ezra was leading the mare up toward where they were standing. He uncoiled a strong rope and tied a loop around the obstructing rock. He tied the other end of the rope to the harness the mare was wearing. He put Jesus in charge of the mare and had him take the slack out of the rope but then wait. He wedged the working end of his great hoe in behind the rock and while he and Joseph pried with the hoe, he signaled for Jesus to drive the mare forward.

The mare leaned into the harness and made only slight progress at first but then lunged forward several steps. "Whoa!" hollered Joseph. "The rope slipped off. Bring her back, Jesus." Ezra took the end of the rope and wrapped it around the boulder three times and tied a secure knot.

"Okay, let's try it again," said Joseph. "Take the slack out slowly. Good. Now pull!"

This time they were successful in dragging the large stone free. Ezra and Joseph cast off the rope and tipped the stone up at one side of the opening so that access to the cave would be restricted to passing behind the bush from the other side. By the time Jesus had untied the rope from the harness and coiled it up, both his father and Uncle Ezra had wriggled out of sight into the cave.

He ran up to the entrance and knelt down to look in. "Are you okay?" he called.

"Yes, come on in," said his father's voice in the blackness.

Jesus was able to go on all fours through the enlarged opening but he went hesitantly. "I can't see anything," he said. He felt a hand on his shoulder.

"You are fine," said his father. "I'm right here."

"I should go get an oil lamp," suggested Jesus.

"We don't need one right now," said his father. "Your eyes will get used to it. I can already see much more than I could at first."

Gradually he began to make out the image of his father, sitting in the darkness. He could hear Uncle Ezra exploring the perimeter of the cave, shuffling and grunting as he went.

"It is so much cooler in here," said Jesus.

"Isn't that nice?" said his father. "Imagine coming in here on a really hot day!"

"That would be wonderful," agreed Jesus. "But imagine how cold it would be in the winter."

"Actually, the opposite is true, from what I understand," said Joseph. "The stones and the earth keep the heat out in the summer but they keep the cold out in the winter. It should offer protection from icy winds and from snow and sleet. Some people use caves as sheep pens because they also protect from wild animals and thieves."

"Then that is why Uncle Ezra is making his sheep pen right here and not on his own place," said Jesus. "I think he wants his sheep to go in the cave at night for protection!"

"This whole project makes sense now that we know about this cave," said his father.

By the time Ezra had finished his inspection, Jesus could see him dimly. When he got back to the opening, he got down on his belly and squirmed out, blocking the only source of light for a moment. Jesus followed him and Joseph came out last.

Jesus signed with his hands to ask if sheep would go into the cave. Ezra nodded enthusiastically. Joseph asked how many sheep. Ezra was ready with the answer. He signed that about 30 sheep would fit in there. He also indicated that there was one narrow opening in the back of the cave that they would have to block off with stones. It might lead to a dead end or it might lead to a drop off. For the sheep's safety, they would have to block that one place.

Before the day was done, they had used the hoe to excavate the opening a bit more so that even Uncle Ezra could go in and out on all fours. They also gathered a few large stones from within the cave and scattered on the hillside. These they used to stop up the only passage in the back of the cave through which a lamb might get into trouble.

The next morning Uncle Ezra brought a wagonload of straw with a load of long poles on top keeping the straw from blowing out. Jesus helped him unload the last of the poles. Ezra set Jesus to work hauling the straw into the cave and spreading it out on the floor. In the meantime, he began using the long poles to connect from post to post, outlining the corral outside the cave. After spreading the straw, Jesus went on to his studies in the scroll of Isaiah.

After lunch, Uncle Ezra proposed that Jesus go with him to get the sheep. Joseph gave his consent and Jesus rode off with his Great Uncle. When they reached Ezra's place, Jesus was surprised to see no sheep. In fact, he saw no sheep pen, either. There were holes in the ground around the outline of what had been Ezra's sheep pen, but the pen and the sheep were gone. He motioned to Uncle Ezra, "Where are the sheep?"

Ezra laughed and pointed to the barn in which he normally kept horses and donkeys. Jesus pointed to where the sheep pen used to be and shrugged his question. Ezra mimed that he had dismantled it to build the new one. That explained why all the materials looked weathered and old. The old water tub still stood where the pen had been. Ezra walked over to it and tipped the water out on the ground. Then he motioned for Jesus to help him load it in the wagon. Then Ezra had Jesus drive the wagon around behind the barn. There, Ezra forked a load of hay into the wagon in front of the water tub.

Only then did he open the door to the barn. Inside was his little flock of sheep. Jesus looked for Samson, Ezra's great, black Arab stallion but he wasn't in his usual stall. Jesus stepped back out of the barn and looked in the corral. There were two donkeys and a pale gelding, but no Samson. He motioned to Ezra to ask where Samson was. Ezra looked at him for a moment and bit his lip. Then he signed that Samson was gone. Jesus was stunned. Samson gone? Where could Samson have gone. He never loaned Samson out, though he was known to loan out other animals to people in need. He would make sure that the borrowers were people who would care for the animals and not use them harshly. But he would never loan out Samson. And it was unthinkable that Samson would be sold. That horse's life was bound up with Ezra's life. Here was a mystery indeed.

Ezra busied himself with catching a ewe that was wearing a halter. When he caught her, he tied a short rope to the halter and swung the door wide open. He led the ewe to the wagon and the rest of the flock followed. He stooped and lifted the ewe onto the back of the wagon where he secured her by the rope. She was complaining loudly, and the little flock of nine ewes and six lambs all responded by adding their complaints and milling about restlessly near the wagon.

Ezra got a shepherd's staff and handed it to Jesus. He indicated that Jesus should follow on foot and keep strays from getting into mischief. Then he clambered onto the wagon and began driving. The entire flock wanted to stay with the ewe that was baaing loudly from the wagon, so they followed readily as Ezra drove slowly away from home. The nine ewes followed as faithfully as if they had all been tethered to the wagon, though they weren't quiet about it. The lambs frolicked and played in every direction and provided Jesus a little bit of concern when their energy would carry them beyond what he considered safe boundaries. He would run to this side and that, wielding the staff to encourage the wayward lambs to rush back to their mothers.

When they got to the new pen, Ezra untied the haltered ewe and lifted her to the ground. He led her by the rope into the pen and all the others followed on her heels. Jesus slid the gate poles across the opening and Ezra released the rope from the halter. Now the flock of sheep were secured in their new home.

Together Jesus and Ezra lifted the water tub off the wagon and set it where the animals could stick their heads through the fence to drink. Jesus set off to haul water from the village well while Ezra unloaded the hay, some inside the pen, and the greater portion just beyond the reach of the animals. On his second trip back up the hill, Jesus saw Ezra pounding some posts into the ground at the entrance to the cave. He stopped to see what his uncle was building. Ezra showed him that this was the second stout post, one at either side of the cave opening, less than a hand breadth from the stone wall of the cliff.

Jesus looked at Ezra inquiringly. Ezra winked and beckoned him to follow. He led him to his father's workshop. There Joseph was putting the finishing touches on a heavy plank door, just big enough to close up the entrance to the cave. James and Joey were fairly bursting with curiosity about the door and it's destined purpose. They had not yet been brought into the secret of the cave.

Joseph showed the door to Ezra, who inspected it and indicated his approval. Then all five of them marched up the hill, Ezra carrying the door under one arm.

James said, "Abba, tell us what the door is for."

You are about to see what it is for," Joseph replied.

"Did you make a play house for us?" asked Joey.

"Not exactly," said their father.

"Jesus, do you know what it's for," asked James.

"You will see what it's for. Just be patient. "

"Why is Uncle Ezra taking it? Is it for his sheep pen?" asked Joey.

"Sort of," said Jesus.

"What do you mean, 'Sort of?'" asked James. "Either it is or it isn't."

"It's too small for the gate of the sheep pen," observed Joey as they approached the pen.

334

"Oooh look," said Joey. "There are sheep in the pen."

"Are they Uncle Ezra's sheep?" asked James.

Ezra opened the gate with his free hand and nodded to Jesus who then waited until everyone was in the pen before sliding the poles into place again. "Yes," said Jesus in answer to James' question. We brought them here this morning."

"But what's the door for?" asked James again.

"Just watch," said Jesus.

The boys watched as Uncle Ezra walked across the pen and went behind the bush. The twins fairly stumbled over each other trying to see what he was doing behind the bush.

"A cave!" they cried out in unison, just as Ezra lifted the door high and slid it down behind the two posts, closing off the entrance to the cave except for a hand breadth at the top.

"That should do nicely," said Joseph. "That should keep the sheep in and keep harm out. Just enough space for a bit of air and light to get in."

Ezra patted Joseph on the back and gave him the sign for "Good job."

"Can we see the cave?" cried James. "Can we go in?"

"Yeah," whined Joey. "We want to see the cave. Please, Abba?"

"Yes, you can go in," said Joseph, sliding the door up and setting it aside. The twins wasted no time in pushing past Uncle Ezra and into the cave.

As soon as they had disappeared into the darkness, Ezra picked up the door and slid it down firmly into place. He, of course, couldn't hear their immediate protests, but he soon saw their desperate fingers clawing at the top of the door and knew his trick was having the intended effect. He roared fiercely through the opening and pinched their fingers, then fell to laughing with merriment at the frightened boys. He soon relented and lifted the door to set the little captives free. They came out angry and in tears, but Ezra laughed at their distress until tears rolled down his cheeks.

Joseph couldn't restrain a smile, but he bent down to comfort his boys and then said, "If you would like to go in and explore a bit, I will not let Uncle Ezra touch the door." James said he would, but no amount of coaxing, not even from James, could persuade Joey to take that risk.

"You see," said Joseph, "it is not intended as a play house but as a secure enclosure for the sheep at night time or during stormy weather. But I don't see why boys can't go in there and play when the sheep are on pasture. And someone will have to go in there from time to time to clean it out and put fresh straw down for bedding."

"Uncle Ezra can do that," said Joey. "They are his sheep."

"Yeah," said James. "And when he is in there we might shut the door on him. See how HE likes it."

"Now, now," cautioned Joseph. "Don't be disrespectful of your elders. He was just having a little fun at your expense."

In the end, James was able to persuade Joey to go back into the cave with him, but only on the condition that their father stay at the entrance with his hand on the door.

While the twins explored the cave, Jesus bent down to pet a lamb that was nibbling on his cloak. Ezra came over and petted the lamb with him. He picked it up in his great arms and made sucking noises with his lips. The lamb stretched his face towards Ezra's and Ezra kissed the lamb on the nose. He pointed out that one of the ewes was pressing against his leg and trying to reach the lamb. Ezra indicated this was the mother of the lamb.

He then proceeded to point out each of the pairings of lamb with mother. He knew every lamb and its family connections. He pointed out that all but one of the ewes were daughters or granddaughters of the old ewe with the halter. The exception was a ewe without a lamb. Ezra indicated he had found her wandering way out in the country when she was just a lamb. He had run across the remains of a ewe that had been killed and eaten by a lion. He suspected that the lamb was orphaned by the predator. He had carried the lamb home by horseback and though he asked around and showed the lamb at the market for two weeks, he did not find any shepherd who admitted to losing a ewe and a lamb. So he had added it to his own flock.

The sun was getting low when James and Joey came out of the cave, babbling about how they wished they could live in the cave and how wonderful it was as long as nobody shut them in. Once the twins had run off to tell their mother and Hannah about their adventure, Ezra showed Jesus how to use the shepherd's staff to move the old ewe toward the side of the pen where the bush stood. It didn't take much persuading to move her up the path and into the cave. And of course, the others wanted to go wherever she was going, so it wasn't a minute before all sixteen sheep were in the cave. When Jesus peeked in after them, he saw that some were already lying down and beginning to chew the cud.

Joseph and Ezra also bent down and looked in. Then Ezra motioned for Jesus to slide the door down behind the posts. Joseph was about to help but Ezra cautioned him not to touch it. The door was heavy and a bit awkward, but Jesus was able to get the door in place by himself. That seemed to be Ezra's intent, for once the task was accomplished, Ezra clapped him on the shoulder and congratulated him. Then he pointed to the east and indicated the next day's sunrise and gave clear instruction for Jesus to come and lift the door to release the sheep into the outdoor pen. Jesus nodded his assent.

As they parted, Joseph said, "I can put a couple of handles on that door so it isn't so awkward for you."

"I can handle it, Abba," said Jesus. You saw me do it, right?"

"Yes, I saw you," said his father. "You are getting to be a man!"

That night after supper, Jesus took an oil lamp and went to check on the sheep. Joseph followed a few minutes later. He found Jesus sitting on the rail of the sheep pen looking up at the stars.

"Is everything alright," he asked.

"The sheep are fine; they are sleeping," said Jesus.

"I'm a little curious, still what Ezra's intentions are," said Joseph. "He has known about the cave since his childhood; why move his sheep here now?"

"And who will be responsible for them?" asked Jesus. "Is he expecting us to take care of them for him?"

"That's a good question."

"Did you notice that all these materials are used?" asked Jesus. "He dismantled his sheep pen and used the materials to build this one. He is not going to keep sheep at his place anymore."

"It's not easy to figure out why he does some things. It's not like you can ask him."

"And Abba, Samson was not at Uncle Ezra's today. When I asked him, 'Where's Samson?' he just went like this," Jesus struck his hands together as if dusting them off. "I think he means Samson is gone. He wouldn't sell him, would he?"

"No, I don't believe he would sell him. That is very curious."

"And he doesn't loan Samson out like he does other horses or donkeys."

"No," agreed Joseph, "he doesn't."

"And he doesn't have many animals there at all. I just saw one horse and a couple of donkeys besides the mare pulling the wagon. I think something is wrong."

"He is getting old; perhaps he is not feeling well."

"You wouldn't know it by the way he has worked to create this sheep pen," said Jesus. "He seems as strong as ever."

"True enough," said Joseph. "We will have to keep an eye on him. If something has happened to Samson, it will upset him deeply. That horse has been his life for what, fifteen years or more."

The next morning, Jesus let the sheep out of the cave at daybreak and made sure they had water in the tub. He was wondering whether he should give them hay or take them out grazing. While he was carrying water, he saw Uncle Ezra bringing another load of building material. He caught a ride the rest of the way up the hill and asked whether he should give the sheep hay or take them out grazing. Ezra indicated he should feed them from the hay pile for three days before leading them out of the pen. By that time, they would begin to know that this new pen was home.

Jesus happily took on the responsibility of feeding and watering the animals and moving them from the pen to the cave at night, but he wondered whether he was now to become a shepherd and how that would impact his studying of the scrolls. Shepherds were usually out in the fields with their flocks from dawn to dusk every day of the week. There would be time to study when the sheep rested, but how can you protect a scroll out in the open country? Perhaps James would have to learn to shepherd the flock. It seemed unlikely that Uncle Ezra would be able to manage them from his place. And it didn't make sense for him to move to Grandmother's house since he needed more open country for his horse operation.

Uncle Ezra set about reinforcing the fence of the sheep pen with the materials he had brought and Jesus went off to his studies. When he came back toward home at noon, Uncle Ezra was busy with his great hoe, leveling more ground outside the pen. Jesus asked him what he was doing. The best he could make out from Ezra's gestures is that he was going to build a storage building for hay. That made sense, but the size of the area Ezra was leveling seemed overly generous for hay storage.

Ezra declined an invitation to lunch and kept on working. Jesus reported Uncle Ezra's new endeavor to his father at lunch. After lunch, the two of them went out to inspect the progress. Ezra had leveled a piece of ground that was as large as Joseph's workshop in just a few hours. He didn't come back that afternoon, but he was there early the next morning with a load of used lumber and soon set about erecting poles to frame a barn. Joseph left off his own projects in the shop to help Ezra and in a few days' time, they had put together not only hay storage, but three stalls for animals.

When Ezra established his mare and the two donkeys in the barn and filled the hay storage, Joseph asked him if he wanted to live in his sister's house nearby. Ezra declined. He asked him what had happened to Samson. Ezra used the same gesture he had used with Jesus. Samson was gone. Joseph asked if Samson had died. Ezra said no. Joseph asked if he had sold Samson. Ezra's response was perplexing. First he said no, then he said yes. Then Ezra got very emotional and broke off the conversation and left.

Ezra didn't come by for a couple of days. He had been there so regularly for a couple of weeks that his absence left a hole in the family. Joseph and Jesus went to his place looking for him. What they saw when they got there was heartbreaking. He had dismantled most of his barn to provide the materials for the new barn on their property. His sheep pen was gone. There were no animals at all and the house was looking run down.

"Did he have any other animals here when you helped him bring the sheep over," asked Joseph.

"He had a pale-colored gelding and two donkeys," said Jesus. "And the mare that was pulling the wagon."

"Well the gelding is the only animal that he hasn't left at our place," said Joseph.

"He's probably away on that one," said Jesus. "Maybe he went to away to buy more horses."

For a week nothing was seen or heard from Uncle Ezra. On market day, Jesus and Joseph were crossing through town when Jesus suddenly said, "Look, Abba! That horse is the gelding I saw at Uncle Ezra's."

"Are you sure?" asked his father.

"I think so," said Jesus.

The animal was being shown by a Berber tribesman who was selling camels and horses. "Excuse me sir," said Joseph. "What do you know of the history of this horse?"

"He's a very fine horse," said the Berber. "He is very young, look at his teeth. He has almost no history at all."

"How long has he been in your possession?" asked Joseph.

"Only one week. I bought him at this market a week ago."

"Can you describe the man from whom you bought this horse?"

"He is a very large man, an older man," said the Berber. "But he can't talk or hear."

"That man is my uncle," said Joseph. "Do you know where I can find him?"

340

"No, I haven't seen him since I bought this horse from him. Sorry!"

Late that afternoon Jesus left off studying the scriptures and went to check on the garden on his way home. He was surprised to find a great pile of straw and dung at one end of the garden. It looked as though Uncle Ezra had scraped up a wagon load of dung from his various animals and brought it here for the enrichment of the garden soil.

Near the sheep pen, Jesus found the wagon but at first he didn't see his uncle. He looked in the stable and found the mare that Ezra usually hitched to the wagon. Noticing that several sheep were standing near the entrance to the cave and looking that way, Jesus wondered if Ezra had gone into the cave. He found him sitting on the ground inside, holding one of the lambs and petting it. When Jesus approached him, he didn't look up, though Jesus knew that he was aware of him. Ezra just kept petting the lamb and looking at it. Finally Jesus sat down beside him. After a few minutes, Jesus reached out to caress the lamb in Ezra's lap. Then Ezra put his arm around Jesus and hugged him tight. They sat there for several minutes petting the lamb together.

When they emerged into the light, Jesus asked him about the dung heap. Ezra indicated that he should just leave it alone until the garden was harvested. After harvest, he was to spread the dung on the garden and then in the spring, he should dig it into the soil.

Then Ezra reached into a bag he was carrying. He brought out a small scroll and handed it to Jesus. It was not sealed so Jesus unrolled it and found a second document inside the first. The one was the title deed to Ezra's land outside of town. The other was his will, leaving all his earthly goods, including land, house and animals to his nephew, Joseph. It had Ezra's mark at the bottom and the signatures of two witnesses.

Jesus looked up at Ezra and asked, "What is this? Are you going away?"

Ezra just smiled and looked away.

Jesus forced him to look at him and asked, "Are you ill?"

Ezra shook his head and started to leave. Jesus grabbed his sleeve and insisted that he come talk to Abba. For a moment Ezra hesitated and then went with Jesus to Joseph's workshop. "Abba, Uncle Ezra has come," said Jesus as he led Ezra into the shop. "And look what he has given me." Joseph greeted Ezra warmly and tried to convey how worried they had been. Then he looked at the documents in Jesus' hand.

"Well, this is extraordinary!" he exclaimed. "Why are you doing this?"

Ezra indicated, "I am old. We all die. You are my nephew."

Joseph and Jesus tried reassuring him that he had many years left, that he was strong and healthy. Ezra tried to make light of the whole thing and dismiss their concerns. He refused to join the family for dinner and left on foot in the direction of his home.

When Jesus and Joseph went to the house for supper, Mary asked, "Isn't Uncle Ezra with you? Hannah said she saw you talking with him."

"Yes, he was just here," said Joseph. "But he declined our invitation to join us."

"Did he say where he had been?" asked Mary.

"No," said Joseph. "But he brought me the title deed to his land and his last will and testament."

"He didn't!" exclaimed Mary. "What is happening to him? Do you think he is joining the Roman Legion again?"

"I doubt that," said Joseph. "I think his fighting days are behind him. And at his age, they wouldn't accept him if he did want back in."

"Well I've heard that there is a Roman camp only a few leagues from here."

"Yes," agreed Joseph. "They've been there for more than a month."

"It wouldn't surprise me if that Roman camp has something to do with how strangely Ezra is acting," said Mary.

After supper, Jesus and his father went to the roof of Grandmother's house to talk and watch the moon come up.

"Abba, I'm worried about Uncle Ezra," said Jesus.

"So am I," admitted Joseph.

"It is so strange that he would stop taking care of animals. He has always surrounded himself with animals."

"Even stranger that Samson is gone. He would never willingly part with Samson. I wish I could get to the bottom of that story."

"We should have asked that horse trader if he had bought any other animals from Uncle Ezra," said Jesus.

As the moon appeared on the horizon, Jesus said, "Watching a full moon rise always makes me feel thankful."

"Me, too," said Joseph "It's a reminder that God is still faithfully watching over His creation."

"Ah Lord God," said Jesus, erupting in prayer. "We praise you that you are One and the only One who reigns and rules in loving benevolence over this earth. Father, we praise you that you know all about what is going on in Uncle Ezra's world. Without speech and hearing, he can't tell us what is troubling his heart right now but you see the thoughts and intents and worries of his heart. Give him peace, give him courage to face his fears. Watch over him and bless him and may we be part of your blessing to him. Help us to understand how we can enter into his suffering and help him bear it. May you gain glory from his life. We thank you for your faithfulness in sending the full moon once again; for giving us the lesser light to rule the night. Blessed be your name forever."

"Amen," whispered Joseph.

After several minutes of silence, Joseph said, "I'm weary. Shall we head home and to bed?"

"May I sleep here under the moon tonight, Abba? Please?" asked Jesus.

"Yes, you may, son. But I think in the morning you and I should pay a visit to Uncle Ezra. He clearly is going through something strange and needs our support."

"I agree," said Jesus. "Thank you, Abba."

After his father had gone, Jesus snuggled down on a roof-top pallet and wrapped his woolen cloak around himself. Directly overhead was a dazzling array of stars. The moon was still below the low wall that surrounded the roof. In waiting for the moon to rise again, this time above the wall, Jesus dozed off. He dreamed that the moon rose above him and smiled down on him with Uncle Ezra's silent face. In his dream, he looked up and spoke to Uncle Ezra, "Hello, beloved Uncle."

To his amazement, Uncle Ezra spoke back to him, "Hello, beloved Nephew," he said. His voice was low and resonant, as gentle as his eyes promised. "Thank you for taking care of my animals. Thank you for what you are going to do."

While Jesus was pondering what Uncle Ezra might mean by "what you are going to do," suddenly Uncle Ezra's face fell from the sky. Jesus woke up with a start and sat up. It was a moment before he realized it had been a dream. He thought, I should have known it was a dream; Uncle Ezra can't talk! The moon had risen above the wall, but a cloud had just covered the moon. Jesus wished he could see it to know if it really resembled Uncle Ezra's face. He tried to shake off the dream but it had left him with a deep uneasiness that kept him awake.

He prayed for Uncle Ezra again and tried to go back to sleep but to no avail. He thought about going home to his own bed but didn't want to risk waking up his family. When the moon came out from behind the cloud, he studied it but couldn't find any resemblance to his uncle's face. Since he couldn't sleep and was too restless thinking about Uncle Ezra being all alone with no animals, he stirred himself to action. He would go see Uncle Ezra.

Twice along the way, the moon again went behind clouds, throwing the path into almost total darkness. When that happened, Jesus stopped and almost turned homeward. But when the moon came out again, he plucked up his courage and went on. The moon was shining brightly when he reached Ezra's home. It was hard to recognize the place with no animals and no sheep pen. A portion of the barn still stood, but much of it had been demolished for the materials to build the new one by the cave.

There was no lamp burning in the house. But at this time of night one would not expect to find one burning. He hesitated; it would make no sense to knock or call out. His Uncle would not hear. If it were daylight, he would just walk in. But if he entered in darkness, his Uncle might lash out in self-defense, not knowing who approached. He thought about turning for home; he would wait until morning and come back with his father. The clouds again obscured the moon. While Jesus waited for the moon to come out again to light his way home, he heard the footsteps of a horse.

The horse was coming nearer at a trot. Jesus hid himself behind the house and waited. The trot slowed to a walk and continued to get nearer. The horse and rider stopped in front of the remainder of the barn and Jesus heard the rider's feet hit the ground. At that moment, the moon emerged from behind a cloud and revealed to Jesus' eye, the forms of Great Uncle Ezra and Samson.

Jesus ran from his hiding place to greet his uncle. When Samson pricked his ears toward the approaching boy, Ezra turned to see what he was reacting to. Jesus threw his arms around his uncle's waist and hugged him tight. Ezra hugged his shoulders and then held him at arms length. He showed amazement that Jesus was not at home in bed. Jesus showed him that his heart was troubled about his uncle and about Samson.

Ezra led Samson into his usual stall in the remainder of the barn and lit an oil lamp. There was no saddle to remove; Ezra had been riding bareback. In the light of the lamp, he showed Jesus numerous welts and lacerations all over Sampson's body. Somebody had horribly abused this noble creature. Jesus recognized the welts as the marks that would be left by a whip and he knew that Uncle Ezra would never have done such a thing. He signed to his uncle asking, "Who whipped him?"

Ezra made signs that were unmistakably intended to portray a Roman officer. Then he set about putting a soothing salve of his own making on the open wounds. He sent Jesus for water from the cistern beside his house. When Jesus placed the water in front of Samson, Ezra added a medicinal brew to the water. Samson greedily sucked it up.

Ezra gave Jesus a brush and showed him to brush gently and to avoid getting too near any of the welts. Jesus murmured soothing words as he carefully worked those parts of Samson's body that were not damaged. When he would get anywhere near one of the wounds, Samson would twitch and move his hooves restlessly.

While Jesus was doing that, Ezra brought grain and dosed it with the same medicine he had put in the water. He put it in a feed bag and hung it on Samson's neck. Samson began to crunch the treated grain and to grow calmer. Ezra patted his neck and scratched around his ears. Samson whickered softly. Ezra removed the feed bag and persuaded Samson to lie down on the clean straw. He sat down next to Samson's head and continued to stroke him and comfort him.

He then indicated to Jesus to stop brushing. He pointed to some gear hanging on a post and Jesus brought it to him. When Ezra separated it out, Jesus recognized two hobbles and a length of rope. He had seen people hobble the front legs of a horse to keep it from wandering off when unattended. Ezra attached the one hobble to Samson's front legs and then crawled toward the rear legs and put the second hobble on them. As he was doing that, Samson's head suddenly swung up with a snort, but Ezra reassured him and got him quiet. Samson seemed to be falling asleep though once in a while he would struggle against the sensation. Just like a nursing baby, thought Jesus.

Ezra then took the length of rope and made a triple loop from one hobble to the other and gradually cinched the loop tighter, pulling the forefeet and hind feet toward each other. Clearly, Ezra did not want Samson to struggle to his feet. Jesus wondered what kind of treatment Ezra was planning to use and how Samson would react. Everyone who knew Ezra was in awe of his way with animals, and especially with horses. Jesus couldn't imagine what Ezra was up to, but he felt privileged to be able to witness it.

Ezra moved to Samson's head and sat down in the straw, lifting Samson's head onto his lap. He continued stroking Samson's neck and ears. Samson's breathing was noticeably slower. Ezra motioned for Jesus to move away from Samson's hooves. Jesus moved to the door of the stall and watched. Ezra brought out a small knife and while holding Samson's head firmly with one arm, he reached down to the base of his neck and made a quick cut. Blood gushed out immediately and Samson struggled for a moment but the hobbles restrained him and Ezra continued to hold his head and stroke his neck.

Jesus was alarmed at the volume of blood being spilled onto the straw. He kept expecting Uncle Ezra to do something to stop the flow but he did nothing except comfort Samson and let the flow continue. Jesus had heard of doctors who let out "bad blood" to try to heal someone of a sickness, but this was so extreme, he wondered if the cure would kill the patient. He looked back at Ezra for some sign of what his intentions were and saw that tears were streaming down his uncles face. Slowly it dawned on Jesus that Uncle Ezra was not trying to heal Samson, but to euthanize him.

He ran to try to pinch the spurting wound closed with his own hands but Ezra pushed him away and warned him not to interfere. So he grabbed Uncle Ezra's shoulders and shook him, asking, "What are you doing? Why?"

Uncle Ezra just continued to stroke Samson's neck and weep. When the flow of blood began to slow, Samson struggled again and tried to raise his head but Ezra held him firmly. Then Samson heaved a great sigh and breathed his last. Then a tremor ran through his great frame and his hooves strained mightily against the hobbles for a moment. Then he lay still. And Uncle Ezra continued to hold his head and weep. Jesus threw himself on Samson's neck and wept, too. Why had Uncle Ezra done this? Samson's wounds had not been life-threatening. And Ezra loved this horse!

After several minutes Ezra roused himself and got up. He gently laid Samson's head back on the straw and cut the rope that had bound the hobbles together. He took off the hobbles and hung them carefully on the post where they had been. He removed the heavy curtain that he had used to close off the stall after the rest of the barn had been taken away. Just the other side of the curtain was a newly dug pit.

Ezra tied the length of rope to Samson's front hooves and motioned for Jesus to stand the other side of the pit and pull on the rope. When Jesus got ready to do that, Ezra took hold of the back legs and lifted. Together they were gradually able to roll Samson's inert body into the pit. By the time they had pushed in the loose dirt and mounded it up over Samson's grave, the morning star was visible in the east.

Ezra hugged Jesus tight and thanked him for his help. Jesus was still bewildered by these events and wished he could understand why Samson had to be put down. Then Ezra looked toward the east and motioned to Jesus that he should run away quickly. Jesus signed that he would stay with him and that Joseph would come in the morning.

Ezra signed his disapproval of that plan and again indicated that Jesus should run away right now. Jesus asked why. Ezra indicated that Romans were coming. Many Romans and the big officer over the Romans would come.

Jesus again wanted to know more. Ezra signed that the officer over the Romans was the one who had whipped Samson. He further indicated that he himself had gone to the Roman camp and had stolen Samson away. Now the Romans would be very angry and would come kill him.

Jesus shook his head in denial and disbelief. He protested that this could not be true. Then Ezra took the oil lamp and led him to another pit that he had recently dug near Samson's grave. He indicated that his grave was for himself. He again indicated that Jesus should run away. Jesus refused to abandon him. He could not believe the story Ezra was telling. Perhaps it was all a mistake. But Samson's blood, drying on his hands was a stark reminder that this was not a dream. He remembered that in his dream a few hours before, Uncle Ezra's face was like a moon that fell from the sky. Did that portend Uncle Ezra's demise?

Suddenly Uncle Ezra's hand tightened on his upper arm. He pointed toward town and Jesus saw the flicker of torches coming toward them. Ezra pushed Jesus away from him and motioned that he should run fast in the opposite direction of the coming Romans. Jesus hesitated. He didn't want to abandon Uncle Ezra to the Romans. Then Ezra ran to him and kissed him soundly on both cheeks. He reached into his pocket and brought out the knife that he had used to open Samson's artery. He pressed it into Jesus' hand and again motioned for him to run.

Jesus pulled on Ezra's arm, urging him to run, too. Ezra shook his head. He was not going to run. He was going to go to his grave. By now, Jesus could clearly hear the footsteps of the marching Romans. Not knowing if it was the right thing to do, he kissed his uncle one more time and ran into the darkness. The moon was setting through a haze of cloud. There was enough light to avoid smashing into a boulder or a tree, but not enough to see every obstacle to his flight, such as cactus or a tree root that could trip him. When he had gone about half a league, he caught his foot on something that sent him tumbling to the ground out of breath.

He lay there panting and praying, trying to figure out what he should do. He had been running uphill and had reached an area that had bushes and small trees scattered here and there. He crept around until he found a vantage point from which he could see the Romans arriving at his uncle's home. There were about a dozen mounted soldiers, three officers, also mounted, and at least fifty foot soldiers. They were carrying so many torches that it was quite possible for Jesus to watch the proceedings from a safe distance.

He couldn't hear what they were saying, but he watched as his uncle showed them the stall where the great pool of blood would still be drying in the straw. Then he showed them the fresh grave where Samson would no longer feel the sting of the whip. Then several foot soldiers were ordered forward to arrest Uncle Ezra. He meekly submitted to their bonds, not offering any resistance at all.

The soldiers stripped him and tied him to the doorpost of the stable. One of the officers dismounted and began to lay stripes across Ezra's great back with his whip. Ezra hung his head and took the beating without a sound, though his body would quake with each stroke. Jesus thought of the marks on Samson's hide and concluded that this Roman officer was the same person who had abused that beautiful stallion. It dawned on him that Ezra had done what he had done to spare Samson from any more abuse. He was willing to take the beating himself rather than let Samson endure it. He hoped that after the officer had beaten Uncle Ezra to his satisfaction, he would let him go and the whole nightmare would be over.

But the officer's anger apparently knew no bounds. When he wearied of beating Ezra, he ordered two of the foot soldiers to continue the beating. Meanwhile, he ordered others to ransack the house and the remainder of the barn for anything valuable. He also ordered the mounted soldiers to pull down the remainder of the barn. They did so and used two of the timbers to construct a rude cross.

The beating continued until Ezra sagged to the ground. The soldiers gathered round him and tried to raise him up to retie his hands higher, but he was so heavy, so bloody that it was impossible to get a good grip on him. And he was so limp, one might assume he was unconscious. But when the officer called a halt to the beating, Ezra crawled toward the cross without coercion. The Romans let out a cheer when they saw that and redoubled the cheer when Ezra lay down on the cross and spread out his arms.

349

Jesus thought of the words of Isaiah, "as a sheep before her shearers is silent, so he opened not his mouth." Though he had never heard his uncle speak a word, except in that dream, he had often heard him roar in playful attacks on village boys who taunted him. He marveled that Ezra didn't roar when they drove the spikes through his hands and his feet. Perhaps Uncle Ezra never roars in pain, he thought, only in play. When he thought about the past month and all the mysterious choices Uncle Ezra had made, Jesus knew that this horrible event was going exactly as Ezra had expected and planned for. The man loved Samson enough to die for him. What was the world going to be like without Ezra in it? And without Samson and Ezra together in it. Suddenly the world felt a lonelier and colder place than it ever had before.

It took four mounted soldiers with the power of their horses to raise the cross. When it dropped into the hole that had been dug for it, it swayed dangerously. The four horsemen were deployed to the four points of the compass to steady the cross while foot soldiers jammed rocks around the base to firm it up. Just like Uncle Ezra setting fence posts, thought Jesus.

Once the cross was secured in the upright position, the officer gave the order and his troops torched the house and the remainder of the barn. Then, leaving one officer and ten foot soldiers to guard the crucifixion, the rest of the Romans formed a column and marched away.

It was quite light now and the sun would be rising soon. Jesus could no longer remain hidden. He wanted to save Uncle Ezra. He couldn't think of a way to do that, but at least he could go be near him, perhaps comfort him as Ezra had comforted Samson in his dying. He hid the knife that Uncle Ezra had given him, marking well the location so he could retrieve it. He used sand to scrub the dried blood off his hands. He walked down the hill wondering if he would be crucified as an accomplice to his uncle's crime of loving a horse too much to watch it suffer.

As it turned out, he was not the only spectator to appear. Others were drawn by the smoke and by the sound of the troops marching through Nazareth back to the Roman camp. But Jesus was the only one who crept up between the smoking ruins of the house on one side and the barn on the other and looked up at his dying uncle. Ezra was still conscious, and though he was in considerable agony, he smiled at Jesus. Jesus felt so helpless before that cross. He had always felt constricted by his inability to communicate with Uncle Ezra verbally. But now Ezra couldn't even do hand signals. Jesus stood there with tears streaming down his face trying to sign to Ezra, "I love you. I understand now. You love Samson." Ezra nodded his head and winked at Jesus.

Suddenly Abba was there at Jesus' side, with an arm around his shoulders. Jesus turned into his father's embrace and said, "Oh Abba…" He sobbed and sobbed in his father's arms.

They kept vigil at the foot of the cross until Uncle Ezra died. It did not take terribly long. He was such a heavy man that within an hour, his shoulders were pulled from their sockets and his efforts to straighten his legs diminished. So before the third hour he suffocated. Jesus and Joseph wanted to offer him water on a sponge because they knew he was suffering thirst. But there was not a sponge or a reed that had escaped the burning.

Bit by bit, as they waited and watched, Jesus whispered to his father the story of what had transpired in the night. "He loved that Samson more than he loved his own life," he said in summary.

"This explains a lot of his peculiar behavior over the last month," said Joseph. "But it still doesn't make sense that Samson had come into the possession of the Roman officer."

"Excuse my intrusion," said a voice behind them. They turned to find a youngish stranger dressed in the style of Jericho. "I am called Nathan, I serve as interpreter for his Highness, Legate Antonius, the commander of the Roman Legion in Nazareth."

"Your clothing would indicate you are from Jericho, is that right?" asked Joseph.

"Ah, very perceptive of you," replied Nathan.

"And you work for the Romans?" asked Joseph.

"I understand that serving them can be offensive," said Nathan, "but please consider the possibility that I was compelled to serve against my will."

"And were you compelled against your will?" asked Joseph.

"I don't have time for that story," said Nathan. "The Legate sent me back here to explain to any concerned locals why this man was executed. You seem to have known him, is that right."

"Yes," said Joseph.

"Are you perhaps related to him?" asked Nathan.

"Before I answer that, I would like to know whether relatives of this man are accused of any crimes," said Joseph.

"Oh, no! Not at all," said Nathan. "He is accused of stealing and killing a very valuable horse that belonged to the Legate. The matter is now settled and no one else will be charged."

"And in what court was this man found guilty?" asked Joseph.

"No court was necessary since the man freely admitted to the crime and the horse's blood was found on his hands and his clothing. The dead horse is freshly buried right here," he said, pointing to the fresh mound.

"And did his Highness the Legate exhume the corpse to determine that the dead horse was indeed his?" asked Joseph.

"Uh, no he did not do that," admitted Nathan in obvious discomfort. "But the criminal admitted that he had done it. Why make any further inquiry when the confession is clear?"

"My point," said Joseph, "is that the horse in question could not have belonged to the Legate. It is a horse that my uncle was willing to die for. He would never have sold him."

"So he was your uncle?" asked Nathan.

"Yes," admitted Joseph.

"And my great uncle," added Jesus.

"Look, I'm not here to defend the Romans and I'm not looking for an argument. Let me tell what I know."

"Speak then," said Joseph.

"His Highness Legate Antonius was transferred from Jericho two months ago. He compelled me to come with him as interpreter. He heard about your uncle from the officers in the camp and he first came to see about having a mare serviced by this great stallion. But once he saw the stallion, he wanted it for himself. He offered your uncle 100 shekels of silver to purchase the horse but your uncle just laughed. The Legate does not like being laughed at and he is accustomed to getting what he wants, so he offered your uncle 200 shekels, believing that he was paying more than the horse was worth but he would not be turned down.

"Your uncle was intransigent and turned his back on the Legate, which he never should have done. Then the Legate was enraged and threw down a bag of 300 shekels of silver and ordered his bodyguard to seize the horse. In his own mind, he was paying double what the horse was worth."

"And in my uncle's mind, the horse was not for sale, so no price was adequate," said Joseph.

"Clearly!" replied Nathan. "For the next morning your uncle showed up at the camp. He returned the Legate's money and demanded his horse."

"And what was the Legate's response?" asked Joseph.

"He laughed at your uncle and had him escorted off the camp."

"And did my uncle then keep the money?"

"No, he refused to accept it. He left it on the ground at the camp."

"And what became of it? Three hundred shekels wouldn't lie around for long."

"The Legate took it back. He said, 'If that cursed fool,' (pardon me, but I'm telling you what he said.) 'If that cursed fool doesn't want the money, I don't have a problem accepting the horse for free.' That's what he said."

"Doesn't it seem to you that the sale was never completed?" asked Joseph.

"It doesn't matter what it seems to me," replied Nathan. "I cannot reason with the Legate. Nor can you or any other short of the Emperor, himself."

"It is very hard to accept the murder of my uncle as the natural consequence of a Roman officer being greedy," said Joseph.

"Please be careful," warned Nathan. "I sympathize, I really do. But you cannot win this battle. And some of these soldiers can understand a bit of Aramaic." He pointed with his chin in the direction of those who were left to guard the site.

"Can you ask the soldiers if we can bury Uncle Ezra now?" asked Jesus.

"His name was Ezra?" asked Nathan. "We didn't know his name. It's hard to converse with a deaf man. My father's name was Ezra."

"Would you please ask them?" said Joseph.

"Certainly."

He went and spoke to the officer over the ten and then nodded in their direction and motioned for them to proceed.

"He dug his own grave right near the one we buried Samson in," said Jesus.

Joseph recruited a few men from among the bystanders and together they took down Ezra's body, washed it, wrapped it in linen and laid him in the tomb he had dug for himself.

"Shouldn't he be buried in the cemetery with his parents and his sister?" asked one of the helpers.

"He dug this grave for himself," offered Jesus. "He wanted to be buried beside Samson."

"And Samson couldn't be buried in the cemetery, of course," said Joseph.

"No, of course not," said the man. "And Ezra always did kind of live apart from people. But he sure had a way with animals."

"Such a pity about that great horse," sighed another. All those present murmured in agreement.

Once the burial was completed, the soldiers ordered the crowd to disperse. Jesus looked around at the now unfamiliar landscape. The ashes of the house and the stable were still smoldering. Smoke rose in two columns that mingled together as the morning breeze swept them toward town as a dark messenger. The news was that an era had ended in sorrow. The great Arab stallion, Samson, was no more. There was no longer a mysterious man who couldn't speak but was a gifted healer of animals. There was no house, no stable, no corral. Just two mounds of fresh earth, two smoldering ash heaps and one cross standing watch over the graves.

"Abba?" said Jesus on the way home.

"Yes, my son?"

"Would it be okay if I go to Grandmother's house and sleep?"

"Don't you want some breakfast?" asked Joseph.

"I'm not hungry and I'm very tired."

"Did you sleep at all last night?"

"Not much. I fell asleep and then had a disturbing dream. When I woke from the dream I was too worried about Uncle Ezra, so I got up and went to him."

"I would like to hear about the dream and all that you experienced last night, son."

"And I would like to tell you, but not now. And I don't want to be the first to bear the news to Mother and the children."

"I can understand that. Go and sleep. I will bear the sad news. And I will check on you at lunch time," said his father, giving him a squeeze around the shoulders.

When Jesus heard the door open he muttered, "I'm not sleeping, Abba."

"And I'm not your abba," answered Mary.

Jesus sat up, blinking in surprise. "Abba said he would come check on me."

"He has come twice," said Mary. "Now that it is almost supper time, I insisted on coming."

"Supper time?" said Jesus. "Have I slept the whole day?"

"I suppose it's because you didn't sleep all night. Oh, Jesus, I am so sad about Uncle Ezra and very distressed that you had to witness that horrible scene. I have worried about you all day and have been terrified over and over at what might have happened to you. Why on earth did you go there in the middle of the night?"

"Oh mother, I had to go. I think I was sent there for a reason. Uncle Ezra needed me to be there," said Jesus.

"Poor Uncle Ezra, God rest his soul," said Mary. "I know he was a drunkard and a violent man in his youth, but since I have known him, he was the gentlest, sweetest, funniest giant on earth. It is just so senseless that he would come to a tragic end."

She wept and Jesus wept with her, squeezing her hands in his.

When he could find words, he said, "Uncle Ezra is at peace."

"What do you mean?" asked his mother.

"He has been planning this for weeks, Mother. Don't you see? Building the sheep pen here and opening the cave that he has known about since his boyhood, bringing all these animals here and selling the rest, he was planning to die this way. It was no surprise to him. He had already dug his own grave and one for Samson. This was his plan and he fulfilled it."

"But it seems so senseless," said Mary, "to die for a horse!"

"To Uncle Ezra, Samson was more than a horse," said Jesus. "Samson was his life partner. They loved each other and he refused to let Samson suffer under a mean tyrant. He put him down so gently and lovingly. He even soothed the welts from the Legate's ruthless whippings with balm before he put him down. I think Samson was so happy to be back in Uncle Ezra's care that he was willing to go, even to death, along with Ezra. And Uncle Ezra was willing to go to death for and with Samson."

"Why, oh why can't these greedy, ruthless Romans go back where they came from and leave us in peace? I can still see Uncle Ezra and Samson galloping along the beach on the way to Capernaum. They were so powerful and full of life. I can't believe they are both gone."

"It's okay, Mother. It will be made right. God's hand is not shortened that He cannot save," said Jesus.

"I know son, but why did he not save Uncle Ezra from this tragic fate?"

"Mother, dear Mother, that is not for us to question. Uncle Ezra seemed to be content with his decision, painful though it was to carry out. The Roman Legate did not take Uncle Ezra's life; he offered it willingly."

"That, I will never understand," said Mary. "Never!"

Jesus bit his lip.

The next morning, Jesus said, "Abba, I would like to let the sheep out of the pen today and see if I can lead them to pasture."

"Where will you take them?" asked Joseph.

"Back to the pastures around Uncle Ezra's place," said Jesus. That area is greening up and the sheep are familiar with it."

"I don't think it is safe," said Mary. "The Romans might still be there."

"The Romans have no interest in that place anymore," said Jesus. "The Legate sought his vengeance on Uncle Ezra and is now satisfied. And besides, Abba now has legal right to that land. May I go, Abba?"

"I will accompany you. If it seems safe, you may pasture the sheep there today. I'm sure they are weary of being penned up and we can't feed them hay forever. If there are any Romans there, we will bring the flock back here."

Jesus tied a short length of rope to the halter on the oldest ewe and led her out the gate. The others followed, baaing eagerly at the prospect of fresh pasture.

"I wonder how long it will take them to get used to your voice and follow you," said Joseph. "They never knew Ezra's voice."

"Oh, he made some noises that they recognized," said Jesus. "They weren't words but the sheep knew him and knew the sound of his voice. "

"I suppose if you care for them and lead them to what they need, they will adopt you as their shepherd. It will take time away from your studies, though."

"It's another kind of studying," said Jesus. "David spent a lot of time with his father's flocks and it didn't prevent him from becoming the king God intended him to be."

"That is true," admitted his father.

When they came within view of Uncle Ezra's place, the scene was peaceful and pastoral. There were still wisps of smoke rising from the two piles of ashes on either side of the cross, but no one was in sight. The sheep fell to grazing and Jesus removed the rope from the halter of the ewe. "With this good grass, they will not wander far," he said.

"We will have a service for Uncle Ezra here," said Joseph.

"When?"

"Probably tomorrow."

"We should gather some stones to mark his grave and Samson's," said Jesus.

"There are plenty of stones here," said his father, "the foundation stones from the house."

"Will we not rebuild Uncle Ezra's house, then?" asked Jesus.

"I think not," said Joseph. "He gathered these stones himself when he built this house. I think he would be honored to have them mark his resting place and Samson's."

The two of them worked together for the next half hour, pulling stones out of the ashes and placing them as borders around the two large graves.

When they were finished, Joseph asked, "Will you be alright here by yourself?"

"Yes, Abba," said Jesus. "I am not alone." Joseph looked at the sheep. Jesus looked at the graves.

"Alright then," said his father. "If you need me for anything, I will be in the shop. Don't hesitate to interrupt me, okay?"

"I'll be fine, Abba. Go in peace."

Jesus followed the sheep for a while and spoke to them as they grazed. He wanted them to become used to his voice so that they would learn to follow him. They didn't seem to miss Uncle Ezra or be upset about the changes to the landscape. The lack of a house, barn and corral didn't keep them from finding plenty of fresh grass to eat.

When they had filled their bellies, they gathered near the spot where the old sheep pen had been and there they lay down to rest and chew the cud. "So you do know this place, after all, do you?" said Jesus. "You no longer have a secure sheep pen here. And you no longer have a great, strong shepherd to defend you. All you have is me. I will do the best I can for you, but I am no Ezra. I have a lot to learn to become a good shepherd."

As he thought about having to defend the sheep, he remembered the knife Uncle Ezra had given him. He got up quietly so as not to upset his small flock. "I'll be right back," he said to the sheep. "I am not abandoning you." The sheep paid him scant attention as he slipped away into the brush nearby. Though it had been dark when he had last been there, it did not take him long to find the spot from which he had watched the Romans arrest and beat his great uncle. He found the spot where he had dug in the earth and buried the knife.

Now, for the first time, he could examine the knife in the light of day. He brushed the dirt off the sheath and discovered Ezra's unmistakable mark burned into the leather. It was a knife of Ezra's own making. The handle was of goat horn and the iron blade had been forged by hammer and anvil. Jesus remembered watching Uncle Ezra's great arms working at the anvil, making sparks fly as he repaired a plow one day for a village farmer. He wondered that such a strong man, armed with such a sharp knife should submit so meekly to the Romans without a fight. Then he remembered that Ezra had not been armed with this knife when the Romans reached him.

He returned to the sheep and sat down near the graves, "Uncle Ezra," he said quietly, "I don't remember if I thanked you for this knife. Forgive me. I was so confused. I didn't know what you were doing or why you were doing it. Looking back, I can see that you had a great plan. If a good shepherd lays down his life for his sheep, you were willing to lay down your life for Samson. You were not willing to allow the Roman legate to destroy your dear companion. So you ushered Samson gently out of this life of suffering, knowing that it would cost you your own life. And then you disarmed yourself so that you wouldn't be tempted to fight against the Romans."

He wiped his tears away with his sleeve and then said, "Thank you for giving me your knife, Uncle Ezra. And thank you for giving us your sheep, the donkeys, the mare, the wagon… even this land. I was blessed to know you. I was blessed to have you for my relative. May you rest in peace."

After some reflection, he prayed, "Thank you my heavenly Father for Uncle Ezra. Thank you for the memories of traveling with him, eating with him, learning from him. Thank you for all that he taught me. Thank you that through Uncle Ezra, you have shown me how to live and how to die. If Messiah has to die for the sins of the people, I should not die in a lesser way than this man died for his horse."

His thoughts were interrupted by the sound of horse and wagon approaching. He looked up to find his father coming. He went to meet him. "Abba," said Jesus, "why have you come?"

"I got to thinking about this cross standing here," said Joseph. "I don't want it standing here tomorrow when we have the memorial service for Uncle Ezra. It's too ghastly a reminder and exposes his blood."

"I agree," said Jesus. "I will help you."

"Besides," said Joseph. "There is good wood in that cross. I can't let it go to waste."

Together, they dug around the cross and removed the portion of blood-soaked earth and buried it at the foot of Ezra's grave. They lowered the cross to the ground and disconnected the cross member. Joseph had brought water with which they washed as much blood as possible from the wood and loaded it into the wagon. "What will you use the wood for, Abba?" asked Jesus.

"I don't know yet," said Joseph. "It will be for something that will honor Uncle Ezra's memory but I don't know what that will be."

They pushed clean dirt back into the hole from which they had removed the cross and smoothed it with their feet. Looking around, Joseph said, "This is not a bad place to graze sheep. It must be much like what this place looked like when Ezra first found it."

"Except for the ashes and the graves, yes," agreed Jesus.

"It's another reminder," said Joseph, "that our lives are like the flowers of the field. A wind passes over them and they wither and fall and their beauty is destroyed."

"But the word of the Lord endures forever," added Jesus. "I will always be grateful for Uncle Ezra. His story will be told in Nazareth for generations."

"True," said his father. "He was one remarkable man."

"I like knowing that he can now hear and speak," said Jesus.

Joseph smiled. "What a joy that must be!"

The two of them sat near the graves and ate their lunch in silence. Then Joseph left and Jesus got up to follow the sheep as they went back to grazing.

Toward late afternoon, Jesus was thinking he might need to catch the old ewe and attach the rope to her halter. How else would he lead them back to the sheep pen and the cave? But before he even approached her, she began to gravitate toward the direction he wanted to take the sheep. And where she went, the others followed. So he said, "Yes, old girl. It's about time to be headed home. Will you follow me?"

He began slowly walking toward home and looked over his shoulder. The old ewe took another mouthful of grass and then followed him tentatively. He walked a little farther and when he looked back, the whole flock was moving in unison in his tracks. Whether it was because of his voice or simply their in-built rhythm of life, he didn't really care. They were coming home to their new pen and their cave. Maybe I am their shepherd after all, he thought.

By the time he got them home and watered and settled in the cave, it was getting toward dusk. Joseph came out to check on him. "How did it go? I see you got them back home okay."

"Yes, Abba. It went very well. I didn't have to tie the rope on the old ewe. She followed me home and all the others followed her."

"Good. And you didn't suffer any anxiety being there where Ezra died and was buried."

"No, Abba. There is something of his peaceful spirit still upon the place, despite the violence the Romans brought to him. I think it is because he died on his own terms. I mean, from the outside, it looks like the Romans had their way with him. But when you look closely, Uncle Ezra defeated the Legate. He took Samson away from the Legate and put him beyond the Legate's reach. The Legate then exacted his revenge on Uncle Ezra but he couldn't get Samson back."

"And for that small victory, Ezra was willing to die?"

"More than willing," said Jesus. "I would say he was content. That's why he didn't flee or resist arrest. For the joy of knowing Samson would never suffer those abusive whippings, he was content to die."

"He sure loved that horse," mused Joseph.

As the two of them were washing up for supper, they were hailed by a traveler. "Is this the home of Joseph the carpenter?"

"It is," replied Joseph. "And I am he. Who is it that seeks me at this time of day?"

"Ah, thank God I've found you, my friend. It is I, Rabbi Zephon of Capernaum."

"Rabbi Zephon!" cried Jesus and ran to greet him. "Welcome, welcome!"

"Rabbi, what are you doing here in Nazareth?" asked Joseph.

"Well, surely even a rabbi has the right to travel a bit in Israel," said the rabbi. "Or did you think that only you and your family were allowed on the roads?"

"Of course, you are more than allowed," said Joseph. "You are welcome. But since we have never had the privilege of seeing you here before, you will allow us to be surprised at your appearance."

"Of course you are allowed to be surprised," said the rabbi. "It was my intention to surprise you. And I bring good news."

"We could use some good news around here," said Joseph. "Please come in and be our guest. Wash your feet and refresh yourself with a bite to eat and then refresh us with your good news. Mary will be delighted to see you."

"Abba, could the rabbi and I sleep at Grandmother's house?" asked Jesus.

"With our own house bursting at the seams with children these days, I think that is our best option," answered Joseph. "And I myself will claim the privilege of joining you. We men need to have a quiet place to visit away from the children."

"Let me stable your donkey," said Jesus. "We have plenty of fodder for him."

"Thank you, Jesus," said the rabbi. "Just let me get my bags."

"Here," said Joseph, "let me take those. You can wash right here."

Jesus led the donkey to drink and then to their recently acquired stable. There he introduced the rabbi's animal to the two donkeys and the mare that were already sharing shelter and fodder. He unsaddled the animal and gave it a good brushing before joining the others at supper.

Mary was just saying, "We have been talking about a trip in your direction, Rabbi. It is past time that Jesus return the scroll of Isaiah that he has been studying."

"Ah, no worries," said the rabbi. "I have brought him the scroll of Jeremiah in case he is ready to trade."

"Thank you, Rabbi," said Jesus. "That is excellent. Yes, I am ready to trade. And I have some questions for you about Isaiah, but those can wait until later."

"Yes, we can get to those questions later. But I don't think we can wait any longer to hear your news, Rabbi. You say that you bring good news?"

"Yes," said the rabbi. "I bring you good news of great joy in the household of the rabbi of Capernaum. The rabbi is no longer childless. Three weeks ago the Lord answered our prayers and my dear wife delivered a beautiful daughter, whom we have named Rebecca."

"Hurray!" shouted the children.

"Mazel tov!" shouted Joseph.

"Oh God bless her," cried Mary. "That is good news indeed. And Elsaba is well?"

"She is very well," said the rabbi. "Her mother is with her in our house, making my presence quite unnecessary for the time being, so I thought it a perfect time to come to Nazareth."

"Absolutely," said Joseph. "We are so glad you have come. And we are delighted with your good news. May the Lord give you many more children. What is it? Five years you have been waiting?"

"Six years," interjected Mary. "Thank God, He has heard our prayers on your behalf. Now when Jesus is finished with the scroll of Jeremiah, I will have to be the one to accompany him to Capernaum so I can visit Elsaba and see this child of yours."

"Your visit would be most welcome," said the rabbi. "Elsaba charged me with the solemn duty to invite you."

"I will gladly come," said Mary. "It may be a few months, but by then she will have regained her strength, God willing."

"But mother, who will escort us in Uncle's absence?" asked Jesus.

"Why in his absence?" asked the rabbi. "Is Ezra not well?"

"Ah," said Joseph, clearing his throat. "It is unfortunate that we have to announce sad news right on top of your wonderful news, but …uh…"

"Uncle Ezra, God rest his soul, is no longer with us," said Mary.

"Oh, I am so sorry to hear this," said the rabbi. "Did he pass recently?"

"Yes, just two days ago," she answered. "But let's not talk about that right now. I want to hear all about Rebecca's birth and Elsaba's health. Tell me about your mother-in-law, too. Did she have to come from far away?"

"Not very far," said the rabbi. "She is from Tiberius. And she is a good woman. But when she and Elsaba are hovering over little Rebecca, there is no room for a man in that house! Besides, I could hardly wait to share the good news with you, knowing that you have prayed and prayed for us to have this child."

"And we are very glad you have come," said Joseph. "We are privileged to share in your joy at the answer to your prayers and ours. But it is also good to have a rabbi here for Ezra's service tomorrow."

"I don't want to talk about Ezra tonight," said Mary.

"Okay, okay," said Joseph. "But we are glad you have come, Rabbi."

Once the smaller children were settled in their beds and the twins were well on their way to the same pleasant fate, Joseph and Jesus led the rabbi over to Grandmother's house for some man to man talk over tea.

As they walked, Jesus explained that Grandmother's house was where he now studied the scrolls. When they stepped through the doorway, Jesus lit a lamp and Joseph offered the seat of honor to the rabbi and poured the tea.

"See, Rabbi Zephon, this is the wooden case in which I keep the borrowed scrolls," said Jesus.

"That's very elegant, Jesus," said the rabbi. "Your father is quite a craftsman."

"Jesus made that himself," said Joseph.

"Really?" said the rabbi.

"Abba taught me and supervised my work," said Jesus.

"That is quite impressive," said the rabbi. "I am comforted to know that the scrolls I loan you are so well cared for."

"And we are more grateful than you know for the generosity with which you loan them," said Joseph.

Jesus muttered his agreement but the rabbi said, "I can't imagine a better use of them. I can only read one at a time. Why should most of them gather dust while an avid scholar suffers from lack of access to the Word of God? But I wonder that a carpenter as skilled as this young man can find time to study at all."

"Actually" said Joseph, "I have released him from being my apprentice so that he can spend more time studying the scrolls. I have begun to train James and Joseph Junior in his stead, but to tell the truth, neither of them shows as much promise."

"But now that we have a small flock of sheep and other animals to tend to, I will still be limited in how much time I can spend studying," said Jesus.

"Oh, did you buy some sheep?" asked the rabbi.

"No, Uncle Ezra gave us his flock of ewes and lambs along with a mare and a couple of donkeys," said Jesus. "I am just beginning to learn the shepherd's trade."

"My goodness," commented the rabbi. "You will be a well-rounded man: a carpenter, a shepherd and a scholar rolled into one."

"I am eager to learn how to care for sheep," said Jesus. "That was David's occupation before Samuel anointed him to be king. But I regret that it means less time to study."

"Well, may the God of Israel be praised," said Rabbi Zephon. "He has prepared a gift for you by my humble hand and has given me the privilege of delivering it to you in person!" As he was saying this, he jumped up and began rummaging around in one of his saddle bags. He brought out a soft cloth bag and placed it in Jesus' lap. "The Lord God knew that you were going to be spending some time with the sheep and He moved me to prepare this gift."

"What is it?" asked Jesus, feeling the heft of the bag and the shape of the mysterious contents.

"Open it and see," said Zephon.

Jesus loosened the drawstring and slipped one hand inside, "It is scrolls," he said, "many small scrolls." He drew one out and untied the cord that kept it rolled small. He opened it and began to read, "The Lord is my shepherd, I shall not live in want…"

"A psalm of David," said Joseph.

"There are three of them on this little scroll," said Jesus as he pulled out a second small scroll and began to open it.

"Such small scrolls," marveled Joseph. "You say that you made them? I didn't know you are a scribe as well as a rabbi."

"My brother Mahli and I both apprenticed as scribes when we were in our teenage years," said the rabbi. "He continued in that trade and works among the scribes at the temple in Jerusalem to this day. Last year when I visited him, he gave me a bag full of small scraps that get cut off when an official book of God's word is finished and dedicated by the priests. He told me that I might find them useful to practice on so that my skills don't diminish with disuse. I have spent many a happy hour since then copying Psalms onto these small scraps. It is one of my favorite ways to spend time with the Word of God. And the Lord told me to bring these and give them to you as a gift."

"They are perfect for carrying with me when I go out with the sheep!" exclaimed Jesus.

"See!" exulted Zephon. "Your heavenly father knew you had need of these and provided the materials through my brother a year ago. And He blessed me with the experience of copying Psalms of David and thus has met a need that only He knew you would have."

"This is wonderful," said Joseph. "Thank you, Heavenly Father, for our brother, Rabbi Zephon and for giving him to us as your personal agent to bless us with this precious gift of your word."

"Amen," said Jesus. "Amen and Amen."

"How many psalms have you copied?" asked Joseph.

"There are forty-three in this bag," said Zephon. "And I have a few unused scraps that I haven't yet used. I am sure I can get more when I go up to Jerusalem for the Day of Atonement."

"Rabbi," said Jesus, "may I ask you a question about this psalm? I have been thinking about it for a long time."

"Which one?"

"My God, my God, why have you forsaken me?"

"Yes," said the rabbi. "What is your question?"

"This part," said Jesus. "Where it says, 'I am poured out like water, and all my bones are out of joint. My heart has turned to wax; it has melted within me. My mouth is dried up like a potsherd, and my tongue sticks to the roof of my mouth; you lay me in the dust of death. Dogs surround me, a pack of villains encircles me; they pierce my hands and my feet.' My question is this; when did this happen to David and what were the circumstances?"

"That's a good question," admitted the rabbi. "I have heard a few opinions on that psalm. Tradition is pretty clear that this never literally happened to David. Most scholars agree that this was hyperbole that David used to describe the inner torment he felt when fleeing from Saul."

"Could it be that David wrote it about someone else under the direction of the Holy Spirit?" asked Jesus. "It seems very literal and specific. The details of bones being out of joint, extreme thirst and piercing of hands and feet? Those sound like David, or someone else was being crucified."

"You have a point," admitted the rabbi. "But we know that David was never crucified."

"Exactly," said Jesus.

"So, do you have an idea of the identity of some other person who was crucified?" asked the rabbi. "Crucifixion was not known among the people of Israel in David's time. Impaling an enemy was known, but not crucifixion. So if this is a description of crucifixion, who could it refer to?"

"The Messiah?" proposed Jesus.

"Oh no, no, no," said the rabbi. "God forbid. The anointed One lives forever and judges the earth. This can't refer to the Messiah."

"Then who does Isaiah write about when he describes the suffering servant who bears the sin of many and makes intercession for the transgressors? Isaiah wrote that 'he was despised and rejected,' that he was 'cut off from the land of the living; for the transgression of my people he was punished.' I can read it to you. I have the scroll right here," Jesus said, laying his hand on the carved box.

"Yes, please do," said the rabbi

Jesus reverently brought out the scroll of Isaiah and opened it to the passage he had read to his father. When he read about the servant "having no beauty or majesty to attract us to him," the rabbi interrupted with, "See, that can't describe the Messiah. We will be consumed by his majesty!"

Jesus read further, "He was despised and rejected by mankind, a man of suffering, and familiar with pain. Like one from whom people hide their faces he was despised, and we held him in low esteem "

"No one can ascribe this to the Messiah," said the rabbi. "The Messiah will be a glorious ruler to whom everyone will pay homage. This passage describes a scoundrel or a failure."

"Of course it is not what we expect of the Messiah," said Joseph. "But listen to the next part. Read on, Jesus."

"Surely he took up our pain and bore our suffering, yet we considered him punished by God, stricken by him, and afflicted," read Jesus.

"Keep going," said Joseph.

"But he was pierced for our transgressions," read Jesus. "he was crushed for our iniquities; the punishment that brought us peace was on him, and by his wounds we are healed."

"Who but the Messiah, takes our sins away?" asked Joseph.

"True, true," said the rabbi. "The Messiah will take away our sin, but the Messiah does not die. This must refer to a king who is punished as a scapegoat for Israel."

"Which king would that be," asked Jesus.

"I don't know," admitted the rabbi. "But here, let me show you another place in the scroll of Isaiah that clearly does speak of the Messiah. You will see that he does not die."

Jesus yielded the scroll to him and he scanned back through it in silence for a while. Then he said, "Here, listen to this, 'Here is my servant, whom I uphold, my chosen one in whom I delight; I will put my Spirit on him and he will bring justice to the nations.' The passage you are reading describes someone who is suffering injustice. But the Messiah clearly brings justice and is upheld by God Almighty. But that is not the best passage to refute your suggestion. Let me look farther. I think it is earlier in the scroll."

He kept scanning back through the scroll for some minutes while Joseph and Jesus waited in silence. "Here it is," said the rabbi triumphantly. "Listen to this. 'For to us a child is born, to us a son is given, and the government will be on his shoulders. He will be called Wonderful, Counselor, Mighty God, Everlasting Father, Prince of Peace.' Is that not clear that this is the Messiah?"

He continued reading aloud, 'Of the greatness of his government and peace there will be no end. He will reign on David's throne and over his kingdom, establishing it and upholding it with justice and righteousness from that time on and forever.'"

"Yes," said Jesus, "but what if the Messiah has to die for the sins of the people in order to take away their sins and then is raised back to life?"

"What part of 'forever' don't you understand?" asked the rabbi. "Forever is forever; The Messiah doesn't die."

370

"Please don't misunderstand my questions," said Jesus. "I am not trying to make trouble. But I do want to understand this. May I read further in the other passage?"

"Certainly," said the rabbi, passing the scroll back to Jesus. "I understand why you would have questions and I am trying to answer them."

"Here," said Jesus after finding his place again, 'Yet it was the Lord's will to crush him and cause him to suffer, and though the Lord makes his life an offering for sin, he will see his offspring and prolong his days and the will of the Lord will prosper in his hand. After he has suffered, he will see the light of life and be satisfied; by his knowledge my righteous servant will justify many, and he will bear their iniquities. Therefore, I will give him a portion among the great, and he will divide the spoils with the strong, because he poured out his life unto death, and was numbered with the transgressors. For he bore the sin of many, and made intercession for the transgressors.'"

"I hear you," said the rabbi. "The part about bearing the sin of many makes it sound like the Messiah, but the Messiah rules on David's throne forever. He doesn't die."

"But," objected Jesus, "combining the Psalm of David that seems to describe crucifixion and this passage about someone whom God was pleased to crush for the sins of the people... doesn't it seem like the Messiah has to be that one?"

"Absolutely not," said the rabbi. "From the Law of Moses we know that anyone who is hung on a pole is cursed and must be removed from the pole and buried before the sun goes down to avoid desecrating the land. Are you willing to imply that the Messiah is cursed? God forbid!"

"But in this instance," said Jesus, "the curse would be because of the sin he was bearing for others, not for his own."

"You know," said Rabbi Zephon, "I am beginning to doubt the wisdom of loaning you scrolls for your independent study. You are very bright and would make a good scholar under appropriate tutelage. But letting you study with no supervision is not in your best interests or anyone else's. If you go astray, the blame will fall on me for loaning you these scrolls."

Jesus looked at Joseph in silent appeal. Joseph very subtly shook his head as if to say, "Drop it."

"Well, it is high time we told you the strange story of Uncle Ezra," said Joseph,"and how he came to his end. For he is one who actually was crucified."

"Oh, God rest his soul," exclaimed the rabbi "What on earth did he do that Rome would mark him out as cursed?"

Joseph and Jesus, by turns, relayed the whole history of Ezra and Samson and how the new Roman Legate craved ownership of the great stallion and would not be denied. By the time they finished the story and answered the rabbi's questions, it was past midnight and the lamp was running out of oil.

"That, my friends, is a most amazing story and a very sad ending of a special life. You have my heartfelt condolences."

"We are sorry to burden you with our grief," said Joseph. "especially since you came bearing good news. I hate that this sadness has marred your joy in the birth of your daughter."

"Nonsense," said Rabbi Zephon. "Grief and Joy seem always to intersect in this life."

"Well, we rejoice with you in the birth of Rebecca and we thank God that you are here to help us with Uncle Ezra's service. We have no rabbi here in Nazareth."

"I am at your service," said Zephon.

Jesus left the house the next morning before the men roused themselves. He took one of the small scrolls of Psalms in his bag along with his lunch. His mother was up and busy in the kitchen of the family home.

"Well, did you have a good visit with Rabbi Zephon last night?" she asked as she got him some breakfast.

"Yes, Mother. Look what he brought me."

"A little scroll? What is it?" she asked.

"He got some small scraps of scroll from his brother who is a scribe. He used them to copy out some of the Psalms. They are perfect for taking with me when I take the sheep out grazing."

"That's wonderful," said Mary. "You can study even while taking care of the sheep."

"But then he threatened to stop loaning me scrolls," said Jesus. As soon as he said it, he wished he hadn't brought up the topic.

"Why did he do that?"

"Well, I asked him some hard questions about a passage in Isaiah and he disagreed with my interpretation. He is worried about responsibility coming back on him for loaning me scrolls to study on my own."

"What passage in Isaiah was it? And what was your interpretation?"

"I'd rather not go into all that right now, Mother. I need to take the sheep out to pasture." He did not want his mother to know that he and Joseph were thinking that the Messiah would have to die. He could not imagine how she would react to such news, but he was sure it wouldn't be supportive.

"Well, I have long wished that we had the opportunity for you to get a proper education. How you are supposed to save our people from their sins without learning is beyond me. Maybe you are supposed to stay in Jerusalem and study under the priests."

"Our Heavenly Father will reveal more knowledge when we need it," said Jesus. "The time has not yet come for me to save the people from their sins. But the time has come for me to go feed the lambs."

"Don't forget, the service for Uncle Ezra is this afternoon at the ninth hour," said Mary.

"I will be there. I am going to graze the sheep on Uncle Ezra's land, so I will be there when everybody comes. "

"Don't you think you should bring them back to the sheep pen before the service?" she asked.

"No, if I time it right, they should be willing to rest and chew the cud while we have the service. And I think Uncle Ezra would be honored to have some of his animals there."

"Okay, I will see you there," said his mother, kissing him as he headed out the door.

Jesus opened the door to the cave and called out the sheep by name. He had no idea if Uncle Ezra had names for them in his own mind. But now that he was their shepherd, he was naming them as he got to know their natures. The older ewe who led the flock, he called Grandmother. And she was a grandmother to most of the lambs. He watered them before opening the gate to the sheep pen and leading them down the path in the direction of Ezra's land. As long as he walked ahead of them, they followed eagerly. When he reached his destination and sat down, the sheep began to graze nearby.

He pulled out the small scroll and found that it contained the first five Psalms. He read each one aloud as though to proclaim the Word of the Lord to this small flock of sheep. Then he began reading them slowly to himself, pondering each word and phrase. In the second Psalm, he was struck by the words which the Heavenly Father used to address the Messiah, "You are my son, today I have begotten you." He had the personal experience of hearing the Father address him in these words, whether it was in a dream, he was not sure. The context of this utterance was that of kings of the earth rebelling against God and wanting to throw off His chains. God's response is to laugh at their puny efforts and to declare that He has established his king on Zion. A king that would rule the nations with a rod of iron and dash them to pieces like pottery.

"Heavenly Father," he prayed. "How am I to be both the suffering servant who dies for the sins of the people and at the same time be your king who rules the nations with a rod of iron? These seem like two different people. How am I to reconcile them? And if Rabbi Zephon is right and I am wrong, show me who this suffering servant is whom Isaiah describes. How am I to save these people? How am I to learn what I must know? Teach me, oh Lord, to walk in paths of righteousness according to all that you have for me. Lead me as I lead these lambs of Uncle Ezra's. You guided him, deaf though he was, and took care of him for many years. I, too, am deaf. I listen for your voice to guide me and yet miss the clues that would give me understanding of the path I am to walk. Open my ears, oh Lord, to your voice alone and make me deaf to the voice of your enemy."

As the ninth hour approached, Jesus saw people beginning to come from Nazareth to honor the memory of Joseph's Uncle Ezra. He brought his small flock into the shade of some nearby brush and got them to lie down. It was their nature to lie down after a good feeding and Jesus had made sure that they got that. It was now time for them to rest and ruminate. Jesus sat with them for a few minutes to make sure they were well settled. Then he joined the gathering neighbors and friends.

Various ones sought him out to express their condolences. Others stared about at the vacancy of Uncle Ezra's land. They were accustomed to seeing it full of animals, some in robust health, some being nursed back to health by Ezra's uncanny gift and home-made remedies. Now the land was cleared of fences, sheds, barn and house. The small flock of sheep that Jesus shepherded and the two graves marked out by stones were left as reminders of what had been. Those and two ash heaps where the main buildings had stood. Soon enough the ashes would nourish new grass, the same grass which would spread over the tops of the grave mounds and, unless mown or grazed short, would obscure the stones which marked the graves.

Uncle Seth and Auntie Hobal sought Jesus out and expressed their sorrow at the loss of Uncle Ezra. "What a good man was this Ezra, God rest his soul," wept Auntie Hobal. "Though he was as strong as Samson, he was as gentle-hearted as a child. He would never harm a fly and he had such a rare gift with animals! Why on earth would the Romans harm him? They are just such an evil lot!"

Uncle Seth held her by the hand and murmured sympathetically but said nothing. His free arm rested across Jesus' shoulders while they both listened to Auntie grieving. Before she was finished, Joseph and Rabbi Zephon arrived and joined their circle. Mary spread a cloth on the ground and settled the children on it to the best of her ability. James and little Joseph sneaked away from her to seek playmates who had come with their parents.

Nearly a hundred people gathered for the service. Joseph stood up and introduced Rabbi Zephon from Capernaum as a friend of the family who would officiate.

The rabbi began with the shema, "Hear oh Israel, the Lord our God is One. He is the Lord and there is no other. We are here today Oh Lord, to commit to your benevolence the soul of our brother Ezra bin Adam bin Matthan, whom the Romans have crucified on this, his own land. We pray that you would receive his spirit and that you would comfort him and give him your great peace. We long for the day when your Anointed one will come and rescue your people from the hand of all who oppress her. We long for the day of judgment when all will be called out of their graves to give an account. Bless Israel this day as we wait like sheep abandoned on a battlefield. We are prey for the nations around us and unless you deliver us, Oh God, we will not be delivered at all. Have mercy on us, Oh God. Have mercy. Amen.

Rabbi Zephon then called upon Joseph as nearest relative to the deceased to say a few words about Ezra's life and the circumstances of his death.

Joseph rose and cleared his throat. "Ezra was my mother's only brother," he began. "He was deaf from birth and therefore never learned to speak. Because of that condition, he never got much of an education in the traditional sense, but was a good and obedient son of my grandfather, Matthan. When he grew up, he fell in with some ruffians who loved to get him drunk and arrange fights for him so that they could win money by placing wagers. Those were very difficult years for him and for the whole family. It is reported that my grandfather, Ezra's father, once prayed that the Lord would take Ezra's life rather than allow him to continue in violence and abuse.

"Perhaps in answer to my grandfather's prayer, a Roman centurion approached Grandfather one day and asked permission to make Uncle Ezra a legionnaire. Though there were many doubts expressed and obstacles to overcome in making a deaf mute a Roman legionnaire, Grandfather could not but believe that this answer was heaven-sent. So he agreed.

"Uncle Ezra trained with the legion in this area for six months and then was transferred to Caesarea and beyond, under the care of the officer who had trained him. During his time with the Legion, Ezra distinguished himself for feats of strength, for fearlessness in battle, but especially in his ability to care for the horses assigned to the Legion. I think all of you here know the story of how he came into conflict with another officer who had acquired the great Arab stallion, Samson, in a campaign in Arabia. The stallion grew to love and trust Uncle Ezra but to hate and fear the officer who owned him and abused him. That conflict culminated in a fight to the death between the officer and Uncle Ezra. When Uncle Ezra won the fight but refused to kill the officer, he was awarded his release from the Legion and ownership of Samson.

"For the last 17 years Uncle Ezra has lived among us as a peaceful and friendly doctor of animals. I would guess there are few of you who have not at some point sought his help and benefitted from his wisdom and his strong, gentle hands. Though he never heard your voice or spoke an intelligible word to you, he loved you and loved your animals.

"Uncle Ezra never married and never had children, but his love of animals was evident to all who knew him. He especially loved horses, and among horses, his love for Samson exceeded all others. We know that King David, in mourning for Jonathon, son of Saul, said, 'Jonathan, your love exceeded the love of women.' I think if Uncle Ezra could have spoken, he would have said, 'Samson, your love exceeds the love of human beings.'

"It was his love of this Samson that led to Uncle Ezra's death. Three months ago, as you surely know, a new Legate was put in charge of the camp just outside of Nazareth. This foreign officer lusted after Uncle Ezra's stallion and tried to buy it. Of course, Uncle Ezra refused. But how can a deaf, mute Israelite withstand the power and will of a Roman Legate? The Roman took Samson by force and threw the money in the dirt at Ezra's feet. Ezra returned the money and demanded his horse, refusing the sale. But the Legate just scorned him and when he wouldn't leave, had him beaten and thrown out of the camp.

"When Ezra saw that Samson was thus consigned to the Legate's brutality and when he saw the welts of the whip all over his beloved's body, he committed himself with deadly earnest to rescue Samson from the brutal Legate, regardless of the cost to himself. Knowing that it would cost him his own life, he set his affairs in order, sold most of his animals, gave the others away and made his last will and testament. Then he entered the Roman camp at night and stealthily stole Samson away, brought him here and humanely put him to death and buried him here in that grave. Next to it, he had already dug this one for himself. Then he calmly waited for the Romans to come and execute him. He willingly laid down his life for his friend, Samson the Arab stallion, who had been the means of his deliverance from the Legion and who had been his constant and faithful companion since that time."

When Joseph finished the story, the crowd sat weeping and murmuring prayers for Ezra's soul and for the deliverance of Israel from the wicked Romans. Joseph sat down and Rabbi Zephon rose. He motioned for silence and then said, "God almighty takes full responsibility for Ezra's deafness. You might ask, 'Why would such a fine man be born with such a terrible disability?' But when the Lord God appeared to Moses on the backside of the desert, he ordered Moses to go and tell Pharaoh to 'let my people go.' You will recall that Moses objected that he was slow of speech and could not do this task. But God answered him and said, 'Who gave human beings their mouths? Who makes them deaf or mute? Who gives them sight or makes them blind? Is it not I, the Lord?'

"So we see that the Lord God takes responsibility for deafness, for muteness and for blindness," continued the rabbi. "We should not, therefore, ask, as some do, 'Who sinned that this man was born deaf?' For reasons of his own, the Lord chose Ezra for this deafness, for this story, which is part of His greater story of Israel and of His entire creation. Therefore, we thank the Lord for Ezra and for his deafness, even as we try to puzzle out the meaning of his smaller story. Even as we weep over how Ezra's story touches our lives and leaves a hole in our community, I charge you not to forget Ezra. Do not forget how he loved Samson and gave his own life to end Samson's suffering. Honor him by coming to these two graves and keeping his story alive. Though he has no children of his own, tell his story to your children and teach them to honor this ancestor of theirs. Yes, Ezra too, is a part of the story of Nazareth. He is a grandfather to all the children who grow up here. He was a good man who lived well here and died well here. Do not let Nazareth forget him."

Then the rabbi quoted the shepherd psalm from memory, closed in prayer and dismissed the crowd.

After the service, the Rabbi and Joseph stood near the grave as the people filed by to convey their thanks to the rabbi and their condolences to Joseph and the family. Jesus stood next to Joseph and Mary next to him. The other children could not be persuaded to participate in these solemnities but scattered through the crowd chasing one another and tagging other children to join in the merriment.

Uncle Seth and Auntie Hobal waited aside until the other guests had left and then came up to the family. "Thank you very much, Rabbi," said Uncle Seth. "I swear I never realized that God himself claimed responsibility for disabilities like deafness. Thank you for pointing that out."

"You are most welcome," said the rabbi. "I was surprised just recently by noting those words. But they are spoken by God himself."

"There's comfort in that," said Uncle Seth. "He makes us each for a different purpose, doesn't He? And he had a purpose in Ezra being deaf, though we can't see what it was."

"And when the day of the Lord comes," said Jesus, "Uncle Ezra will hear as well as any of us. He will come out of this grave and give glory to God."

"That is true," said the rabbi.

"I wonder what Uncle Ezra's first words will be," wondered Uncle Seth.

"He'll probably look around and ask, 'Where's my horse?'" said Joseph and they all chuckled in spite of the solemn occasion.

"Forgive me if I'm being nosey," said Uncle Seth, "but I'm curious. How did he put that horse down humanely? I mean, I know he would but... were there any witnesses?"

"There was one," said Joseph. "He wishes to remain anonymous, but he described the process to me. First he put soothing salve on all the whip welts and gave him grain and water with medicine in them. Then he got Samson to lie down, hobbled him well to restrain any struggles. Then he opened a vein in his neck and bled him to death."

"God bless his soul and give him rest," sighed Uncle Seth. "Treating Samson's wounds before he took his life blood! He was an amazing man."

All of them muttered their agreement. Mary began trying to gather her wandering children as they all prepared to leave the graves. Jesus was about to go back to the sheep when one last visitor approached them. It was Nathan of Jericho, the translator for Legate Antonius.

"You are here?" said Joseph.

"Y-y-yes," stuttered Nathan. "I could not stay away."

"I don't mean to be rude," said Joseph, "but I wonder what business you have here. Are you to go and report to the Legate what you have witnessed?"

"No, no," said Nathan. "Nothing of that sort."

At the rabbi's questioning look Jesus whispered, "He is the translator for the Legate. He was here with the Romans when they beat Uncle Ezra and crucified him."

"I-I-I am n-no longer in the Legate's employ," said Nathan. "I have quit my job and I'm going back to Jericho."

Joseph looked at him for a moment before answering. "That cannot have been an easy decision," he said. "It could be hard to find another job with that kind of pay."

"The pay was not enough for what I had to endure," said Nathan. "Listen, I have come here to tell you… to try to convey to you… how sorry I am for what happened to your Uncle… I never imagined the story would end like it did. If there had been a way for me… I didn't know what to do! I swear I would have saved him if I could have!"

There was an awkward silence but then Joseph, seeing the man's torment, said, "And how much was your pay supplemented by what was stolen from my uncle's house?"

"What? There was nothing of value stolen from his house. The troops ransacked the house and were frustrated as they found nothing worth stealing," said Nathan.

"My uncle had sold at least seven horses and four donkeys in the past few weeks as he prepared to die for that stallion. There had to be some money in that house."

"If there was, no one found it," said Nathan.

"Or one found it and concealed it," suggested the rabbi.

"If that happened, it was completely hidden from me. The soldiers were all grumbling that they got nothing for their trouble." Nathan fell on his knees before Joseph and pleaded, "Please forgive me. I never intended your uncle any harm."

Joseph looked at him for a moment and then said, "I forgive you. Go in peace."

"I don't know if I can forgive myself," muttered Nathan.

"You are not guilty of Uncle Ezra's blood," said Joseph. "You were not given the authority or the power to defy the Legate. Go back to Jericho and do whatever God tells you to do. Go back to your family. You had no power to save Ezra and you have no power to bring him back. I forgive you for what role you did have in this messy story. Just go home and sin no more."

Nathan bowed his head to Joseph and whispered, "Thank you, sir. Shalom." Then he walked away.

"Already we see," said the rabbi when Nathan was out of earshot, "that at least one story is being impacted for good by Ezra's story."

"The Legate will find a new translator," said Joseph

"True enough," said Jesus. "But Nathan has found a new life."

That night after supper, Joseph and Jesus again accompanied the rabbi to the house where Joseph's mother had lived out her days of widowhood.

"Thank you so much for conducting the service this afternoon, Rabbi," said Joseph over tea.

"I was happy to do it," said the rabbi. "Your uncle was a remarkable man."

"And we are sorry that our situation here has tempered the joy of your announcement. We are delighted with the news of your daughter's birth. May the Lord bless her and keep her and make her to be a mother in Israel."

"Bless you for your blessing," replied the rabbi. "I need to hurry back tomorrow and see how she and her mother are faring."

"I thank you for the little scrolls of Psalms," said Jesus. "I took one with me this morning when I took the sheep out. While they were grazing I started memorizing the first five Psalms."

"You are more than welcome. It pleases me to see your zeal to know the word of God."

"And please don't stop loaning me scrolls to learn more. I promise you I won't become a heretic," said Jesus.

"I didn't mean to imply you would become a heretic," said the rabbi. "But it would be much better if you could study in a proper school instead of always reading by yourself. I should introduce you to some people in Jerusalem. Are you planning to go up for Day of Atonement?"

"That is still more than three months away," said Joseph, "but we always try to go. If we have the means and if we are healthy, we will be there."

"We should try to meet in Jerusalem then," said the rabbi. "I'm sure we can find a situation where Jesus could study under some proper rabbinical scholars. He really does show promise."

"I suppose it wouldn't hurt to talk with them and visit their schools," said Joseph. "But we have no means to pay for such an education and I'm not sure his mother and I are prepared to give him up."

"Who said anything about giving him up?" asked the rabbi. "But if he gets a good education, he might in a few years come back to Nazareth and provide this place with a proper rabbi."

"But…" Jesus started to object. When he saw his father's solemn look and subtle shake of the head he faltered.

"But what?" asked the rabbi.

"But…who would take care of the sheep? And Grandmother's garden? I am needed here."

"Your brothers can grow into those roles," said the rabbi. "Such skills as you possess should not be squandered in the sheep pen, young man. You have a gift! Now, how will I find you in those crowds in Jerusalem?"

Joseph told him about the garden at the foot of the Mount of Olives. "We always camp there; you shouldn't have any trouble finding us."

"Okay then," said the rabbi. "We will meet in Jerusalem and I will help you find a good school."

When they finally retired for the night, Jesus found it impossible to fall asleep. When he could hear the rabbi snoring and he thought Joseph was asleep, too, he crept up to the roof to look at the stars. He was surprised a few minutes later to find Joseph joining him.

"Son, are you okay?" asked Joseph softly.

"Yes, Abba. I just couldn't sleep."

"I can't either."

"I'm very disappointed at Rabbi Zephon's interpretation of that Isaiah passage," said Jesus. "Why won't he tell us who else it could refer to?"

"Because he doesn't have any idea," said Joseph.

"The more I think about it the more I am sure that the suffering servant is Messiah."

Joseph replied, "I can't tell you how much it frightens me to think you may be right."

"I was tempted to tell the rabbi that I am called to be more than a village rabbi," confessed Jesus.

"That's what I was afraid of," said his father. "I don't think the time is right. He is a good friend and may be an ally in the future. But I can't predict his reaction if we were to bring him into our secret."

"Abba, do you think I should go study in Jerusalem?"

"I don't think I could handle leaving you there, Jesus."

"Does any prophet die outside Jerusalem?" asked Jesus.

"Don't say that," admonished Joseph. "I am not prepared to even think of you dying. The Lord will guide us as to schooling. He has guided us this far, has He not?"

"He has. He has indeed," said Jesus. "Shall we pray for wisdom together?"

"Yes," said his father. Right then and there the two of them sought the wisdom of heaven for the future.

In the months that followed, it became Jesus' routine to tend the sheep during the day and tend the garden in the evening. He studied the Psalms from the small scrolls while the sheep were grazing and studied the Jeremiah scroll by lamplight after dark. He often slept at Grandmother's house and Joseph joined him not infrequently. When the weather was fair they slept on the roof under the stars. Together they watched the changing phases of the moon that marked the progress of the season toward the Day of Atonement. They talked from time to time about what it would look like for Jesus to stay in Jerusalem and study under rabbis, priests and scribes.

"One of the biggest obstacles to your studying," said Joseph one night, "is the expense. I don't mind telling you that I am struggling to keep enough food on the table for all these mouths. And we will have to buy hay for feeding the animals through the winter. I am in debt to Jonas for wood and I don't know when I will be able to pay him. I just don't see any possible way that I could pay for you to study in Jerusalem."

"Do you need me to help you in the shop?" asked Jesus. "We could probably hire Uri to take care of the sheep for half of the wool at shearing time."

"No, that's not a solution," said Joseph. "I don't have enough work for the two of us. If we tend the sheep ourselves, then we get all the wool. That is a help. Just keep doing what you are doing. But I'm just saying that I can't pay for schooling."

"Well, if the Lord wants me to study, He will provide a way," said Jesus.

"At some point you will probably have to study," said Joseph. "But I don't think that time has come."

As the time came near for their going up to Jerusalem, the financial burden on Joseph grew more oppressive. He had not had paying work for more than a month. He stayed busy training James and little Joseph in the workshop, but there was no income.

One evening he and Jesus were reading through Jeremiah. "Oh, listen to this, Abba," said Jesus "'This is what the Lord says: "If I have not made my covenant with day and night and established the laws of heaven and earth, then I will reject the descendants of Jacob and David my servant and will not choose one of his sons to rule over the descendants of Abraham, Isaac and Jacob. For I will restore their fortunes and have compassion on them."' That means His promises are as secure as are the laws of nature."

"Amen!" said Joseph. "And the sun came up again this morning. If it comes up again tomorrow, then the promised Son of David is still securely given."

"Abba?" said Jesus. "You, too, are a son of David. Did you ever wonder whether you were called to save the people from their sins?"

"I don't think there has ever been a son of David who didn't wonder that," said Joseph.

"So how did you know that you weren't called?" asked Jesus.

After a moment, Joseph answered, "I guess it was when the angel told me that you were going to be born to Mary and that you would be the one. Up until that time I, like everyone else in Israel, wondered from time to time who would be the anointed Son of David and I considered whether it might be me. But the thought was always overwhelming."

"It overwhelms me, too," admitted Jesus. "Are you ever a tiny bit jealous that I am the one?"

"Absolutely not!" cried his father. "I am well contented with my role of being your abba. And I don't even feel adequate for this role, let alone yours! Who on earth is adequate to be the abba of the anointed one?"

"You are perfect for your role, Abba. And I love you so much! I thank God for you every day."

"By God's grace, I am what I am. I swear I am doing all I can for you but I don't know how to prepare you for what comes next. I don't even see how we are going to make it to Jerusalem next week."

"But we promised Rabbi Zephon we would be there," objected Jesus.

"I know, I know," said Joseph. "That promise weighs on me, too. Even more, the duty and the desire to be present at the temple on the Sabbath of Sabbaths weighs on me. But financially, I don't know how to pull it off."

"This year we have a horse and wagon along with two donkeys," said Jesus. "We would not have to borrow animals as we have in the past."

"That would be fine, but that is not our only expense. Jonas is pressing me to make a payment on my loan so that he can go up. I don't have any way to get that money. If we don't go up, Rabbi Zephon will just have to be disappointed and wait for another occasion."

The next morning as Jesus was taking the sheep out, he paused to look at the garden. It had not done well this year. A worm had gotten into the cucumber vines and destroyed them. The melons had produced a few edible fruits, but were now withering and almost overwhelmed with weeds. It had not worked out well for him to try to take care of the sheep and the garden. The garden had suffered some neglect. He decided that the time had come to put the garden to bed for the winter.

He brought the flock home a little earlier than usual that afternoon. He penned them and made sure that they had plenty of water. Then he went to harvest the last of the garden fruits and vegetables. Then he uprooted weeds by the handful and threw them in a pile to dry. When they were thoroughly dried he would burn them to prevent the seeds from germinating. Then he took a hoe and thoroughly turned over the garden soil. It was quite dark and his muscles were aching by the time he finished. He was exhausted and hungry but had the satisfaction of a job completed and the prospect of a new beginning in the garden.

The next morning as he was leading the sheep past the garden he glanced at the clean, freshly turned soil and at the pile of weeds for burning. Then his eye fell on another pile: the dung pile that Uncle Ezra had hauled in as one of the last gifts before his death. "Oh," he thought, "now is the time for using that dung pile on the garden. Uncle Ezra told me to wait until the garden was harvested and the soil turned." He resolved to spread the dung thickly on the garden when he brought the sheep back in the evening.

During the day he pondered the lesson in Jeremiah that he and Abba had recently studied. Though Jeremiah had warned the people of terrible devastation at the hands of the Babylonians, he had also promised a bright future. "Then this city will bring me renown, joy, praise and honor before all nations on earth that hear of all the good things I do for it; and they will be in awe and will tremble at the abundant prosperity and peace I provide for it."

As he meditated on those words, he prayed, "Lord God of Israel, we see that you are going to provide abundant prosperity for Jerusalem. We don't know when that day will come but perhaps it is coming soon. Would you please provide a little bit of that prosperity to my Abba so that we can go up to Jerusalem to praise you? This is not a hard thing for you though we see no way in which you might do it. Your ways are not our ways, your thoughts are so much higher than our thoughts. All wealth belongs to you. But if it is not your will for us to go to Jerusalem at this time, may we be filled with joy and peace in believing that all your ways are right and righteous. Amen."

At the end of the day he was so tired and his muscles so sore from the garden work the day before that he almost put off the promised garden work for another day. But when he found that supper was going to be a bit later than usual, he roused himself to action and began spreading the dung thickly over the turned soil of the garden. "How generous dear old Uncle Ezra was," he thought as he worked. "Even giving us the very dung pile from his little farm. He wanted nothing to go to waste, not even the droppings of his animals."

As he neared the bottom of the pile, his tool struck a resisting object that gave off a subdued 'clink' sound. "What on earth is this?" he thought. "It looks like an old piece of animal hide but it is covering up something heavy." He squatted low to pull away the hide and found that it was a leather bag with Uncle Ezra's distinctive mark burned into it. Jesus knew in a flash what had happened to Ezra's missing money. He quickly covered the bag back up and set out on a run to fetch his father.

"Abba, Abba, come quick. I have something to show you," he said as he burst into the shop where his father was cleaning up the chips and dust from another day of work.

"What is it?" asked Joseph in surprise.

"We're going to Jerusalem," said Jesus. "Uncle Ezra left us one more gift."

"What are you talking about?" said Joseph, following Jesus out the door.

Jesus ran all the way back to the garden without saying another word. When Joseph arrived, Jesus was scooping the manure pile away from the bag with his bare hands. "Look!" he cried. "Just look what Uncle Ezra hid in the manure!"

"Well," gasped Joseph, out of breath from running. "That wily old Uncle Ezra fooled the Romans in this, too! He knew they wouldn't dirty their hands to look for his money here! Bless his heart!"

"And he instructed me not to touch the dung pile until the garden was finished," added Jesus. "That allowed time to pass and people to forget all about the money."

"God be praised for giving Uncle Ezra such canny wisdom!" exclaimed Joseph.

"And God be praised for abundantly providing us the means to go to Jerusalem," said Jesus. "We can go now, can't we?"

"We surely can and we surely will," said Joseph. "We will pack up your mother and all the children and..."

"And I will get Uri to watch our flock," added Jesus.

"Yes, that would be good." agreed his father. "As soon as I go and make a payment to old Jonas, we can pack our bags and go."

"Hurray!" shouted Jesus. "Thank you, Heavenly Father! We are going up to Jerusalem to sing your praises!"

The next day was a whirlwind of activity. Jesus contacted Uri the shepherd and arranged for him to add their little flock to his responsibilities for the days they would be gone. Joseph added a tailgate to the wagon Ezra had given them in order to ensure safety for the smallest travelers. Mary was busy baking bread and mending clothes for the family's travels. James and Little Joseph were sent to cut grass for the animals.

The journey was always exciting because there were so many travelers on the road. But this time it was made even more exciting because when they reached Scythopolis and were setting up camp in the shadow of Mount Gilboa, they happened to meet a large contingent of Mary's family. Her older sister, Esther and her husband, Carmi, had six children and lived on the eastern side of the sea of Galilee. The children were mostly older than Jesus but there was a boy named Josiah that was six months younger. Along with Esther and her family was a cousin, Tabitha, with her husband Jonadab and their eight children who had recently moved from Seleucia to the region of the Gadarenes.

There was a great deal of laughing and weeping and telling of stories among the adults that evening around the campfire. Jesus and Josiah sat together listening to the adults and smiling shyly at each other. When there was a lull in the stories, Jesus asked, "Do you live right on the sea?"

"We live in the town of Hippos," said Josiah. "It is near the sea but not on the shore."

"Is your abba a fisherman?" asked Jesus.

"No, he works in leather. He makes saddles and harnesses, sometimes sandals. He made these sandals for me," said Josiah, showing his feet.

"Those are very nice," said Jesus. "My abba is a carpenter. He makes and repairs all kinds of wooden things."

"Does he teach you to do that work?" asked Josiah.

"Oh yes, but lately I have been shepherding a small flock and haven't had much time in the wood shop. And I spend some of my time studying. Do you study?"

"No," said Josiah, "but I wish I could. "There is no rabbi in Hippos."

"There is no rabbi in Nazareth either," said Jesus. "But Abba has taught me to read. We borrow scrolls from a rabbi in Capernaum and study them together."

"Wow," said Josiah. "You are lucky. I wish I could read."

"I can teach you," offered Jesus. "I have some small scrolls with me that have some of the psalms written on them. We could make a start."

"I would love that," said Josiah.

The friendship was sealed on this agreement and all the way to Jerusalem the two boys were inseparable. They would ride together in one wagon or the other as Jesus read psalms to Josiah and coaxed him to begin learning his letters from the tiny scrolls Rabbi Zephon had given him. When they camped, he would have Josiah spelling out words in the dust with his finger. They ate together, played together and slept rolled up in their blankets next to each other near the fire. It was a new experience for Jesus to have a cousin who was so congenial and so compatible.

When they camped at the foot of the Mount of Olives, Rabbi Zephon was waiting for them. "Shalom, Shalom! Welcome to Jerusalem," he said. "I have been here two days already. I was beginning to think you weren't coming."

"And we almost didn't come," said Joseph. "I was under such terrible financial pressure I didn't think it would be possible, though I hated to disappoint you. I always try to keep my promises."

"So how did the Lord deliver you from that pressure?" asked the rabbi. "You have brought your whole family, so He must have answered your prayers."

"You remember the missing money from Uncle Ezra's estate?" asked Joseph. "He had hidden it in a leather bag at the bottom of a manure pile. He told Jesus not to bother the pile until the garden was harvested and then to spread it on the garden. Jesus did that just two days before we left and there was the Lord's provision where no one would ever look!"

"Praise be to the Almighty!" said the rabbi. "On the mountain of the Lord it will be provided. And God can make mountains into dung hills or dung hills into mountains! I have often thought of your Uncle Ezra, God rest his soul, since we were last together."

"Rabbi Zephon, I want to introduce you to my cousin, Josiah," said Jesus. "I have been teaching Josiah to read from the little scrolls of psalms you made for me. Josiah, this is the rabbi from Capernaum who loans us scrolls to study and who made these little scrolls of psalms for me."

"Shalom, young man," said the rabbi. "May the Lord give you a double portion of the spirit that is upon Jesus. If you receive it, you will become a scholar of great renown."

"Shalom, Rabbi," said Josiah. "I cannot read at all, sir, except a few words that Jesus has taught me on the way here."

"Well with such an apt teacher, I'm sure you will get on well," said the rabbi. "We are going to see about getting Jesus enrolled in a proper rabbinical school here in Jerusalem."

Josiah looked with new admiration at his accomplished cousin.

"Will you camp with us, Rabbi?" asked Joseph.

"No, no, I am already staying with my brother, Mahli, who, as I told you, is a scribe here. He has been telling me about various yeshivas which we should consider for Jesus."

"We will be happy to learn about possibilities," said Joseph, "but we are far from ready to commit Jesus to the care of anyone else at this young age."

"Nonsense," said the rabbi. "Many boys younger and less capable than he are already studying here in Jerusalem while their families live far away."

"I'm just saying that we have not made a decision, yet," said Joseph.

"I understand. Once you have reliable information, you will be in a better place to make a decision. Will you be going up to the temple early tomorrow?"

"Yes, about the third hour is our plan," said Joseph.

"I will watch for you by the south gate," said the rabbi. "When you are finished at the temple we will dine with my brother and you can hear his recommendations."

"Thank you so much, Rabbi Zephon. You are too kind."

The next day the entire family visited the temple in preparation for the sacrifice on the high holy day. It was a time of confessing their sins and cleansing their consciences. It was a declaration of their identification with the nation of Israel and their desire to be covered by the sacrifices to be made by the high priest.

When they met Rabbi Zephon on their way out, Mary and the smaller children made their apologies and headed back to the garden while Joseph and Jesus went with the rabbi to his brother's house.

"Did your wife and daughter accompany you here," asked Joseph.

"No, we decided not to expose little Rebecca and her mother to the press of the crowds here in Jerusalem just yet," said the rabbi. "They are healthy enough, I'm sure it would be fine. But they are staying with Elsaba's mother in Tiberius until my return."

"God bless them and keep them," said Joseph.

"Thank you, my friend. How was your time at the temple?"

"It was good, if a bit hectic," said Joseph. "The crowds are so great and so impatient this year that by the time we saw the priest, we had a few more sins to be cleansed of, I'm afraid."

"I know what you mean," laughed the rabbi. "Last year at Passover I was nearly trampled by a man leading a great ox to be sacrificed. And when I dodged out of his way, I was butted by a goat that had escaped from a teenaged boy."

"Worshiping God is not always comfortable," said Joseph. "Just think how uncomfortable our father, Abraham, must have been as he obeyed God's command and was about to sacrifice his son, Isaac!"

A chill went up Jesus' spine as he thought about that Biblical story. Soon they turned into a narrow street of two-story houses.

"This is it," said the rabbi and ushered his guests into his brother's house. "Mahli, this is Joseph and his son Jesus of Nazareth. Joseph, this is my older brother Mahli about whom I told you."

Greetings were exchanged. Jesus studied Mahli. He resembled Rabbi Zephon in height and facial features, but was becoming quite bald and what hair he did have was salted with grey.

"Please sit down," said Mahli. "The tea will be brought in a moment." The four sat down on the floor around a cloth.

"We are very grateful for your brother, Mahli", said Joseph. "Though we have no rabbi in Nazareth, we benefit greatly from your brother's wisdom and generous hospitality when we travel to Capernaum."

"And he has told me a bit about you," said Mahli. "How is it that you, being a carpenter, are skilled in reading the scriptures?"

"My father taught me," said Joseph. "He was a scripture-reading carpenter before me. Some of my best memories of him involve reading and discussing the scriptures."

"All of Israel would benefit if there were more men like your father," said Mahli.

"That's true," agreed the rabbi. "Though I never met your father, God rest his soul, I believe that Nazareth is a better place because of the legacy he has left you and Jesus."

At that moment a young man appeared from the back of the house with a tray. On the tray were small glasses, a pot of tea and a dish of raisins.

"This is my son, Gershom," said Mahli. "He is studying at the same yeshiva where my brother and I once studied."

"We are interested in hearing from you about educational opportunities here," said Joseph. "I'm not sure we are ready to leave Jesus here and go back to Nazareth, he being only twelve years old. But being better informed cannot do us any harm."

"That is not too young," said Mahli. "I was only eleven when my parents came from Caesarea and left me here to study under Rabbi Gamaliel. How old were you when you came, Zephon?"

"I was ten," said the rabbi, "but by then you were fourteen. I don't think Abba would have left me here at that age if I had not had you."

"Right, and I found it easier once you came," said Mahli. "Just having a brother in the same yeshiva can relieve the loneliness, even if it is a younger brother who needs a lot of coddling."

"Hey," said Zephon, "I was very mature for a ten-year-old. I think Abba left me here to keep you from getting into trouble and to make sure you applied yourself to your studies!"

Mahli laughed and slapped the rabbi on the back. "Those were good times, were they not? And now look at us; you're a rabbi and I am a scribe. Neither one of us turned out too badly. We watched out for each other, did we not?"

"We did," agreed the rabbi.

"Who is this Rabbi Gamaliel?" asked Joseph.

"Oh, he is a good man," said the two brothers simultaneously.

"Gamaliel bin Simeon, bin Hillel," said Mahli. "He was recently elected to the Sanhedrin."

"He is from Caesarea, like our father," said Rabbi Zephon. "He is very conservative in interpreting the scriptures but is not a rabid exponent of pharisaism like the leaders of some of the yeshivas. You have seen how I am very tolerant of the fishermen who go out on the lake on the Sabbath. Rabbi Gamaliel would not have a problem with that. He emphasizes that the word of God should penetrate our hearts rather than our outward practices."

"In that, he must be a most unusual rabbi," said Joseph. "The rabbis I have seen tend to be pompous men who build their own reputations at the expense of God's reputation. Present company excepted, of course," added Joseph, blushing as he nodded in the rabbi's direction."

"You are not unfair in describing many rabbis in such unflattering terms," said Mahli. "I could name half a dozen yeshivas here in Jerusalem led by Pharisees who are guilty of that behavior. But there are others. I know of two that are led by Sadducees. They don't believe in angels or visions or the raising of the dead. And then there is one who is led by a zealot named Joshua who is almost more a political activist than a rabbi. But if you are of a more conservative bent like my brother and myself, you would do well to consider letting your son become a disciple of Rabbi Gamaliel. His name means 'gift of God' and there are many who believe the name suits him well."

"We are very serious about God and His word," said Joseph. "We are not zealots and certainly not Sadducees. We want our son to know the scriptures by heart and to follow God more than following a particular rabbi."

"Then I would recommend that you and your son visit Rabbi Gamaliel and see how he runs his yeshiva," said Mahli. "For a rabbi with a following of disciples, he is quite a humble and gentle man. If he had been harsh or arrogant, my brother and I would not have continued with him. We probably would not be in the professions we have chosen, were it not for Rabbi Gamaliel, isn't that right, Brother?"

Rabbi Zephon concurred. Then dinner was served.

Over dinner, Joseph asked, "How expensive are the fees at Rabbi Gamaliel's yeshiva?"

"They are very reasonable compared to many other yeshiva's," said Mahli. "Rabbi Gamaliel is more interested in training scholars than in making money. I get a discount for Gershom because I myself was a student of his. But I know of at least one young man whose parents are very poor and because the young man is very promising, the rabbi educates him for free. His parents only provide for his living expenses. When you meet with him, you can negotiate the financial terms."

"And where do students from outside of Jerusalem find accommodation?" asked Joseph.

"Each family arranges something according to their means," said Mahli. "Your son could live with us if he wishes to study under Rabbi Gamaliel. We have the room as my daughter just got married last spring. Then Gershom could be a big brother to Jesus just as I was to Zephon."

"That is very generous of you," said Joseph. "Thank you very much for your offer. What do you think, Jesus," he asked, turning to his son. "Would you like to meet this Rabbi Gamaliel?"

"Whatever you wish, Abba," said Jesus glancing at Gershom. "I would work at any opportunity available to me to help earn my keep. And I'm sure it would be helpful to have an older brother who knows this city and this school." Gershom smiled at Jesus and nodded enthusiastically.

"Tomorrow is the great day of the feast," said Mahli. "Why don't the two of you come here at the second hour on the day after tomorrow. Gershom can take you to the yeshiva and introduce you to Rabbi Gamaliel. I will send him a message to expect you."

"Thank you, we will do that," said Joseph.

On their way back to the garden where they were camping, Joseph spoke up, "Well son, what did you think of Mahli the scribe and his son Gershom?"

"They seem very nice," said Jesus. "I think Gershom could be a good friend. And his father seems very familiar, due to the similarity to his brother, Rabbi Zephon."

"And what did you think of the yeshiva of Rabbi Gamaliel as they described it?"

"I don't know what to think," said Jesus. "So much depends on the character of the rabbi who leads it."

"True," said Joseph.

"If he is a kind and patient man like you, Abba, I could benefit from studying with him. But if he is at all like the rabbi we had for a while in Nazareth..."

"If he is at all similar to that man," interrupted Joseph, "I forbid you to study under him or cross his shadow in the market place!"

"Thank you, Abba."

When they got back to camp, Mary and the other women were busily preparing the meal that would initiate their fasting period of twenty-four hours. Jesus was about to offer to help.

"There you are," cried a young voice. Jesus looked up; it was his cousin, Josiah.

"Hi," said Jesus.

"What did you find out about yeshivas today?" asked Josiah. "Are you going to stay here and study?"

"We haven't decided yet," said Jesus. "We will visit a yeshiva day after tomorrow."

"I wish I could stay here with you and study," said Josiah. "But my parents won't let me stay. I asked them."

"Speaking of studying," said Jesus. "Would you like another lesson right now?"

"Yes, of course! Can you read me the story of Abraham when he almost sacrificed Isaac?"

"I don't have that scroll," said Jesus. "But we can study one of my little scrolls of Psalms."

"Okay."

Jesus brought out one of his small scrolls and read from it the psalm that begins, "My God, my God, why have you forsaken me." As he read, he pointed to each word so that Josiah could see the shape of the words he was reading. When he got to the part that says, "In you our ancestors put their trust ... and you delivered them," he thought of the story Josiah had asked him to read. Isaac had asked his father why they did not bring a lamb to be sacrificed. Abraham had answered that the Lord himself would provide the lamb. That showed Abraham's trust. He wondered if Isaac had felt just as confident about the Lord's provision while his father was tying him up. He remembered that one of the names for God after that incident was "the Fear of Isaac."

After reading the psalm aloud, he began showing Josiah the individual letters that formed the first words of the psalm. Before they got very far, they were called to the meal that would be their last until sundown of the following day. The Day of Atonement was to begin as soon as they had eaten.

They arrived at the temple early the next morning, so early that the gates were not yet opened. Even Mary and the small children were with them. There had been no breakfast to prepare and eat, no dishes to be cleaned up. It was a solemn day of fasting and repenting. Jesus wondered how he could get a place in the temple from which he could observe the proceedings. When he had been small, Joseph had hoisted him onto his shoulders so that he could see over the heads in front of them. He was now too big for that but not big enough to see over the others.

"Abba," he said, "I could take Simon on my shoulders so that you can hold Hannah."

"Are you sure?" asked Joseph. "It might be too much for you; it's a long day."

"I wouldn't have to hold him the whole time," said Jesus. "Just when there is something happening. And if I get a place near the front, we will both be able to see quite well."

Joseph and Mary agreed that it would be okay if they didn't wander out of sight. Jesus promised to be very responsible and to bring Simon back to his mother if he became too restless. When the gates opened, Jesus was one of the first ones in with his little brother riding on his shoulders. They secured a spot on the temple steps, from which they could see everything, including their parents peering over the heads of other worshipers nearby.

It was a long wait in the morning sunshine as more and more people packed themselves into the courtyard surrounding the temple. Priests and Levites were kept busy in making preparations and in guiding the burgeoning crowd while preserving enough space for the ceremonies.

Finally, a trumpet sounded and the crowd grew quiet. Then the high priest emerged from the temple in shining garments of gold. He was attended by numerous priests as he offered the ordinary morning sacrifice the honor of which on other days he would have yielded to lesser priests. The priests then attended him as he washed his hands and feet, changed into white linen garments and washed his hands and feet again.

His ablutions having been scrupulously attended to, the priests now led forward the bull for the sin offering. The high priest leaned over the head of the bull and confessed his own sin and that of his household, placing the guilt of the sins on the head of the bull and pronouncing the name of God, Yahweh. At the utterance of the name, the whole crowd prostrated themselves to the extent that the crowded conditions permitted. Then taking a large ceremonial knife, the high priest cut the throat of the bull and his assistants caught the flowing life-blood of the bull in a basin until the bull collapsed.

As Jesus watched the blood flow, a pang shot through his heart and he was transported back to the night when Uncle Ezra had slain his beloved Samson. The confusion and anguish of that night rose in his throat and he began to moan. When Simon burst into tears on his shoulders, it brought him back to the present. Simon was covering his face and trying to turn away from the scene before them. Jesus took him down into his arms. Simon buried his face on Jesus chest. "It's alright, Simon," said Jesus. "You are okay. No one is going to hurt you." He wondered whether Simon had been upset more by the sacrifice of the bull or by the reaction of his big brother who was holding him.

He reminded himself that Ezra had not sacrificed Samson as a sin offering. Rather, he had released the horse from suffering, knowing that he was sacrificing his own life for that privilege. He wondered if Isaiah's suffering servant was to sacrifice himself in a very similar quest. A shiver went up his spine.

They watched as the high priest then drew lots at the Eastern Gate to determine which of two goats would be the offering for the sins of the priests and which would be the scape goat. He tied a red band around the horns of the scapegoat, representing the sins of the entire people.

Next the High Priest prepared a shovel of embers from the altar and a vessel with a double handful of incense and entered the holiest of holies. The incense was not placed on top of the embers until the High Priest had entered the most holy place. The shovel of embers would be placed where the Ark of the Covenant would have been in the original temple built by Solomon. Then the incense would be placed on the embers and the high priest would wait until the chamber was filled with the aroma of the burning incense before emerging.

Upon emerging, the High Priest took the bowl of blood from the bull and went into the holy of holies again to sprinkle the blood there. Leaving the remaining blood on a stand outside the most holy place but still in the temple, he emerged again to sacrifice the goat for the sins of the priests. When the high priest confessed the sins of the priests over the head of the goat, he again pronounced the name of the Lord, Yahweh, and all the people prostrated themselves. Little Simon again buried his face on his brother's shoulder when he saw the High Priest take up the knife. Jesus hugged his little brother tight and tended to him rather than watch the blood being caught in a second bowl.

He knew from stories his father had told him that the High Priest would do the same thing with the goat's blood that he had done with the bull's. And that after sanctifying the most holy place, the remaining blood would be used to sanctify the larger portion of the inside of the temple.

When the High Priest came out the next time, the scapegoat for the sins of the people was brought to him and he confessed over it the sins of all the people. For the third time, he pronounced the otherwise avoided name, Yahweh, and all the people prostrated themselves. Simon again turned from the scene, anticipating another bloodbath. "No, no," said Jesus. "It's alright. He won't cut this one." Simon's big eyes watched in wonder as the goat with the red band on its horns was led out of the temple courtyard.

"Where's he going?" asked Simon.

"This one will be let loose in the wilderness," said Jesus. "It is to symbolize the sins of the people being removed from them as far as the east is from the west, as it is written in one of the Psalms." He didn't tell Simon that this goat would actually be pushed over a cliff to its death. That was a convention someone had come up with after some previous scapegoat had not been inclined to wander in the wilderness, but instead had wandered back into Jerusalem with the symbol of the people's sins displayed on its horns. Jesus again wondered how he, as Messiah, was to remove the people's sins from them as far as the east is from the west. He thought of the suffering servant about whom Isaiah had written, "It was the Lord's will to crush him and cause him to suffer, and though the Lord makes his life an offering for sin, he will see his offspring and prolong his days and the will of the Lord will prosper in his hand." The end of that passage came back to him, too: "After he has suffered, he will see the light of life and be satisfied; by his knowledge my righteous servant will justify many, and he will bear their iniquities. Therefore, I will give him a portion among the great, and he will divide the spoils with the strong, because he poured out his life unto death, and was numbered with the transgressors. For he bore the sin of many, and made intercession for the transgressors."

Jesus suddenly felt very weak and thought he was going to swoon. He knew it wasn't from fasting but thought it might be exacerbated by the fasting. He suddenly wanted to get out of the crowd and away from the temple. He had quite enough of the rituals and the blood. Carrying Simon on one arm, he made his way through the crowd to Joseph and Mary. "Abba, with your permission, I would like to take Simon back to the garden."

"Is he not feeling well," asked Joseph.

"He is okay," said Jesus. "I am not feeling well."

"You don't look well," said Mary. "What is it?"

"Probably a combination of things, Mother. Seeing all that blood reminded me of Uncle Ezra and Samson and..."

"Oh, of course," said his mother. "I hadn't even thought of that. Listen, Hannah has had about enough, too. I will come with you."

"I can take both of them if you want to stay, Mother," offered Jesus.

"No, no. Now that you have put the thought of Uncle Ezra in my head, I don't want to see any more blood either. Joseph, can you handle the twins?"

"Of course," said Joseph. "We will be along soon enough. You go on ahead."

On the way back to the garden, Jesus carried Simon and held Hannah's left hand while his mother held her right. As he thought about bearing the sins of such people, he was strengthened in his spirit. But he knew that he didn't want them to watch him as he died.

Early the next morning, Joseph and Jesus presented themselves at Mahli's door. While they were still approaching, his son Gershom peeked out the door. "They're here, Abba," he called over his shoulder. He hopped down the steps as his father appeared behind him.

"Shalom, my friends," said Mahli. "I see you are punctual. That will be in your favor with Rabbi Gamaliel."

"Shalom," said Joseph. "We dare not sully your reputation with the rabbi by showing any disrespect."

Gershom and Jesus greeted each other with bright smiles in the shadow of their fathers and then they were off. The three of them traveled at a boyish pace, Gershom happy to be the guide through a part of Jerusalem that was not familiar to the Nazarenes.

"Do your lessons start so early every day?" asked Jesus.

"Lessons don't start until the third hour," said Gershom. "We are arriving early so that you and the rabbi can get acquainted and get your questions answered."

"Is he expecting us," asked Joseph.

"Yes, Abba sent me to him with a message right after you left day before yesterday," said Gershom.

They approached a respectable looking house on a broad street. Joseph pointed to it with his chin and winked at Jesus but Gershom led them right past it. Then he turned in to a rather humble looking synagogue just down the street. He knocked at the door and entered without waiting for an answer, but they found no one inside.

"Here is where we hold yeshiva," said Gershom. The rabbi lives next door. I will tell him you are here."

So saying, he left them standing in the entrance and turned, not toward the respectable house, but in the opposite direction.

"I would have thought a rabbi of his reputation would live in that fine house back there," whispered Joseph. "I wonder what kind of man he is."

Soon enough they heard footsteps. A man appeared in the doorway but was strongly backlit so that not much detail could be seen. "Shalom," said the rabbi in a warm and friendly voice. "Welcome to our synagogue and my yeshiva, I am Rabbi Gamaliel."

When he closed the door behind him, it took a few seconds for Jesus' eyes to adjust. Then he saw a man almost as tall as his father and of a similar age, but rather slender and slightly stooped. He had bushy, high-arching eyebrows that made him look surprised, but his eyes were kind and merry. His beard was full and greying, but could not be described as flowing. And despite the beard, his smile was visible and welcoming.

"Shalom, Rabbi," said Joseph. "Thank you so much for making time for us in what must be a very busy schedule. I am Joseph of Nazareth and this is my son, Jesus."

"Shalom, Rabbi," said Jesus and made a little bow in his honor.

"Shalom to you, young man. Welcome. I am told you are already something of a scholar, but look at your hands! They are strong and rough like your father's."

Jesus blushed and hid his hands behind his back.

"No, no," said the rabbi, "I don't say that to shame you. I can see from your hands that you do not shy away from hard work. That is a good quality. Look at my hands! I have devoted so much of my life to study that my hands are as soft and weak as a woman's! If you can work with your hands and improve your mind by study at the same time, I envy you."

"You have no need to envy us, Rabbi," said Joseph. "We envy you the opportunity you have had to devote your life to the study of God's word."

"It is a privilege, for sure," said the rabbi, "and I am grateful for the pleasant lot that has fallen to me. But I regard craftsmen as children of the same Heavenly Father. And if they exercise their calling to the best of their ability, they should not be looked down upon."

"That is a refreshing attitude for a rabbi, if I can be pardoned for saying so," said Joseph.

"Ahhh," sighed the rabbi. "No pardon needed. There are plenty of pompous rabbis out there who have no calling from God, just a great ambition to be praised by the people."

"I thank God that you are not one of them," said Joseph.

At that moment, Gershom came in carrying a tray of glasses and a teapot.

"Please, please, sit down. You are my guests. I shouldn't keep you standing in the doorway."

As Gershom poured the tea, the rabbi continued, "Tell me how it is that you are seeking a yeshiva for your son here in Jerusalem,"

"My own father, God rest his soul, was a carpenter in Nazareth and I have followed in his footsteps," said Joseph. "He was literate and had an old copy of the first scroll of Moses that he had purchased from a rabbi when it was so worn out that the rabbi had to replace it. He used to read to me when I was very small and later taught me to read, as well."

"Abba," asked Jesus. "Do you still have that scroll? This is the first I have heard of it."

"No, son," said Joseph, 'when we got back to Nazareth from… from afar, my father, God rest his soul, had passed away and I don't know what happened to the scroll."

"So you lived some place other than Nazareth for a while?" asked Rabbi Gamaliel.

"Yes, for a couple of years," said Joseph.

"Travel is very educational. May I ask where you were?"

"Uhh… actually we lived in Egypt for a while when Jesus was quite small," said Joseph.

"So your father taught you to read and you have returned the favor to your own son," said the rabbi. "I commend you for your contribution to Israel's enlightenment. But without the scroll you mention, on what have you relied for material?"

"We have had the great privilege to be befriended by a former disciple of yours," said Joseph. "Mahli's brother Zephon, Rabbi of Capernaum. He loans us scrolls to study."

"Ah, Zephon! God bless him," cried the Rabbi. "He was an excellent scholar. I am glad to hear that you have a connection to him and that he is being generous with God's word."

"He it was who recommended your yeshiva to us," said Joseph. "We only met his brother Mahli and this, your current disciple, Gershom, a couple days ago."

"Well, well. What a coincidence," said the rabbi. "Yes Mahli was my disciple as well and now Gershom his son is following well in the footsteps of his father and his uncle."

"We owe Gershom's uncle no small debt of gratitude," said Joseph. Jesus nodded in Gershom's direction.

"Well, Jesus," said the rabbi, "how would it be if I asked you to give us a sample of your reading ability?"

Jesus swallowed a lump in his throat and nodded. "Okay, I'll try."

"Gershom, bring me the scroll of Isaiah."

Gershom reverently brought the scroll and handed it to the rabbi. The rabbi kissed the scroll, and handed it to Jesus. Jesus kissed it as he had seen the rabbi do and then opened it.

"From the beginning?" he asked.

"Yes, from the beginning," said the rabbi.

Jesus began to read: "The vision concerning Judah and Jerusalem that Isaiah son of Amoz saw during the reigns of Uzziah, Jotham, Ahaz and Hezekiah, kings of Judah. Hear me, you heavens! Listen, earth! For the …" Jesus hesitated. "Rabbi, may I ask you a question," he said.

"Certainly," said the rabbi. "Speak."

"Is it a great sin to read the name of God aloud when it is clearly written in the scripture? Why do most people substitute "the LORD" instead of saying God's name?"

"And I will ask you a question," said Rabbi Gamaliel. "Were you not at the temple yesterday?"

"I was," said Jesus.

"And did you hear the high priest read the name of God aloud?"

"I did," said Jesus. "And all the people prostrated themselves at the sound of the name."

"So tell me," said the rabbi. "What are your thoughts about the matter."

"I don't think it is a great sin to read the name aloud or the High Priest would not commit such a sin in front of all the people." The rabbi nodded. Jesus continued. "But I suppose it would be a great bother to read a long passage aloud with many mentions of God so that the people would be prostrating themselves every other line. But when God revealed himself to Moses on the back side of the desert, he told Moses his name and told him to tell the Israelites his name and he went on to say that by that name he would be known forever. How will the people of future generations know what His name is if only the High Priest pronounces it and only on the Day of Atonement each year?"

The rabbi laughed out loud. "Just look what a scholar you have created, Joseph," he said. "In my twenty years of yeshiva, I have never been asked such questions!"

"I admit that he comes up with questions that baffle me," said Joseph. "That is one of the reasons we are considering bringing him to you."

"If you don't mind, Rabbi," said Jesus, "I stopped reading just now when I came to the name. When Abba and I study together, we read the name aloud and though we reverence God's name very highly, we don't prostrate ourselves every time we read it. Once Rabbi Zephon invited me to read the scriptures in his synagogue in Capernaum and I read the name aloud as is my custom with Abba, but it upset some of the men there. They expected me to substitute 'the LORD' for Yahweh. Why should it be considered a sin to pronounce the name of God, when God said that is the name by which He is to be known?"

"Son, I don't believe it is a sin to pronounce the name. Nowhere in the scripture is it stated that we should not pronounce the name of God, only that we should not use it in vain. But our traditions are very strong and in order not to use the name of God in vain, we have developed a tradition of not uttering it at all."

"And what should we do if our tradition is in violation of scripture?" asked Jesus.

"Scripture should always be honored above tradition," said the rabbi. "But I am not sure that avoiding the pronunciation of the name is a sin any more than pronouncing it is. Sometimes we go along with traditions so as to avoid giving offense to others who are less enlightened."

"So in your yeshiva, disciples are expected to avoid pronouncing the name?"

"At the present time, yes;" said the rabbi, "that is our custom. But traditions sometimes change."

"Thank you, Rabbi," said Jesus

"Well, son, you certainly read fluently enough to be a disciple in this yeshiva. And it is clear that you have a curious mind. I think you would be a good addition to my school."

"And he could stay with us," offered Gershom. "My father already offered. My sister got married last spring so we have room for him. And I would help him with his studies."

"We are not entirely sure that this is the right time for Jesus to leave home," said Joseph. "And you have not mentioned what it would cost to enroll him here."

"I try to make enrollment here affordable to the right kind of disciples," said the rabbi. He mentioned a figure that they never could have considered before Ezra's generous bequest but that now was within reach, all things considered.

"His mother and I will certainly pray about this very tempting offer," said Joseph. "I appreciate your generosity and it seems clear that you are a man to whom we could entrust his education. But we have only begun to consider the possibility of being separated from our son. Please don't misunderstand if we hesitate to say yes. It is not because we doubt you or your qualifications. It is only a question of whether we can live without him in Nazareth."

"I certainly understand that dilemma," said the rabbi. "If you decide to send him to me, I will gladly receive him and do my very best to guide him into paths of righteousness. I trust the Father will make it clear to you the path you are to take."

"Bless you, Rabbi," said Joseph. "We trust the Father will make it clear. Thank you again for your hospitality."

"Well," said Joseph after they started back to the garden, "what did you think?"

"I like him," said Jesus. "What did you think?"

"He is refreshingly unlike what I expected him to be," admitted Joseph. "And between Mahli's offer of housing and the rabbi's reasonable fees, I think we could make it work. But I was serious when I told him that I'm not sure I can live without you."

"Oh, you will be fine," said Jesus. "One of the twins can help you in the shop and you can send the other out with the sheep. You could even alternate every six months so that both learn both trades."

"That's not what I mean," said Joseph. "You are not a servant in my house who can be replaced by someone else. I still feel so responsible for leading you into your calling… so responsible and so unsuited to the challenge. I don't know how to help you take the next step."

"This is something the Lord began and the Lord will have to complete it," said Jesus. "You have not been given all the answers, neither has mother and neither have I. By faith we have to ask for guidance and follow whatever God gives us each day."

"That is truth," agreed Joseph. "Let me talk to your mother tonight. And we will pray."

"I will pray, too, Abba," promised Jesus.

The camp in the garden was a bustle of social activity that day. Mary and her sister, Esther, along with cousin Tabitha combined their efforts to feed the men and children a common meal. That way they could catch up on women's talk while they worked. The children were running here and there. The ritual obligations were all taken care of and the shyness of the children had worn off. This was their chance to revel in the abundance of playmates. That revelry would continue on the shared road out of Jerusalem the next day, but today was special in the relative freedom to roam about the garden and play in the creek.

Jesus spent nearly two hours teaching Josiah more of his letters in the sand by the creek. Then they dabbled their feet in the water and told each other stories of their adventures. Josiah was fascinated by Jesus' story of night fishing on the sea of Galilee and how deaf Uncle Ezra had proved himself a worthy seaman.

"Mother and I crossed the lake one time to visit a cousin in Tiberius," said Josiah. "But we didn't have a storm or catch fish or anything. I had expected a great adventure but it was a bit dull, really. There wasn't enough wind so the men had to row most of the way."

"Believe me," said Jesus, "it can get exciting."

"Have you ever been to Tiberius?" asked Josiah.

"We pass through it on the way to Capernaum and back," said Jesus. "But the most exciting thing we have ever done there is eat lunch on the beach. Who did you say you visited there?"

"A cousin," said Josiah.

"If you visited a cousin of your mother's, she would be a cousin of my mother, too."

"No, Aunt Miriam is a cousin of my father's. She wouldn't be related to you."

Soon they were called to supper where the whole clan of six adults and nineteen children were chattering, eating and laughing. It wasn't until very late that Joseph and Jesus were able to sit quietly and talk with Mary about their visit to the yeshiva of Rabbi Gamaliel.

"What kind of man is this rabbi?" asked Mary.

"He seems to be very kind," said Jesus.

"And wise," added Joseph.

"And humble," said Jesus.

"How old a man is he?"

"I think he is about my age," said Joseph. "He was recently elected to the Sanhedrin, so you know that he is very highly respected."

"Is he harsh? Is he rigid?" asked Mary.

"He seems gentle and reasonable to me," said Joseph.

Jesus told her about their discussion of pronouncing the name of God, Yahweh, as opposed to substituting 'The LORD.' "He seems to value scripture above tradition," said Jesus, "which is very good. But he believes that we have to honor traditions where they do not violate God's word. And he allowed the possibility that traditions might change. Hopefully, he believes that God's word does not change."

"All in all," said Joseph, "I think that if we were to leave Jesus here to study at a yeshiva, Rabbi Gamaliel's would be a good choice. I'm just not reconciled to leaving him here so young. He was entrusted to us for these years of training."

"But what kind of training are we affording him?" asked Mary. "He is learning to be a carpenter and a shepherd, but how does he learn what he needs to know to save the people from their sins?"

"I'm not sure that Rabbi Gamaliel or anyone else can teach him that any more than we can," said Joseph. "If God does not reveal it, who on earth is up to that task? None of the rabbis or priests, for that matter, have ever seen a Messiah, let alone raised one!"

"I acknowledge our dependence on God," agreed Mary. "I think we should continue to pray about it. Let God's will be revealed.

"Amen!" said Joseph.

Sleep was elusive that night for Jesus. The trek home to Galilee would begin in the morning but he was torn. He was convinced that saving the people from their sins would involve shedding his blood but he didn't know how to put himself in the position to make that sacrifice. And he was conflicted in his desire to obey his Heavenly Father and yet to spare his family, and especially his mother, the agony of witnessing the bloody details. He was convinced that he would be raised from the dead, but could not tell the timing of that glorious future. He didn't know what would happen to Abba, to his mother and brothers and sisters after his death and before his resurrection.

He imagined himself moving in with Mahli and his family, of being younger brother to Gershom and studying at the yeshiva. But then he imagined speaking the name of Yahweh out publicly in the yeshiva and creating a great disruption. He imagined asking who the suffering servant was in the passage of Isaiah and having Rabbi Gamaliel chastise him for having studied the scriptures alone, just as Rabbi Zephon had done and threatened to take the scrolls away.

"Oh Father in Heaven," he prayed. "May your name be hallowed; may your will be done on earth just as it is in Heaven. May you be glorified in my life and in my actions, thoughts and words. May I know what I am to do and may I have the courage to do it. Help me not to shy away from death if it is death that you are sending me to. I am but a child; I do not know the way I am to walk. Grant me clarity to recognize your voice among all the noises of this earthly existence. If I am your Anointed One, let me do exactly what you have sent me to do, no more and no less. And may you be glorified. Amen"

Even after that prayer, he tossed and turned most of the night. He got up before dawn and went to the creek to sit and pray where he wouldn't disturb those family members sleeping in the camp. When they began to wake up, he went to help his father with the packing and loading. He was torn between going back to Nazareth and the familiar routines of village life on the one hand, and the challenge of an adventure in the big city where he knew he had a daunting role to play at some point. As he helped his father pack up bedding and food stuff for the journey home, he was inclined to join the homeward journey. But when James and Little Joseph started squabbling for the privilege of riding the donkeys instead of being in the wagon, he was inclined to stay in Jerusalem. He wondered what it would be like to have Gershom to deal with instead of the twins. It was tempting.

He went to see to the animals. They needed watering and brushing. He always brushed the donkeys before saddling them, lest a burr or a tangle of hair should chafe under the saddle and become an open sore. He couldn't be around horses or donkeys without thinking of all he had learned from Uncle Ezra. The very smell of a stable seemed to bring Ezra's memory to the fore. He talked to the animals as he brushed them. "How does that feel, little donkey? Does it make you remember Ezra like it does me? He loved you so much! It delighted him to know that you were content. We are going back to Nazareth starting today. I will take you to graze near where he is buried. There where the happy days of your youth were spent grazing in security and leisure."

When he had saddled the donkeys, he tied them to the back of the wagon and hitched the little mare to the front. His mother called him to get a bite of breakfast before they cleaned up the dishes.

He had taken only a couple of bites when he said, "Mother, I'm not that hungry but thank you for your good work. I want to run say goodbye to Josiah before they leave for Hippos."

"They have already left," said his mother. "You just missed them but we will catch up with them tonight and camp with them again."

Jesus jumped up and ran after the departing family group. "I need to talk to Josiah," he shouted over his shoulder. Mary saw him catch up with her sister's family as they started the climb up Mount of Olives.

"Where is Jesus?" asked Joseph a few minutes later as he came up from the creek.

"He ran after Esther's family," Mary said. "He said he needed to talk to Josiah. We probably won't see him again until we catch up with them this evening."

"Well, he has done his chores here," said Joseph. "I guess he will be alright."

When Jesus caught up with Josiah, they were just beginning to climb up the steep part of the trail. "Hey," said Jesus, "I just wanted to say goodbye and wish you a great journey home to Hippos."

"We will see each other tonight when we camp, won't we?" said Josiah.

"Yes, probably…" said Jesus. "But just in case we don't, I wanted to wish you well. I have enjoyed our time together."

"So have I," said Josiah. "Why don't you hop on behind me? I'll give you a hand up."

"Your donkey is working hard enough on this slope," said Jesus. "If the road were level and smooth I would ride with you. But on this trail it would be cruel to add my weight to yours."

"I suppose you're right," said Josiah. "But we can take turns."

"We'll see about that," said Jesus. "Here," he said, reaching into his bag. "I've got a gift for you." So saying he handed his cousin one of his little scrolls.

"What is this?" asked Josiah. "It's one of the scrolls we have been studying! Thank you so much! Are you sure you won't miss this one?"

"I have already memorized the Psalms on that one," said Jesus. "When I get more cut-offs from Rabbi Zephon, I can write out another copy from memory."

"Or I can copy this one onto a scrap of leather from my father's shop," said Josiah. "Then I can return this one to you next year in Jerusalem."

"Don't worry about that," said Jesus. "Just keep studying every chance you get."

"I will. Thank you so much for helping me get started."

"Well, here is a short cut back to the garden. I'd better go help Abba get our family on the road."

"Okay," said Josiah. "See you tonight."

"Probably so," said Jesus and scampered down the steep path toward the garden at the bottom of the mountain. When he got to the garden his family was gone. Jesus ran forward to where he could see the bottom of the road. He saw the twins on the donkeys first. They were climbing steadily in pursuit of Josiah's family. Then he saw the mare pulling the wagon with his father, mother and the smaller children. He shouted and waved. He thought Abba looked right at him but he did not return the wave. Jesus began to run after them but then stopped after a moment.

He wondered whether his father intended for him to stay behind. Why didn't he wave; surely he saw me. Did he not want to draw Mother's attention to me? Was he signaling me to stay?

"Lord you know that I was conflicted about whether to stay or to go. But you also know that I didn't intentionally stay without saying goodbye. I was willing to go back to Nazareth. Is this something you have arranged? If so, help me to bear whatever you have in store for me. And help Abba and Mother to bear what you have for them."

He realized that he was still standing with his hand waving in the air but the wagon had begun to turn a corner. Nobody in the wagon could see or hear him now. He went back to the now empty garden and looked around. The place didn't seem near as welcoming once his family had left for Galilee. He wandered down to his favorite place by the creek. There he sat on a rock with his feet in the water and he cried.

When he was finished crying, he dried his tears on his sleeve and continued to sit in the quiet of the garden. He heard birds singing in the trees above him. He sat very still and tried to see what kind of birds they were. A motion upstream some fifty cubits caught his eye. He froze, moving only his eyes and no other part of his body. A fox appeared, its every move furtive and silent. Its eyes were searching and ears at high alert. He could see the fox's nose working as it sought information that could warn of any danger. Or of any prey, he thought. The cool morning air was flowing downstream, thought Jesus. So there is no likelihood of her catching my scent from upstream. "I wish I had a nose such as yours," whispered Jesus. "I would have smelled you before I saw you!"

At that instant a fly landed on Jesus' nose and it tickled so badly that he had to shoo it away. Of course the motion startled the fox and she turned tail and fled. Jesus quietly got up and made his way to where the fox had appeared at the stream's edge. He studied the footprints and began to follow them through the brush that bordered the garden. He was able to follow them for maybe half an hour before he found a den with tracks coming in and out. "So this is where you call home," said Jesus. "At least you have a home. And the little birds have nests in which to sleep. But I am now without a home, no place to lay my head."

He thought about Mahli's home and the offer of housing that still stood open. He was reluctant to presume upon them without his father's arranging it. He couldn't just show up without his father and say, "I have decided to take you up on your offer." They would surely ask about Joseph and what would he say then? Besides, the housing was bound up with him enrolling in the yeshiva of Rabbi Gamaliel but he was not enrolled. Could he tell the rabbi, "I have decided to enroll?" He could not. And the rabbi would ask, "Has your father sent you to me?" And he could not truthfully say he had. Why had his father not waved? Perhaps he didn't see me. But almost surely he had…

He found his way back to the garden where they always camped. He knew that he didn't want to camp there alone. It might not even be safe. And he would miss his family more here than anywhere else in Jerusalem. He decided to go up to the city.

He took stock of what he had with him. He had a piece of bread and a hard lump of cheese that he had put in his bag at breakfast when he had had so little interest in food. He had one change of clothing and a woolen wrap that could serve as a covering at night. He had several of the little Psalm scrolls that Rabbi Zephon had given him and Uncle Ezra's knife. That was it.

"Heavenly Father," he prayed. "I am a poor boy in a mostly strange city. I have only these few resources and you. I do have you. Thank you that I have you. Since I have you, I have everything I need. I don't need a den or a nest, for I have you. I don't need a lot of food for I have you. I don't need any gold or silver for I have you as my priceless treasure. You are my strong tower. You are my shield and my refuge. I have everything that I need."

On the strength of that prayer and that faith, twelve-year-old Jesus left the garden and went to seek his fortune in the great city of David. He did not go to Mahli's house nor to Rabbi Gamaliel's yeshiva. He wandered throughout the city asking the Lord to guide his steps and lead him to a place where he could sleep that night. He thought of the story of Uriah the Hittite who, when he had come from battle, would not go enjoy his own home but slept "at the palace gate with all the King's servants." Sleeping at the gate of Herod's palace did not seem to Jesus as safe and welcoming as King David's palace must have seemed to Uriah. He searched for and eventually found the market where he and the Samaritan girl had taken refuge just two years prior. But the basket merchant was no longer there. Perhaps she had even passed away, she was so old.

Eventually, he was drawn to the temple in the late afternoon. There he saw an old blind woman begging on the steps outside the gate. He sat down beside her and asked, "Mother, has no one given you anything today?"

The toothless woman turned toward him and asked, "Who are you that you call me mother?"

"Are you not a mother in Israel?" he asked.

"I was a mother once," she lamented. "But now I have been alone these seven years and I'm just waiting for the Lord to call my name."

"What is your name, Mother?" asked Jesus.

"Call me Mara," said the woman. "For the Lord has dealt bitterly with me."

"I see you know the story of Naomi," said Jesus. "Has the Lord not given you a Ruth?"

"No, my son," she said. "He has only left me to die but He won't even give me the release of death."

"Can you eat this?" Jesus asked, handing her the bread and cheese from his bag.

"God bless you, son, I haven't had a bite of anything since before the Day of Atonement."

"So you have fasted more than the High Priest!" said Jesus.

The woman laughed and said, "I am sure that everyone in Jerusalem and Judea fasts more than the high priest." She began to break off bits of bread and suck on them to soften them.

Jesus said, "I am going to take your bowl for alms and wash it out to bring you a cool drink of water."

"Bless you, my son. What did you say your name is?"

"You have told me your name in riddle," he said. "So I will do the same. I am called Emmanuel."

She grasped his wrist and wept. "Surely you are God with me," she said.

When he brought her bowl back full of water, she drank greedily and began to eat the bread and cheese more readily. "You sound like you have a Galilean accent," she said.

"Yes, I am from Nazareth."

"What are you doing here? The feast is over."

"I am listening for the voice of God." said Jesus. "It is said that if you want to hear the voice of God, go near His temple in the city of David."

"You sound young," she said. "How old are you?"

"I am twelve," said Jesus.

"Just twelve?" she said in surprise. "Where are your parents? Don't you have a family?"

"They have gone back to Nazareth," said Jesus.

"Well, I would think you are an angel except that I never heard of an angel who spoke with a Galilean accent."

Jesus laughed. "I am no angel, I assure you. Tell me, Mother, where do people sleep in Jerusalem when they have no home here?"

"If they have money, they stay in inns. There are many that would have room now that the festival is over."

"And if they have no money?" asked Jesus.

"Then they sleep wherever they find a place to lay their heads."

"Where do you sleep, Mother?"

"Up until two months ago, I slept beside the pool of Bethesda, near the Sheep Gate. Many sick and injured stay there waiting for the waters to be stirred by the angel. Each day a friend of mine would bring me here to beg for alms, but one day she didn't come back for me in the evening. I'm afraid she must have died. So now I sleep here."

"Can you walk?" asked Jesus. "I could lead you back to the pool of Bethesda."

"No, my son. I won't go back there. I don't have that much more time to live. I want to die here beside the temple of the Lord."

"Listen, Mother," said Jesus. "I am going to try to get us something to eat. I will be back before dark."

"Go in peace and return in prosperity," mumbled the woman.

Jesus followed his nose to a vendor nearby who was cooking a big pot of lentils and onions. The vendor was a heavy set Arab with drooping mustache and only one good eye. "Sir," Jesus said, "is there any work I can do or service I can perform for you in order to earn a little soup for myself and my friend?"

"You can surely do me a service if you're a mind to, but the soup costs money," he replied.

"And how much money will you pay me to wash all those bowls from your previous customers?" asked Jesus.

The Arab stared at Jesus for a moment and then asked, "Do you know your way around this city?"

"A bit," answered Jesus.

"Do you know the synagogue on the road called "Flat" that is by Rabbi Gamaliel's house?"

"Yes, as a matter of fact, I do."

"Three houses down from the synagogue is a small house with a blue door. If you will take this food to my children there, I will give you soup and bread for yourself and your friend."

"I will do it," said Jesus.

"And give them this medicine for their mother," added the Arab. "She is not well. When you get back you must tell me my mother-in-law's father's name to prove that you actually did deliver this to them."

"Agreed," said Jesus.

Jesus delivered the food and medicine to the designated house with some trepidation, lest he should meet Gershom or Rabbi Gamaliel. He thought about trying to approach the house from the other end of the street to avoid them. But then he thought, if I meet them, I meet them. Then the Lord will have to give me the wisdom to answer their questions. He needn't have worried. The trip was uneventful and he saw no sign of anyone who would ask questions.

When he got back he went right up to the Arab vendor and said, "Your family sends you their gratitude and your mother-in-law's father's name is Sabri."

"Ha! Good boy! I thought I could trust you. See, I've already served up your portion. Just bring back the cups when you are done."

"Thank you very much, sir."

After Jesus and Mara enjoyed their supper together on the steps of the temple, Jesus washed the cups in the public fountain and returned them to the Arab. By that time the sun was down and the gate to the temple was closed. Jesus put on his change of clothes over the ones he was wearing and tucked his woolen wrap around the woman to keep her warm. "Do you mind if I sleep here beside you, Mother?" he asked.

"I would be honored, Emmanuel. Highly honored," she said and leaned on his shoulder as he recited Psalms in her hearing.

The Lord ordained that that was to be the woman's last night on earth. When Jesus rose in the morning, Mara was already rejoicing in Abraham's bosom on the other side. Jesus closed her eyes with his finger and waited for the Levites to open the temple gates. The morning air was chill and Jesus had to retrieve his woolen wrap for his own comfort. He hated to take it back from Mara, but he reasoned that she no longer needed it and he surely did. Even with it, he was shivering when the Levites opened the gate to the temple courtyard.

"Please sirs," he said, addressing the two men. "This poor woman has died in the night and I don't know what to do for her."

"Are you her family?" asked the older of the two.

"No sir, I don't believe she has any family."

"How do you know her?"

"I met her yesterday here on the steps," said Jesus.

"Well, she has been begging here for quite some time," said the Levite. "She used to have someone bring her here every morning and take her away every evening, but for the last few weeks, she has just stayed here."

"She told me that her friend failed to come for her about two months ago so she just stayed here. She suspects the friend stopped coming because she herself died."

"Well, that's sad," said the Levite. "Do you know her name?

"She called herself Mara, but I don't think that was her real name," said Jesus.

"Okay," said the Levite with a sigh. "I will get someone to take care of the burial."

Jesus waited with Mara's earthly remains until the grave diggers came to carry her away. He reasoned that she had already spent too much time alone. And he didn't want stray dogs to bother her while she waited. People came and went from the temple but no one looked at him or Mara twice. When the grave diggers did arrive, he watched over her as they put her on a cart and followed them to a simple cemetery for indigent people outside the city wall. After they had buried her, he wept over her, not because he knew her, but because nobody did.

Upon leaving her graveside, Jesus made his way to the pool of Bethesda where many sick and disabled people waited under the colonnades surrounding it. He approached a group of elderly women and asked, "Does anyone here know the blind woman who calls herself Mara?"

"She doesn't come here anymore," said one of them, a woman with only one leg.

"Then you knew her?" asked Jesus.

"Knew? Then she has died?" asked the woman.

"Yes," said Jesus.

"God rest her soul. When?"

"Last night."

"Where did she die?"

"On the steps of the temple. I offered to bring her here but she said she wanted to die there," said Jesus.

"It is too sad. The girl who used to take her to the temple each day just disappeared. She may have died, too. Did she die alone?"

"No," said Jesus. "I was with her. Do you know her real name or anything about her?"

"She just called herself Mara. We don't know what her real name was or anything about her," said the woman with one leg.

"Well, she is now buried in the little cemetery outside the wall on the western side. If anyone comes asking about her, you can tell them that she is at peace."

"Thank you, young man. Tell me your name?"

"Jesus. Jesus of Nazareth."

He went back to the temple mid-afternoon and looked for the Levite he had talked to that morning. He found a Levite near the front gate but it was not the same one.

"Excuse me, sir," said Jesus. "I would like to speak to one of the Levites who opened the gates this morning."

"They are no longer on duty," the man replied. "The new shift came on at the sixth hour. Is there something I can help you with?"

"I wanted to ask him more about the woman who died on the steps last night," said Jesus.

"Someone died last night?" asked the Levite. "Was it the old blind woman who has been there forever?"

"Well, not forever," said Jesus, "but for the last two months or so."

"She has been coming here every day for at least a year and a half," said the Levite. "But she used to go away at night. For the last little while she never left. I don't even know where she went to the latrine."

"Did you know her name?" asked Jesus.

"No, I never spoke to her," said the Levite. "What would one say to a woman like that?"

"One might ask her if she would like a cup of cold water," said Jesus, beginning to get angry.

"Look, son. That's not our responsibility. If people want to give her alms or something, they are free to do so. Our responsibility is to make sure she doesn't bother the worshipers or desecrate the temple or anything."

"So you are not sons of Abraham?" asked Jesus.

"Hey boy, don't get sarcastic with us," said the other Levite standing nearby. "We can throw you out of here."

"What's going on here? Is there a problem?"

Jesus turned to see who was speaking. It was a priest.

"This boy is trying to make us guilty of something with regard to that old beggar woman," said the first Levite.

"Which one," asked the priest.

"You know the blind one who has been living on the steps for the past two months, not even leaving at night?" asked the Levite.

"Yes," said the priest.

"Well I guess she died last night and this boy is interrogating us as if we killed her."

The priest turned to Jesus, "Did you know her? Are you her kin?"

"No sir, I only met her yesterday," said Jesus. "And I wasn't trying to make these men guilty of anything. I was only astonished that she had been living on these steps for two months and these men didn't even know her name."

"That's not our job as gatekeepers," said the one.

"We aren't nursemaids," said the other.

"It's not your job as gatekeepers," said Jesus, "it is your duty as brothers and sons in Israel."

"I see we are beginning to draw a crowd," said the priest. "Young man, why don't you come with me to a more private place. I will deal with these men later."

So saying, the priest put his arm across Jesus' shoulders and turned him toward the temple. Over his shoulder he gave a knowing look to the Levites who quickly dispersed the crowd.

"What's your name, young man?" asked the priest as he brought him into a side room in the temple.

"My name is Jesus."

"Is that a Galilean accent I hear?" asked the priest.

"It is. I am from Nazareth."

"Did you come up for the Day of Atonement?"

"Yes we did."

"Where is your family today?" asked the priest.

"They have gone back to Nazareth," said Jesus. "They left yesterday morning."

"And left you here? Are you studying in one of our yeshivas then?"

"I might be," said Jesus. "The arrangements have not been finalized."

"What do you know about the woman who died on the steps?"

"I met her on the steps yesterday afternoon. We shared a cup of soup and some bread along with our stories.

"What did you learn of her story?"

"She used to stay at the pool of Bethesda hoping to be healed. A friend of hers used to bring her to the temple to beg but one morning she left her here and never came back. I offered to take her back to the pool last night before dark but she said she would rather die near the temple."

"So she knew she was dying?" asked the priest.

"I don't know if she knew when she would die, but she knew it wouldn't be long," said Jesus.

"And what was her name, Jesus?"

"She called herself Mara, but I don't think that was her real name. She said the Lord had dealt bitterly with her. The same thing Naomi said when she returned from Moab after the famine."

"How old are you, Jesus?"

"I am twelve."

"I must say, I have not met any twelve-year-old your equal. Not even in Jerusalem, let alone from Galilee. Would you like a glass of tea?"

"I would like that very much, sir."

The priest left the room for a few minutes. When he came back in, he was accompanied by a servant with a tea tray and three other priests.

"My fellow priests," said the first one, "behold Jesus, an Israelite in whom is no guile."

Jesus was surprised at this accolade and asked, "How do you know me?"

"In the few minutes I have conversed with this young Galilean," continued the priest without answering Jesus' question. "he has revealed a genuine compassion for the poor, has called into question the training of our Levite gatekeepers and has demonstrated a familiarity with the story of Naomi and Ruth. I invite you to make his acquaintance."

"Galilee, you say?" asked the tallest of the priests. "How can any good thing come out of Galilee?"

"Why do you call me good?" asked Jesus. "Only God is good."

"Aha! Well said!" cried the eldest of them.

"Who are you, son?" asked the third priest. "Tell us about yourself."

"I am Jesus, son of Joseph, son of Jacob, of Nazareth. My grandfather was a carpenter, as is my father. I have been apprenticed to my father since my youth."

"I would speculate that you are still in your youth, Jesus. Who is your rabbi and under whom did he train?" This was the eldest speaking again.

"Nazareth has no rabbi," said Jesus. "My father taught me to read as his father once taught him. We read the scriptures together whenever we get a chance."

"It does not surprise me that there is no rabbi in Nazareth," said the older priest. "But you must admit that a carpenter who reads and teaches his son to read is news to all of us. Where does your father get these scriptures that you read together?"

"He borrows them,' said Jesus. He thought about showing them the little scrolls with Psalms on them but he was afraid they would be confiscated.

"What's this about your compassion for the poor?" asked the tall one.

"I found him disputing with the gatekeepers because they did not know the name of the blind beggar woman who died on the steps last night," said the first priest. "He was chastising them for their failure to their duty as brothers and sons in Israel."

"Was this woman a relative of yours, Jesus?" asked the old one.

"I only met her yesterday," said Jesus. "But she was a mother in Israel and she shouldn't be left like living rubbish on the steps of the temple."

"Well said, young man. Well said," cried the tall one.

"May I inquire," said Jesus, "how many of you knew her name?"

There was an uncomfortable silence and then the old one cleared his throat. "Dear Jesus, I'm afraid we are as neglectful as the gatekeepers in this matter. But surely not out of malice."

Jesus said, "in the story that God gave Nathan with which he trapped David, our Heavenly Father reveals how he cherishes and nurtures every lamb that belongs to Him."

"Please say more," said the eldest priest.

"There is a poor man in the story who owns only one lamb, a ewe which he had bought. He raised it like a daughter. It slept with him, ate out of his hand and drank from his cup. That is how the Lord cares for each sheep of His and how he cares for the woman who died on your steps."

"That is an extraordinary interpretation of that story," commented the tall priest.

"The greedy rich man is a picture of Satan who won't feed his guest with his own flocks, which are many; but he steals the poor man's lamb which the man had bought from him at a fair price."

"I'm not sure about your interpretation of that story," said the old priest. "But your point is well taken that we are all guilty of neglecting this beggar woman whom God values."

"There is a member of the Sanhedrin, a highly respected rabbi in our midst who may know her name," said the original priest. "I have seen him stop and give her food or alms. Likely he will know her name."

"I confess that we failed to honor this woman as we should have done. Thank you for bringing this failing to our attention," said the old one. "For myself, I promise you that I will make a better show in the future."

Jesus nodded in his direction. "May the Lord keep you true to your promise," he said. After a momentary silence, he continued. "I did not anticipate having the honor of an audience with priests today, but I have a number of questions that I would love to ask."

"You have our attention," said the old priest. "Ask!"

"First of all," said Jesus, "you know my name but I do not yet know yours."

"My apologies," said the priest who had first addressed him. "I am Joseph Caiaphas and this," indicating the oldest of the four, "is my father-in-law, Ananus ben Seth, High Priest of Israel."

Jesus acknowledged this announcement with a look of surprise and confusion. "I… I should have recognized you, sir, having seen you performing the ceremony on the Day of Atonement."

"It was likely the fancy ceremonial robes I was wearing," said Ananus.

"That and the fact that I never expected to meet the High Priest," added Jesus.

Joseph then indicated the tall man and introduced him as Alexander and the fourth as John. "They are also of our family," said Joseph.

"I am very honored to make your acquaintance, all of you," said Jesus.

"And we, yours," said Joseph. "Now you had some questions?"

"Uhh… yes, if you don't think me disrespectful…"

"Not at all," said Ananus. "Ask!"

"One question concerns a Psalm of David," said Jesus, "the one that begins, 'The Lord said to my lord, "Sit at my right hand until I make your enemies a footstool for your feet."'"

"Yes," said the High Priest, "What is your question?"

"This is about the Messiah, is it not?" asked Jesus.

"It is," agreed the High Priest.

"Then why do we call the Messiah 'Son of David' when David himself calls him 'Lord?'"

"It's a good question, Jesus," replied the High Priest. "It is very clear from many scriptures that the Anointed One will be a descendant of David. Thus we call him a son of David or even The Son of David as being a very special, specific one. But in honor and power and authority, the Messiah will greatly exceed his ancestor, King David. For in the scroll of Isaiah it is written, 'the Redeemer and Holy One of Israel — to him who was despised and abhorred by the nation, to the servant of rulers: "Kings will see you and stand up, princes will see and bow down, because of the Lord, who is faithful, the Holy One of Israel, who has chosen you."' Thus David can call him 'my lord' because he has greater honor than kings, and greater honor than King David."

"That is a good answer," said Jesus, "but it brings up another question. Why does Isaiah say that the Redeemer and Holy One of Israel was 'despised and abhorred by the nation?' And in another place Isaiah writes at length about a suffering servant who is despised and rejected but who dies to take away the sins of the nation? Can that be the Messiah? Must the Messiah die?"

At that moment the door opened and the servant who had brought the tea came into the room and said, "I beg your pardon for the interruption, but it is time for the evening sacrifice. The people are waiting."

"Ah. yes. Thank you, Ebenezer. We are coming." To Jesus he said, "Young man, I am astounded at your very insightful questions. Will you come again tomorrow morning? I regret that we cannot take more time now for this discussion."

"We have a meeting of the Sanhedrin tomorrow morning," said Joseph.

"What time is that to be?" asked Ananus.

"At the fourth hour."

"Young man, if you can come at half past the second hour, perhaps we can have this very fascinating discussion before the Sanhedrin gathers. Will you come?"

"Of course," said Jesus. "Thank you very much for your time."

Upon leaving the temple, Jesus nodded in the direction of the gatekeepers whom he had challenged for their heartless attitudes, but they pointedly looked the other direction.

Suddenly realizing how hungry he was, he sought the Arab vendor. He was in his usual spot by the busy intersection. "Hello, little friend," said the Arab. "Are you still here?"

"I am," said Jesus.

"Still with empty pockets, I suppose?"

"Yes," said Jesus, "but still willing to run errands or wash dishes. Any work, really."

"Then take this to my children," said the Arab, handing Jesus a basket of food. "Bring the basket back to me."

"Along with the name of your mother-in-law's father?" asked Jesus.

The Arab laughed. "No, I already know his name. And I already know that you can be trusted. Go!"

Jesus delivered the food and brought the empty basket back to the vendor.

"So, two cups of soup again?" asked the Arab.

"Just one today," said Jesus.

"Your friend is not hungry today?"

"No, she will never be hungry again," said Jesus.

"God rest her soul!" said the Arab.

"Yes," said Jesus, "God rest her soul."

After Jesus had eaten, he washed the cup and returned it to the vendor and bade him good night. He didn't want to sleep on the steps of the temple that night, but didn't want to return to the empty garden where his family always camped, either. He wandered the city for a while and found himself at the Pool of Bethesda. At one corner of the pool, he saw a group of men huddled together for warmth.

"May I join you?" he asked.

"Stay away," they said. "We are lepers."

"I'm not afraid of you if you are not afraid of me," Jesus said.

"If you are not afraid, then you are welcome here," said one of them. "But if anyone asks, you must reply that we warned you."

"That's fine," said Jesus. "I will do that."

Then they welcomed him.

The next morning Jesus went to the temple and sat on the steps where Mara had died, waiting for the appointed time. The gates were already open and the gatekeepers studiously avoided making eye contact with Jesus. When it was almost time for his meeting with the priests, he saw Rabbi Gamaliel approaching.

"Shalom, Rabbi," said Jesus.

"Young Jesus! Shalom to you," exclaimed the rabbi. "I am surprised to find you still here. I assumed you and your family were back in Nazareth by now."

"My family left," said Jesus, "but I stayed."

"Are you staying with Mahli? I'm surprised you have not come to yeshiva with Gershom!"

"The arrangements were not finalized before my family left," said Jesus.

"From a distance, I thought you were the blind beggar woman who is usually in this spot," said the rabbi.

"Did you know her then?" asked Jesus.

"Not well," said the rabbi. "But I took pity on her, she was so helpless and pathetic."

"She died night before last," said Jesus. "Did you know her name?"

"She told me to call her Mara," said the rabbi, "because the Lord had dealt bitterly with her."

"That's what she told me, too," said Jesus. "But I don't think it was her real name."

"It wasn't," said the rabbi. "Her real name was Martha. I only coaxed it out of her after many brief visits. How do you know her?"

"I only met her here on the steps a few hours before she died," said Jesus. "We shared some soup and I tried to keep her warm that night. She was dead in the morning. She is buried in the small cemetery outside the city wall."

"God bless you for your kindness to her on her last night on earth," said the Rabbi. "She was a mother in Israel."

"That was my thought," said Jesus. "What are you doing here, Rabbi? I thought you would be teaching yeshiva."

"My disciple is doing that in my stead," said the rabbi. "I was invited by the High Priest to meet with them before the Sanhedrin meets. It seems he has someone he wants me to meet."

"What time is your meeting?" asked Jesus.

"Half past the second hour," said the rabbi. "Right now."

"Well then I think you might have already met that someone," said Jesus. "I have a meeting with him and his family right now, too."

"Really? Well then let's go," said the rabbi. "It would not be good to keep the High Priest waiting."

They were received by Joseph Caiaphas and ushered into the same private chamber where Jesus had met with them the day before. "I see you two have already met," he commented on the way in.

"Yes, this young man is already known to me," said Gamaliel. "His father brought him to visit my yeshiva a couple of days ago."

"Really?" said Joseph. "One of the reasons we invited you this morning is that we thought he might be a candidate for your yeshiva."

'We seriously considered it," said Jesus. "But then my father left for Nazareth before we made a final decision."

Tea was brought in by a servant of the High Priest. Soon the High Priest himself and the other two priests came into the chamber and the rounds of greetings and explanations started all over again.

The High Priest opened by saying, "Rabbi Gamaliel, we invited you here this morning to meet a most surprising young Galilean who, at the age of twelve, is literate in the holy scriptures and has a social conscience that humbled me and my staff yesterday in the matter of compassion toward the indigent. Specifically, he took my gatekeepers and even us to task for not knowing the name of a blind beggar woman who died on the steps of the temple night before last. Having seen you conversing with her on multiple occasions, I speculated that you might know the woman's name and something about her. I and my staff could take a lesson from you."

"I cannot say that I knew much of her story," said Gamaliel. "But I do know her name. She asked me to call her Mara because the Lord had dealt bitterly with her. But her real name was Martha. She was of the tribe of Issachar and had two children, a son and a daughter, both of whom preceded her in death. Her husband died before the children, very much parallel to the story of Naomi. But Martha had no Ruth and no Boaz to take care of her in her old age. She lost her sight progressively some ten years ago and was reduced to begging at that time."

"Thank you for paying attention to her," said the High Priest. "And thank you for bringing her to our attention, Jesus. I regret that she came to our attention too late for us to do anything for her. Rabbi Gamaliel, this young Jesus is someone we would like to recommend to you as a potential disciple in your yeshiva. Since he and his father have already met with you, you know what potential he has. He has many questions about the Law and the Prophets with which I believe you are very well suited to deal."

"I am honored that you would think of me in those terms," said Gamaliel, "especially since I am a Pharisee and you and your family are adherents of the Sadducees' party."

"Despite your party affiliation, you have our respect," said Ananus. "I am guessing that Jesus is not particularly devoted to either party at his tender age. Or am I wrong, Jesus?"

"I am not familiar with party distinctions, sir. I only want to know and follow God."

"I wish it could be that simple for myself," said the High Priest.

At that moment the door opened and the servant of the High Priest came in. "Pardon, your excellency," he said. Then he hurried to the High Priest and whispered in his ear. The eyebrows of the High Priest betrayed the fact that something very surprising was afoot."

"Bring them in," he responded to the servant.

The servant swung the door open and stepped out of the way. Joseph and Mary appeared in the doorway.

"Jesus!" shouted Mary and immediately burst into tears as she raced into the midst of this august company and buried her face on his neck. Joseph followed quickly in her wake but was rendered speechless by his anxiety for his son and the surprise of finding him here.

"Mother? Abba?" stammered Jesus. "What are you doing here?"

"How could you do this to us?" wailed Mary. "Your father and I have been searching for you anxiously!"

"Why did you search for me?" asked Jesus. "Didn't you know that I had to be at my father's house?"

"We came here because an Arab street vendor where we stopped for breakfast told us to look in the temple. Please forgive us this awkward intrusion," said Joseph. "We left here two mornings ago with a large group of relatives. Until we camped that night, we assumed Jesus was with his cousin. When we found that he had never joined the party, we left our other children camping there with Mary's sister and family so that we could rush back here to look for our son. We apologize for distressing you with our family disturbances."

"Not at all," said the High Priest. "We have all been intrigued by your most unusual son. He is a bright and shining star in Israel for one so young. Tell me, are you really Galileans?"

"We are," said Joseph.

"I hear that you have already visited Rabbi Gamaliel's yeshiva," said the High Priest. "I would strongly encourage you to enroll him there so that his talent, which is undeniable, can be nurtured."

"My offer is still open," added Gamaliel.

"Thank you so much," said Joseph. "But I think that having lost him for these few days has made us aware of how unprepared we are to be separated from him at this age." His explanation was clearly illustrated by Mary's grief. She wouldn't let go of Jesus and couldn't stop crying.

"If you change your mind," said Gamaliel, "you know where to find me."

"Yes. Yes, we do," said Joseph. "Perhaps in a year or two…"

"As you wish," said Gamaliel.

The three of them bade their farewells and gushed their thanks as they left the private chamber of the High Priest and began, anew, their journey home.

"Son, why did you not join us?" asked Joseph.

"I tried to," said Jesus. "Why did you not return my wave?"

"Return your wave? What wave? I never saw you."

"I had run to say goodbye to Josiah when his family left ahead of us," said Jesus. "I walked alongside of him almost to the top of the Mount of Olives. Then I took the shortcut back to the garden to join you, but you were already gone. I saw you driving up the lower part of the mountain and I yelled and waved. You looked right at me and didn't return my wave. I didn't know what that meant, and I …"

"Son, at that time of the morning and driving up that road, the sun is squarely in my eyes. I could barely see the road to drive. I did not see you wave. Why didn't you run after us? You would have caught up with us on that steep road."

Jesus didn't know what to say. "I guess I wasn't sure what I was supposed to do," said Jesus. "We had talked so much about the possibility of staying here to study and we hadn't really made a clear decision and ..."

"And what?" asked his father.

"And you know, our little secret..."

"What secret?" asked Mary

"Yes, what secret?" added Joseph.

"You know... the suffering servant passage in Isaiah."

"No!" said Joseph, very firmly. "That can't be what you were thinking!"

"Of course that is what I was thinking," said Jesus. "That's all that I have been thinking about for months!"

"What is this suffering servant passage?" asked Mary. "What secrets have you been keeping?"

Joseph explained to Mary that months ago while reading through Isaiah the two of them had become curious about whether a certain passage that referred to a suffering servant was the Messiah."

"The suffering servant dies for the sins of the people and redeems them to God," said Jesus. "How can that not be the Messiah who takes away the sins of the world."

"Oh God," murmured Mary, choking up again. "So you stayed here thinking that you would die for the sins of the people while your family calmly returns to Nazareth, oblivious to the whole thing? What were you thinking? I am your mother!"

Then Jesus burst into tears. "We kept it a secret partly because Rabbi Zephon did not agree with our interpretation," said Jesus. "But mostly because I didn't think you could handle it. And I … I didn't think I could die with you watching."

They stopped in the middle of the street and hugged each other and wept. When they recovered somewhat, Joseph said, "Son, did you never ask your mother that question I told you to ask?"

"What question, Abba?"

"About what Simeon told her when we dedicated you here in the temple..."

"Oh… I did forget," admitted Jesus. "What did he say, Mother?"

"He said, 'Lord, now you can let your servant depart in peace for my eyes have seen your salvation.'"

"I know that part," said Jesus. "What else?"

"'Which you have prepared in the sight of all nations: a light of revelation to the Gentiles, and the glory of your people Israel," continued Mary. "Then he turned and looked me right in the eyes and said, 'This child is destined to cause the falling and rising of many in Israel, and to be a sign that will be spoken against, so that the thoughts of many hearts will be revealed.'"

"That is consistent with the suffering servant who is 'despised and rejected,'" said Jesus.

"And his last words to me were these," said Mary. "'And a sword will pierce your own soul, too.'"

Jesus shuddered. "He said that?"

Mary nodded, holding back her tears.

"Did he mean a literal sword?" asked Jesus.

"I don't know," sniffed Mary.

"I wanted to spare you… and myself…" muttered Jesus.

"Son, you are going to save me from my sins," said Mary. "I am clear on that. But you cannot save me from my sorrow."

They all heard a shout and looked up. The one-eyed Arab vendor was hailing them from across the street. "I see you found him!" he shouted with a grin as wide as his face.

"Yes," replied Joseph. "We've found him. Thank God!"

Christmas 2015

About the Author:

Terry Todd grew up at the foot of the Rocky Mountains in Littleton, Colorado. As a young man he served with Wycliffe Bible Translators and became their expert on Kurdish dialects. At the time of this publication, he and his wife, Nancy, shepherd cross-cultural workers in various parts of the world through Barnabas International. He enjoys wood carving, woodworking, hiking and riding a tandem bicycle with Nancy.

Made in the USA
San Bernardino, CA
29 January 2017